Under The Pope's Windows

A REX DALTON THRILLER

BOOK TEN

JC Ryan

ISBN: 9798642587836

About Under The Pope's Windows

They stole it. He's going to take it back—by force.

In October 1943, Hitler's SS troops surrounded Rome's Jewish Ghetto and plundered the Jews' most precious heritage: two ancient libraries containing unique books and manuscripts dating from before the birth of Christ, from the time of the Caesars, the emperors, and the early popes.

The Nazi ambassador to the Vatican reported to his masters in Berlin that the looting and deportations took place *'under the Pope's windows'*.

Now, Rex Dalton and his wife, Catia, and Digger, their military dog, set out on a quest to find the stolen libraries and return them to the Jewish community of Rome.

But before long, they cross paths with modern-day Nazi diehards, anti-Semites, and a secret organization of super-rich elite who will kill to keep the past a secret.

DEDICATION

Dedicated to my good friend Mitch Pender, a military dog trainer, for giving me the idea for this series and guiding me through the intricate and amazing capabilities and psychology of those majestic four-legged soldiers.

Mitch has a lifetime of experience and exceptional depth of knowledge as a military dog handler and trainer.

CONTENTS

About Under The Pope's Windows 2

Dedication 3

Contents.....................................4

Prologue.....................................9

PART I 12

Chapter 1 - A singular event....................13

PART II 25

Chapter 2 - His atonement was finally over 26

Chapter 3 - Not in our lifetimes 34

Chapter 4 – Books books books 40

Chapter 5 – Among those who escaped 49

Chapter 6 – Under the Pope's windows..........59

Chapter 7 – Stocking the Museum...............66

Chapter 8 – That look.........................71

Chapter 9 – Are you serious? 78

Chapter 10 – Vague concepts 89

Chapter 11 – I know a few people 95

Chapter 12 – Could be worth billions............100

Chapter 13 – Time to arrange a meeting 112

Chapter 14 – Only three people................117

Chapter 15 - A black-ops-assisted Ph.D. 123

Chapter 16 – We might stir the hornet's nest 132

Chapter 17 – Family matters................................138

Chapter 18 – German precision 144

Chapter 19 – I burned it all 153

Chapter 20 – We'll need legal advice......................160

Chapter 21 - A text message from Josh 165

Chapter 22 – We need to talk 171

Chapter 23 – Make that three 179

Chapter 24 – His home was bugged.........................186

Chapter 25 – You only copied it 193

Chapter 26 – A pocket watch and a diary 200

Chapter 27 – Music to a man's ears.......................204

Chapter 28 – We'll have to do it at night 211

Chapter 29 – I get the exclusive 217

Chapter 30 – It was a novel................................223

PART III 231

Chapter 31 – The beginning of the end 232

Chapter 32 – Please give me a bit of time 237

Chapter 33 – Some got charged for war crimes 249

Chapter 34 – A blanket 253

Chapter 35 – Take it or leave it 263

Chapter 36 – Write it down 267

PART IV...271

Chapter 37 – Geneva, here we come......................272

Chapter 38 – A cause as deserving as this 277

Chapter 39 – They're still alive and well today 285

Chapter 40 – Reason to be concerned......................289

Chapter 41 - Continue the investigation....................298

PART V...305

Chapter 42 - Germany was doomed 306

Chapter 43 - Zehnhaus Consultants..........................311

Chapter 44 - Innately superior to others 316

Part VI 319

Chapter 45 – Too close for comfort 320

Chapter 46 - The troubleshooter 329

Chapter 47 – I can already see the headlines 335

Chapter 48 - They never forget what they've smelled340

Chapter 49 – Find them 351

Part VII 356

Chapter 50 - What's that boy up to? 357

Chapter 51 - Well played Dalton...............................366

Chapter 52 – Initiating the mission 374

Chapter 53 – Where is Catia Romano? 378

Chapter 54 – Zechariah is late..................................383

Chapter 55 – Warn Catia...389

Chapter 56 - Flaming with a frightening rage 392

Chapter 57 – Prost 398

Chapter 58 – Josh's primates 407

Chapter 59 - No doubt that he has 411

Chapter 60 – It's them 419

Chapter 61 – He'll have us killed 425

Chapter 62 – I want them alive 439

Chapter 63 – Modern-day Scharnhorst members 444

Chapter 64 – Where should we take them? 449

Chapter 65 - The six-hour mystery.........................453

Chapter 66 – Trauffer was asleep 457

Chapter 67 – The power of suggestion 459

Chapter 68 – What libraries John?.........................469

Chapter 69 – A speedy apprehension 473

Chapter 70 – There was nothing to say 479

Chapter 71 – The aftereffects 484

Chapter 72 – The summit.......................................490

Chapter 73 – Disclosure of a secret 494

Chapter 74 – Tying up loose ends 501

Fact or Fiction 505

Rex Dalton's Next Adventure..................................506

More Rex Dalton and Digger...................................507

Also by JC Ryan...509

Your Free Gift 514

About JC Ryan 516

Copyright 517

Prologue

Jewish Ghetto, Rome, Italy

October 14, 1943

THE NAZIS HAD an insatiable lust for books, especially esoteric books such as the books of the *Biblioteca della Comunità Israelitica,* the library of the Jewish community of Rome, and the *Biblioteca del Collegio Rabbinico Italiano*, the Italian Rabbinical College Library; books and papers including incunabula and scrolls covering more than two thousand years of the history of the Jews of Rome.

On 30 September 1943, two uniformed Nazi officers turned up at the Jewish Ghetto and demanded to see the libraries. They visited again on 1 October to inspect the libraries again, and on the second they visited the chief rabbi's home, where they examined and confiscated all the books and papers they found there.

On 11 October, the two officers were back, this time in the company of a man purporting to be a German scholar with expertise in book publishing. An eyewitness of the events wrote of this man: *...He too is escorted by SS troops and appears to be just another German officer, but with an extra dose of arrogance that comes from having a privileged and, regrettably, well-known 'specialty.'*

This elusive, dread-inducing character makes his way into the synagogue building. While his men commence ransacking the libraries of the Rabbinical college and the Jewish community, the officer, with hands as cautious and sensitive as those of the finest needlewoman, skims, touches, caresses papyri and incunabula, leafs through manuscripts and rare editions, peruses parchments and palimpsests. The varying degrees of caution in his touch, the heedfulness of his gestures, are quickly adapted to the importance of each work. In those aristocratic hands, the books, as though subjected to the cruel and bloodless torture of an exquisite sadism, revealed everything. Later, it became known that the SS officer was a distinguished scholar of paleography and Semitic philology.

On 14 October the Nazis were back, it was the day when the Community Library and a portion of the Rabbinical Library were removed as the president, secretary, and sexton of the Jewish community looked on, helpless.

The rabbi ripped his shirt, threw himself to the ground, and poured dust on his head. When the sexton urged him to rise, he moaned, "How can a people live when the knowledge of their past is taken from them?"

"Some will perish, but our people *will* survive. It is written; 'I will bring back all the people unto thee.'"

The rabbi scooped up another handful of dust and poured it on his head. "It is also written; 'My people are destroyed for want of knowledge! Today the knowledge has been taken from them.'" He scooped up another handful of dust and poured it on his head.

"It was not you who stole the books, rabbi."

The rabbi remained inconsolable. "It is written; 'Where there is no vision, the people perish.' My people will perish because we lost the books... 'Ye shall perish among the heathen'."

Helplessly, the sexton repeated, "All is not lost. The Torah remains."

***

OŚWIĘCIM, POLAND - AUSCHWITZ EXTERMINATION CAMP

OCTOBER 21, 1943

The rabbi got the first bitter almond whiff of the Zyklon-B gas, hydrogen cyanide. In the airtight room many of the condemned vomited and retched and convulsed and banged their heads against the walls. He merely leaned against the wall, murmuring, "My people. The books! The books! The boo . . k . . .s . . . .s . . . . .s."

PART I

THE SURPRISE

Chapter 1 - A singular event

ROME, ITALY

SATURDAY, MAY 7, 2016

"WHAT'S THAT?" SHE asked a few seconds after entering the room. She was pointing at the dress on the bed.

He struggled to hide his nervousness. This was the situation they could not plan for—it was the potential single point of failure of this entire mission. Nevertheless, he managed to keep a poker face. "If I'd have to venture a guess, I'd say it's a wedding dress."

"For whom?"

"I'd have to make another guess. I'd say it's for you."

She approached the dress slowly, picked it up, held it against her body, looked in the mirror, and whispered, "When?"

"Today."

"But... what about... I mean... you... the guests... a rabbi... what..." Then she turned and smiled. He could see her eyes had turned aquamarine—the color they changed when she was very happy. Then she was in his arms and they were whispering to each other.

"Let's do it. I've been fretting too much about it for far too long," she said.

He made no reply; instead, he kissed her.

"How much time do I have?" she asked.

"As much as you need."

"What time is it now?"

"Six oh five."

"What time is sunset?"

"Eight fifteen."

"We'll start at eight twenty. Five minutes after the Sabbath is over."

He left and entered the next room with a grin on his face that said it all and told his accomplices they were on.

As he walked away, he quoted the famous words of the actor George Peppard, the cigar-chomping leader of the A Team in the popular TV series of the '80s, Colonel John 'Hannibal' Smith; "I love it when a plan comes together."

***

IT HAD BEEN a very special occasion, unique in many ways—weddings usually are. This was a small one—private, essentially a secret affair—attended only by a few close friends and no family. The couple had no family, no father to walk the stunning bride down the aisle.

Despite the absence of family, it was a joyous occasion which could easily not have taken place at all. The idea of a surprise wedding had been around for a while. It was a straightforward concept—the couple invites their guests to an event under the pretense of a party, dinner, or brunch, and then surprises them by announcing a matrimonial celebration.

In this case, however, due to the groom's misinterpretation of what a surprise wedding entailed, it was not the guests who got the surprise but the bride. That the groom had purposefully misconstrued would be proven beyond a reasonable doubt in the aftermath of the event.

Traditionally couples go to great lengths to make their big day a memorable one. Every now and then a pioneering couple will come up with an idea so outlandish it will get media attention—scuba diver fanatics getting married underwater, skydivers during a freefall from ten thousand feet, in an airplane a few miles up in the sky, in a hot air balloon a few thousand feet up—people seemed to never run out of avant-garde ideas.

If the media had been allowed at this wedding, which they were most definitely not, the choice of venue would have gotten some mention. It was on a luxury yacht, the TOMATS, at anchor in Roma Marina Yachting. That was the first marina to be built in Rome's historic, 2,000-year-old Port of Civitavecchia, also known as the Port of Rome, about fifty-five miles from the city center. The name TOMATS was derived from the first letters of Ernest Hemingway's classic short novel, *The Old Man and the Sea*.

The hybrid Christian-Jewish ceremony, co-officiated over by a rabbi and a Roman Catholic priest, was not unusual. It was the security clearances of both clergymen that would have been extraordinary to the media.

Some of the guests would have gotten a lot of media attention too. After all, it was quite possible that history was made by the French Prime Minister, Lucien Laurent, accompanied by his niece, deputy minister Margot Lemaire, and her little daughter, Rowena, attending a wedding within Italy's territorial waters.

Other notables among the guests were the deputy director of the DGSE, the French equivalent of the American CIA; the captain of the TOMATS, a former Navy SEAL; and the head of the Collections department of Mossad, Israel's intelligence agency.

Christelle Proll, the dazzling deputy director of the DGSE, was in the company of John Brandt, the CEO of a top-secret black ops American private military contractor known as CRC, Crisis Response Consultancy.

Declan Spencer, the captain of the TOMATS, former Navy SEAL Commander and life-long friend of John Brandt, was accompanied by Simona Bellucci, another one of the beautiful women who graced the yacht that day. Simona was formerly known as Sophia Maiorani from Naples.

The Mossad's deputy director, Yaron Aderet, had no companion, but he was the man whose arm the bride was holding when she walked into the room where the ceremony took place.

The bride, as usual, stole the day. At 5' 9" she was tall for a woman, only two inches shorter than the groom. In the high heels she was wearing, she looked the groom straight in the eyes. There was no dissension; she was the fairest of them all. Her shoulder-length waves of stunning auburn hair, flawless creamy skin, scattering of light freckles across her nose attesting to the natural red in her hair, and a near-constant dazzling smile that lit up her face made her breathtakingly beautiful. The groom would have told anyone who wanted to listen that her eyes were the color of the Mediterranean, blue at times and aquamarine at others, as they changed with her mood and what she wore.

The groom, at 5'11", with penetrating dark eyes, black hair, tan skin, the physique of a gymnast, and a stern-looking face, was not movie star attractive but certainly a very handsome specimen.

Everyone found the big black Dutch shepherd dog, who brought in the wedding rings on a dainty white satin cushion balanced on his nose, adorable.

That Rex Dalton, the groom, an American citizen, was a former black ops field agent and assassin in the employ of CRC, and his bride, Catia Romano, an Italian Jew, a former Mossad agent, now Ph.D. student at Sapienza (aka the

University of Rome), would certainly have been newsworthy to journalists of any stripe.

***

IN RETROSPECT, CATIA recognized all the signs she should have picked up about the surprises awaiting her from the moment her fiancé of four months, Rex Dalton, turned up at her apartment located in one of the side streets off the *Piazza di Spagna,* Spanish Square, on that Jewish Sabbath morning of Saturday, 7 May 2016. Not that Catia was an observant Jew, but she respected those who were.

The surprises of the day started with Rex's brand-new Ducati Streetfighter S motorbike which he had been vowing to buy for the past few months. A motorbike enthusiast and owner of a Ducati Streetfighter S herself, she was immediately smitten by the bike.

It was only a few minutes later, after she had a good look at the bike, that she asked why Digger, Rex's best friend, the big black military-trained Dutch shepherd, didn't accompany him. He told her he couldn't bring Digger along because he had come to take her for a ride on his new bike and dinner on the TOMATS to give her a bit of a break from her studies. Digger would be eagerly awaiting her arrival.

Catia didn't need much encouragement; she needed the break from her studies and the tedious wedding planning. And she had not seen Rex in more than eighteen hours—a very long time for two people as madly in love as they were. And then, of course, there was the offer she couldn't refuse—Rex told her she could drive, as he would be more than happy to have his arms around her as the passenger.

***

TWENTY MINUTES LATER they were on the new bike, cruising through the streets of Rome, stopping at a park for a walk and later at a street café for an espresso and pastries as they slowly made their way in the direction of the TOMATS.

From Catia's perspective, she and Rex had a short courtship—three months—before they got engaged in January that year.

Rex had a slightly different view. He was of the opinion the courtship, at least from his side, had lasted for more than four years.

The first time Catia listened to his opinion about it, she was a bit perplexed by his calculations. "How did you arrive at that?"

His answer, given with a big grin on his face, was, "It's called telepathic wooing."

"What... telepathy, as in..."

"Yep, for more than four years I've sent you daily telepathic declarations of love. That's courtship, isn't it?"

Digger's long, noisy yawn had prompted Catia's response. "Rex, even Digger thinks it's poppycock. However, come to think of it, maybe I did get the messages, but they got stuck in my subconscious mind and came to the fore only when you turned up in August last year. That could explain how I fell in love with you in just three months."

Rex laughed. "There, you see it's been four years, not three months."

Ever since they got engaged, Catia had been dividing her time between her studies and wedding plans and managing her Airbnb. Fortunately, the latter didn't require much of her time due to an excellent job done by the assistant she had hired when she commenced her Ph.D. studies.

Rex was expected to participate in the planning of the wedding. After a few days of being subjected to wedding planning, he thought out loud that it might be much easier to pull a team together and plot the whole thing out.

But Catia was not charmed. "Rex, a wedding is not a mission."

"Of course, it is," he said. "It's a mission to get married."

Since then, Rex's contributions to the planning were relegated to *only* giving his opinion, *only* when he was asked, and *only* about the options Catia presented to him.

And he soon discovered it was best to agree with every idea she had, even if he hated them or they conflicted with previous ideas. The result was that three months later they had a choice of venue ranging from the *Tempio Maggiore di Roma*, the Great Synagogue of Rome; the *Piazza di Spagna;* the *Piazza del Popolo Forum Romanum,* to any one of the legion of public gardens in Rome, even on top of one of the famed Seven Hills of Rome.

Rex found it surprising that Catia, who was always so organized and logical, could be so disorganized and illogical when it came to the planning of her own wedding. He made no mention of it, he just accepted it as part of the excitement of finally getting married to the woman he had been wanting to marry for almost five years

At the rate the guest list kept growing, Rex at times feared it would soon include the entire Jewish community of Rome and many others.

Maybe we could ask the authorities to restore the Colosseum, he thought but wisely didn't say.

The dress, the bridesmaids, the menu, and such changed by the hour, it seemed.

When they got engaged, they talked about a date—in vague terms—it would be in the spring.

It was about mid-April, two weeks before the start of spring, during one of their planning sessions, when Catia let out a long despondent sigh and said something that was music to Rex's ears. "I wish we could just have a very small wedding with very few guests."

"That sounds like a *very* good idea," Rex replied as impassively as possible.

"I'm glad you like the idea," she said. "Let me think about it and come up with some options."

Rex almost groaned—after four months, he knew what those words meant—they would still be considering options when winter arrived.

That afternoon, when Catia had left the TOMATS on her motorbike to do some research at the university library, Rex spoke to Spencer, told him what he had in mind, and they called a mission team together.

Rex and Spencer were in the operations room of the TOMATS. Everyone else had dialed in via secured video links from America, Paris, and India.

On the big screen was one photo, Catia's.

"In three weeks, on Saturday, May the seventh, I'm going to marry this woman," Rex started.

"Finally!" John Brandt shouted from CRC headquarters in Arizona.

"Congratulations!" some of them shouted in chorus.

But it was Christelle Proll from Paris who rained on their parade. "Rex, where is Catia? I would've thought she'd be very interested in these discussions."

Rex shrugged and said, "She doesn't know anything about it."

The silence was deafening.

***

AS EXPECTED, DIGGER was there to welcome Catia and Rex when they stepped off the gangplank onto the TOMATS. As he rushed toward her, his claws clattered on the deck, his perky ears shifted forward, and his bushy tail fluttered wildly. He was too well-mannered to jump on her, but he sat down at her feet and looked up adoringly, before glancing at Rex. She leaned over to scratch his ears.

Unexpected though, was to find Marissa Bissett and Rehka Gyan in the small lounge where Rex had led her. Catia couldn't stop a shriek of delight when she saw her friends. "Rex didn't tell me you'd be here! This is such a nice surprise."

The three of them had become very good friends the year before when, as part of a team based on the TOMATS, they prevented a major terrorist plot that would have thrown the world into chaos and probably started World War III.

Marissa, also a trained CRC agent, was engaged to one of Rex's friends, Josh Farley, a former colleague at CRC. Rehka, Rex's IT expert and business administrator, was the daughter of a friend from Bilaspur, India. Rex and Rehka had met when he and Digger liberated her and six other women from a Saudi Arabian prince who held them in captivity as enslaved concubines.

A moment later, Simona Bellucci entered the room with a big smile on her face. Another surprise. Catia had known Simona for almost five years. They met the night Rex had delivered her to the doorstep of a Mossad safehouse close to the Jewish Quarters in Rome. Back then, in 2011, her name was Sophia Maiorani. Catia was responsible for creating a new life, a new face, and a new identity for her, in order to hide her from the Camorra of Naples.

Before Catia could ask her friends what brought them to Italy again, Marissa, with a big grin on her face, said, "There's another surprise for you, Catia. Rex will show you."

Catia looked at Rex. He held his hand out for her and led her to one of the yacht's staterooms.

What Catia would eventually get out of the innocuous-looking guests, piecemeal, during the reception, was that every one of them, including the rabbi and the priest, were involved in the conspiracy—and for that she loved them.

PART II

THE LIBRARIES

Chapter 2 - His atonement was finally over

Rome, Italy

Thursday, July 14, 2016

THE ENGINES OF the two black Ducati Streetfighter S motorbikes were purring softly as they moved slowly along the street in search of a parking space. The bikes, their riders, and passenger turned more than just a few heads that morning. The two bikes, marvels of Italian engineering, certainly contributed to some of the onlookers' curiosity, so did the riders, a man and woman, dressed in matching black helmets and jackets. Another attraction probably was the seemingly very happy big black dog, with his rear shifted into the man's lap, front feet on the handlebars, sporting a pair of big wraparound dark goggles, referred to as doggles.

An old man had stopped walking when the two bikes pulled into the parking space a few yards ahead of him. He started shaking his head and laughing, said to no one in particular, "A dog with dark glasses on a motorbike..."

The man on the bike had his helmet off by then, heard what the old man was saying, and smiled at him. The dog also had a big smile on his face, but the rider wasn't sure the old man would have recognized the lolling tongue and bared teeth as a smile.

The old man turned and continued along the street still laughing and shaking his head, mumbling, "Now I've seen everything."

The woman had witnessed the exchange, raised the visor on her helmet, and asked, "What was that?"

"I think the old guy has never seen a dog on a motorbike," the man replied.

She laughed. "Maybe it's Digger's doggles he finds so amusing."

"Yes, he mentioned that. Look at Digger, I don't think he cares much about his looks, just as long as he's the center of attention."

Catia had removed her helmet and waves of auburn hair had tumbled down to her shoulders.

On the street that morning, there was not a man with a pulse in his wrist and blood pressure in his veins within sight of her who didn't take a second look—many just stared unabashedly.

As if a curious first-time visitor, Rex rotated slowly and made a mental inventory of his surroundings and the people in it—a second-nature habit fostered over many years in his previous profession. A profession he believed he had finally parted with five months ago when Operation Badr ended.

As he conducted the surveillance, it didn't escape him that Catia was also familiarizing herself with her surroundings, and that she had caused quite a stir on the street. It brought a smile to his face as he saw that she seemed to be wholly unaware of it. Her unassuming nature was one of the many attributes which had him madly in love with her.

When they had packed their gear into their small backpacks, locked their bikes, and leashed the dog, Catia took Rex's hand, pointed at a small bakery with a sign in cursive writing saying *Boccione*, and said, "I suggest we start our tour with an espresso and *ricotta e visciole*. It's a cake made with ricotta and wild cherries."

"Good plan. Digger and I are famished." Rex put his arm around her waist, gently pulled her closer, and kissed her on the cheek.

They were in the enclave known as the Roman Ghetto, often called the Jewish Ghetto or Jewish Quarters—a stone's-throw from the Vatican. The word ghetto was not inappropriate; that's what the locals called the four cramped blocks around the *Portico d'Ottavia*, wedged between the Theatre of Marcellus, the *Fontana delle Tartarughe*, *Palazzo Cenci*, and the Tiber. It hosted the Grand Synagogue of Rome or *Tempio Maggiore*, one of the most important religious and cultural symbols of the Jewish community in Rome, as well as kosher bakeries and Jewish-Roman trattorias offering some of the best cuisine in the city.

The friendly faces and convivial atmosphere in the modern-day Ghetto gave few hints about its sad history of suffering, suppression, and humiliation.

Catia Romano was born and bred in Rome from a lineage of Jews living in the Eternal City for more than four and a half centuries. She had completed a master's degree about the history of the Jewish Community in Rome in 2014 at the Sapienza University of Rome, often referred to as Sapienza or just the University of Rome.

Her research for her dissertation left a lasting impression on her about the small Jewish community which survived more than two millennia of malevolent emperors and popes, Garibaldi's red shirt radicals, Mussolini's fascists, Hitler's extermination squads, and 21st century terrorists.

It was also during her master's degree studies that she formulated the topic of her doctoral studies—the missing books of the *Biblioteca della Comunità Israelitica,* the library of the Jewish community of Rome, and the *Biblioteca del Collegio Rabbinico Italiano*, the Italian Rabbinical College Library. She had become fixated on finding out what had happened to those books, and if they still existed, to find and return them to their rightful owners, the Jewish community of Rome.

At the time of her enrollment for her Ph.D. studies she had worked for the Mossad as a mission support specialist, known as a *sayan*. A small intelligence agency compared to those of the USA, the UK, and other western European countries, the Mossad, always cash-strapped, had devised a brilliant plan to overcome their limitations by recruiting helpers, *sayanim,* Jewish volunteers across the world. The *sayanim* were bankers, restaurateurs, homeowners, hoteliers, owners and managers of guest houses, rental car companies, travel agents, lawyers, doctors, nurses, journalists, and many others. Across the globe, they numbered more than 10,000 and whenever needed, provided mission support to Mossad's covert operations—free of charge in most cases.

But Catia was no ordinary *sayan* who only owned an Airbnb in Rome which the Mossad could use for a safehouse; she was one of their agent trainers. She was skilled in hand-to-hand combat and use of weapons, in street-craft, surveillance and counter-surveillance, in setting up weapons caches, and in providing false identity documents when required by operatives. She was also trained to lead surveillance teams to collect information about targets.

At the end of 2014, when she was accepted into Sapienza's Ph.D. program, she had handed her resignation to her handler, or *katsa* as they were known in Hebrew, to devote her time to her studies. He had not been very happy to hear her request. Although she was young, thirty-one, she was one of his best *sayanim*. But he also understood her ambitions and agreed to her request.

Rex and Catia first met in 2010, when she provided part of his European tradecraft training. At the time, Rex worked for the Arizona-based organization Crisis Response Consultancy, CRC, a private military contractor specializing in black operations on behalf of their clients such as the CIA and other US security agencies.

At the end of Rex's training in Rome, he and Catia, although they didn't say so, both knew that much more than a tutor-student relationship had developed between them. But they also knew the rules. No fraternizing between agents and handlers. It could get both killed.

In 2011 Rex was on a joint CIA-Mossad mission in Italy to stop a weapons-for-drugs deal between the Camorra of Naples and Hezbollah terrorists. Catia provided the mission support. Since the end of that mission, more than four years had elapsed without any contact between them, but Rex thought of Catia every day. For the first two years or so after saying goodbye to her, Rex was still working for CRC and prohibited from contacting her. For the remainder of the time since they last saw each other, Rex was on the run under various fake identities and couldn't contact her because that would've blown his cover.

In 2014, while on a mission in Afghanistan, Rex and his men were betrayed and led into an ambush that killed his entire team except Digger, a military trained Dutch shepherd owned by the former Australian SAS operative, Trevor Madigan, Rex's good friend, who was also killed that night. Digger was now Rex's trusted companion because of the promise Trevor extracted as he lay dying. Rex had been afraid of dogs before that, and even as he promised to care for the dog, he hadn't known how he'd do it, or whether Digger would accept him. But Rex had little to worry about; Digger soon accepted him into his pack and they quickly became best friends as they set out in a new life, away from those who had betrayed him and his men. With a certificate to back it, Rex passed Digger off as his service dog, complete with yellow vest, as they traveled around the world for more than two years.

Although he and Digger had left Afghanistan and set out for a life of peace and quiet, it seemed that wherever they went they landed in a situation where they had to use their special skills to help someone in trouble. Many days Rex found himself wondering if it was his destiny or his curse for the many killings he'd done over the years before. Atonement for his sins? —a standing duty of care to everyone who crossed his path in life?

Case in point, about nine months ago, on August 31, 2015, in an enigmatic confluence of events, Rex and Digger turned up at the right place at the right time to rescue Catia and Simona from a team of Camorra thugs trying to apprehend them.

But for the past eight months, after stopping a terrorist plot which could have started the apocalypse, Rex had settled into an unaccustomed peaceful existence—he was married to the woman he loved, they'd had a blissful seven-week honeymoon traveling all over Europe on their motorbikes, and no one in trouble requiring his help had crossed his path.

Rex could be forgiven for thinking that his atonement was finally over.

ROME, ITALY

THURSDAY, JULY 14, 2016

DIGGER WAS SITTING on the ground next to the table between Rex and Catia, eagerly waiting for them to share at least some of what they were enjoying so much. But none of it was going his way, because neither the *ricotta e visciole* nor the espresso was good for a dog's digestive system. While Catia was talking, Rex was feeding Digger small pieces of Italian beef jerky. He seemed to be moderately happy with that.

"The history of the Jewish community of Rome, the oldest surviving Jewish community in the world, goes back to before Christian times. The first record of Jews in Rome dates back to 161 BC, when Jason bin Eleazar and Eupolemus bin Johanan were sent from Jerusalem to Rome as Judah Maccabee's envoys." Catia was in full lecture mode.

"They left when Claudius expelled the Jews from Rome, but soon returned."

Rex had an intense interest in history. He graduated at the top of his class in 2003 with a double major in history and linguistics and a master's in political science in 2004. He was spellbound by the words of the most stunning lecturer he ever had.

When Catia had told Rex about her studies and her desire to find out what happened to the Jewish libraries, and her desire, although admittedly potentially a fanciful notion, to find them and give them back to the Jewish people of Rome, Rex immediately offered his and Digger's services. Not that Rex at the time had any idea in what manner Digger would be able to contribute to the research work required for a Ph.D.

Digger's love for Catia was a source of great pleasure for Rex. From the very first day Digger met Catia, he had shown immediate affection for her. It was as if he had known her his entire life. Rex had never seen Digger take so much of a liking so quickly to a stranger.

This visit to the Jewish Ghetto, to be followed by a visit to the *Centro Bibliografico* later in the day, was to get Rex up to speed with the research that Catia had already completed.

Catia had her tablet out and glanced at it every now and then to get the correct details. "Decreed by a Papal bull, *Cum nimis absurdum*, by Pope Paul IV on 14 July 1555, the Jewish quarter was established as the only residential area for Rome's two thousand Jews of the time. The area was walled off and the two gates to it locked at night."

She took Rex's hand while they strolled slowly along the street. Digger was walking on her other side, very protective of the new member of his pack.

Rex looked around at the buildings with new-found interest. Catia had told him a few days before, when they were discussing the approach to her research, that it was important to understand the history of the Jewish Community in Rome, especially the history of the Ghetto. "Because," she had said, "the books of those libraries were in the *Collegio Rabbinico Italiano*, the Italian Rabbinical College. here in the Ghetto, whence the Nazis removed them.

"The cost of the wall's construction, three hundred silver coins known as Roman scudi, had to be paid by the Jewish community so that they could be locked up in their own prison.

"And as you can see, the area chosen for them to live in is one of the most undesirable parts of the city, subject to constant flooding by the Tiber.

"With Pope Paul IV's bull many of the rights of the Jewish people were revoked. They were prohibited from owning property. Restrictions were placed upon the occupations that they were allowed to perform. They were allowed to work only at unskilled jobs such as ragmen, secondhand dealers, fish mongers, etcetera. They were strictly forbidden to practice medicine on Christians, and it was compulsory to attend the Catholic Church sermons on the Jewish Sabbath.

"Life in the Roman Ghetto was one of severe overcrowding, crushing poverty, and terrible hygienic conditions. The plague of 1656 killed twenty percent, about eight hundred, of the four thousand inhabitants. Whenever the Jews went outside the enclave, men had to wear a yellow cloth, known as the *sciamanno,* and women a yellow veil—the same color worn by prostitutes.

"Every year the Jews had to petition the authorities of Rome for permission to continue living in the ghetto and had to pay a yearly tax for the privilege. Every year, on the *Campidoglio,* one of the Seven Hills of Rome, in front of the populace of Rome, the Rabbi had to pay homage to the chief of the city councilors, the *Caporione*. After doing so the Rabbi had to turn around and bend over so that the *Caporione* could kick his ass as a sign that the Jewish community had been mercifully granted one more year to stay in the Roman Ghetto."

Rex was shaking his head in disgust.

"Every year, at the Arch of Titus, they also had to swear loyalty to the pope. That was especially significant, because it was Titus who had sacked Jerusalem.

"Over a period of more than two millennia, the Jews of Italy had often fallen on hard times as they were stripped of their basic human rights, discriminated against, persecuted, humiliated, and exterminated.

"It was only in 1848, at the outset of Pius IX's papacy, when Jews were permitted to live outside the Ghetto. After the unification of Italy in 1870, Jews were granted the right to citizenship of Italy. It would take another eighteen years, until 1888, before the Ghetto walls were torn down and the place almost completely demolished to make room for the new Synagogue of Rome and apartment buildings to be erected.

"The Roman Ghetto was the last remaining ghetto in Western Europe until the Nazis reintroduced them across Europe.

"On a single day in 1943, the Nazis deported more than a thousand Jews from this area and sent them to the gas chambers of the extermination camps. Only sixteen survived. Today, Rome has fewer than twenty thousand Jews of which only a few hundred live here."

Rex was shaking his head at the harrowing tale of misery and whispered, "The eternal hatred of Jews. Is it ever going to end?"

Catia paused and shook her head slightly. "I don't think so... not in our lifetimes. It was from here," Catia continued, "in 1943, that the Nazis removed, or rather, looted, two of the most priceless artifacts of all their looting raids across Europe, the contents of the two libraries: the Library of the Jewish Community, and the Rabbinical College's library.

"The entire contents of the Community Library remain missing to this day. Some of the contents of the Rabbinical College's library was recovered in 1947, but much of it is still missing."

She looked at her watch. "We've got about an hour and a half before our meeting with Zechariah."

"Enough time for lunch," Rex said.

Digger woofed once in support of Rex when he heard the word *lunch*.

Catia laughed. "Sounds like you and Digger practiced that one. There's a nice little place just around the corner."

Chapter 4 – Books books books

Thursday, 14 July 2016

THE *CENTRO BIBLIOGRAFICO*, Bibliographic Center, owned by the Union of Italian Jewish Communities, was in a house built in the 1700s, on the west bank of the Tiber, not far from the landmark Ponte Sisto bridge.

Zechariah was a bespectacled, tiny, almost fragile old man with disheveled gray hair. He had a rumpled face matching his clothes which, apparently, he had retrieved directly from the tumble dryer that morning. If Catia hadn't told him before, Rex would have guessed Zechariah's age to be somewhere between 95 and 110. He was 86, a friendly man whose face lit up like a Christmas tree when Catia hugged and kissed him on both cheeks.

In Hebrew, to help Rex get more practice in conquering yet another new language, Catia, with a beaming face, introduced Rex to the old man as "The man I told you so much about, the love of my life, my husband, my friend, and my hero."

The old man she introduced to Rex as "Professor Zechariah Nachum, the man I told you so much about. The man who is like a father to me, my study mentor since I started my post graduate studies. Without him I would never have completed the master's, and without him I'll never complete a Ph.D."

Zechariah shook Rex's hand, welcomed him, and congratulated the two of them on their marriage. He looked at Digger and got a smile from him. Then he looked back at Catia and Rex and said, "Which one of you is responsible for not inviting me to your wedding?"

Rex opened his mouth but noticed Catia's index finger already pointing to him. All he could do was listen to her saying, "Thanks to my beloved husband, it was a surprise wedding—I got the surprise, not the guests. There was no time to send out invitations."

The old man, still smiling, said nothing, his gaze just shifted and rested questioningly, maybe even a bit accusatorily, on Rex, who made no reply other than a nodded admission of guilt.

"I'll make sure Rex makes it up to you, Zechariah," Catia said, struggling to look and sound serious. "You have my word on that."

Rex feigned submission.

Zechariah laughed. "I'm going to hold you to that."

He led them to what Rex thought some people might have described as a study, where Zechariah moved toward a mountain of books below which Rex presumed was a desk. Zechariah proceeded toward a big chair, facing two others on the opposite side of the pile. It was impossible to make out what kind of desk it was, if there was one, because none of it was visible beneath the books, scrolls, parchments, and other unidentifiable objects.

Rex looked back at the door through which they had entered and concluded that his first theory about a dump truck tipping the contents of the room in there, was flawed—the door was too narrow. In that case, how the room came to be in such a state of chaos could only have been caused by some force of nature. Words such as earthquake, tornado, and tsunami entered Rex's mind. It was only much later, and much to his surprise, when he would learn that although Zechariah's filing system could not have been the Library of Congress or the Dewey Decimal organizational systems, there must have been some kind of system in operation in that room. Zechariah never had to search for anything—he knew exactly where every item in that room was at any given time.

The room smelled of old paper, dried leather, vellum, ink, and a few others Rex could not identify. Even Digger seemed to be intrigued by the unfamiliar odors as he moved around the room, taking a sniff at every new scent.

Zechariah's eyes were fixed on Digger as the dog made what Rex always thought of as a fragrance surveillance run. A routine which Digger always followed when he entered new environs. He moved around slowly and with extreme care, as if he knew what Rex still had to find out—anyone who moved anything in that room without

Zechariah's permission, even by a hairbreadth, was doing so at peril.

Catia walked to one of the shelves, looked at Zechariah to get his blessing, and at a slight nod and smile from him, she very gently retrieved one of the ancient books written on vellum—calfskin—caressed, and smelled it. She let out a soft squeak of pleasure. "I can't get enough of touching, feeling, and smelling these old books. It's almost as if they're talking to me from across the abyss of the centuries."

At this stage, Digger had paused his reconnaissance and looked at her attentively. It was as if he was taking note of the pleasure Catia was getting out of handling the book. He sidled up to her. She looked down at him and lowered the parchment for him to smell. "Yes Digger, it's incredible—this one's six hundred years old."

When Catia had finished, the old man motioned for her and Rex to take a seat. Digger sat down on the floor between them.

Thanks to Catia's briefing the day before, Rex knew Professor Zechariah Nachum was the world's foremost scholar on the history of Italian Jewry. He was born in the Jewish Ghetto in 1929 and was there on 14 October 1943, when the Nazis came to remove the Library of the Jewish Community of Rome, and part of the Italian Rabbinical College's library. He was also there two days later, on the morning of October 16, 1943 when the Nazis came again, this time to arrest 1,023 Jews and cart them off to Auschwitz.

***

"IT WAS THE winter of 1939. World War II was three months old," the old scholar said in a surprisingly strong voice. "That was when it began. Books, books, books, screamed the headline of the Deutsche Allgemeine Zeitung.

"The Nazis had a feverish lust for books. They were driven by a fanatic mania to collect books, which was fueled by their desire to control people's lives, memories, and thoughts to own their past, and to take away their ability to write their own history. Hitler's henchmen plundered Europe's books by the tens, hundreds, thousands, and millions. They hauled them away in crates, even in potato sacks, by the truckload and trainload.

"It was the biggest theft of books in history."

He interrupted himself. "Apologies, I have forgotten my manners. Can I get you something to drink, espresso, tea, wine?"

"Thank you, Zechariah, Rex and I just had lunch and coffee at the Jewish Quarters," Catia said with an endearing smile.

"Okay, maybe later then. Mhh... where was I?"

"The biggest book theft in history," Rex said.

"Yes, of course. You see, Hitler's Nazis were not the first to plunder the art and cultural heritage of the nations they conquered. Looting had been part of warfare since time immemorial. The Nazis, however, were the most efficient at it.

"Apart from the billions-worth of art, gold, precious stones, jewelry, money, properties, and other valuables, the Nazis also pillaged books, manuscripts, letters, diaries, maps, scrolls, photographs, and recordings. Not only that, they also stole the inventories and registers and catalogues of libraries and collections and dispersed the books within, causing context to be lost."

Zechariah had a sad look on his wrinkled face when he continued. "Jewish prisoners were put to work to catalogue and organize the loot, but it was an overwhelming task as the trucks and trains arrived quicker than the workers could process the cargo.

"In some cases, they deliberately didn't catalogue their spoils. In other cases, vast quantities were simply burned, pulped, or left to rot. Bibliocide is the word Alon Confino used to describe the Nazis' public burning of books that began with the work of banned authors in May 1933."

Zechariah paused for a while as if ordering his thoughts before he continued. *"'As good almost kill a man as kill a good book; who kills a man kills a reasonable creature, God's image; but he who destroys a good book kills reason itself.'* A quotation from the *Areopagitica*, published in

1644 by John Milton, an English author, one of history's most powerful and fervent advocates for the right to freedom of speech and expression.

"In 1823, a hundred and ten years before the Holocaust, German essayist, journalist, and poet Christian Johann Heinrich Heine wrote: *'Dort wo man Bücher verbrennt, verbrennt man auch am Ende Menschen* – Where books are burned, in the end, people will also be burned.'"

"An eerie premonition of things to come," Rex whispered.

"Quite so," Zechariah said. "You see, the atrocities of the Holocaust didn't begin when Jews and others were sent to the gas chambers of the extermination camps; it started, as the United States Holocaust Memorial Museum rightly points out, six years before the war, in 1933, the year of the nationwide book-burning program to eliminate foreign influence in Germany. Where, ironically, copies of Heine's books were among the many burned on Berlin's *Opernplatz*."

The conversation was still conducted in Hebrew and Rex didn't have too much difficulty following it. He had a natural talent for learning new languages. And with one handy little quirk; when he learned a new language, he, unconsciously took on the accent of his teacher, which was why Rex spoke Hebrew with a distinct Italian accent, like Catia.

"After the war," Zechariah continued, "due to the efforts of various governments, private organizations, and individuals, much of the stolen goods were tracked down and returned to their legitimate owners. But despite their efforts, of the estimated twenty percent of the art of Europe looted by the Nazis, there remain well over a hundred thousand items that have not been returned to their rightful owners yet.

"Among them are the contents of the Jewish Community Library and the Italian Rabbinical College's Library, the subject of Catia's Ph.D. studies. Part of the Rabbinical College's library was discovered in 1947 and returned, but every single item of the Community Library remains missing to this day."

***

IT WAS AROUND 5:00 P.M. when Rex and Catia invited Zechariah to join them for dinner at the BellaCarne, a kosher restaurant on Via del Portico d'Ottavia in the Jewish Quarter. It didn't take much to persuade him. His wife had passed away ten years before. His daughter, Hannah, an only child, lived more than an hour away by train; he only saw her, the grand- and great grandchildren over weekends. Weekday evenings he had only his books, his TV, and a friendly neighbor, Luisa, for company.

Zechariah accepted the invitation but, on the condition that they wouldn't expect him to be a passenger on one of their motorbikes.

Catia booked a place for three, one accompanied by a service dog, for 6:30 P.M. At 6:15 P.M. she and Rex saw to it that Zechariah was in the taxi Catia had ordered and that the driver understood where he had to go. They followed on their motorcycles.

CHAPTER 5 – AMONG THOSE WHO ESCAPED

ROME, ITALY

THURSDAY, JULY 14, 2016

OVER DINNER, WHICH extended late into the night, while enjoying the exquisite traditional Jewish Ghetto food, Zechariah and Catia continued Rex's education.

"Both libraries were housed at the Great Synagogue of Rome at Lungotevere De' Cenci," Zechariah said.

"The Rabbinical College Library, transferred from Florence to Rome in the 1930s, was a teaching library of close to ten thousand volumes. The Community Library, consisting of items previously held by five different synagogues here in the Ghetto and other locations in the Jewish community of Rome, was kept on the second floor of the synagogue.

"The Community Library consisted of about seven thousand rare or unique books and manuscripts, many dating back more than two millennia. It was the most important Jewish library in Italy and one of the most important in the world.

"Among them were a quarter of all the work of the Sconcinos. They were Jewish-Italian printers from the sixteenth century who later worked out of Salonica and

Constantinople. There were also the sixteenth century works of Daniel Bomberg, Alvise Bragadin, Nicollet, and many more."

Zechariah paused. "I'm going to eat some of my food before it gets cold. Let's see how much Catia remembers of what I've imparted to her over the years."

Catia smiled. "I'll try my best not to disappoint my professor."

Digger was on the floor next to Catia. He had enjoyed the bits and pieces of the kosher dinner everyone had been slipping to him, surreptitiously so that the waiting staff wouldn't notice. His pack was relaxed; he sighed softly and closed his eyes.

"On 8 September 1943, Italy surrendered to the Allies. Germany still occupied northern and central Italy, including Rome. One-fifth of all Jews in Italy, about eight thousand, lived in Rome at the time. The Nazis had not yet quenched their thirst for books, and the libraries of the Jewish community in Rome got their attention.

"On 26 September 1943, *Oberstleutnant* Herbert Kappler, the head of the German police, the Gestapo, and the Schutzstaffel, the SS in Rome, called the Jewish leaders in and put an ultimatum to them. Hand over fifty kilograms, about one hundred and ten pounds, of gold within thirty-six hours or the deportation of Rome's Jews to the concentration camps would commence.

"The impoverished Jews, with the help of non-Jewish friends and sympathizers, flocked to the synagogue in their thousands and handed over their jewelry. They managed to collect the amount of gold and delivered it by the stipulated deadline, midday, 28 September."

Zechariah's stare into middle space didn't escape Rex—he was sure the old man's mind was back to the days when it happened. He would have been fourteen at the time.

"The elders of the Jewish community believed that with their demand for the gold, the Nazis had demonstrated their intentions—they were after the money, not the people. They were wrong. Kappler had lied to them—the deportation orders had been issued two days before."

Zechariah put his knife and fork down and interrupted Catia. "What the Jewish leaders didn't understand was that the SS conducted their operations like a business, and they were very successful at it. How could they not be profitable? They had fourteen million people to harvest from. Six million Jews, five million Russians, two million Poles, half a million gypsies, and half a million others. The latter group comprised of Germans and Austrians who were mentally or physically handicapped or dissidents, enemies of the Reich, Communists, Social Democrats, liberals, editors, reporters, priests, and such.

"They harvested from them in three stages. In stage one they robbed them of all their earthly possessions. In stage two they put them to work and extracted from them, with as little food as possible, as much productivity as possible for as long as the prisoners were capable of working. Stage three was when the captives were no longer in a physical state to work anymore. That's when their final journey began, through the gas chambers to the furnaces that never stopped burning. Before entering the gas chambers, all their clothes and spectacles were removed, providing the SS with trainloads of shoes, socks, shirts, blouses, dresses, jackets and trousers. The condemned got a last haircut—the hair was shipped to the boot factories to make felt boots for the German troops. And finally, before burning or burying the corpses, their gold teeth fillings were ripped out of their mouths with pliers, melted down, purified, and formed into gold bars. Complete with the stamp of the eagle of the Third Reich and the twin-lightning symbol of the SS."

Zechariah retrieved his handkerchief, removed his glasses and wiped the tears from his eyes.

"Sorry, Catia, I interrupted you. Please continue."

Catia was struggling to keep her emotions at bay. She took a sip of sparkling water, cleared her throat, and picked up the thread.

"On 29 September, the day after the gold had been delivered, forty soldiers in trucks accompanied by two tanks surrounded the synagogue. The officers in charge walked into the office of Ugo Foà, president of the Jewish

Community of Rome, and told him they had information that the Jews of Rome were collaborating with the enemy. They conducted a thorough search of the synagogue. So thorough that they destroyed one of the arks inside and broke into the charity boxes and helped themselves to the cash. They also confiscated the historical records which included the contact information of almost every Jew in Rome. That was probably the entire objective of the raid of that day.

"The day after, on 30 September, two uniformed Nazi officers turned up at the synagogue and demanded to see the libraries. They visited again on the first of October to inspect the libraries again, and on the second they visited the chief rabbi's home, where they examined and confiscated all the books and papers they found there.

"The librarian of the time, Rosina Sorani wrote in her diary: *'They turned to me and told me that they had seen very well how many books there were in the libraries and in what order. They declared the library under sequester, that within a few days they would come to get the books and that all was to be as they left it; if not, I would have to pay with my life.'*"

"On October 11, the two officers were back. This time in the company of a man purporting to be a German scholar with expertise in book publishing."

"Who were they?" Rex asked.

"We don't know the names of the two officers, but Zechariah is of the opinion that the third man, the one who was there on the eleventh, was Doctor Karl Bauer, chief of the Hebraica collection at the Frankfurt Institute's library, head of the Rosenberg Taskforce, *Einsatzstab Reichsleiter Rosenberg,* ERR. An organization led by the chief ideologue of the Nazi Party, Alfred Rosenberg, dedicated to sequestering the cultural property of France, the Benelux countries, Poland, the Baltic States, Greece, Italy, the Soviet Union, and Ukraine.

"But you must keep in mind that in the Nazi book looting saga the names of several villains feature prominently such as Alfred Rosenberg, Karl Bauer, Reinhard Heydrich, and Franz Alfred Six. And, of course, there were their gofers, an army of well-organized thieves.

"The next time the Nazis turned up was on 14 October. That was the day when the Community Library and a portion of the Rabbinical Library were removed as the president, secretary, and sexton of the Jewish community could do nothing but look on." Catia paused while she retrieved her Samsung tablet from her handbag, swiped the screen, and searched for a document. "Here is what Giacomo Debenedetti, a journalist, literary critic, author, and eyewitness of the events of 14 October 1943, wrote.

It would be interesting to know more about the strange figure who appears at the offices of the Jewish community on October 11. He too is escorted by SS troops and appears to be just another German officer, but with an extra dose of arrogance that comes from having a privileged and, regrettably, well-known 'specialty.'

This elusive, dread-inducing character makes his way into the synagogue building. While his men commence ransacking the libraries of the Rabbinical college and the Jewish community, the officer, with hands as cautious and sensitive as those of the finest needlewoman, skims, touches, caresses papyri and incunabula, leafs through manuscripts and rare editions, peruses parchments and palimpsests. The varying degrees of caution in his touch, the heedfulness of his gestures, are quickly adapted to the importance of each work. In those aristocratic hands, the books, as though subjected to the cruel and bloodless torture of an exquisite sadism, revealed everything. Later, it became known that the SS officer was a distinguished scholar of paleography and Semitic philology.

"It required two railroad cars to move the contents of the libraries north, presumably through Switzerland to Germany. The services of a freight company, Otto and Rosoni, were apparently acquired to organize the transport, and the movers were threatened with death if they removed a single volume of those libraries.

"Debenedetti's translator, Estelle Gilson, reports: *Though the books, like all Holocaust victims, traveled in sealed cars bound for Germany, they were carefully treated—stacked in layers with corrugated sheets between and packed in wicker cases.*"

Catia paused, switched the tablet off, and took a spoonful of her dessert before she continued. "They were unable to complete their pillaging in one day. On 23 December, the officers returned to finish the job by removing the remnants of the Rabbinical College Library. Only a few items, hidden by members of the community or overlooked by the Germans, survived the looting.

"All pleas by the Jewish community to Italian authorities including the Vatican to stop the removal fell on deaf ears—the authorities didn't even respond to the supplications."

Catia looked at Zechariah and said, "How am I doing so far, professor?"

The old man grinned. "Outstanding. I'd award you a distinction so far; even your intonation was perfect."

Rex laughed and noticed Digger smiling as well.

Zechariah's facial expression was melancholic as he took over the exposition. "On the morning of 16 October 1943, the SS and Gestapo surrounded and sealed off the Ghetto. *Hauptsturmführer* Theodor Dannecker, an associate of Adolf Eichmann, was in charge. Dannecker had recently been appointed as the chief of the *Judenreferat*, Jewish Affairs, in Italy. His job was the implementation of the Final Solution, the extermination of the Jews, in Italy. His orders were to clear out the Ghetto.

"Some managed to escape over the rooftops.

"One thousand two hundred and fifty-nine were captured. Some of that number were not Jews and were released. Three hundred and sixty-three men, six hundred and eighty-nine women, and two hundred and seven children, all Jews, were transported to the Palazzo Salviati in Trastevere. When the trucks with the captives drove past the Vatican they screamed and shouted at the pope to help them. To no avail. Two days later, they were loaded onto Holocaust trains at Tiburtina station headed for Auschwitz. Only sixteen survived—fifteen men, one woman and no children.

"You were among those who escaped," Rex said in a whisper.

The old man nodded slowly. "But not my parents, neither my younger brother nor my little seven-year-old sister... I should've been with them, but I ran away when the soldiers turned up. My family died without me. I... I... should've..." His voice had broken down and he stopped talking.

Survivors' remorse. Rex had seen it many times. He had a hard time controlling the emotion of rage that had been building inside of him as he listened to Zechariah. He couldn't help but relive March 11, 2004, the day when his parents and siblings were killed by terrorist bombs at the Madrid train station. Catia had a similar story. Both her parents were killed in 2005 by terrorists working for the Jihad Council, the military wing of Hezbollah.

"Oh my God!" Catia's hand had flown to her mouth. "Zechariah, you never told me that. I'm so sorry..."

It was after 11:00 P.M. when Rex asked for the check, paid, and left a nice tip for their server of the evening while Catia ordered a taxi for Zechariah.

CHAPTER 6 – UNDER THE POPE'S WINDOWS

ROME, ITALY

FRIDAY, JULY 15, 2016

THEY WERE IN Catia's apartment near the *Piazza di Spagna*. Since the day of their wedding they had not set foot on the TOMATS. Not that they didn't like to be on the TOMATS, on the contrary. But they were on a seven-week honeymoon, and since they returned to Rome, they had to make a few alterations to the apartment to accommodate Rex and Digger, and then they got busy with Catia's research project.

Besides, the day after the wedding, Declan Spencer, the captain of the TOMATS, with three passengers, set out on an extended cruise in the Adriatic Sea, visiting the ports on the east side of Italy from Bari in the south to Venice in the north, after which they would cruise down the west coast of Croatia making stops at various islands and ports along the way.

Spencer gave no set return date.

Rex smiled when he thought about that.

It was not surprising that no return date had been set— the passengers were John Brandt—he and Spencer were best friends since their childhood—and Brandt's love interest, Christelle Proll, the deputy director of France's DGSE. The third guest was Simona Bellucci. That was a bit of a surprise to Rex, but Catia told him the vibes between Simona and Spencer were clear as daylight, right from the beginning, for everyone to see, except of course Rex. He was quick to point out that obviously he missed it because he only had eyes for Catia. That earned him a passionate kiss.

According to Catia, Simona and Spencer enjoyed each other's company despite the eighteen-year age gap.

The day Rex and Catia got engaged, they made a promise to each other – no secrets between them, not about past lives and not in the future. No exceptions. Therefore, Catia knew the history of the TOMATS—Rex had liberated it from Prince Mutaib bin Faisal bin Saud, an international black-market arms dealer and human trafficker—a scumbag whom Rex had killed in 2014.

Catia also knew of the special arrangement between John Brandt and Rex about the TOMATS. CRC owned and operated the yacht and Rex had permanent board and lodging on the yacht for the token amount of one dollar per year for life. An arrangement which now included Catia as well.

When Rex and Catia talked about their finances, they had concluded that neither of them *had* to work. Between the two of them they were worth a little more than $7 million. Rex's contribution was a little over $4 million, a sum which included the inheritance from his parents and siblings, savings while working for CRC, and the $1.5 million dollars in severance pay from CRC. Catia, an only child, inherited the apartment block which she had turned into an Airbnb plus the proceeds of life insurance policies and savings which contributed about $3.5 million to their nest egg. With no rent or mortgage or any debt, they were free of the money-worries so many young couples had to deal with. They were free to come and go as they wished and pursue the things they chose.

The first thing they wanted to tick off their to-do list, before setting out on an around the world cruise with Captain Declan Spencer on the TOMATS, was Catia's Ph.D.

They did talk about having children, somewhere in the future. Rex was almost 36, Catia had just turned 32. Catia was excited about having children; Rex also, though he was worried about his ability to be a good father.

What kind of father would I be? As a former assassin, what kind of father could I be? Is it even fair to a child if all you have is a history of death and destruction? were thoughts that often crossed his mind.

He told Catia about his emotional battles. She was not alarmed; she knew Rex would be the world's best father, he only had to believe it—and she was quietly working on that.

***

IT WAS ALMOST 1:30 A.M. Rex's mind was in overdrive as he lay on the bed staring at the ceiling and working through the day's information dump. Catia sat next to him on the bed with her back against the headboard, her long legs stretched out in front of her, the tablet PC on her lap, sipping on a glass of chilled white wine.

"I have lots of questions," Rex said.

"Such as?"

"I couldn't help but notice that you and Zechariah use words such as 'estimated' and 'believed to be' when you talk about the contents of those libraries. I got the impression neither of you know exactly what's in them."

"That's because we don't. In fact, as far as we know, no one knows. You see, those libraries were never catalogued—not fully. We can only go on people's memories."

Rex frowned. "Why would they not have catalogued them?"

"Part of the Community Library was catalogued in 1934. But Zechariah suggests, and I agree with him, the lack of full catalogues was probably deliberate. The Jewish community had two thousand years of experience to draw on. Their books, the ones they couldn't hide in time, had been banned, confiscated, and burned frequently. The Catholic Church was the culprit on many occasions. It is quite possible that their paranoia and maybe some premonition led to the view that without catalogues there was a better chance that the libraries might survive."

"Makes sense. Tell me about the partial catalogue."

"It was created in 1934 by Isaia Sonne, a Jewish historian, bibliographer, and teacher at Jewish colleges across Italy. He emigrated to the United States in 1938, where he taught at the Hebrew Union College in Cincinnati until his death in 1960. Sonne's catalogue names a little over four thousand seven hundred volumes, but you must remember that Sonne himself bemoaned the fact that he had been only permitted to see the second-best items in the collection.

"Rex, that library contained two thousand years of Jewish history in Rome. Not only that, it also contained history of the beginnings of Christianity."

She scrolled to a document on her tablet and read a quote from Robert Katz's book, *Black Sabbath*. "'*Among the known material were the only copies of books and manuscripts dating from before the birth of Christ, from the time of the Caesars, the emperors, and the early Popes. There were engravings from the Middle Ages, books from the earliest printers, and papers and documents handed down through the ages.*'"

"It's going to be a bit of a challenge, not insurmountable, but a challenge nevertheless, to track down books if we don't even know what titles we're looking for," Rex said. "However, I guess, if we can find one or more it might lead us to the rest."

Catia nodded. "Yes, that's what Zechariah and I are hoping for."

"Another question. Where did the Catholic Church, specifically Pope Pius XII, stand on this? Surely he must have known about the atrocities committed against the Jews of Rome?"

"Not only the Jews of Rome, the Jews of Europe," Catia said. "No doubt the pope knew about it. The pope's silence about the *Shoah* is the subject of much controversy. The thing is, he could've done something about it. The Nazi military commander in Rome was hesitant to act against the Jews of Rome for fear of condemnation from the church, but it never came.

"The members of the Catholic Church all over Europe, and especially in Italy, had a lot of sympathy with the Jews. They helped thousands of them to flee or hide from the Nazis. But the voice of the Supreme Pontiff, leader of the worldwide Catholic Church, the Vicar of Christ, was never heard about the genocide of the Jews and others.

"Listen to this. It's an extract from a piece written by the Swiss diarist, De Wyss, on 14 October 1943. *'The population is half crazy... Everybody is in a cold sweat. Young men and families look desperately for hiding places, get them, then look for a better one... convents and seminaries have become the most sought-after hideouts.*

Another one is the lunatic asylum. People have entered and filled it to bursting point.' Yet, the pope remained quiet.

"Michael Phayer, the author of the book *The Catholic Church and the Holocaust*, wrote, *'The question of the Pope's silence has become the focus of intense historical debate and analysis because the deportations occurred 'under his very windows.'* The term *'under his very windows'* is based on an actual quotation from the report of Ernst von Weizsäcker, the German ambassador to the Vatican, reporting to his masters in Berlin that the looting and deportations had taken place *'under the Pope's windows.'''*

"It's less than two kilometers from the Ghetto to the Vatican," Rex whispered. "Under the pope's windows indeed."

Chapter 7 – Stocking the Museum

Rome, Italy

July 2016

IN THE DAYS following their visit to the Jewish Ghetto and Dr. Zechariah Nachum, Rex got busy reading through every bit of information Catia had collected over the years.

He soon learned that the joy the Nazis took out of destroying Jewish books didn't end with the book burning orgy of May 1933. In March 1941, the Frankfurter Zeitung reported, "For us it is a matter of special pride to destroy the Talmudic Academy, which has been known as the greatest in Poland [Yeshivas Chachmei Lublin]. We threw out of the building the great Talmudic library and carted it to market. There we set fire to the books. The fire lasted for twenty hours. The Jews of Lublin were assembled around and cried bitterly. The cries almost silenced us. Then we summoned a military band, and the joyful shouts of the soldiers silenced the sounds of Jewish cries."

But they didn't burn all the books they laid their hands on. In 1940, Hitler instructed the man with a Jewish sounding surname, who was no Jew but a misguided Nazi philosopher and ideologist, Alfred Rosenberg, to seize "all scientific and archival materials from the ideological foe."

Thus, the *Einsatzstab Reichsleiter Rosenberg*, ERR, was founded. Their goal—to collect books and cultural items of Germany's enemies, Jews and others, to stock the shelves of *Hohe Schule,* schools of higher learning, where they were to be studied. There was such a school in Hamburg for colonial research, another in Halle was for religion, another in Stuttgart studied biology and race.

The ERR workers followed Hitler's armies across Europe as they conquered one territory after another, collecting the spoils of cultural treasures from the enemies of the Reich. Moneywise, art theft was their biggest crime. Trainloads and truckloads of paintings, artifacts, antique furniture, carpets, tapestries, and such were carted to Germany, destined for its museums and private collectors, many of them high-ranking Nazi officers and officials such as Hermann Göring, one of the most powerful figures in the Nazi Party.

In March 1941, Rosenberg opened the Institute for Research on the Jewish Question in Frankfurt, of which he said, "The library for the Jewish Question not only for Europe but for the world will arise in Frankfurt."

It was Rosenberg's delusional dream to create the largest library of Jewish books in the world. However, his dream never materialized. As the Allied bombing of Germany intensified toward the end of the war, large quantities of books were destroyed by the bombs. Even so, vast numbers were moved by Rosenberg's cronies to

German occupied territories or stored in underground bunkers.

By April 1941 Rosenberg's team had followed the German army into the Balkans where they confiscated massive amounts of books and Judaica from the ancient Salonika *kehillah*.

It was while Rex was reading about the books of Salonika that he came across the name of Dr. Karl Bauer, director of the Hebrew Department of the Nazi Institute for Jewish Research in Frankfurt, again.

Rex sorted through the documents and extracted all information pertaining to Karl Bauer.

Bauer was an enigmatic and contradictory character who went from being an ordained Catholic priest to a passionate Nazi and anti-Semite, the destructor of Jewish heritage.

Born in Cologne, Germany in 1904, he studied Catholic theology in Bonn where he attained a doctorate for his study about Messianism and the prophet Ezekiel of the Old Testament. He was ordained as a priest in 1927 and received a vicariate in Essen. Two years later, he attended the Pontifical Biblical Institute in Rome where he graduated with another doctorate in Bible and Language Studies. In 1931 he received a scholarship from the Görres Society to further his studies at the Oriental Institute in Jerusalem where he also worked for the German Association of the Holy Land.

It was in Jerusalem where he met his future wife. She was part of the community of German colonists who had been living in Palestine since 1868.

In 1934, Bauer and his wife-to-be returned to Germany where Bauer was discharged from his clerical position and they married. By 1935, with his language skills and academic record, he was working as a lecturer in Hebraica at the Prussian State Library in Berlin. He became enamored with Hitler's National Socialism and wrote articles which were published by the Institute for the Study of the Jewish Question, as well as for the anti-Semitic weekly, *Der Sturmer*.

He joined the Nazi Party in 1940 and in 1941 his path crossed that of Alfred Rosenberg, the founder of the *Einsatzstab Reichsleiter Rosenberg*, ERR and he was offered a job.

Working for the ERR, Bauer traveled to occupied territories to collect useful writings for the Institute. In this capacity, in January 1942, Bauer was instrumental in the robbery and destruction of the Jewish cultural heritage in Vilnius, Lithuania. He selected 20,000 of the most valuable books and manuscripts and shipped them to Frankfurt for Rosenberg's planned museum. The rest, about 80,000 volumes, he sold to a paper mill for twenty marks a ton and the lead printing blocks of the famous Rohm printing house he sold as scrap metal.

Bauer and his underlings committed similar crimes in France, the Netherlands, Poland, Czechoslovakia, Greece, Russia, and elsewhere. And, Zechariah suspected, he was probably also involved in the theft of the two libraries in the Jewish Ghetto of Rome during 1943.

To Rex it was clear, although Rosenberg was head of the ERR, its daily operations were headed by Dr. Karl Bauer, the man responsible to stock the Nazi museum, the fervent spokesman for the concept of *Judenforschung ohne Juden*, Jewish Studies without Jews.

CHAPTER 8 – THAT LOOK

ROME, ITALY

THURSDAY, JULY 28, 2016

"WOULD HAVE BEEN nice if those scumbags were still alive. Digger and I could pay them a visit and have a nice chat with them. Catia would be able to complete her Ph.D. in record time," Rex mumbled.

"What was that?" Catia asked from her desk.

"Just daydreaming."

"About what?"

"How nice it would've been if Rosenberg and Bauer and the rest of the friendly Nazi book robbers were available for a chat."

Catia smiled. "Yep, that would've made things so much easier. But I'm afraid we'll have to do it the hard way—without their help."

Rex laid back in the reclining chair and started scratching Digger's back. They both closed their eyes; Digger because of the sheer joy any dog will get out of a backrub and Rex because he wanted to concentrate so that he could recall a few facts.

"I've just finished reading the history of those scoundrels. Some of them got what they deserved, but some of them literally got away with murder," Rex started. "For instance, Reinhard Heydrich was fatally wounded in Prague on May 27, 1942. He started a war and he died in it. Justice.

"The guy in charge of the *Judenreferat*, in Italy, Theodor Dannecker, escaped a Nuremberg trial by committing suicide after being captured in December 1945. Good riddance.

"Dannecker's successor, Friedrich Bosshammer, disappeared after the war but was found working as a lawyer in Wuppertal, Germany, and was brought to trial in 1968. It was only in 1972 that he was sentenced to life in prison for his involvement in the deportation of three thousand three hundred Jews from Italy to Auschwitz. But then he escaped it all by dying a few months after the verdict without spending any time in prison. Cheat.

"Franz Alfred Six went on trial in Nuremberg for war crimes. There was not enough evidence to link him to atrocities. So, instead of the death penalty he got twenty years in prison which was commuted to ten years by a clemency board. In the end the bastard served seven and a half years from the day he was arrested—about thirteen and a half days for each of his two hundred victims. He died in 1975, in Italy. Injustice."

Catia was shaking her head slightly; she was still getting used to Rex's photographic memory.

"Alfred Rosenberg, the chief engineer of Hitler's book marauding enterprise, the man who convinced the Führer that the Jews were a greater threat to the Nazi Reich than Russia, author of *The Myth of the Twentieth Century*, the second-most popular all time blockbuster in Nazi Germany after Hitler's *Mein Kampf*, also went on trial in Nuremberg. He got the death penalty and was executed on October 16, 1946—to the day exactly three years after the theft of the libraries from the Ghetto. Poetic."

Catia smiled; she was also still getting used to Rex's dry sense of humor.

"And that brings me to my favorite Nazi uncle, Doctor Karl Bauer…"

"Uncle?"

He shrugged. "I'm half German, from my mother's side, as you know."

Catia smiled. "Ah, I see…"

"Okay, so this guy was obviously Rosenberg's chief cook and bottlewasher…"

Catia burst out in laughter.

"Why are you laughing?"

"The image of Bauer with a *toque blanche* on his head, cooking for Herr Rosenberg."

Rex grinned and continued as if there was no interlude. "What bugs me about this guy is that there is very little information about his life after the war.

"He was captured in 1945, interned for a year and released in October 1946, a week or so after his buddy, Rosenberg, was executed. Bauer, Rosenberg's manager of operations, never went on trial. Apparently, the investigators couldn't find enough evidence against him. Even in the city of Frankfurt and at the university library, where Bauer has spent so much time, everyone suffered from amnesia. They couldn't remember him. I smell a rat.

"After his release, still very much in love with books, he found a job as a publishing editor for a German academic publishing house, Franz Steiner Verlag. He was also on the editorial board of the *Duden*, a dictionary of the German language.

"It seems Doctor Karl Bauer, the former priest and Hebraic scholar who forsook the Catholic Church to become a devout Nazi and Rosenberg's head of operations, the man who stole and destroyed millions of books and might've been responsible for the deaths of at least two Jews, came full circle when he returned to the patronage of the Catholic Church which he had left in 1934, and lived out his days in peace, as a free man, until he died on January 30, 1960 in Wiesbaden, Germany."

"Rex, what are you thinking? I've seen that look on your face before."

"What look?"

"The one that says, I've got an idea..."

"Oh, that one. It should be there. I've got an idea, but..."

"No buts. No secrets, remember?"

Rex grinned. "Yes, of course, no secrets, I was just hoping to get my ducks in a row, maybe a bit more reading, before I tell you about it."

"Well, then you shouldn't have screwed that I've-got-an-idea-look onto your face."

Rex laughed. "Okay, here're some of my thoughts.

"From what I have read, Bauer definitely got 'special' treatment after the war. I'd like to know why. It is as if someone had wiped out the man's past to ensure there was nothing left to use as evidence in a trial. And not only that, after the war, someone—it could be the same someone or a successor—made sure that Bauer remained in obscurity. He was married but I couldn't even find his wife's name. Did they have children? I couldn't find anything about it. I'd like to know who that someone was."

"Are you thinking of something like ODESSA?" She was referring to the codename coined in 1946 by the Americans who had derived it from the German: *Organisation der ehemaligen SS-Angehörigen,* meaning: Organization of Former SS Members. It was an underground organization, they believed, responsible for assisting prominent Nazi SS officers escape from Germany at the end of the war. It was an idea that became a popular theme for novels and movies, notably Frederick Forsyth's best-selling 1972 thriller, *The Odessa File*.

"Yeah, something like that. Except that it seems ODESSA never existed."

"Yep, apparently not. But as you probably know, there is enough proof that the Nazis did get support from actual ODESSA-like escape networks such as *Konsul, Scharnhorst, Sechsgestirn, Leibwache,* and *Lustige Brüder.*"

Rex got up from the recliner, went to the kitchenette, poured two glasses of red wine, and handed one to Catia.

She had her tablet in front of her looking at the screen and said, "Uki Goñi is an Argentine author who researched the role of the Vatican, the Swiss authorities, and the government of Argentina in organizing 'ratlines,' escape routes for Nazi criminals and collaborators. In his book *The Real Odessa*, he described the role of Juan Domingo Perón, the former Argentine General who later became president, in providing cover for Nazi war criminals with cooperation from the Vatican, as well as the Argentinean and Swiss governments. According to Goñi, Perón even had his agents set up a secret office in Bern, Switzerland, to run an operation that stretched from Scandinavia to Italy."

"Ratline…," Rex said softly, deep in thought. "Bauer didn't need a ratline to get to South America or any of the other favorite Nazi holiday destinations. He got his ratline in Germany."

"And you're thinking of finding it?"

"Only if you'll allow me."

Catia laughed. "Permission granted, on condition you take me along."

"Wouldn't dream of doing it without you," Rex said. "But before we go down that rabbit hole, I'd like to do a bit more reading, especially about the attempts made to find the libraries in the post war era."

"Prepare yourself to be disappointed," Catia said. "But don't let my pessimism stop you. Have a read of it. Unlike me, your mind is still untainted. You might just pick up something Zechariah and I've overlooked."

ROME, ITALY

SATURDAY, AUGUST 6, 2016

THE POST WAR American military government in Germany established the Monuments, Fine Arts and Archives Division, which managed to recover many looted items from the central Offenbach Archival Depository outside Frankfurt am Main and tried to return them to their owners or countries of origin. There were many other organizations, Jewish and non-Jewish, who got involved in the recovery efforts.

The Communist dominated countries were less cooperative in the effort to recover and restore the harvest of the depredations of the ERR and the *SS-Reichssicherheitshauptamt*, RSHA. The RSHA alone had collected almost three million books from Nazi enemies, which, according to them, included churches, Freemasons, Marxists, and Jews. The RSHA shipped most of their booty to the Theresienstadt ghetto outside Prague. After the war, when the Hebrew University Library of Yerushalayim started negotiations with the Czech government for the return of the books, they got a ransom demand to the tune of 936,736 korunas, Czech crowns.

According to a report by the Jewish Museum in Prague, by 1951, about 100,000 books had been recovered, but it was unclear whether all of the books were from the Theresienstadt collection.

In 2003, 48 years after the war, the Austrian National Library returned 52,403 books to their rightful owners, and as recently as May 2010 agreed to pay 135,000 euros for thousands of books looted by the Nazis but determined to be ownerless.

Over the years the resolve and hard work of some of the individuals and organizations involved in the restoration process paid some dividends. But, by all accounts, hundreds of thousands of books remained unaccounted for.

As for the effort to recover the libraries of Rome's Jewish Ghetto, Catia was right. It was disappointing, to say the least. The obvious lack of urgency to recover the two libraries left Rex with the sense that their concealment could have been orchestrated.

In 1947, twenty *incunabula*, books printed before 1501, belonging to the Rabbinical College Library, were recovered and returned. But that was it—to this day nothing else had been recovered. Those books were part of the second shipment of books from the Roman Ghetto, in December 1943.

Eighteen years later, in 1965, some short-lived excitement ensued when two manuscripts with the

Community Library's diamond-shaped stamp were acquired by the Jewish Theological Seminary Library in New York. The subsequent investigation brought to light that although the two books were listed in Isaiah Sonne's 1934 catalogue, they were removed from the library in 1935, long before the Nazis turned up in the Ghetto. None of the material present in the Community Library in 1943 was ever recovered.

Nothing else happened for thirty years, until the late 1990s when, like many other European nations, Italy finally also established a public committee to investigate the plundering of Italian Jewish property during the war. But the committee didn't achieve much.

It was not until 2002, under pressure from the Jewish community, that a special commission was put together to find the Community Library. The commission ended up producing only more conjecture and no answers.

Nevertheless, sources were consistent about the fact that the libraries were removed from the Ghetto in two batches. The first on October 16, 1943 when the entire Community Library and part of the Rabbinical College Library were removed. The second removal happened on December 22 and 23, 1943 when the remainder of the latter library was removed. As to the destination of the first shipment there was no consensus—it could have been Berlin or Frankfurt.

Proof of the destination of the second tranche was found in a report addressed to the ERR dated 21 January 1944, which stated: *Monthly report December 1943 - thanks to a special operation in Rome, what remained of the library of the Synagogue has been loaded onto a wagon and sent to the Institute for the Research into the Jewish question in Frankfurt am Main.*

The special commission investigated the possibility that the first shipment, of October 16, went to Frankfurt, or Berlin, or Frankfurt via Berlin. The Frankfurt option, they concluded, was the less likely one. Of the millions of books stolen by the Nazi's, 1.2 million were found by the Americans at Hungen, about 30 miles from Frankfurt. Among those were the 20 *incunabula* belonging to the Rabbinical College Library. However, none of the books of the Community Library or the rest of the books from the Rabbinical College Library turned up at Hungen or anywhere else for that matter.

The commission concluded it was quite possible that the contents of the two rail cars of October 16, 1943 were destroyed in Allied bombing raids. Alternatively, the contents went to Berlin from where it was evacuated to Ratibor, Silesia, now known as Racibórz, Poland, which eventually came under Soviet Union control. The Soviet Union refused to assist with requests to return Nazi loot to their rightful owners, neither did the post-Soviet Russian government. They refused investigators access to important archives such as those of the Russian Federal

Security Service. That, of course, gave rise to the theory that the Russians had something to hide—therefore, the libraries could be located somewhere within the current Russian Federation.

Rex's attention was drawn to the writing of Estelle Gilson, the translator for Giacomo Debenedetti, the journalist and eyewitness of the events of October 14 and 16, 1943. "History has made it poignantly clear that Jewish books had a far better survival rate than did Jewish human beings."

"Except, it seems, in the case of the libraries of the Jewish Ghetto," Rex countered her under his breath.

Nevertheless, it was Gilson's notes about the commission's investigation of the rumors that the freight train carrying the first haul from the libraries toward Germany was bombed by the Allies which Rex found of interest.

The diary of Rosina Sonari, the secretary of the synagogue in Rome, contained an entry which read: *They were even used to seize two capable railway wagons. In them the books were arranged neatly in layers. Sheets of corrugated paper were interposed between the layer and the layer. [...] The wagons, once filled, were carefully sealed and sent to Germany. The staff [...] could not do anything but write down the numbers and destination of the wagons. Here they are: DRPI / Munchen / 97970 / G DRPI / Munchen / 97970 / C. 27*

The commission consulted the Italian State Railway to find out more about the train, but the railway authorities were unable to produce any documentation about it—not about its departure, neither about its destruction, nor about its destination or its arrival. As far as they were concerned there was no such train. On the other hand, a report by American officers who visited the Hungen depot in April 1945 stated that a trainload of materials from Italy had been expected but never arrived.

This time Rex was a bit more audibly vocal with his comments. "A train of which the Italian State Railway have no records, could have departed from Italy—or not. But, if it did, it never reached Germany, if that were its destination. What happened to the ghost train? There's no record of its destruction... in fact, there is no record of it at all."

"Rex, you have that I've-got-an-idea-look on your face again," Catia said. "Tell me about it."

Her voice shook him out of his reverie. "What have you heard?"

"Something about a ghost train."

Rex told her what he had been thinking and added, "I'm not inclined to support the idea that the Russians have the libraries. I agree with Harvard professor Patricia Grimsted's notion that it is just too easy to blame the lack of an answer on the greed of the Russians, or even the notorious obscurity of their archives."

"So, what's her theory?"

"She reckons the Russians had no interest in Hebraica at that time. She said if the Russians came across it during the war, they would've left it out in the snow. She believes the libraries ended up in Frankfurt where they were stashed in Nazi bomb shelters in which case they could have been destroyed, or if not destroyed, they could very well have ended up in the hands of one or more individuals."

"I take it she gave no explanation about the mystery of the missing train, did she?"

"No, unfortunately not..."

"But I get the feeling you have a theory of your own. Right?"

"Yes, I have. Two actually. One, what if the train left Italy, did go to Germany, Berlin or Frankfurt doesn't matter, but on the way wherever it made a stop to unload some of its cargo?"

"Where?"

"Switzerland..."

"Switzerland?" Catia frowned.

"Well, I've been brought up with the idea that Switzerland, as a neutral country during the war, provided sanctuary to the persecuted, the wounded, and the refugees. And while that part seems to be true, since my school days I've learned that was only half of the Swiss story. The part that we never hear of is that they also profited hugely from the war. The Swiss didn't care who they did business with. The Nazis squirreled much of their stolen *objets d'art* to Switzerland, with the full knowledge of the Swiss authorities.

"And the Swiss finally confessed it, albeit more than half a century after the war. In 1996, fifty-one years after the fact, their federal assembly ordered the creation of an Independent Commission of Experts to investigate Switzerland's involvement in the handling of looted items. The commission's conclusion? —Switzerland was a trading hub for looted art during the war. Of course, the commission's brief was limited to the events of World War II; therefore, it was not necessary for them to mention that they're still involved in it to this day."

Catia nodded slowly.

"Arthur William 'Douglas' Cooper, who sometimes published under the name Douglas Lord, was a British art historian, art critic, and art collector. He was assigned by the Allies to a unit that investigated Nazi looted art, and this unit was quite successful. One of their most significant discoveries was the Schenker Papers. The Schenker Company, during the war, was tasked with the transport of stolen art to Germany and elsewhere, including Switzerland. They were one of the most important enterprises engaged in the German pillage and plunder, aggressions and mass crime, throughout Europe.

It was Cooper's investigations into the activities of the Schenker Company that exposed the roles of Paris art dealers, Swiss collectors, German experts, and museums in the looting of Jewish property for the likes of Hitler, Hermann Göring, and many others.

"There's no doubt that the Swiss banks accepted looted gold from the Nazis, much of it ripped from the teeth of their victims on their way to the gas chambers. The Swiss banks, using the gold as collateral, provided Hitler with Swiss francs, the only universally accepted currency during the war. That money kept Hitler's war machine going for another year when it should have come to a screeching halt in the autumn of 1944.

"Millions more died because of the Swiss financiers.

"Much of the world's gold and silver and most valuable collectibles lie in the vaults beneath the streets of the banks of Switzerland. Not to mention what's hidden in the Geneva Freeport."

Catia raised an eyebrow. "Geneva Freeport?"

"It's a warehouse complex in Geneva, used for the storage of not only art but all kinds of valuables and collectibles, some say even vintage cars. It's the oldest and largest freeport facility in the world. Described as the foremost place to store valuables—the place where collectors go for the security and stay for the tax benefits. It's been in existence since 1888 and it is estimated that the value of the artworks stored there today would exceed one hundred billion dollars. It has been called the world's best museum that no one will ever see."

"An extension of the secret Swiss banking system...," Catia whispered. "Your Swiss hypothesis is as good as, if not better than, any of the others put forward. But before we discuss that in more detail, what's your second idea?"

"The train never left Italy."

"Wow! Signore Dalton, you certainly have some novel ideas. I love it. Where in Italy?"

"I have a general location in mind, but I think I know who might be able to give us the exact spot."

"Come on, don't be like that. I love you, you can tell me. Don't make me sing for my dinner."

Rex grinned. "The Vatican."

Catia's wide-shot eyes betrayed her surprise. "Rex Dalton, are you serious?"

He nodded.

Digger woofed once, probably because he heard the word dinner, but Rex thought it was in support of his idea.

Catia's gaze swiveled between Rex and Digger as if she was trying to unearth a conspiracy between them. Apparently, she didn't find one. "The Swiss dish I might be able to consume; the Vatican dish needs a lot of seasoning."

Rex started laughing. "Something tells me you're hungry."

"That I am. Let's go down to the trattoria. I've been craving their ossobuco for weeks now."

"Ossobuco?"

"Yes, it's a bone-in veal shank, cooked over low heat, very slowly, in a broth of meat stock, white wine, and veggies. Delicious."

"Two ossobucos it will be." Rex looked around for Digger and saw him standing at the door already. He had his leash in his mouth.

CHAPTER 10 – VAGUE CONCEPTS

ROME, ITALY

SATURDAY, AUGUST 6, 2016

TO ANYONE OBSERVING the three of them, they would have been the quintessence of contentment. Digger because he was with his pack, his pack was happy, and, of course, small pieces of food were being fed to him stealthily. Rex and Catia because they were newlyweds, madly in love, and, of course, the ossobuco was every bit as delectable as Catia said it would be.

"Okay," Catia started after she had a few bites of her food and a sip of red wine. "You were going to explain the Vatican connection to me. I'm all ears."

Rex gave Digger another piece of veal under the table. "We spoke about the role of Pope Pius XII in the war a few days ago. I've thought about it and read a bit wider since. I'm of the opinion we have to look at the history of the relationship between the Vatican and Jews, especially here in Rome. A topic you know much more about than I do. Nonetheless, my appraisal is that it's been a checkered history. Many atrocities were committed against Jews, including the banning, confiscation, and burning of Jewish literature. From your previous studies, you know much better than I do that the Catholic Church didn't only have it against Jewish literature, they also had

89

it against the Jewish people themselves— 'the God killers.'

"I'm aware of the arguments in support of Pius XII's reticence about the Nazis' extermination camps. But as far as I'm concerned there is no argument that weighs as much as the lives of fourteen million people, among them European Jewry, six million of them. No argument can justify that, absolutely nothing. And it's not as if the pope didn't know what was going on; he knew. The plights of the condemned reached his ears every day.

"What's more, some of the pope's priests, bishops, and cardinals openly supported the extermination of the Jews, thus indirectly taking part in the Holocaust. And when the concept of an independent Jewish state in Palestine came to the fore, the Vatican opposed the Jews' only bolt hole. The Vatican was against the Nuremberg trials, and its common knowledge that there were high-ranking clergymen and officials who helped the Nazis escape from Europe in the last days of the war... and long after. Pope Pius XII never excommunicated a single Nazi leader.

"I know that the Italian Jews received help from Catholic Church members and were not slaughtered to the same extent as the Jews in the rest of Europe. At Eichmann's trial a witness said, 'Every Italian Jew who survived owed his life to the Italians.' But that described the Italian people and *some* of the clergy. Helping the Jews escape from the Nazis was not official Vatican policy. The church's efforts, when they came, were late in the war. By then, millions had already perished in the death camps, and aid was mostly limited to Jews who had converted to Christianity."

Catia put her wineglass down slowly. "I agree. It was not the Vatican's proudest moment. But what led you to the idea that the Vatican had something to do with the disappearance of the libraries and are still hiding it?"

"Look at their actions after the war.

"In the last months of the war, eighty percent of the SS leaders disappeared. They abandoned their positions, got rid of their uniforms, and vanished in the chaos of post-war Germany. The SS gold bars stashed away in the banks of Switzerland, Morocco, Argentina, Liechtenstein, Beirut, and others, now came in handy for the various secret organizations helping the SS criminals to get false identity documents, money, and paid passage to their new homes in friendlier climes such as South America and elsewhere.

"The Catholic Church had a hand in it. One doesn't have to search much further than the Austrian bishop of Rome, Bishop Alois Hudal, a 'ratliner' par excellence. He helped many an SS officer get Red Cross travel documents, issued through the intervention of the Church. One of his favorite hiding places for his charges was the Franciscan monastery at the Church of San Bonaventura al Palatino.

"A few of his notable clients were SS Captain Eduard Roschmann; Josef Mengele, the 'Angel of Death' at Auschwitz; Gustav Wagner, SS Sergeant at Sobibor; Alois

Brunner, organizer of deportations from France and Slovakia to German concentration camps; and Adolf Eichmann, the man in charge of the enterprise to exterminate all of European Jewry.

"There exists a letter written by Hudal to the Argentinian President, Juan Perón, in August 1948 requesting five thousand visas: three thousand for German and two thousand for Austrian soldiers. In that letter, Hudal takes great care to explain his request was not for Nazi refugees, but for 'anti-Communist fighters', whose wartime 'sacrifice' had saved Europe from Soviet domination.

"Hudal was not the only one; there's a lot more evidence of the church's involvement in the escape of prominent Nazis.

"The current pope is the sixth since Pius XII. Seventy years have passed since the end of the war, and there has been only one, and I'd call it half-hearted, apology for the church's role in the Holocaust."

"The 1998 'We Remember: A Reflection on the Shoah' by Pope John Paul II," Catia said quietly.

"Yep, and it took them eleven years to draft it," Rex added.

Catia continued. "The document called on Catholics to repent of past errors and infidelities regarding the Jews and to renew their awareness of the Hebrew roots of their faith. It also declares deep sorrow for the sufferings caused to the Jewish people during the war and states clearly that the Shoah was a permanent stain on the history of the century, and it offered to help heal the wounds and rectify the injustices."

"Yes. And as a Jew, how do you feel about that statement?"

"Although I welcome the gesture and accept the apology, the problem I have with that document is the lack of details about the kind of help the church had in mind to heal the wounds and rectify the injustices."

"Exactly," Rex said. "That statement came up short on the details, which is why after more than seventy years, nothing more than a vague statement has happened. That statement is already eighteen years old, and the Vatican has done nothing to help. To this day, the Vatican has steadfastly refused to unseal the archives of Pope Pius XII. Every attempt by independent scholars to get access to the Vatican's Secret Archives to research the controversy surrounding Pius XII has been rejected."

"It's a pity we'll never get into the archives," Catia sighed.

"Well, where there's a will there's a way."

Catia frowned. "Tell me you're not thinking of breaking into the Vatican's Secret Archives."

Rex smiled. "Don't worry, it's not Plan A."

"You already have plans?"

"Nah, only vague concepts."

"Okay, you can tell me about them later. I think we need to have another chat with Zechariah." Catia said.

"Agreed."

Chapter 11 – I know a few people

ROME, ITALY

MONDAY, AUGUST 8, 2016

ZECHARIAH LISTENED TO Catia and Rex in silence. When they had finished, over his lowered wireframe glasses, he stared at them for a long while before he started speaking. "You two seem to have a plan. Tell me a bit more. Maybe I can be of assistance."

Catia nodded for Rex to explain.

"I wouldn't call it much of a plan yet—more like a fact-finding mission. As Catia explained before, there's a big gap in our knowledge of Doctor Karl Bauer."

"I'm still listening," Zechariah said.

"At the Nuremberg trials, the ERR was branded a criminal organization. Bauer admitted he had worked for them during the war. In fact, Bauer's own reports to Rosenberg about the ERR's acquisition activities were used as evidence in Rosenberg's trial. They found him guilty and executed him.

"There is enough evidence of Bauer's criminal behavior during the war to have warranted a trial for him as well. The mystery is, the ERR's prime looter was released—he never stood trial for anything. For some hitherto inexplicable reason the Allies were not interested in prosecuting the staff, the rank-and-file looters of the ERR."

Zechariah nodded slowly.

Rex continued. "After his release, Bauer kept a low profile. We know he worked in Wiesbaden on the editorial staff of a publishing company until his death on January 30, 1960. And that's more or less all we know about him.

"It seems he never returned to Berlin or Frankfurt, the cities where he had made a name for himself, nor did he establish contact with his former ERR colleagues. It's possible that he evaded trial by avoiding prominence and socializing, but I think there is more to it."

"Such as?"

"Well, living as a recluse could've kept him out of court, but what did he do to obliterate his personal information? We know nothing about his wife or his children, if there were any. Nothing about relatives, friends, and associates either. It looks as if there had been a deliberate and well-executed effort to hide or destroy that information. And I'm not convinced he would've been able to do it on his own. He must have had some help... in high places."

"You have a point," Zechariah said. "We know many of the Nazi fugitives never left Germany. They just got false names and papers and went undercover until the Allies handed the governance back to the German people."

"Yes, but Bauer didn't change his name, nor did he get himself false documents; nevertheless, it's obvious he went to some trouble to stay out of the limelight and get his records deleted."

"A type of ratline...," Zechariah murmured.

"Exactly. And my question is: in exchange for what?"

"The ratline, you mean?"

"Yes. You see, if there was one man who could tell the world what happened to all those books he'd stolen so diligently, it was Bauer. But apparently no one ever asked him."

There was a big grin on the old scholar's face. "Not your first... what's the word the Americans use?"

"Rodeo," Rex said with a grin.

"Yes, that's the word. Not your first rodeo?"

"In fact, this *is* my first. I've never been a research assistant for a Ph.D. student before, let alone for one as beautiful as Catia," Rex deadpanned.

Zechariah chuckled and left it at that. He knew Catia was a *sayan* just like he was and was convinced that Rex had some kind of military, probably Special Forces, background. He turned his gaze to Catia and said, "If I understand your husband correctly, the two of you intend to start by filling in the gaps in Bauer's personal file?"

She nodded. "What do you think?"

"Rex has certainly brought a new perspective to the search, and I'd say we would be remiss if we didn't investigate it. I'll give you all the help I can."

"The first thing that comes to mind is to pay a visit to Germany and see if we can dig up the old registers," Catia said.

"What remains of them," Zechariah said. "Keep in mind the Nazis deliberately destroyed as much of the records of their senior officers and officials as they could get their hands on in the final months of the war. My understanding is that there are a significant number of records missing. The records you might get access to may not contain the information you're looking for.

"Furthermore, it's my personal experience that getting any information about prominent Nazis is a bureaucratic nightmare, probably more appropriate to call it a communal resistance to divulge information about an appalling past."

Catia looked a bit crestfallen.

"But there are other ways to get it. I know of three people who made it their business to conduct investigations into looted Holocaust assets. Between those three, over the years, they had been able to get billions of dollars in settlements from the financial institutions of Switzerland and Austria and managed to return a lot of stolen property. They might have come across information about Bauer.

"Unfortunately, two of them are already dead. But it might be worth trying to find their families to see if you can get access to their research. There could be some leads. The person still alive has just turned 94; he is not in good health, but his mind is still clear. Abraham Heilbron. He's in Geneva. We've met on a few occasions, and we keep in contact. I can make an introduction if you want to."

"That would be great," Catia said.

"Good. I'll give him a call and let you know his answer."

"Thanks for that."

"Now, I don't want to sound paranoid, but I'm afraid it's a congenital trait of the Jews who survived the war; I want to caution you to be careful. Those private investigators, and for that matter everyone else who was involved in the restitution of loot, made many enemies across Europe and elsewhere. Some were brutally assaulted."

CHAPTER 12 – COULD BE WORTH BILLIONS

ROME, ITALY

MONDAY, AUGUST 8, 2016

BACK AT THE apartment Rex called Rehka on his secured satellite phone. She was his technology expert, virtual assistant, researcher, and friend. With a master's degree in computer sciences, she had exceptional skills in programming and online research. If anyone anywhere left a digital footprint, be it on social media, email, or online searches, she could track that person down. She had enough black hat and gray hat skills to operate anonymously on the Darknet and get unfettered access to some of the most secure private, government, and law enforcement databases across the globe without leaving so much as a hint that she had been there. And since she had met CRC's IT guru, Greg Wade, and worked with him on two missions, she had gone from strength to strength.

Since taking on the position as Rex's IT doyenne a few years before, she had equipped them both with encrypted satellite phones. Rex's phone was encased in a shockproof and waterproof casing, because he would be out and about in nature and some rough places with his phone. Hers was daintier and looked like a normal mobile phone. The ringers were set to sound like a normal smartphone.

It was not impossible to tap into their conversations, but to do it, one would need one of the phones in hand, need to know the password to unlock it, and know the passphrases which Rex and Rehka had agreed on.

"Rex! What a surprise," Rehka shouted after they'd exchanged the passphrases. "How is married life agreeing with you?"

"It's a bliss, Rehka, I can only recommend it highly to anyone who's in love." Rex hinted at the budding romantic relationship between her and Greg.

She ignored it and, Rex had no doubt, with a smile on her face, said, "I'm glad to hear that. How's Catia?"

"She's here right next to me. I'll put the phone on speaker."

The next five minutes Rex couldn't get a single word in. He gave up, sat back, and listened to the ladies babbling excitedly. When there was a quiet moment in the conversation, Rex knew it was not a sign that they were finished, it was just for them to take a breath so that they could continue. He finally interrupted. "Sorry, ladies, would you mind if we talk business first? Then the two of you can take the rest of the day to catch up while Digger and I go for a run."

Between Rex and Catia, over the course of the next hour, they explained to Rehka what they were after.

***

LANCY, SWITZERLAND

ZECHARIAH HAD PHONED Catia early on Tuesday morning to let her know Abraham Heilbron was excited to meet them. Rex, Catia, and Digger were on an Alitalia flight from Rome to Geneva late on the same afternoon. Rex rented a Europcar in his name, signing the documents after being made aware that the car was fitted with a GPS tracking device and showing his passport. He didn't like the idea of being tracked, but then reminded himself that his days of clandestine operations were over.

A minute or so before 10:00 A.M. on Wednesday, Rex, Catia, and Digger in the rental car pulled up in front of Abraham Heilbron's house in Lancy, a small town in the canton of Geneva.

The lady who opened the door for them was probably somewhere in her mid to late fifties and very friendly. With a big smile on her face she welcomed them, told them her name was Charlotte, and apologized that the only languages she could speak were French and German, languages Catia didn't know. Rex told Charlotte, in Parisian accented French, that there was no reason to apologize; he would translate between her and Catia.

Digger and Charlotte were introduced to each other in French. Rex had no idea how much French Digger understood—apparently enough to sit down and extend his right paw to Charlotte to shake. She laughed and

102

shook the proffered paw, saying, "Pleased to meet you, Monsieur Diggaire."

Rex was trained in paying close attention to people's micro-expressions to detect when they were deceitful, but since he and Digger had teamed up, he had come to realize that Digger was much better at it. The dog was a living breathing four-legged lie detector that outstripped any man-made device or human observations. It was reassuring to see that Digger took an immediate liking to the woman.

She invited them in, and while leading them to the living room where Abraham was waiting, she explained that Abraham was her uncle and she was his caretaker. She and her husband lived in the house next door.

The two houses were contemporary single-story semi-detached dwellings situated in the heart of a well-kept garden. Abraham's place was spacious and comfortable, with a sunny living room, fireplace, and open-plan kitchen.

It was obvious to Rex and Catia that Zechariah did not exaggerate when he told them Abraham's health was failing. He was in a wheelchair, a frail, bony man with silver-gray hair. The horn-rimmed spectacles with impossibly thick lenses testified to his failing eyesight. Despite his health, he was in good spirits and noticeably excited to welcome them in his home. He spoke English fluently albeit with a German accent. And it soon became apparent that Zechariah didn't exaggerate either when he told them Abraham's mind was still as sharp as someone half his age.

Zechariah had given Rex and Catia a bit of background about Abraham. He and his wife were German-Jews, Holocaust survivors of Auschwitz and Dachau. They met shortly after the war and got married in 1948 after which they moved to Switzerland. They never had children – the result of the inhumane medical experiments performed on her by Auschwitz's SS physician, Josef Mengele, better known as the Angel of Death. His wife had died ten years ago.

It was after moving to Switzerland that Abraham set out on his private pursuit to track down as much of the Nazi loot as he could and return it to their owners. Zechariah wasn't privy to the details of Abraham's successes, but he knew enough to tell Catia and Rex that the value was estimated to be in the billions.

After Charlotte had served them coffee, she had left them to converse in private and enjoy the plate of typical Swiss pastry, *Appenzeller Bärli-Biber*, gingerbread with a unique taste derived from the almond filling and a secret spice mix.

"Catia, Zechariah told me a little about your research. It's a praiseworthy endeavor you're embarking on, and I'd be honored to help you in any way I can. It might be best if you could tell me what you have gathered so far and let's see where I can fill in gaps or make suggestions."

A little over two and a half hours later, the *Bärli-Biber* and their second cup of coffee a distant memory, Charlotte came in and invited them all over to her place for lunch.

Finally, after lunch, they got to the topic of Dr. Karl Bauer and Rex's ideas about the anomalies surrounding the man.

Abraham told them he had known about Bauer's involvement in the looting of books across Europe and always had him on his list to be investigated. However, there were just too many Nazi criminals for one man to study, and in the end his health and rapidly fading eyesight caught up and prevented him from really getting into the Bauer project. "Over the years, as I worked on other projects, bits and pieces about Bauer came across my desk, occasionally. I filed them in a folder I kept about him. Yesterday, when I heard about your visit, I had Charlotte read the file to me to refresh my memory. But I'm afraid it doesn't contain much more than what you already know."

Abraham handed the Bauer file, all of it in German, to Rex to read out loud and translate into English for Catia's sake.

It contained, as Abraham had said, not a lot of information. There were twenty or so sheets of paper, some photocopied from other documents, some Abraham's handwritten notes. One of the handwritten notes suggested that Bauer's wife's name could have been Gertrude. But there was no explanation where the information came from.

Abraham looked a little embarrassed when he said, "Since yesterday I've been thinking hard to remember where I got that information from, but, I'm sorry, unfortunately, my mind is not what it used to be. I simply can't remember."

"No need to apologize," Catia said. "From what I've observed so far today, yours is in much better shape than mine."

The old man chuckled.

Rex continued and translated the remaining notes. "Catia, listen to this." It was another handwritten note. "It says, after Bauer was released in 1946, he went back to Cologne where he was born. It seems it was there that he rejoined or tried to rejoin the clergy as he became active in the local parish of the Catholic Church. He lived for a time in a church compound on the outskirts of the city. And it seems it was only in 1953 that he had relocated to Wiesbaden."

"Could it be he was not married anymore at that time?" Catia speculated. "I mean, he got kicked out in 1934 for getting married, I assume. To get back in I guess one of the first conditions would have been no wife."

Abraham nodded. "Sound argument."

Rex agreed. "The question is what happened to her or if they had children?"

Abraham shrugged. "Sorry, I don't know the answer to any of those."

"Gertrude, if that was her name, disappeared out of the picture after they got married in Germany in 1934. There must be a reason," Catia said.

Rex added, "I'd think, either she died during the war, of which there is no public record, or she had left him, of which there is no public record either."

"Maybe she returned to her family in Jerusalem," Abraham suggested.

"Even so, it is as you have said, strange, highly suspicious, that there is nothing in the public sources about her life after getting married to Bauer." The old man closed his eyes for a short moment before continuing. "It's not impossible that Bauer, knowing full well he could be arrested and tried at any moment, had arranged a ratline for her and a child or children, if there were any. But to where?

"Be that as it may, I agree with you." He looked at Rex. "I've got no reservations; Karl Bauer got help from somewhere."

"We've also considered the money angle," Catia said. "But as far as we know, Bauer was not into stealing gold, jewelry, art, and money—his vice was other people's books, especially Jewish books. There could not have been much money to be made out of Jewish books, which were probably not of much value to anyone but the Jewish community at large."

Abraham was shaking his head. "I wouldn't be so sure of that. In monetary terms, unique antique books are just as valuable as old art pieces..."

"Yes, but you can't sell them at Sotheby or other public auctions without proper provenance, can you?" Catia said.

"You're right, if you want to buy and sell them legally. If you were trading on the black market, provenance plays no role. Over the years I've come to the conclusion that the market for illicit *objets d'art,* including the type of books you're talking about, is enormous. I dare say it's bigger than the legitimate market."

Catia was frowning.

"Some collectors have strange habits; they'll go to great lengths to stay anonymous," Abraham said. "They'd never show their collections to a living soul. For some of them, provenance is of no concern. Just to own the artifact is enough satisfaction.

"In the underworld of art, unprovenanced artifacts sell for around ten percent of their provenanced market value. It might not sound like much until you think of the multi-million price tags those items fetch at public auctions. Ten percent of a fifty-million-dollar painting is five million—still a lot of money."

"But books? I mean... they never fetch those prices, do they?"

"You might be surprised. Let me give you a few examples." He reached for a folder on the coffee table next to him and held it out for Rex to read and translate. It contained newspaper clippings of book auctions and private sales gathered by Abraham over the years.

Within seconds of opening the folder, Rex's jaw had dropped. "The first atlas, also known as the Cosmographia, Geographia or simply the Geography, written by the Greco-Roman, Claudius Ptolemy, considered the world's first printed atlas, sold for almost four million US in 2006.

"The Babylonian Talmud, one of only fourteen complete multi volume sets from the early sixteenth century, sold for seven and half million just last year after it had been sitting at Westminster Abbey for some four hundred years. Apparently, no one knew how valuable it was. It was the most expensive piece of Judaica to ever sell at auction.

"In 1987, the Gutenberg Bible, the first complete book to be printed from movable type in 1455, sold for five point four million, about twelve million in today's money.

"It seems Bill Gates bought the most expensive book ever in 1994—Leonardo da Vinci's Codex of Leicester, also known as the Codex Hammer, written in 1510. It set him back thirty point eight million. Gates had it digitally scanned and released some of the images as screen savers and wallpapers for Microsoft's computer operating system, Windows 98 Plus."

Catia was shaking her head. "I had no idea."

"Neither did I," Rex agreed.

"That means the Jewish Community Library of thousands of unique works could be worth billions," Catia whispered.

Abraham nodded slowly. "Yes, it could. And I'm sorry to tell you, but you will probably agree with me, bringing money into the equation has just extended your list of potential suspects to include a significant number of unsavory collectors worldwide."

Catia and Rex agreed. What Abraham said made a lot of sense.

It was obvious that Abraham didn't get many visitors, and visitors who wanted to talk about his life's work probably less frequently. But Catia noticed that Abraham looked tired, and suggested it was time for them to leave.

He didn't want to let them go but had to admit that he was tired. However, he extracted a promise that they would visit again and keep him up to date with their progress. He also told them about other private investigators whom he had met and worked with over the years. Both of them had passed away, but he had contact details of relatives and offered to make introductions if they wanted.

Finally, before they left, like Zechariah, Abraham cautioned them. "You have to be careful who you talk to and what you say. I suggest you keep your research secret and trust no one. Over the years, I had more than just a few threats and attempts to harm me, even to kill me."

In the car on the way back to the airport, Rex brought up the matter of their safety. "Catia, I think we need to take heed of Abraham's parting advice about our security."

"You took the words out of my mouth," she said. "I agree, let's rather be safe than sorry."

"Okay, so from now on we make sure none of your research is on a computer connected to the internet. We start using alternative IDs for air travel, accommodation, and rental cars..."

"I can talk to Yaron to arrange with *sayanim* to organize those for us in the future," Catia said.

"Even better."

CHAPTER 13 – TIME TO ARRANGE A MEETING

ROME, ITALY

WEDNESDAY, AUGUST 10, 2016

EARLY EVENING, SOON after arriving back from Geneva, Rex got a call from Rehka on his satphone. He put it on speaker after their usual greetings and witticisms.

"It's a nightmare to deal with German bureaucracy," Rehka reported when she and Catia had greeted.

"You sound a bit demoralized," Catia said.

"Not demoralized, but definitely frustrated. Let me tell you, everything you've ever heard about German precision, and doing things by the book or not at all, is true. And to that you can now add the fact that Germans don't like to share their pedigrees."

"Doesn't sound like you've made much headway with Herr Bauer's history," Rex said. "Have you spoken to Greg yet?"

"I've made no progress at all. As for Greg, that's the reason for my call. Will it be okay with you if I ask him to help? We'll need to use unconventional methods to get the information."

Rex looked at Catia to see what her thoughts were. She knew Greg very well; she had worked with him on the Badr mission the year before, and she trusted him without hesitation. She nodded.

"We're both good with that, Rehka. But I'd like you to hang on for a day or so, I'd like to have a word with John Brandt first. I've been thinking of asking him for a few more resources."

Rehka laughed. "Good luck with that." Until they had met in person at the wedding, she had only ever dealt with John Brandt over secured video and audio communication links. Notwithstanding, she had seen enough of the apparent hostile interactions between Rex and Brandt to know it was just a charade; they loved each other like father and son. But it didn't mean she expected Brandt to easily agree to make CRC resources available to conduct research for a Ph.D., even if the student was Rex's wife.

Rex smiled. "Yeah, I know I'm going to need it. That's why I haven't contacted him yet—I'm still preparing my opening statements and closing arguments."

Rehka laughed. "I can already hear him tell you, 'Dalton, CRC hunts terrorists, not old books and dead Nazis.' I'd give anything to be a fly on the wall during that conversation."

"Aha, thanks for that. You just gave me an idea—if things become too rough for me to handle, I'll invite you to the meeting. Your presence might just soften the old man's heart."

"Well, if you want to soften him up in that manner, Catia is all you need there. Brandt thinks of you as his son and Catia as his daughter-in-law."

"Well, his daughter-in-law already agreed to be part of the meeting. I wouldn't dream of doing it without her."

"If she's there, you'll get what you want."

Catia was just shaking her head.

"Okay, Rehka," Rex said. "Thanks for the call. I'll leave you and Catia to chat. I'm taking Digger out for a walk."

***

ON THE WAY back, after walking Digger in one of the nearby parks, Rex stopped at one of their favorite trattorias near Trevi Fountains and ordered two takeaway pizzas and two slices of tiramisu for dinner. While he waited for the food to be prepared, he popped into a liquor store and got a six-pack of cold Peroni Gran Riserva, an Italian double malt bock beer that they both liked.

Back at the apartment, he laid the table, opened two of the beers, poured Catia's into a glass, took a sip of his own straight from the bottle, and said, "Dinner's ready, Missus Dalton."

After a few bites of pizza and a sip of beer, Catia said with a big smile, "So you're going to turn the research work of my Ph.D. into a black ops mission?"

Rex grinned. "Yes, like our wedding mission."

He got a kick under the table for that.

"You're going to make academic history. Your Ph.D., as far as I know, will be the first ever to require the services of a team of black ops specialists."

"You mean a complete team with field agents, snake eaters, door kickers, shooters, computer specialists, fully armed, and even a military dog?" Catia laughed.

"Exactly. I don't like half-measures."

Catia smiled. "Well, I guess since the Nazis stole the libraries with the backing of their military, I think it's befitting that we have the backing of military forces to get them back."

They would have been perturbed to know how true the adage, many a truth is spoken in jest, would prove to be.

"Catia, I know you've set your heart on finding those libraries, but you'll have to allow for the possibility that they have been destroyed, as some scholars suggested."

Catia nodded. "Don't worry, Rex, I've made peace with that possibility. It would be a great disappointment, but then I'd like to at least prove it beyond a shadow of doubt."

"That's good. Okay, I think it's time to arrange a meeting with the Old Man. Two days ago, when I checked, the TOMATS was on the way to Venice. I think it's probably best if we fly over there and have a face-to-face meeting. What do you think?"

"Agreed. It would be nice to see Venice again. I haven't been there for more than ten years. Maybe we can spend a day or two?"

He agreed. "And maybe this time Digger will enjoy it more. Last time we were in Venice, Digger was refused entry to one of the museums. He wasn't happy about that, I know, because I was also upset."

A few minutes later, Rex had Declan Spencer on the satphone. The TOMATS was indeed at anchor in Marina Santelena, Venice. They intended to stay for at least a week.

Rex smiled when Spencer told him, "Everyone on the TOMATS will be looking forward to your arrival."

If John Brandt had been part of the conversation, he certainly would have told Spencer, "Speak for yourself."

CHAPTER 14 — ONLY THREE PEOPLE

VENICE, ITALY

THURSDAY, AUGUST 11, 2016

ARRIVING ON THE TOMATS, Rex got a handshake from Spencer and Brandt, kisses on both cheeks from Christelle and Simona, plus a hug from the latter. Catia got kisses and hugs from everyone. Digger got an ear and back scratch from everyone, including Brandt.

When Rex saw Brandt's enthusiastic welcome of Catia and Digger, he grinned slightly. *Excellent. I'm going to need all the allies I can get.*

Shortly after 10:00 A.M., after dropping their luggage in their stateroom, the three of them joined Brandt, Spencer, Christelle, and Simona in the big lounge, where the kitchen staff had provided snacks and hot drinks.

After the how are you doing and the inevitable how's married life treating you questions and accompanying repartee, when there was a lull in the conversation, Brandt looked at Rex and said, "Out with it, Dalton."

"Out with what?" Rex feigned surprise.

"Son, I know that look on your face."

"What look would that be?"

"The one that screams 'I'm up to something.'"

"I wouldn't know about that. But now that you've mentioned it, I just remembered there is something I'd thought to discuss with you while we're here."

Brandt grinned. "I thought so. In private?"

"No. Everyone in this room is good, but you have to promise it stays between us."

Rex waited until he got the nod from all of them before he continued. "It's about Catia's Ph.D. Strange as it might sound, we need CRC's help with the research."

Everyone looked puzzled, staring at Rex, waiting for an explanation.

"I think its best if Catia gives you the background of her Ph.D. topic. I will fill you in on the rest."

Catia was neither surprised nor disappointed that none of them had even heard about the missing Jewish libraries before. There were not many people outside the Jewish community of Rome who knew about the libraries and their fate.

It took the best part of four hours, including lunch, to get everyone informed about Catia's studies, the research done so far, and what still had to be done.

"Expecting trouble, Rex?" Spencer asked out of the blue.

"Nothing specific that we know of right now. But both Zechariah and Abraham have cautioned us to keep the research secret and to be very careful. Both have received death threats in the past. Although they were unable to say who exactly was responsible for the threats, they have strong suspicions they came from one or more secret organizations with roots in anti-Semitism."

Christelle said, "Unfortunately, anti-Semitism didn't end with the fall of the Third Reich. It's still alive and well across Europe. That certainly is one possibility.

"Another possibility is the money involved. There are billions of dollars' worth of loot from the war still unaccounted for. Many of the stolen artifacts are still out there in bank vaults, warehouses, and private homes. The people who have them in their possession would go to great lengths to keep it secret. And degenerate collectors would commit horrendous crimes to get their hands on it.

"Make no mistake, there's a vibrant and thriving global black market for stolen artifacts of any kind, and that would include those unique and ancient books in those libraries you are seeking."

"Pretty much exactly what Abraham told us as well," Catia said.

Simona added, "And don't forget, organized crime syndicates also dabble in this industry in a big way. I know, from personal experience, that the Camorra is deeply involved in the illicit art trade. That's one of the ways they launder their drug money."

"So do many terrorist organizations. Art, antiquities, and drugs are how they fund much of their operational expenses," Brandt added.

Spencer looked at Rex. "It's clear those books could be worth billions, and where money is involved, often the worst traits of humanity are in operation as well."

"And Rex hasn't yet mentioned that he and Zechariah are of the opinion that we shouldn't put this beyond some ranking members of the Catholic Church," Catia added.

Their audience stared at them in near disbelief.

"The church, you said?" Brandt frowned, deep in thought.

Rex grinned and said, "Okay, it's official, you've now managed to scare the living daylights out of us."

"You'll have to agree, the two of you could be unleashing a cascade of trouble here," Brandt said.

"Right. We intend to conduct the research as surreptitiously as possible, but we expect once we start asking questions the miscreants will crawl out of their holes. So that's why we're here, to ask for help."

Brandt said, "My first thoughts were to tell you, CRC's in the business of hunting terrorists and their cronies, not old books and dead Nazis. But…"

Rex and Catia exploded in laughter.

"What the hell's so funny?"

When their mirth subsided, Rex answered, "Those were Rehka's exact words, almost verbatim, when she predicted what you would say when we told her we're going to ask you for help."

Brandt growled and mumbled something almost unintelligible that sounded a lot like, "So now even Rehka reckons she's got me figured out," before he said, "So, who do you need and what are they supposed to do?"

This is a lot easier than I thought it would be. "Only three people," Rex started.

"Greg, Josh, and Marissa, right?" Brandt interjected.

"Very perceptive of you, John. Rehka is already on the team; she needs Greg's help. Josh and Marissa can help Catia and me follow up the leads we got from Zechariah and Abraham."

Brandt said, "Okay, I'll make them available, but on the understanding that if I need them for a higher priority mission elsewhere, I'll have to pull them off your project for as long as needed."

"We can live with that," Rex said.

"Thank you so much, John; I really appreciate it," Catia said with a smile of relief.

It was John's "Don't mention it," that made Rex do a double take at Brandt's face and sense the Old Man was up to something of his own. Rex didn't say anything; he knew Brandt would spill it at the time of his choosing.

Brandt looked at the clocks on the wall. It was 7:00 A.M. in Arizona. He took out his secured satellite phone and called Chris McArdle, CRC's second in command. It took him a few minutes to explain what he wanted and instruct McArdle to get Greg to get in touch with Rehka and for Josh and Marissa to report to Rex in Rome the coming Monday.

Rex was getting more and more perplexed by Brandt's affable behavior. The presence of Christelle Proll, clearly very much enamored with Brandt and vice versa, obviously had something to do with it, but Rex was sure Christelle was not the only factor in the Old Man's uncharacteristic behavior.

We're here for two more days. He will tell me when he's ready.

Chapter 15 - A black-ops-assisted Ph.D.

Saturday, August 13, 2016

THEIR FLIGHT BACK to Rome was scheduled for mid-day. The Dalton family were up early and went for a jog through the streets of Venice with Digger on leash. They stopped at one of the dog-friendly parks to give Digger a chance to run around without the leash and claim a large part of the park as his territory by lifting his leg against every tree and shrub in sight.

They were back on the TOMATS shortly after seven. After taking a shower, they went in search of coffee and breakfast. They found Brandt in the dining room, sipping on an espresso, deep in thought.

Catia joined him at the table while Rex got two cups of espresso from the machine and carried it over to them. The chef came in and announced breakfast would be ready in half an hour to forty-five minutes.

When the swing door had closed behind the chef, Brandt cleared his throat and shifted on his chair as if he were uneasy. "I... mhh... was actually planning to have this conversation with Rex... alone... I mean... I wanted to talk to him first... ah... and then to both of you," he started.

Rex instantly recognized this as the matter he had detected on Brandt's face a few days ago. And he found it a little amusing to see the Old Man at a loss for words—not a sight he had seen often.

They stared at Brandt with raised eyebrows.

"But I guess it makes no difference.... You see, the thing is I'm past my 'best-by' date. I had my innings and I did my bit for God and country. There was a time when I firmly believed I'd stay in the fight until I was killed or died of natural causes..."

Catia opened her mouth to respond, but Brandt held his hand up and said, "Hear me out."

Catia nodded.

"I've come to realize it's time to step aside and let someone younger take over the reins. I'd stay on as consultant to provide input as required, but we need a new CEO.

"My kidnapping and torture last year had more of an impact on my physical and mental health than I cared to admit for a long time. My mind is not what it's supposed to be for the CEO of a black ops organization such as CRC. It's in the best interest of our country and the men and women of CRC to have an intelligent, young, and vibrant CEO.

"The threats against our country, and for that matter all of the civilized world, have not subsided—they have only increased and mutated as the international political climate has changed. It's no longer only the Middle East we have to keep our eyes on; Russia and China have entered the fray as well."

Rex and Catia were listening intently. Rex could see Brandt was serious. And he found what the Old Man was saying a little unsettling. CRC was one of the go-to private military contractors for the CIA and several other security agencies of the United States. In the world of black ops, CRC had a storied reputation for getting things done that the security agencies, due to the meddling of politicians in their business, were not allowed to get involved in—not directly.

As far as Rex was concerned, CRC's track record stood to the credit of one man, John Brandt. He was the founder of CRC. His selection of candidates and his training and his mission control were unrivaled in the industry. The Old Man's retirement wasn't something Rex had ever given much consideration—CRC was John Brandt, and John Brandt was CRC.

"How soon, John?" Rex asked, almost whispering.

Brandt grinned. "Depending on the outcome of this conversation, within the next two years, I hope."

"Outcome of this conversation... what does that mean?" Rex asked. "Do you need our opinion about your choice of CEO? In that case I'd say..."

Brandt stopped him. "No, Rex, I don't want your opinion. I want *you* as the new CEO."

Rex's mouth opened and then closed, and Catia's face displayed shock.

There was a protracted silence as the three of them stared at each other.

Digger must have sensed the sudden onset of tension in his pack, got up from where he had been sleeping, and sat down between Catia and Rex. He looked at the three of them in turn as if to ask, "Anything I can help with?"

Catia saw he was unsettled and started to rub his back in silence and Digger relaxed.

Rex eventually got his equanimity back and said, "I can't speak for the physical issues you're experiencing, but as for mental health issues, I can. My diagnosis is: you've lost your mind, John. You're in need of a new brain.

"I can't even manage a one-man ice-cream stand. I don't know what's the difference between debit and credit. I have never met, let alone talked to, a politician. I... never mind, I'm out of the industry. You know as well as I do it's no life for a married man, not to mention a married man with children."

Brandt raised his eyebrows.

"No, Catia is not pregnant. Not yet, but we're planning on accomplishing that in the not too distant future." Rex paused and smiled. "Digger can't be an only child."

"Why not Chris McArdle?" Catia asked.

"I spoke to Chris, not to offer him the job but to hear his opinion. And it might surprise you to know, he insists, just like I do, that Rex is the only person who could and should step up to the plate. He is, just like I am, firm in his belief that Rex is the only one he knows and trusts who would make a success of it."

"You've missed your calling, John. You should've been a snake oil salesman," Rex said.

Brandt ignored him. "McArdle is a good man, honest and trustworthy, solid as the rock of Gibraltar. And I admire those traits, but what I admire most about him is his understanding and acceptance of his own strengths and weaknesses. He's an unrivaled administrator and support specialist, not a CEO. His words, verbatim, were, 'Tell Rex Dalton it would be an honor to serve as his second in command or any other capacity, for that matter.'"

Rex shook his head. "John, surely you..."

Brandt interrupted. "And, before I forget, Rick Longland is your next and equally ardent supporter. He also, without hesitation, promised undivided loyalty to you when you take over as CEO."

Rick Longland was CRC's resident psychologist. He was not just a shrink with no idea of what the men were doing out in the field. He himself was a trained Delta Force operator and had passed through the grueling CRC training and taken part in more than a few missions before he was appointed to his current role. He knew what made a good agent and what they were up against when on missions. And he knew what was required of a good CEO to lead those agents. Over the years, he'd become the Old Man's confidant and soundboard.

"When you take over?" Rex said. "You make it sound as if the date has been set and I just have to turn up. Do I have a choice in this?"

Brandt ignored the question. "With Catia by your side, between you, McArdle, and Longland, CRC would continue to be a force that can take the fight to our enemies and decimate them."

Rex took Catia's hand, looked into her eyes as if searching for an answer, and was momentarily surprised to find not shock or resistance in them, but what he thought was support for Brandt's idea. He and Catia had both suffered the loss of their loved ones at the hand of terrorists. Both had given all of their adult lives so far to fight the forces of evil who killed their loved ones. But since the last mission, after which they got engaged and married, there was a tacit understanding between them that they had bidden farewell to their lives as field operators for covert organizations.

Even so, Rex knew neither of them would decline a request for help to combat those evil forces. But the thought of running an organization such as CRC was something totally different. It was downright terrifying.

Rex tried another escape route. "I take it your sudden retirement plans were brought on, in no small measure, I suspect, by a certain Madame Proll?"

Instead of the usual, *none of your business*, or *mind your own business*, Brandt smiled and said, "Absolutely. The Badr mission last year brought us together after many years. Our time together since then was enough to rekindle the feelings we had for each other in our young days. The days before the Atlantic Ocean and our careers got in the way."

Catia smiled. "Is it just my imagination, John, or am I hearing tiny bells in the background?"

"What bells?"

"Those that sound like wedding bells."

Brandt's face lit up with a big smile. "That, my dear Catia, depends entirely on the answer Christelle gives me when I ask her a certain question tonight."

"Catia, let's postpone our return flight. Seeing this old coot's face when Madame Proll says yes is something I don't want to miss for the world," Rex said.

"You seem to be rather sure that's going to be her answer," Brandt said. "Do you know something I don't?"

Catia laughed. "John, it might come as a surprise to you, but she's been waiting for you to ask. Rex and I've been watching the two of you closely the last few days, and we're a bit surprised you haven't asked already."

"Tell you what," Rex said through the chuckles. "If she says no, I'd agree to take over CRC tonight, because you wouldn't be in the mental state, which, by your own admission, is already iffy, to manage the outfit in any event."

John laughed and was about to retort when the chef pushed the breakfast trolley into the room.

Catia phoned the airline and rescheduled their flight for the same time the next day before helping herself to the food.

A few minutes later, Digger herded Christelle, Simona, and Spencer into the dining room.

***

SHORTLY BEFORE 10:00 P.M. Rex, Catia, and Digger were in the small lounge still talking, as they had been almost the whole day, without coming near an answer to Brandt's bombshell proposition that morning, when Digger alerted them of the arrival of Brandt and Christelle, who were returning from their dinner at L'Alcova, one of Venice's best restaurants.

Stepping off the gangplank, Rex and Catia immediately saw on Brandt and Christelle's faces that Rex was not going to take over the job as CEO of CRC that night.

Rex told Digger to go and fetch Spencer and Simona.

A few minutes later, Digger arrived with the two of them in the lounge. And soon after, the popping sound of champagne being uncorked was heard.

After Rex had clinked glasses with Brandt, he leaned in closer and said quietly, "I want our discussion of this morning put on hold until after Catia's graduation ceremony. And please note; that doesn't constitute acceptance in any way, shape, or form."

Brandt smiled. "No worries. Understood. But I want *you* to take note; I'm going to see to it that your wife gets a fast-tracked, security-cleared, black-ops-assisted Ph.D. I intend to get it all done and dusted before my wedding day."

Catia only heard the last bit and asked, "You've set a date already?"

"Not specifically, but neither of us believe in long engagements... nor in protracted Ph.D.'s."

CHAPTER 16 – WE MIGHT STIR THE HORNET'S NEST

ROME, ITALY

MONDAY, AUGUST 15, 2016

JOSH AND MARISSA had arrived in Rome on a direct flight from DC the evening before. Rex was glad to see Josh had made a full recovery from the bullet wound in his left upper arm, sustained during Operation Badr in October the year before. Catia had put them up in the second bedroom in her apartment. Their transport in and around Rome, when required, was going to be Catia's second motorbike, a Ducati Multistrada 1200 S Touring.

At about 6:40 A.M. the four of them were sitting around the dining room table sipping homemade espressos and talking about everything except Catia's Ph.D. It was a topic, Rex and Catia had agreed, that could not be discussed with novices on an empty stomach. But it was way too early for a trattoria in their neighborhood to be open for breakfast, and the Daltons had not had a chance to go grocery shopping since their return from Venice late the previous afternoon.

The first trattoria would open around eight. Catia suggested they all go for a walk around the *Piazza di Spagna,* Spanish Square, about fifty or so yards away from the apartment. Josh and Marissa had been to Rome before, but always on missions—they hadn't seen much of the city yet.

When Rex reached for the leash, Digger let out a yelp of excitement. It was noticeable how invigorated Digger had been since Josh and Marissa's arrival. It must have been the joy of having almost all of his pack with him. Rehka was the only one missing.

About an hour later, they were all sitting at the top of the Spanish Steps, one of the renowned features of the *Piazza di Spagna,* looking out over the picturesque Eternal City as it slowly awoke.

Rex and Josh were smiling as they listened to Catia's animated telling, and Marissa's running commentary, of the memorable engagement of John Brandt and Christelle Proll.

Josh shook his head and started laughing when Catia finished. "Rex, you wouldn't believe the torrent of verbal diarrhea Marissa and I had to endure from the Old Man when I told him we were engaged. I'm going to rub his nose in his own words the moment I see him again."

"That'll be poetic justice; he deserves it." Rex chuckled.

He and Catia had agreed to make no mention of Brandt's retirement plans or his ideas for his replacement.

"Ah, Amos and Rosanna opened ten minutes early today," Catia said excitedly, pointing to a trattoria on the other side of the square. "Let's go." She had known Amos and his wife, Rosanna, for many years. They always made her feel welcome, and they had been quite excited when Catia turned up there one day and introduced Rex and Digger, with whom they became fast friends as well.

Over a continental breakfast of fresh bread with butter and honey, Italian pastries, cheeses, and cured meats, and a constant stream of espressos, the conversation finally turned to the reason for Josh and Marissa's presence in Italy.

As with Brandt and them on the TOMATS, it took quite a few hours to get Josh and Marissa acquainted with Catia's Ph.D.

They were long back in the apartment when Catia's chronicle ended.

"Chris didn't tell us what we were supposed to come and do over here; he didn't know. But of all the things Josh and I have considered, this would not have come up in a thousand years. It's exciting. I like it," Marissa said with a big smile.

Josh grinned. "Rex, and there I was sitting through the entire flight gearing myself up for another door-kicking, bad-guy-shooting mission. But it seems to me there ain't gonna be no door-kickin."

Rex smiled. He and Josh had come a long way together as CRC field agents. Josh had been recruited into CRC a few years after Rex. Rex had given him some of his training, and Josh was an outstanding operator. One of CRC's best. Between the two of them, they had more than just a few war stories to tell and the battle scars to show for it. Among their many joint missions was the one to rescue John Brandt about 14 months before, when Rex fractured his leg. And Operation Badr about 11 months before, when Josh was wounded in the arm. Rex and Josh trusted one another without reservations.

Marissa was the best of CRC's handful of female agents. And she was beautiful—shoulder-length, raven hair and azure eyes suggested French heritage, and her forty-something years gave her an alluring mantle of maturity. She was almost ten years older than Josh, but one would had to have seen her birth certificate to know that.

She was an expert social media analyst and spy and, if necessary, could handle herself in a fight. She also spoke two languages besides English: Arabic and French. The latter she had spoken along with English since her childhood, thanks to her French father. She and Josh had gotten engaged in September the year before and had set their wedding date for December 17.

They obviously believed in longer engagements than John Brandt and Rex did.

Rex said, "I'm sorry I can't promise you anything as exciting and adventurous as any of our previous missions. However, that might change very quickly."

Josh and Marissa frowned.

Catia told them about the threats Zechariah and Abraham had received and about Christelle and the others' speculations about the potential antagonists they might encounter, including officials of the Catholic Church.

"So, here's what Catia and I came up with so far. We're reasonably certain that Bauer was involved in the removal of those libraries. What happened after that is what we must prove—either the libraries were destroyed, as some people suggest, or they still exist.

"If they were destroyed, we want to know the exact circumstances. The more information and evidence we can gather about it, the better. We need to remove the speculation. We think Bauer would've known the details and hopefully recorded them somewhere. We must try and find them.

"We *do* know that before and during the war, Bauer was a devoted anti-Semite, absolutely smitten with the collection and study of ancient Jewish writings—he was also the architect of the concept of *Judenforschung ohne Juden*, Jewish Studies without Jews. Maybe he stashed the libraries himself.

"The bottom line is we believe if there were someone who would definitely know, it would've been Bauer."

"If my understanding is correct, the immediate goal is to get as much information about Karl Bauer as possible?" Marissa asked.

"Yes," Catia said. "And we hope as we collect Bauer's information, we might come across more leads to follow."

Josh nodded. "And that's how we might stir the hornet's nest?"

"Right," Rex said.

Within a few hours they worked out a rough plan. The first step was to introduce Josh and Marissa to Zechariah and ask him to arrange with Abraham for letters or calls of introduction to the family members of the late private investigators who had worked on the recovery of stolen World War II loot.

The plan was that while Josh and Marissa would visit the contacts, Rex and Catia would go on a fact-finding mission to Germany to investigate the life of Karl Bauer. They would start in Cologne, his birthplace on February 6, 1904, and try to follow his trail from there to his death. Where did he get married? Who was his wife? Any children? If so, where are they or any grandchildren? Any friends and family? What happened to his research?

Greg and Rehka would conduct the online research and, if required, hack into the electronic records of any person and organization of interest.

CHAPTER 17 – FAMILY MATTERS

COLOGNE, GERMANY

TUESDAY, AUGUST 23, 2016

IT WAS A beautiful, cloudless, warm, late-summer's day when Rex, Catia, and Digger arrived at the Cologne-Bonn Airport on a direct flight from Rome. This was their first stop in their quest to find out more about Doctor Karl Bauer.

Cologne, *Köln* in German, was a 2,000-year-old city in western Germany spanning the Rhine River. With a little more than one million inhabitants, it was the largest city of the federal state of North Rhine-Westphalia and the fourth most populous city in Germany after Berlin, Hamburg, and Munich.

After collecting their car from the *sayan* at the airport, a Volkswagen SUV, they made their way to the Marriott Hotel in Johannisstrasse where they had a reservation under fake names, made by another *sayan*. By 2:00 P.M. they had unpacked their stuff and were ready to take a self-guided tour of the city.

During the past week, Catia had arranged for Marissa and Josh to meet Zechariah. The two then had to assimilate the mountain of information collected by Catia and Rex. By the end of the week, they made it known that it felt a lot like cramming for an exam back in their university days.

By Monday morning, the list of subjects to be interviewed had been contacted by Abraham, and it was time to start knocking, very gently though, on their doors.

When the Daltons arrived in Cologne, Josh and Marissa were already in Vienna, where they had an appointment with Laura Fabelsohn the next day at 10:00 A.M. Abraham told them that he had some difficulty to persuade Frau Fabelsohn to meet with them and that they should expect her to be a bit apprehensive.

Rehka and Greg had been working tirelessly to collect background information about the interviewees. On the conference call the night before, Greg and Rehka reported they had collected and uploaded to the secured CRC servers the information about the people to be interviewed. They had not made any breakthroughs worth mentioning into the computer systems of any of the tightly secured German registry offices yet.

***

OVER THE PAST few weeks, Rex frequently had thoughts about his German heritage. Thanks to his mother, he spoke German fluently, with a Munich accent. Even so, as a keen scholar of history, he had no excuse for his superficial knowledge about his own ancestry. He knew his mother, Mareike's, maiden name was Riesch and she was the only child of Gunter and Madleen Riesch.

However, he also remembered that his mother told him that her parents had changed their surname from Weingart to Riesch when they moved to America.

He had only vague memories of his grandparents, as both had passed away before his eighth birthday. He knew his grandfather was born in 1934, five years before the war, and his grandmother in 1935. The two of them met in 1955, married in 1956, and immigrated to America in 1958, a few months after his mother's birth.

His mother got married to his father, Richard Dalton, in January 1979.

The Dalton surname originated from English or Irish, meaning "from the valley town", although some believed the name derived from a place in England called Alton. Rex had never met his paternal grandparents; they had passed when his father was about eighteen. His father was also an only child.

Rex was born on October 29, 1980, he was almost 36, and that was more or less the extent of Rex's knowledge of his own lineage.

It was close to 10:00 P.M. They had returned from their tour of Cologne about an hour before and had a room-service dinner. Catia was in the bathroom getting ready for the night. Digger was fast asleep on his blanket in the dining room area of their suite. Rex was on his back on the bed reading on his tablet PC through a long list of German-Jewish surnames on a website when he discovered his mother's real maiden name, Weingart, was actually Jewish. He was surprised.

When Catia came out of the bathroom a minute later, it took Rex more than a few moments to catch his breath that got taken away when he had looked at his stunning wife in her negligée. When he eventually got his mind back to task, he said, "I never told you about my mother's maiden names, did I?"

"No, but what do you mean by maiden *names?* Aren't women supposed to have only one of those?"

"Well, my mother's maiden name, according to all her official American ID documents, was Riesch. But she told me, I think it was when I was about ten or so, that her parents had changed their surname from Weingart to Riesch when they immigrated to America."

"Ah I see. Interesting. You know Weingart is a German-Jewish surname?"

"I didn't until a few minutes ago when I found this website where it says so. But I'm puzzled. My mother never mentioned to me that she was of Jewish descent. She never followed any Jewish traditions or taught us any."

"You have to keep in mind that Orthodox and Conservative Judaism follow Jewish law, *Halakha*—a matrilineal system which dictates a person is Jewish if their mother is Jewish."

"Ah, I forgot about that. In other words, if my grandmother were Jewish, my mother would've been Jewish and so would I. The problem is that I don't know if my grandmother was Jewish. It'd be interesting to find out."

"Were your grandparents alive during the war?"

"Yes, but they were children; Grandpa would've been five when the war started and ten when it ended. Grandma would've been four and nine. They moved to the States in 1958, a few months after my mother's birth. I'm ashamed to admit I never asked how my grandparents survived the war."

"Well, one explanation could be that your grandparents, if they were Jewish, due to the horrible persecution of the Jews during the war and the realization after the war that anti-Semitism didn't end when the last shots were fired, might have decided to conceal their Jewish origins. My understanding is that many Jews did that to protect themselves and their families."

"I can only hope we don't get any nasty surprises about the maternal side of my family while we're delving into Nazi history."

Catia smiled, put her arms around his neck, pulled him closer, kissed him, and said, "Family, Rex, we can't choose them."

"Right. But I can kick myself for not learning more about my family when my parents were alive."

"Water under the bridge," Catia said as she took the tablet out of Rex's hand and put it on the bedside table on her side and then snuggled into his waiting arms.

CHAPTER 18 – GERMAN PRECISION

COLOGNE, GERMANY

WEDNESDAY, AUGUST 24, 2016

GOVERNMENTS HAVE SYSTEMS to keep track of the three main events in the lives of their citizens: birth, marriage, and death. For many centuries, in Germany and across Europe, until the late 1800s when governments took it over, the churches kept the registry. In Germany the government stored the information in what they called civil registration records: *Standesamt*.

Rex and Catia's first visit was to Cologne's *Standesamt* in search of copies of Bauer's birth, marriage, and death certificates. But what they expected to be a simple request, easily fulfilled, started off with an exercise in anger management.

On arrival, Rex told the receptionist, in German, what they wanted. She barely looked up from her computer screen. "Take a number and wait until you're called."

Although they were the only people in the waiting area, it took twenty minutes before their number was called. Across a counter, Rex and Catia faced a portly, bald, bespectacled man in his mid-fifties who had a permanent sour facial expression bespeaking his annoyance about having to talk to them or anyone for that matter. He insisted on speaking only German.

In German, therefore, Rex explained what they wanted.

"For what purpose?" the man asked.

"Academic research."

"Full names?"

"Karl Bauer."

"Date of birth?"

"February 6, 1904."

"You can't have it."

"Why not?"

"We don't have it."

"Do you know where we could find it?"

"State Archive."

Rex was about to ask for clarification but decided, for the sake of this man's well-being, and to keep himself out of a German prison for strangling an official, not to test his own patience any further. He said, "Danke für deine Hilfe," thanks for your help, took Catia's hand, and led her and Digger out of the building.

"I gathered that didn't go very well?" Catia said when they got outside.

"It didn't. But at least we can't complain about the service—there was no service. Let's hope we find a more cordial official at the State Archive; I'm not sure how much more of this kind of bureaucratic efficiency I can withstand."

Half an hour later, Rex's wish was granted when they arrived at the Cologne State Archive and were attended to by a friendly, dark-haired lady in her early thirties, with a big, beautiful smile. She was also happy to speak English to them.

This time Catia did the talking and explained what they came for and expressed the hope that she might be able to help them.

"You're probably at the right place," the lady began. "But before we conduct a search, it might be worth giving you a bit of background about the German civil registration records system." She didn't wait for them to respond. "Since the keeping of civil registration records became a government duty in the late 1800s, there were several changes to regulations. The latest change came into effect at the beginning of January 2009.

"That change determined that birth certificates older than a hundred and ten years, marriage certificates older than seventy years, and death certificates older than thirty years have to be handed over to the state archive. Only authenticated copies of those documents can be released."

"Good. Karl Bauer was born in 1904," Catia said, "more than a hundred and ten years ago. He died in 1960, more than thirty years ago. He got married in 1934 more than seventy years ago. In other words, his records should all be here at the Cologne State Archive. Right?"

"Well... yes and no."

Here we go again. Rex struggled to keep the grumble inaudible.

"You see, Germany has no central repository for civil records of births, marriages, and deaths. Records of those events are created and kept at the *Standesamt* of the city or region where the event; birth, marriage, and death, occurred. So, unless Herr Bauer was born or got married or died in the jurisdiction of Cologne, you won't find any record of him here."

"We know he was born here in Cologne," Catia said. "We're almost sure he got married here, and we know he died on 30 January 1960 in Wiesbaden."

"Good. In that case we might have his birth and marriage records here."

"Might?"

"Yes. The problem *we* have is, on 3 March 2009, Cologne's State Archive building collapsed along with two neighboring apartment buildings. It was caused by the construction of a new underground railway line. Two people were killed and an unknown number injured. About ninety percent of the documents and artifacts were buried in the rubble. Although we were able to recover and restore much of it in the aftermath, some was lost forever."

"Only one way to find out then," Catia said.

The friendly lady asked them to take a seat while she ran a search on her computer.

Digger, sensing Rex's growing irritation, sidled up next to him and pushed his wet nose against Rex's hand. Rex looked down and grinned when he realized Digger was trying to comfort him. "Thanks, buddy," he whispered softly and started scratching Digger's ears. "I'll be okay."

From where they were sitting, they could see the facial expressions and body language of the woman as she worked on her computer. Rex leaned over and whispered to Catia in Italian, "Is it just me or do you also get the impression she's not going to find Bauer's records?"

"Uh huh… doesn't look good."

A few minutes later they got the news. "I'm so sorry, but there's no record of a Karl Bauer born in Cologne on 6 February 1904, in our system."

Catia started to get up, but Rex managed to keep the testiness out of his voice and asked, "Is that the end of it? I mean are there no other ways to get Bauer's records? We are almost one hundred percent sure he was born on that date in Cologne."

"There is another possibility," she said. "The microfiche records. They're in the building next door. You'll have to fill in some forms and pay a fee if you want it done today."

"We'd very much like to have it today," Rex said. "And we'll be happy to pay for it."

"I can call one of my colleagues and ask him to assist you?"

"Thank you, we'd appreciate that very much," Catia said.

Two hours later, with the help of the lady's colleague who was not entirely as friendly as she was but helpful nonetheless, they had paid the fee of €80 for a fast-track process and had completed and signed a stack of forms in duplicate and triplicate. It took another half an hour or so before they left the building in possession of an authenticated birth certificate of Karl Bauer. No marriage certificate though.

"One down, two to go," Rex mumbled when they got into their car. "I'm not sure I can take much more of the antics of the German resistance movement."

Catia smiled, put her hand on his arm, and said, "Remember how to eat an elephant, Rex?"

"Yeah, yeah, I know. One bite at a time. I'll try and keep my cool."

"At least we've now confirmed Bauer was born in Cologne, and we've also learned who his parents were," Catia said.

"Right."

"Okay, let's grab a quick coffee before we go to the offices of the Archdiocese," Catia said.

***

THE CLERK AT the Archdiocese's office was a friendly and loquacious gray-haired man of medium height and build. He was dressed in a dark pinstriped suit, white shirt, and bowtie, as if he were going to attend some kind of formal event. He explained to them that they got these types of requests often, but that Germans, although known for their precision in everything they do, had to admit that when it came to civil registration records, they were, unfortunately, not able to achieve a high degree of precision. Simply because of the destruction of records as collateral damage during the war and of course the deliberate destruction by the SS and others.

While he tried to regale them with his knowledge of the history of the Archdiocese of Cologne, he scanned through the computer records and, based on the church records of Bauer's baptism, confirmed that the details on the birth certificate they had were correct. However, he was very sorry to inform them, he couldn't find a record of his marriage.

"There is one more place we can look," he said. "The wedding register. You see, in those days the church kept a handwritten register of all weddings and baptisms."

About twenty minutes later, Rex and Catia let out a joint sigh of relief when the man said, "Got it!" Even Digger smiled.

The man turned the old leather-bound register around and showed them the entry of Saturday 9 June 1934, the marriage of Karl Bauer and Gertrude Schulte.

Catia asked if she could take a photo with her mobile phone and the man agreed.

Two bites of the elephant down, Rex thought.

"Why would it be that the marriage had been noted in the church's register but not in your computer system or at the State Archive?" Catia asked.

"It's difficult to say. You must remember the information was manually entered into the computers many years ago. The person making the entries could've made a mistake and missed it."

Yeah right. So much for German precision. Or purposeful oversight, Rex thought but kept his own counsel. However, he did ask if there was any information about Bauer's stay in Cologne after his release from the POW camp.

Again, the friendly clerk conducted an extensive computer search, but it came up empty.

The Daltons next stop was Wiesbaden where Bauer had worked from 1953 until his death in 1960. It was an hour's drive from Cologne.

CHAPTER 19 – I BURNED IT ALL

VIENNA, AUSTRIA

WEDNESDAY, AUGUST 24, 2016

AT THE SAME time that Rex and Catia were being initiated into German bureaucracy in Cologne, Josh and Marissa were 460 miles to the southeast in Vienna where they were to meet with Frau Fabelsohn, the first interviewee on their list.

They didn't know what to expect from the meeting. Abraham told them that he could not give Frau Fabelsohn much detail about the meeting over the phone and that she reluctantly agreed to meet with them only because of his relationship with her late father. Notwithstanding, she had insisted on meeting with Josh and Marissa only with her husband present and not at her house but in a public park.

None of them knew what the other looked like, but Frau Fabelsohn had described to Abraham a specific bench in the park. Her husband would be carrying a black walking stick and she would have a silver butterfly brooch pinned to her blouse.

"This woman is obviously very nervous about something," Marissa said after Abraham told them about the meeting arrangements.

"Mhh… yeah. It sounds a lot like a Cold War spy-and-handler meeting, park bench and all," Josh said.

"She can't be a spy."

"How'd you know?"

"She left out the newspaper under the arm and the mystical code phrases."

Josh laughed. "Yeah, and don't forget to be on the lookout for the invisible ink pen and poison-tipped umbrella."

***

MARISSA AND JOSH reviewed the background information of Laura Fabelsohn one more time while in the back of the taxi on their way to the meeting.

According to Rehka and Greg, Frau Fabelsohn was the daughter of Heinz Eberhard, Abraham's friend. Heinz was born in 1928. He was twelve in 1940, when his parents fled from Germany to Turin, Italy, where they were given refuge by an Italian Jewish family for the duration of the war.

Five years after the war, the Eberhard family returned to Austria where, in Vienna, Heinz went to University and afterward set up his loot recovery business. He was successful in recovering large sums of money and countless artifacts. He was married. They had only one child, Laura. Heinz had passed away at the age of 85 in 2013. His wife passed away in 2014.

Laura Eberhard married Berend Fabelsohn, an Austrian Jew. She was a primary school teacher and Berend an electronics engineer. She was 60, her husband 61, and they had two adult children not living with them.

It was interesting to note that the Fabelsohns had an almost non-existent social media footprint. Either they didn't catch on to the technology trends that had swept the world since the advent of the internet, or they wanted to remain anonymous.

The taxi dropped them off at the entry to the park. There were only a few people. Josh and Marissa spotted the Fabelsohns as soon as they entered the park. They walked over and introduced themselves.

Neither Josh nor Marissa could speak German but the Fabelsohns' English, although accented, was fluent.

As agreed, Marissa would do most of the talking. But despite Marissa's friendly mannerisms, the Fabelsohns were visibly tense.

Frau Fabelsohn started by making sure Marissa and Josh understood that she and her husband were inconvenienced by the meeting and that they only agreed to it because of her father's friendship with Abraham. She looked at her watch and then at Marissa.

Marissa got the message; Frau Fabelsohn's loyalty had a time limit.

Marissa, still using all her charms, spun their story. They were freelance journalists doing research about the work of people who are or were involved in the recovery of Holocaust loot. They felt strongly that those people, like her late father, deserved tribute for their work.

The look of terror on the Fabelsohns at hearing the words 'Holocaust loot' was unmistakable.

"Have you lost your mind?" Frau Fabelsohn almost shouted. "Do you have any idea what you're doing? You're playing with fire.

"Yes, we're Austrian Jews. Yes, our people were slaughtered by the Nazis and we hate them for it. The Nazis lost the war, Hitler is dead, but never forget that they left a legacy of hatred for the Jews behind. They are still out there; they've never gone away. They still hate Jews. *We* want nothing to do with this."

As Frau Fabelsohn launched into the tirade, Josh worried that the woman was about to have a nervous breakdown.

Marissa tried to calm her down. Josh also tried, but to no avail. When the Fabelsohns started to get up, Marissa said, "Please accept our sincere apologies. We had no idea that we're putting your lives in danger. We're…"

"Not only ours, young lady, yours as well," Herr Fabelsohn retorted. "Do you have any idea how much anti-Semitism there is in this world?"

Marissa and Josh knew all about it, but they wanted to keep the Fabelsohns talking. Feigning ignorance, they shook their heads in unison. It had the desired effect.

Frau Fabelsohn, the teacher, launched into a lesson about the history of anti-Semitism. "Since time immemorial to this day, libelous claims of blood sacrifice and ritual murder have been leveled against us. Jews are accused of murdering Christian children to use their blood as part of religious rituals. Those and other horrific lies have been used as justification for the persecution of Jews in Europe."

"Not only during the war," Herr Fabelsohn added, "but for millennia before, and it continues to this day."

Frau Fabelsohn continued. "Part of the reason for the continuance of anti-Semitism after the war was the fear that returning Jews would attempt to reclaim property stolen during the Holocaust or that they would expose those who gave assistance to the Nazis, the SS specifically. That's the work my father did and that almost cost him his life—on several occasions. Their hatred and threats were not only aimed against him, but against my mother and me as well. We lived in constant fear of reprisal. But my father was too stubborn to let it go."

Herr Fabelsohn added, "Incidents of anti-Semitism have been rising significantly in Europe since 2000. Verbal attacks and vandalism such as graffiti, fire bombings of Jewish schools, and desecration of synagogues and cemeteries have increased. Physical assaults against Jews including beatings, stabbings, and other violence have increased markedly in several cases resulting in serious injury and even death.

"If you don't believe me, just look at a report issued in 2015 by the State Department of your own country, America, declaring that, 'European anti-Israel sentiment crossed the line into anti-Semitism.'"

Frau Fabelsohn told them that the rise in anti-Semitic attacks was caused partly by Muslim anti-Semitism among Europe's growing Muslim immigrant population, and partly by the rise of far-right political parties. She rambled off some examples and concluded the lesson with, "By 2012, in ten European countries polled, anti-Semitic sentiments reached levels of between seventeen and fifty-three percent of the population."

Josh and Marissa were nodding when she finished. Marissa apologized again. She knew there was very little to zero chance that the Fabelsohns would give them access to Heinz Eberhard's research, but she had to ask—just in case.

However, before she could ask, Frau Fabelsohn said, "My father was obsessed with revenge and getting the stolen property back. The older he got, the more fanatic he became. His passion for revenge destroyed his health and his mind, and all he got for it was threats to his life and the lives of his family. He was attacked on occasion leaving him with broken ribs and a broken arm. He had to spend a week in the hospital.

"As the only child, I inherited everything including his documents and research. I burned it all. That's it. Please don't contact us again. And please don't mention his name or ours in your article at all."

Chapter 20 – We'll Need Legal Advice

Wiesbaden Germany

Thursday, August 25, 2016

IT DIDN'T TAKE much effort to find the academic publishing house, Franz Steiner Verlag. Founded in 1949 in Wiesbaden, its specialty was history, but it also published works in geography, philosophy, law, and musicology.

Within a few hours, Catia and Rex had the confirmation; Bauer had indeed worked there from 1953 until his death in 1960. And in minimalistic fashion, Franz Steiner Verlag kept record only of what was necessary to show that Bauer had worked there 60 odd years before. Other than his service record and pay slips they knew nothing about him, not even an old photo.

At their next stop, the offices of the Duden, a group responsible for the upkeep of a dictionary of the German language, Rex and Catia only got confirmation that Bauer had indeed served on the editorial board. It was a volunteer position. They didn't have record of anything else.

Their third stop was at the Wiesbaden State Archive where, to their surprise, they got hold of an authenticated copy of Bauer's death certificate in less than an hour.

Their final stop was the cemetery where they found Bauer's grave and confirmed his dates of birth and death as noted on the certificates.

They were back at their hotel in time for lunch.

"It was nice to see Wiesbaden," Catia said while they were waiting for their lunch to be served. "But it's disappointing that we couldn't get more information."

"Well, at least we've proven our theory that someone went to great trouble to edit out Bauer's information from history. But I've been wondering how the German law of succession works. Bauer must've left something behind, and someone must have inherited it. There could have been a will. If not, I guess in Germany it works more or less the same as in other countries; if there are no familial heirs, everything goes to the government."

Catia smiled. "Rex, you're a walking treasure chest of ideas! I think you're onto something."

Rex's, "I am glad I still have the ability to impress you," earned him a playful punch in the shoulder. "Well, brilliant as I might be, we'll need legal advice."

"You're right. Maybe I should give Yaron a call and ask if he could recommend a lawyer who is a *sayan*?"

"Now that's what I'd call an excellent idea," Rex said with faked nonchalance. This time it earned him a kick under the table.

Digger wasn't disturbed by any of it; he was fast asleep on the floor between Catia and Rex.

Catia took her secured mobile phone out and sent a text message to Yaron Aderet asking when she could phone him. He was one of the deputy directors of Mossad. He was in charge of the organization's largest department, Collections, tasked with all the many aspects of conducting espionage overseas. He and John Brandt were good friends.

Aderet had taken Catia under his wing the year before when her *katsa*, handler in Hebrew, David Sternberg, suffered a stroke and had to go on early retirement. During Operation Badr, Aderet took a quick liking to Catia, as if she was his daughter. It was therefore no surprise that he didn't hesitate when Rex, through John Brandt, asked him to lead Catia down the aisle at her surprise wedding earlier in the year.

***

WIESBADEN GERMANY

THURSDAY, AUGUST 25, 2016
ADERET'S TEXT REPLY came just when they finished lunch.

I'LL HAVE HALF AN HOUR FOR YOU IN TEN MINUTES.

Ten minutes later they were in their hotel room. Before Catia made the secured call to Aderet, Rex scanned the room for bugs and found none. Fortunately, she didn't have to spend much time on giving Aderet background information. He knew about her Ph.D. studies, supported her in the endeavor, and had offered any help she might need when he saw her last, at the wedding.

Even so, mindful of the time limit, Catia gave him a quick high-level summary of what they had been doing and asked him to recommend a *sayan* lawyer familiar with German law of succession.

Aderet told her he would text a name and then asked her to use the rest of her time to tell him a bit more about the research she had conducted so far. He was quite happy to hear that Rex and Digger were by her side and that his friend John Brandt had supplied them with resources.

"It will be a momentous occasion of immense significance to the Jewish people if you can track down those libraries, Catia. Anything I can do to help you, just let me know."

"Thanks, Yaron, much appreciated. For now, all I need are the contact details of that lawyer and an introduction from you."

"No problem. I must run to another meeting now. I'll text the details to you soon. At some stage, soon, I'll set up a time with you so you can brief me fully on your progress."

"That'll be my pleasure. Thanks for your help."

ZURICH SWITZERLAND

FRIDAY, AUGUST 26, 2016

RENATE TREITELFELDT WAS a *sayan* and a lawyer who knew all about German, Austrian, and Swiss inheritance laws. She was more than happy to see Rex and Catia on short notice after receiving a personal call from Aderet. She was in her mid-fifties, good looking, professional, friendly, and very helpful.

As they entered her office, Rex had surreptitiously activated the scanner on his phone and confirmed there were no bugs before they started asking questions.

She explained, "I won't bore you with all the intricacies of the German law of succession. In summary it comes down to this; if Karl Bauer had a will, the terms of the will would have been executed and his inheritance would have been distributed to the heirs mentioned in his will.

"If he died intestate, without a will, the proceeds of his estate would have been distributed to his family members. First to his wife and children; failing them, his parents; failing them, his siblings; failing them, his nieces and nephews; failing them, his grandparent; failing them, his uncles and aunts or cousins; and if there were none of those, his whole inheritance would've gone to the German government."

"How can we find out if he had a will and who inherited from him?" Catia asked. "There must have been something, at least some money and some personal effects. We'd very much like to know what happened to it."

Renate smiled. "The winding up of his estate would've been recorded in the German court system. I'll make a few enquiries with some of my lawyer acquaintances in Germany and let you know."

"Thanks, Renate, that would be great," Catia said.

"Now tell me a bit more about your research. I'm very much interested. Yaron didn't have time to tell me more and suggested I ask you."

Catia explained that they had learned that Bauer had somehow miraculously escaped prosecution. He had been in custody for about a year but was set free and left in peace for the rest of his life. It was abundantly clear that Bauer's history had been wiped out. How it was possible that Bauer, so well-known for his contribution to the Nazi book-looting rampage, could all of a sudden, after the war, have no record and no witnesses against him, was part of what they were trying to find out.

"Apparently the Allies' investigators couldn't find enough evidence against him to bring him to trial even though his own reports helped to convict his boss Rosenberg. Even in the city of Frankfurt and at the university library, where Bauer has spent so much time, no one could remember him," Catia said.

Renate nodded. "In our modern society where everything is computerized and social media tracks people's every move from cradle to grave, it sounds impossible to wipe out someone's records as thoroughly as Bauer's have apparently been wiped out. But if you go back to the time of the war and many years after, before the dawn of computers and the internet, it's not so unbelievable that personal records could've been destroyed. They were generally kept in only one location.

"Nevertheless, let me give you a modern-day example: East Germany. The Records of the State Security Service, known as the Stasi Archives, are open to the public today. However, very few people know it's not the entire record. You see, in the final days of the East German regime, the Stasi shredded files. Seventeen thousand bags full.

"In the dying months of the Second World War, thousands of SS murderers who were supposed to be put on trial, of whom well over eighty percent deserved a death sentence, managed to escape."

"You make it sound as if it was easy for them to get away. Was it?" Rex asked.

"Yes, surprisingly easy. They had secret organizations, and some of the members of those organizations who helped them escape were government officials. Others were clergymen of the Catholic Church. There were tens of thousands of Germans and Austrians without identification papers. Some had genuinely lost their IDs and, of course, some had lost them intentionally.

"Now, normally to get new ID documents one had to produce a birth certificate, However, millions upon millions of records, including birth certificates, were destroyed by the Allied forces in bombing raids and artillery barrages, and when those came to an end by 1945, the SS went to work and selectively destroyed more records.

"Therefore, in order to give people IDs as soon as possible, the Germans devised a very simple process. If you had lost your ID all you had to do was get two witnesses to swear that you were who you said you were and a new ID would be issued in the name of whoever you claimed to be.

"It was impossible to check the veracity of the claims. There were just too many of them. Of course, this messy situation perfectly served the purpose of those who wanted to conceal their real identities."

"Messy indeed," Catia said. "But Bauer was in a POW camp. They would've known who he was."

"Well, many POWs had no papers either. On their release from the camps, all POWs got a signed release paper stating the name of the prisoner. Which, of course, was the name given to the Allies when arrested. The POWs used those papers to apply for new IDs. At the end of the war, SS members, in droves, discarded their uniforms and ranks, got themselves normal German Army or Luftwaffe uniforms of ordinary soldiers, and when arrested claimed to have lost their IDs.

"On the strength of the new IDs, passports were applied for and issued, and thus many of the killers escaped."

"But the thing is, Bauer, as far as we could tell, never changed his name. Yet in some way he succeeded in wiping out much of his history," Rex said. "What we're trying to establish is who did it and why."

"You have to understand that many senior SS officers and Nazi officials had escaped the country by using false IDs. But many of them never left Germany; they only assumed a new ID, got the documents for it, and started a new life.

"The die-hard Nazis outside and inside Germany started working on the establishment of the Fourth Reich. They soon launched secret organizations and started infiltrating their members, former Nazis, into all facets of the new German society. Into the civil service, judges, police, doctors, local government, banks, you name it. They were everywhere.

"From those positions they succeeded in building a network, a brotherhood of former Nazis, to protect each other from investigation and arrest. And soon they started controlling vast sums of money and much of the economy and politics."

"That would help to explain how Bauer could get out of prison without a single charge brought against him," Rex said.

"Exactly. Maybe one more interesting fact, just to show how much influence they still have in modern-day Germany. For many years, up until recently, no German politician who had called for the prosecution of Nazi criminals had ever been elected to the party hierarchy of the CDU, the Christian Democratic Union of Germany. They are the liberal-conservative political party, the major catch-all party of the center-right in German politics. Coincidence?"

"Probably not," Rex and Catia said in unison.

Ten minutes later, Rex and Catia thanked Renate for her time and stood to leave. She declined their offer to pay for the consultation. *Sayanim* very seldom charged for their services to the Mossad.

As they got to the door of Renate's office, Rex's satphone vibrated—a text message from Josh.

Chapter 22 – We need to talk

Zurich, Switzerland

Friday, August 26, 2016

ABOUT AN HOUR or so before Rex and Catia arrived at Renate Treitelfeldt's office in Zurich, Josh and Marissa had knocked on the front door of David Sulzberger's house in Zurich. Sulzberger was the second person on their list to be interviewed. They had gone straight from the airport to Sulzberger's home close to the university. The *sayan* had made a reservation for them at the same hotel as Rex and Catia, the Widder Hotel in Zurich Old Town, in the City Center, near the famous Bahnhofstrasse shopping street. The plan was that the four of them would meet at the hotel after their respective meetings to compare notes.

Again, Rehka and Greg had done the prior research about Sulzberger's background. David was the younger brother of Leonhard Sulzberger. David was now 79, Leonhard died 5 years ago at the age of 82. When the war ended, Leonhard was 16, and David, 8. Leonhard became an accountant and David a history teacher and later a lecturer at the University of Geneva.

David was married. His wife, Meike, was still alive, and they had three adult children not living with them. Even before their marriage, Meike had been a lecturer in the same history department at the same university, so that was probably where she and David met. They were both retired.

Leonhard never married.

As with the Fabelsohns, the Sulzbergers kept a very low-key online profile.

When they were seated in the family room and Frau Sulzberger had served them coffee, Herr Sulzberger asked how he could be of assistance.

It had completely slipped Josh's mind to scan the room for bugs. He would realize his blunder only later.

Marissa repeated the same cover story about them being freelance journalists working on a story about the work of people involved in the recovery of Holocaust loot. They felt strongly that those people, like Herr Sulzberger and his brother, deserved much more acknowledgement for their work and what they had achieved than what they were getting.

If Herr Sulzberger found their story questionable, he didn't show it. Perhaps the personal phone call from Abraham Heilbron and the letter with his signature on it was all he required to relax and trust them.

It was obvious that the Sulzbergers felt much safer in Switzerland than the Fabelsohns in Austria. Herr Sulzberger didn't have any qualms about opening up and telling them about his and his brother's work.

He told them that Leonhard was 15 and he, 7, when, in 1944, the SS troops stormed into their city, Lörrach, to arrest the Jews. He explained that Lörrach was a city in southwest Germany, in the valley of the Wiese, close to the French and the Swiss borders. He and his brother had managed to hide in the garden shed of German neighbors, without them knowing, for two days until the SS had left. That night the two of them made their way over the border into Switzerland.

A sympathetic Swiss-Jewish family living in Riehen, about 3 miles from Lörrach, took them in and gave them food and shelter for the rest of the war. Their parents, though, were not so lucky. They were arrested and shipped to Auschwitz, where they were selected for extermination immediately on arrival.

When the war ended, Leonhard was 16, and David, 8. Their Swiss family, which was well-off, helped them to get through school and university. When Leonhard finished university, the two brothers started their business working on the recovery of Holocaust loot.

They'd found many art pieces and artifacts as well as stolen money and jewelry and other valuables over the years and restored them to their rightful owners. Leonhard was the man who tipped Douglas Cooper off to investigate the Schenker Company, leading to the uncovering of the notorious Schenker Papers.

Sulzberger concluded, "Make no mistake, much of the ill-gotten booty still lies beneath the streets of Zurich, guarded by the complacent and self-righteous bankers of this city."

"You and your brother did amazing... no, valiant... work, Herr Sulzberger," Josh said. "It's laudable, and it's such a pity that you never got recognition for it. I won't even begin to tell you what choice words I have for the authorities who one would have expected to do this work but didn't move a finger."

Sulzberger grinned and said, "They, the authorities, were more often than not the main cause of our headaches, with their stonewalling tactics, and in some cases, flat-out refusal to help us. Nonetheless, it was gratifying to play a small part in rectifying the injustices of the past."

Marissa fixed a disarming smile and said, "One more question, Herr Sulzberger, if you don't mind?"

"Not at all," Sulzberger said.

"I've got a Jewish friend who told me about a very interesting piece of history that I didn't know about. She told me it happened in 1942... could've been 1943, when the Nazis, when they occupied Rome, had confiscated two libraries from the Jewish Ghetto. Umm... she gave me the names, but it has escaped me now. Apparently, some books were recovered and returned to Rome after the war, but the rest of them were never found.

"I was wondering if you'd ever come across information about those libraries?"

Josh was struggling to subdue the smile threatening to take over his face as he listened at Marissa spinning the real reason for their visit.

Sulzberger had his eyes closed for a long while before he said, "I know about those libraries. If my memory serves me correctly it was the Jewish Community Library and the Italian Rabbinical College Library. I think a few books belonging to the latter were found in Frankfurt and returned to the Jewish community of Rome. The Community Library remains missing in its entirety and so does the rest of the Rabbinical College Library.

"I can vaguely remember seeing some information about the libraries coming across my desk over the years, but I can't remember the details. I gave up the loot hunting business a few years ago. At the time, I put all my research work on a portable computer hard drive and locked it away in a safety deposit box at my bank. If you want, I can get the disk, and if you come back tomorrow, we can look through all the information in more detail."

"Thank you so much, Herr Sulzberger," Marissa said. "We'd be grateful if you could do that. But, please, we don't want to inconvenience you."

Frau Sulzberger laughed and said, "Inconvenience him? Not likely. He lives for this stuff."

"It's settled then," Herr Sulzberger said. "See you tomorrow at 8:30 A.M."

***

CROSSING THE UNIVERSITY campus to get to their rental car, Josh saw him—a follower. He took Marissa's hand and whispered, "We've got a fan."

"Uh-huh, I've made two so far," Marissa replied.

Then it dawned on Josh, he had forgotten to scan the Sulzbergers' family room for bugs. He could kick himself.

They were in operational mode.

Josh put his hand around Marissa's waist and gently pulled her closer. They had slowed down to a slow stroll, looking around at the architecture of the old buildings on the campus. Every now and then one of them would stop and excitedly point at some feature.

When they passed a coffee shop, they decided to make an impromptu stop for coffee and that delicious-sounding gingerbread pastry Catia told them about. And, while they were at it, they might as well get a better look at their followers.

Within minutes, before their order had arrived, they knew what their three admirers looked like. A short, fat, blond-haired guy, around his mid-thirties and the demeanor of a well-known English dog breed. Josh dubbed him Bulldog. The other guy was a nondescript, skinny, medium height, dark-haired, ponytailed creature in his late twenties, maybe early thirties. He got the unimaginative moniker of Skinny. The third was an almost good-looking woman with blonde hair of medium height and build. She had apparently tried her level best to look young—like a student—but she had failed miserably. From her blouse, her small backpack, her jeans, to her sneakers, she would have been cool among students 10 years before. Maybe that was when she was a student, but she definitely was not a student now. For her effort, though, Josh bestowed on her the title of Miss Uni.

Josh and Marissa discussed options over the coffee and pastry, which were every bit as delicious as Catia said they would be. One option was to lose the tail, an easy feat for the two experienced CRC operatives.

"But that's like throwing the baby out with the bathwater," Marissa said.

Josh agreed. "We have to keep them in tow but take care that they don't know we've made them. They're obviously amateurs, and it shouldn't be much of an effort to turn the tables and put tabs on them. They could be a rich source of information."

"Agreed," Marissa said. "Let's get hold of Rex and Catia and find out if they're available for a bit of excitement."

Josh typed a text message to Rex. WE NEED TO TALK. URGENT.

Rex's reply arrived before Josh could take another sip of coffee. 2 MINUTES.

CHAPTER 23 – MAKE THAT THREE

ZURICH, SWITZERLAND

FRIDAY AUGUST 26, 2016

"WHAT'S UP, JOSH?" Rex said when Josh answered the phone.

"Marissa and I have been to see David Sulzberger. I'll give you the details of the meeting later. After leaving Sulzberger's house, on the way to our car, we picked up an entourage of fans."

"How many?"

"Three; Bulldog, Skinny, and Miss Uni."

Rex smiled. Josh would never let an opportunity pass to impart some witticisms.

"So, with three such wonderful admirers, we've decided to not disappoint them by shaking them off. Who knows, we might be able to have a nice chat with them at some stage? At the moment, our procession is at this coffee shop on the university campus. Marissa and I were wondering if the Dalton family might want to join the convoy?"

"Text the address," Rex said, as he started the car. "We're on our way. We don't want to miss any of it."

Rex handed his phone to Catia, who put it on speaker. By the time Rex and Catia arrived at the coffee shop, they had a plan in place. Marissa would make a reservation at another hotel, and then she and Josh would get into their car and drive to their new hotel, slowly. They didn't want to lose their fans.

Rex found parking in a spot overlooking the coffee shop on a terrace below. Over the phone, Josh quickly pointed the three out to them before he and Marissa paid their bill and walked to their car.

Catia immediately got on the phone to their *sayan* to make a new reservation for Josh and Marissa. Within fifteen minutes the *sayan* told her the new reservation was at Hotel Rütli in Zaehringerstrasse, about a mile away from the Widder Hotel where Rex and Catia would be staying.

Soon after, Rex and Catia saw Josh pull out of the parking area, the car with Bulldog in the driver's seat and Miss Uni as the passenger pulled out as well. Not far behind the car was Skinny on a motorbike. Catia was still snickering about the names Josh gave them.

Catia and Marissa each had a phone on speaker in their cars so that the four of them could stay in touch.

Rex and Catia followed the followers to the Hotel Rütli. Bulldog and Miss Uni parked in the street opposite the hotel. Skinny parked the motorbike a hundred or so yards away and got himself an outside table at a street café.

"A stakeout, Swiss style, in progress," Rex mumbled.

Rex and Catia parked outside another street café, about midway between Bulldog's car and Skinny's motorbike.

Josh and Marissa parked in the driveway in front of the hotel and went inside to book in. They carried their own luggage to their room, and Josh swept the room with his mobile phone. There were no bugs.

"We need to get tracking devices on that bike and car," Rex said.

Everyone agreed.

Just then Miss Uni got out of the car and walked across the street into the hotel's foyer. "Probably to find out in which room you are," Catia said.

A few minutes later, Miss Uni reappeared and walked across the street back to the car. It was impossible to tell if she got the information she went for. Rex thought she didn't get it because she was standing next to the car looking up at the façade of the hotel, probably trying to figure out which room Josh and Marissa were in. Catia thought she did get the information and was only counting the windows to figure out which one was room 405.

"Hang on. I'll give her a clue," Marissa said.

Next, Rex and Catia saw the curtains of room 405 being drawn; Marissa stood in full view, looking out over the city. Josh appeared next to her. She pointed at something in the distance and then put her arms around Josh's neck, and in full view of the audience, kissed him.

Catia laughed. "Well, Marissa, if those jokers don't know which room you are in after that show, we'll have to bring them up and introduce them."

"Okay," Rex said. "Now I think we need to try and get them away from their vehicles so we can plant tracking devices."

Less than 30 minutes later, Josh and Marissa were in the foyer, talking loudly to the bellhop, asking for directions to the Zurich Central Library.

Hand in hand, like loving couples do, they walked out and turned in the direction of the Zurich Central Library on Zähringer Place, about four blocks away. A taxi slowed down, and the driver asked, with gestures, if they wanted to get in. Josh waved him away, indicating politely that they wanted to walk. He didn't explain they were walking because they wanted to make sure their admirers could keep up with them.

Miss Uni had gone back to the hotel, spoken to the bellhop, pushed something into his hand, probably a tip, and then followed Josh and Marissa on foot, talking on her cellphone.

A minute or so later, Bulldog got out of the car, locked it, and followed Miss Uni by about fifty steps on the opposite side of the street. When he passed the café where Skinny was sitting, he tried his best to avoid eye-contact. A few minutes after Bulldog had passed him, Skinny got up and joined the parade.

Rex left Digger in the car with Catia so the followers wouldn't notice the large dog, and he too joined the procession down Zaehringerstrasse, about fifty or so yards behind Skinny.

When Rex was about hundred yards away, Catia and Digger went to work. They got out of their car and walked to Bulldog's car. Catia was right next to the car when she stopped and turned around slowly as if she was a bit lost. She took her small backpack off, opened it, and retrieved something from it, but then whatever it was dropped out of her hand and landed on the road right next to the left rear wheel of the car. She bent down to pick it up.

Digger was watching her intently.

"Car's tagged," she said into her earpiece.

"Excellent," said Rex.

Catia was still close to the car, putting on a show for anyone who could be watching, as she was searching on her mobile phone and then turned back in the direction from which she had come—heading for the motorbike.

She was wondering what ruse she could come up with to get a tag on the motorbike unnoticed. *Maybe just pass very close to it, bend down in stride, and put the magnetic device under the mudguard quickly and keep on walking.*

She was still thinking about it as they approached the bike, when Digger started pulling on the leash going straight for the bike. Catia instantly decided she would let him sniff the bike. That would be her opportunity to plant the tag.

Why Digger did it she would never know. Rex would later say it was because Digger was a genius and knew what had to be done after Catia had shown him once. Catia thought maybe Digger recognized the motorbike and associated it with the good times he always had when on such a vehicle with Rex. Maybe he thought Catia wanted to take him for a ride.

Whatever the reason, it turned out that Digger didn't only want to sniff at the bike; he also raised his leg against the rear wheel. Catia admonished him for it and bent down to look at the damage but couldn't see any urine anywhere. She got up, looked at Digger, and found him smiling at her.

While scratching Digger's head, she said softly, "Digger, I'm not sure what exactly just happened, but if it is what I suspect it is, you're the Leonardo Da Vinci of the canine species."

Digger bathed in the praise and pushed his wet nose against her face.

She reported, "The bike's tagged, thanks to Digger. We're going back to the car."

"Digger can put tracking beacons on vehicles?" Josh asked incredulously.

Catia laughed. "After what I just saw, I'll testify under oath that he can."

"I'd like to hear that story," Marissa said.

"That makes two of us," Rex said.

"Make that three," Josh said.

On the way back to their car, Catia checked her mobile phone and confirmed that it was receiving the signals from the tracking devices on the car and motorbike.

CHAPTER 24 – HIS HOME WAS BUGGED

ZURICH, SWITZERLAND

FRIDAY, AUGUST 26, 2016

JOSH AND MARISSA spent a little over an hour at the Zurich Central Library where one of the friendly staff helped them find the books they were looking for and make photocopies. They walked back to their hotel, slowly so as to not lose their tail, especially Bulldog who was hopelessly obese. His gait resembled a waddling duck more than a walking human.

Back in their room, Josh swept it for bugs again and was not surprised to find four of them. One in the headboard of their bed, one in the bathroom, and one on each of their bedside lights. He left them in place and showed Marissa while talking about their dinner plans.

He sent Rex a text. ROOM NOW BUGGED. 4 OF THEM.

Rex replied. EXCELLENT.

Entertaining as it was to match their skills against a bunch of amateurs, they knew it meant that either they had missed another follower, or a member of the hotel staff was working with the followers. Probably the latter.

Shortly after, Skinny left on his motorbike. Bulldog and Miss Uni were now on watch duty, it seemed.

Rex and Catia followed Skinny in their car. The signal from the tracking device had a range of ten miles; therefore, it was not necessary to stay right behind the bike. Catia drove and Rex navigated. About twenty minutes later, they saw Skinny pull up in the parking lot of an apartment block five miles from Hotel Rütli and enter a unit on the ground floor.

"Okay," Rex said. "Now we have to wait for him to come out and go somewhere so that we can return the favor and plant bugs in his place."

The bugs Josh had found in their room were not the latest and greatest in technology, but they were sensitive enough to pick up almost any sound in the hotel room and would broadcast for more than 100 yards. Bulldog and Miss Uni were well within range. For the sake of their listeners, Josh and Marissa kept up the playact of two lovebirds on a research trip in Europe.

It was almost 5:30 P.M. when Josh announced that he wanted to read the documents they had copied at the library and Marissa said she wanted to watch a bit of TV and then take a shower and get ready for dinner. She switched the TV on and plonked down on the bed. Josh sat in the armchair by the window reading American news on his tablet PC.

By 7:00 P.M. they were showered and dressed, ready to leave for the restaurant where they had reservations.

***

IT WAS SHORTLY after 7:00 P.M. when Catia got the alert on her phone that Skinny was on the move. It could be their opportunity to get into his apartment and bug it.

When they reached Skinny's apartment building, Catia and Digger waited in the car, keeping a lookout, while Rex approached the unit. The signal on Catia's phone showed that Skinny was at a shopping mall about three miles away.

The door lock on Skinny's apartment surrendered to Rex's lock picks within 30 seconds. Rex told Catia he had access, and Catia confirmed that Skinny was still at the shopping mall. His motorbike was stationary.

It took Rex less than two minutes to plant the bugs and start a manual sweep of the apartment. He wore latex gloves as he worked his way through the rooms quickly and efficiently, making sure he didn't leave any sign of his visit.

Skinny's name, according to some of the mail on the kitchen counter, was Matteo Wittwer. He was obviously a very neat and tidy guy—his apartment was spotless; his bed was made almost military style, there were no dirty dishes or clothing, everything was nice and tidy and packed away. Not a speck of dust or dirt in sight. What gave away his twisted political views were the neo-Nazi posters on the bedroom walls and a life-size black and white poster of Hitler saluting his goose-stepping troops at the Brandenburg Gate in Berlin.

Wittwer was a lousy countersurveillance operator. His laptop was on the kitchen table, switched on and logged in, with no password needed. Rex only had to move the mouse to get full access to the computer.

A nice windfall.

Rex got Rehka and Greg on the line and told them what he had found. Rehka told him how to find the computer's IP and MAC addresses, and three minutes later they had full access. A minute later they told Rex it would take them about 30 to 40 minutes to copy all the data, leaving out the video and music files. They would load the copied data to the secured CRC server and let Rex know when they were done. They would also make sure there were no traces left of their visit to Wittwer's computer.

By the time Wittwer returned to his apartment later that night, a copy of his entire electronic life history, including the passwords to all his online accounts, had been stored on the CRC servers in Arizona. Rehka and Greg were able to start analyzing it—bank accounts, internet browsing history, searches, emails, as well as social media activities. Very soon there was going to be very little they wouldn't know about Matteo Wittwer.

***

BACK AT THEIR hotel, after they had swept their room for bugs and found nothing, Rex texted Josh at 8:30 P.M. CONFERENCE?

They decided not to meet in person. They wanted to keep their fans relaxed and oblivious. CRC had several secured and encrypted teleconference numbers for cases like this. All participants phoned the same number, followed the prompts, put in their pin codes, and they could all talk to each other.

Josh replied. YEP. GIVE US 5.

Catia ordered room service dinner while they waited.

Josh and Marissa were seated in a very quiet corner of the restaurant enjoying the soft music, romantic candlelight, and the exquisite food.

The last time Josh and Marissa saw them, Bulldog and Miss Uni were outside in the parking lot in their car where they would probably stay until the end of the dinner. "Poor suckers. Must be extremely boring for them," Marissa said. "What do you say, Josh, shall we send them a bottle of wine to keep them in good spirits while they wait for us?"

Josh laughed. "Not on our first date. Maybe another time, when we know each other a bit better." Taking a sip of wine, he pushed the speed dial button for the conference number on his phone, Marissa did the same.

Rex and Catia were already waiting for them. Rex started. "Catia and I assume that David Sulzberger's home is under some kind of surveillance and that's how you earned yourselves the admiration of the three stooges."

"We reached the same conclusion," Marissa said. "But how to explain the bugging of our room?"

"I'd say it could have been one or more of the hotel staff," Rex said. "I saw Miss Uni give the bellhop something. It could have been the bugs, the instructions, and some bribe money."

"If so, I don't think the bellhop is part of their team," Josh said. "He probably only did a bit of moonlighting and earned a few bucks on the side."

Josh and Marissa were putting on a brilliant playact that would have misled even the keenest of observers into believing that the two of them were talking only to each other.

Rex said, "Okay, we've got Skinny—by the way, his real name is Matteo Wittwer—under electronic surveillance. We got a nice little windfall; his computer was on and logged in. Rehka and Greg copied everything and are already working through it."

"Hopefully the information from his computer and the tabs on his phone will help us find out who these people are and who employ them," Josh said.

"Yep," Rex said. "The posters I saw on the walls of his apartment led me to believe they're part of a neo-Nazi group. As you know, there are many delusional people belonging to neo-Nazi organizations across Europe and America. They share a common hatred for Jews and worship Adolf Hitler. They hate gays and lesbians, and blacks, and even sometimes Christians, but the Jews are their cardinal enemy."

"Well, that could be one explanation of why they're so keen to follow us. Be that as it may, it seems, for now, they're happy to just follow us and listen to the conversations in our room."

"Right," Rex said.

"So, tell us how your meeting with David Sulzberger went?" Catia asked.

Marissa and Josh told them about the meeting and that they had to meet with Sulzberger again the next morning, and that they would have to warn him that his home was bugged.

They spoke for another ten or so minutes and ended the call when Josh and Marissa had finished dessert.

CHAPTER 25 — YOU ONLY COPIED IT

ZURICH, SWITZERLAND

SATURDAY, AUGUST 27, 2016

SHORTLY BEFORE JOSH and Marissa left their hotel to meet with David Sulzberger, there was a shift change among the watchers outside. When Bulldog and Miss Uni drove away, Rex and Catia followed them.

At precisely 8:30 A.M. Josh knocked on the front door of the Sulzbergers' home. Marissa had her laptop with her in a bag. Matteo Wittwer, formerly known as Skinny, was on a park bench across the street from the Sulzbergers' home.

When Herr Sulzberger opened the door, Josh handed him a small, folded piece of paper. Sulzberger invited them in, closed the door behind them, and unfolded the note in his hand.

We think your house is bugged. Keep the conversation normal. We're going to invite you and your wife to join us for breakfast in one of the cafés nearby. We can work out a strategy when we're there.

Sulzberger's face momentarily displayed shock, but he kept his composure and nodded his understanding. He started talking about the weather and an upcoming holiday in Malta he and his wife had planned and how excited they were.

Josh was impressed with how well Sulzberger handled the news. He showed him a thumbs-up.

Marissa proposed that they all go out for breakfast. Sulzberger immediately accepted and said he would have to ask his wife if she would like to join them. He said that he vaguely remembered her saying something the day before about meeting with a friend.

He was still talking when his wife appeared in the kitchen door and spoke to her husband in German. Josh and Marissa didn't have to understand German to make out that Frau Sulzberger was chiding her husband about his forgetfulness. She then switched to English and thanked them for the invitation, but very politely declined because she had an appointment with her sister, not a friend as her husband had told them.

A few minutes later, the three of them left the house and walked to a nearby restaurant. Of course, they were duly followed by Matteo Wittwer, formerly known as Skinny.

After taking their seats at a table in the restaurant, Josh took his phone out and pushed a few buttons, ostensibly to switch it off or put it on silent. He was actually scanning for surveillance bugs—there were none. Assuming that Sulzberger was under surveillance and that it could include his mobile phone, Josh would have preferred to switch Sulzberger's phone off and remove the battery. But that would have raised the old man's tension exponentially. Therefore, he switched on the jammer app on his phone.

The mobile phone jammer or blocker application transmitted signals on the same radio frequencies as mobile phones. This one had a range of a few yards, blocking the receiving and transmitting of signals, thus effectively disabling mobile phones within the range of the jammer. Jamming and blocking of cellphone signals was an illegal activity in many countries, including the EU, but not Switzerland which is not part of the EU.

Wittwer ambled into the restaurant a few minutes later and sat at a table in the opposite corner, facing them but looking very busy reading a newspaper.

Of course, David immediately wanted to know about the bugs in his home and why they suspected there were any. And how they came to suspect it.

Marissa explained, "Abraham warned us that there might be people who wouldn't like what we're doing and would try to stop us from publishing our article. We're taking Abraham's warning seriously and we're more than a little nervous.

"The thing is we're writers, journalists, not secret agents, we don't know anything about surveillance and countersurveillance and all that cloak and dagger stuff. We kept looking around trying to remember people's faces and clothes. We saw these three people yesterday after we left your home, and then later we saw them again outside our hotel. Two of them, a man and a woman, were still there, in a car outside the hotel, this morning when we woke up. The two in the car drove off half an hour or so before we left to meet with you. We thought we could've been mistaken about being followed, but then we saw the skinny man we saw yesterday following us on a motorbike."

Marissa lied without blinking an eye, touching her nose or ears, or showing any of the other telltale signs of deceit.

"Josh and I thought the only way those people could've known about our visit to you yesterday is if they had some kind of surveillance equipment in your house... We..."

Sulzberger leaned forward and said, in a whispered tone, "Where's the man on the motorbike now?"

Josh told him it was the man who came in a few minutes after them and was now seated in the far corner from them.

Sulzberger, who was facing Wittwer, glanced at him quickly and turned his gaze back to Josh. "Can't remember that I've seen him before."

"Well, he's one of the three," Josh said. "The others might be close."

Marissa said, "Herr Sulzberger, we are a bit worried about being followed, and we are now also worried about your safety. We don't want to give up on our research, but we don't want to put you in any danger. Up till now, they haven't given any indication that they're aggressive."

Sulzberger raised his hand to stop Marissa. He was angry. "Listen, my brother and I've been threatened and assaulted by these cowardly idiots for all of our lives. The police were never able to apprehend a single one of them. We always had to fend for ourselves. We've never given in to them, and I don't intend to start now. I will fight these bastards with every bit of strength left in me as long as I'm alive."

Josh thanked him and said, "Okay, let's finish breakfast and go back to your house. But we'll have to keep the ruse up for anyone who's listening. We were thinking you and I could talk about your research while Marissa searches for the information on the hard drive you got from the bank. Is that okay with you?

"No problem at all. That's why I got the disk from the bank."

"Will it be okay if I copy some of the information over to my computer?" Marissa asked.

"No problem. Now, what should I do about the bugs in my apartment? I'd hate to leave them there. I'm not doing research anymore. Visitors who are interested in our work, like yourselves, I haven't had since my brother died.

There is nothing the scumbags can learn from listening to my private life."

It was Josh's turn to lie. "We don't have the expertise to help you. But if you know someone in the police or in security it's probably best to contact them for help. That's of course if there are bugs. It's possible that only your phone is bugged."

"I'll do that."

Half an hour later, they had finished their breakfast and were ready to return to the house. A quick glance at Wittwer told them that he had finished the coffee he had been sipping for the past 45 minutes.

Back in the house, Josh looked out the window and saw Wittwer back on his bench in the park. Earphones were plugged into his ears. Maybe he was listening to the conversation going on in the house, or maybe he was just listening to music or one of Hitler's rousing speeches to kill the time.

Marissa made sure that the internet connection on her laptop was disabled before she plugged Sulzberger's portable hard drive in.

Sulzberger was playing along nicely and kept the conversation going while Marissa searched the hard drive and copied over information. She quickly found twenty-four records containing Bauer's name and four mentioning the libraries.

It took about ninety minutes to complete the searches and copying.

They thanked Sulzberger for his time and willingness to help them.

"I wish we could help him get rid of those bugs," Marissa said when they were outside the house.

"Yes, I feel the same. But at least he knows about them now, and I'm sure he has some trustworthy friends or acquaintances in the Jewish community who know someone who could take care of it for him."

"I hope so."

"Was there information about Karl Bauer and the libraries on that hard drive?"

"Yes, my searches returned a number of results, but instead of searching and copying selectively, which would've taken a long time, I copied the entire disk to my laptop. I know that's not exactly what Sulzberger agreed to, but I'm sure he would've agreed if I'd asked."

Josh smiled. "Yeah, I'm sure he would've."

"It's not as if I *stole* his research, Josh," Marissa said, looking at him as if she wanted him to exonerate her.

Josh grinned. "Right. You only copied it."

Marissa saw the grin and punched him in the shoulder.

CHAPTER 26 – A POCKET WATCH AND A DIARY

ZURICH, SWITZERLAND

SATURDAY, AUGUST 27, 2016

THEIR NEXT INTERVIEW was scheduled for Monday in Berlin, with a journalist by the name of Erhard Bachenheimer. Josh and Marissa were getting fed-up with playing follow the leader with the three stooges, not to mention the invasion of their privacy with the bugs in their room. They were hoping that Rex and Catia would be able to put the tabs on Bulldog and Miss Uni before the day was over so that they could ditch their three fans and go to Berlin, hoping that their fans wouldn't tail them there.

Josh was driving. Wittwer was on his bike a hundred or so yards behind them. Marissa texted Rex to join them in a teleconference.

A few minutes later, in the conference, they filled Rex and Catia in on the meeting with Sulzberger. Marissa told them that she uploaded the information to the CRC servers where they could access it.

Rex and Catia told them that they had followed Bulldog and Miss Uni and got their address. They lived in different apartment blocks not far apart. "They're probably sleeping now and might go back on watch duty tonight," Catia said. "If they do, Rex and I'll take care of the bugging of their apartments."

Before they could continue their discussions, Catia's phone vibrated. It was a text message from Renate Treitelfeldt, the lawyer. HAVE INFORMATION. 2:00 P.M. MY OFFICE?

Catia replied. SEE YOU AT 2.

It was 1:30 P.M.

"Sorry, I have to break up our party. We got a text from the lawyer, looks like she has information about Bauer's estate for us," Rex said. "We have to be at her office in half an hour. Let's have another catch-up after."

***

A FEW MINUTES later, Rex and Catia were rushing over to the lawyer's office in their rental car. Digger was on the back seat staring out the window.

Renate was waiting for them in the lobby of her office building. When they were seated in her office, she got to the point right away. "My lawyer friend in Wiesbaden emailed me with the information I requested, and I thought you would want to hear about it immediately."

"Thank you so much, Renate, and for seeing us on a Saturday afternoon. We really appreciate it very much," Catia said.

Renate continued. "My pleasure. Apparently, my friend had little trouble finding out that Karl Bauer indeed had a will. He got a copy of it which he has emailed to me." She printed a copy and handed it to Rex and Catia.

It was a very simple will, in what could have been Bauer's own handwriting, signed in the presence of two witnesses. It stated: *I bequeath my entire estate to Heinrich Bödeker, the oldest son of my late sister, Emely Bödeker.* It was dated November 15, 1959, two and a half months before Bauer's death on January 30, 1960.

"My friend also managed to get a copy of a record showing the assets and liabilities in the estate." She printed a copy and handed it to Rex and Catia.

The estate consisted of the proceeds of Bauer's savings account which was 3,650 Deutsche Marks; the original manuscripts, signed by him, of all books Bauer had written; the originals of his two Ph.D. theses, also signed by him; a bundle of all articles he had ever published; a pocket watch; and a diary. There were no debts.

The diary was immediately of interest to Catia and Rex. And, of course, they wanted to know if Renate's friend had perchance mentioned anything about Heinrich Bödeker's last known address. Unfortunately, he didn't.

They thanked Renate, and again she politely turned down their offer to pay for her services. She wished them the best of luck and told them they were welcome to contact her anytime they needed legal advice or assistance.

On the way back to their hotel, with Rex driving, Catia called Rehka and Greg and placed the phone on speaker. The request was simple. "Find Heinrich Bödeker, the oldest son of Karl Bauer's sister, Emely Bödeker."

"We're onto it," said Greg. "Watch this space."

CHAPTER 27 – MUSIC TO A MAN'S EARS

ZURICH, SWITZERLAND

SATURDAY, AUGUST 27, 2016

BACK AT THEIR hotel, Rex was about to text Josh and Marissa to set up another conference to continue their last discussion and bring them up to date with the news from the lawyer, when Catia told him Bulldog's car was moving.

"Okay, let's see where he's going."

Catia followed the signals emitted by the tracking device on Bulldog's car on her phone. Bulldog went to Miss Uni's apartment, presumably to pick her up, and then the two of them made their way to the Hotel Rütli in Zaehringerstrasse, probably to relieve their teammate, Matteo Wittwer.

Catia texted Marissa. WE THINK THE CHANGING OF THE GUARD IS ABOUT TO TAKE PLACE. KEEP A LOOKOUT AND LET US KNOW.

A few minutes later, Catia got the confirmation text from Marissa. THEY'RE HERE. W GONE. B & MU ARE WATCHING.

Catia replied. GREAT. WE'LL GO AND BUG THEIR PLACES.

Marissa replied, OKAY. WE'RE GOING OUT FOR SIGHTSEEING. WILL TAKE B & MU ALONG :)

It took Rex and Catia less than thirty minutes to get to Bulldog's apartment. His unit was on the second floor. In broad daylight, entering through the lobby posed a bit more of a challenge than getting into Wittwer's apartment the day before. Fortunately, there was no reception desk and staff. The only obstacle was the front door where a unique code, which Rex didn't have, had to be entered to get access.

It was a job for Rehka and Greg. CRC's team of computer hackers, under the leadership of Greg, were among the best in the business. With a few keystrokes, they could create havoc, black out a city, take control of their traffic lights, enter their databases and extract the plans for any building, and much more. They were not going to break a sweat to overcome the electronics of this door.

Rex thought the seven minutes it took for Greg to phone him back with the access code was much longer than he would have expected. "What took you so long, Greg? Are you losing the touch? I'm used to having you solve little problems like this in less than a minute," Rex bantered.

Greg laughed, and Rehka, who was also on the line, started giggling softly.

Rex said, "Aha. Greg, don't worry, Rehka just answered my question."

Three minutes later, Rex opened the door to the lobby with the passcode provided by Greg. He took the stairs up to the second floor and was standing inside Bulldog's studio apartment half a minute later.

The place was a pigsty. There was a nauseating smell emanating from rotten food, dirty dishes, unwashed clothes, and the lingering body odor of someone uncaring about personal hygiene.

How the hell does Miss Uni survive the smell in the confines of a car for hours on end?

Rex had his handkerchief over his nose as he quickly planted the bugs and looked around. The walls were covered with Neo-Nazi posters, swastikas, and extremist slogans. Bulldog's real name was Oskar Bächler, but there was no computer to be found in the mess. To Rex it seemed as if Bächler spent his days eating junk food, drinking beer, and watching TV.

Explains his physical condition.

A quarter of an hour later, he was back in the car with Catia and Digger.

Catia pulled out of the parking lot and headed to Miss Uni's apartment.

On their way, Greg told them what to expect at her apartment. The building had a revolving door in the front and a building manager at a reception desk in the foyer. But each floor had an emergency exit to a staircase that led to the ground in back. Greg couldn't tell if the outer door was locked, but he could tell that there was no alarm attached to it. There were also no security cameras in the staircase or in the hallways.

Miss Uni's apartment was on the fourth floor.

The emergency exit door was locked, but that only halted Rex's progress for ten seconds. Miss Uni's front door slowed him down by another ten seconds.

Stepping inside her one-bedroom apartment, Rex was relieved and took a deep breath of the fresh, clean air— *such a contrast to Bulldog's place*. This one was tidy, clean, well-organized, and with functional furnishings. No offensive odors. On the walls were only posters of nature scenes. No signs of Neo-Nazis anywhere.

Rex quickly planted the bugs and conducted a search. Her name was Lisa Marolf. She had a laptop, it was switched on, but locked.

Greg and Rehka stepped Rex through a routine of shutting down and restarting the laptop. A few minutes later, the two of them had remote access to it and told Rex it would take them about an hour to copy the contents of the hard drive to the CRC servers. He could leave; they didn't need him to get the job done.

Rex was back in the car with Catia and Digger within twenty minutes.

As Catia pulled away from the curb, Rex's phone started ringing. It was Rehka.

"Problems, Rehka?"

"No, not at all. When you phoned earlier, Greg and I were just about to let you know we've tracked down Heinrich Bödeker."

"Rehka, you're a star! Wait, let me put you on speaker. Catia will want to hear this." To Catia he said, "She found Bödeker."

"Excellent, Rehka!"

"Thanks. It wasn't difficult," Rehka said. "The man and his wife are social media addicts. They've got every possible social media account out there, and they're active on them all. I'm surprised they get anything else done.

"We've got their whole routine, when they go to work, when they sleep, eat, go out, even when their children are visiting them. All of it on Facebook and Instagram and Twitter."

"Wow! Thanks for that, Rehka," Catia said.

Rehka gave them Bödeker's address in Berlin and said she would create a document with their detailed background information and routines and upload it to the CRC servers.

"Let me know if you need anything else," Rehka said. "Greg and I will start analyzing the data we got from Miss Uni's computer. So far, Mateo Wittwer's computer and phone only confirmed Rex's suspicions. He's indeed involved with some demented neo-Nazi group who calls themselves the FRV, Fourth Reich Vanguard. But we still have a lot to go through."

When the call ended, Rex looked at Catia and said, "I think we're done here in Zurich. What do you say?"

"Yes, I'm itching to go to Berlin. Any ideas how we're going to get our hands on that diary?"

"The old-fashioned way," Rex said with a grin on his face. "We're going to steal it. Or do you have other ideas?"

Catia smiled and shook her head. "No, my ideas are in alignment with yours."

"Music to a man's ears," Rex said.

Catia laughed.

Rex texted Josh to join them in a conference call. He and Marissa were still in their car driving around Zurich with Bulldog and Miss Uni in tow.

When they joined the call, Rex told them about the bugging of the apartments and the news that Rehka had tracked down Heinrich Bödeker and that there was nothing to keep them in Zurich any longer.

Marissa and Josh let out a joint hallelujah!

"You would not believe how wholeheartedly hacked off we are with these jokers following and listening to us all day," Marissa said.

"Okay," Rex said. "You're scheduled to leave for Berlin on Monday morning to meet with Erhard Bachenheimer. But I think we should change that. We'll need your help to put surveillance on the Bödekers to figure out how we're going to get our hands on that diary."

"Anything to get away from our loving but overbearing fans." Marissa chuckled. "I'll reschedule our flight for tomorrow morning."

"Good. Let me know when you have the details. Catia and I will try to get seats on the same flight. But let's not make contact with each other again until we get to Berlin and we know whether you have any raving fans over there as well. We can book accommodation when we get there and know what the security situation is."

On the way back to their hotel, Marissa phoned the airline and changed their Monday morning flight to the next morning at 8:15 A.M. She texted the details to Catia, who immediately got on the phone and booked herself, Rex, and Digger on the same flight.

Chapter 28 — We'll Have to Do It at Night

Berlin, Germany

Sunday, August 28, 2016

THE DALTONS WERE at Hotel Rütli very early that Sunday morning and followed Bulldog and Miss Uni, who were about a hundred yards behind Josh and Marissa, to the airport. At the airport they observed Bulldog and Miss Uni watching Josh and Marissa as they parked their vehicle in the parking lot. When the two got on a bus to go to their terminal, Bulldog and Miss Uni left.

Catia tracked their signal on her phone for a while and reported, "Looks like they've given up and are returning home."

"Let's hope we've seen the last of them," Marissa sighed.

The tracking devices would lose their power within the next 24 hours and would drop off the vehicles the first time they hit the smallest of bumps.

Rex and Catia also parked their car in the parking lot, left the key in it, and made their way to the departure terminal where they had to get Digger booked in before they could do so themselves. When they finally got to the waiting area, they located Josh and Marissa and kept them under surveillance until they boarded their plane and were somewhat relieved when they couldn't find any signs of a tail on their friends. They could only hope that wouldn't change when they get to Berlin.

One and a half hours later, after landing at Berlin-Tegel Airport, the city's main international airport, Rex, Catia, and Digger made their way to the luggage area. They soon got a view of Josh and Marissa, who still seemed to be without any followers.

After collecting their luggage, Rex and Catia followed their friends at a distance. Josh and Rex collected a car from a *sayan*. They agreed, via text messages, to meet each other for breakfast at the popular restaurant, House of Small Wonder at 20 Johannisstrasse if they were not followed. If they were, Rex and Catia would not stop at the restaurant, and they would book in at different hotels again.

"I thought the two of you were famous. But it appears your fanbase is limited to the Neo-Nazis of Zurich," Rex quipped when he and Catia joined their friends at their table in the restaurant. "I thought you would've gained more of an international following by now."

Marissa laughed. "Yeah, well, just wait until they see our first performance. There's no telling what lengths our admirers will go to after that."

A few minutes later, Catia had phoned the *sayan* to book two rooms for them at Hotel Riu Plaza, at 1 Martin-Luther-Strasse in the center of the city.

After checking in and dropping their luggage off in their rooms, the first order of business was to stretch their legs in a nearby park and let Digger have a run and visit a few trees and shrubs.

While Digger was running around enjoying himself in the deserted park, they discussed their plan of action.

As promised, Rehka had created a document containing the background information about Heinrich Bödeker and saved it on the CRC server.

Bödeker didn't follow in the academic footsteps of his famous uncle. He had dropped out of school early and had been in and out of jobs his whole adult life. Currently he was working as a salesperson at a furniture store. Born in 1950, he was 66 and had about a year before retirement. His wife was a few years younger. She worked as a caregiver at a nursing home. They had three adult children who didn't live with them.

Their house was in Lichtenberg, a middle-income residential suburb about five miles from the Berlin city center.

According to Rehka's document the Bödekers lived a monotonous life of work between 8:00 A.M. and 5:00 P.M. five days a week. Wednesday nights, like clockwork, they went out for dinner, and on Saturday nights, without fail, they went to the movies. The rest of their time was probably spent on social media and watching TV.

They looked at the online maps and satellite images of the Bödekers' house and neighborhood and decided to visit the area to see what it looked like in reality.

An hour or so later, they were all in the SUV that the *sayan* had provided for them. Digger, on the back seat, had his head out the half-open window. His lolling tongue and pricked ears signaled that he was very happy.

The sprawling Lichtenberg area was known for the Stasi Museum, the former headquarters of East Germany's secret police, and the Hohenschönhausen Memorial, a former prison now open for tours. There was a plethora of produce markets, clothing shops, and restaurants. Lichtenberg also hosted the famous Friedrichsfelde Central Cemetery where many socialist leaders were buried.

The Bödeker home was at the end of a quiet cul-de-sac. The small two-story house bordered on a public park in the back. They parked the car and took Digger for his second park visit of the day.

It didn't take them long to scout the park and find that it had various entrances and that the vegetation provided the ideal cover to get undetected access to the Bödeker property.

"We'll have to do it at night," Rex said. "I can't see that we'd be able to get in there unnoticed during the day."

"Agreed," Josh said.

"Okay, let's take Digger for a walk along the fences bordering the park to see if there are any dogs we should be worried about," Rex said.

As they moved along the fences of the houses bordering the park, they talked loudly, and Digger went sniffing along every fence. If there were any dogs, they were either used to people making a lot of noise in the park or they were inside the houses where they couldn't hear anything. It was also possible that there were no dogs at all.

On the way back to their hotel, Rex said, "If Rehka's information is accurate that Wednesday nights are the Bödekers' date night, it seems to be the ideal time to hit their house."

They all agreed.

Back at the hotel, Rex phoned Rehka and Greg and asked them to put tracking on the Bödekers' mobile phones to see where they were at any given moment. With the CIA technology available to CRC, it was a surprisingly easy thing to do. Much, much easier and a lot less red tape to navigate than tapping into their phones and listening to their conversations.

Within three hours of Rex's request, Rehka and Greg confirmed that they had it all set up. The Bödekers were at home at the moment. They remotely installed the tracking software on the phones carried by Rex, Catia, Josh, and Marissa and showed them how to use it.

Chapter 29 – I Get the Exclusive

Monday, August 29, 2016

HAVING PLACED THE tabs on the Bödekers, knowing where they were at all times, knowing where they lived, and how to get into their home, there was nothing more to do but wait for Wednesday night, hoping their subjects would stick with their routine and go out to dinner.

The four of them had breakfast together and then took the short stroll from their hotel to the famous Brandenburg Gate, the 18th-century neoclassical monument built on the orders of Prussian king, Frederick William II. The gate gave entry to *Unter den Linden*, a thoroughfare lined by linden trees leading to the City Palace, home of the Prussian rulers.

Throughout its existence, the Brandenburg Gate had been the site of major historical events, and in modern times it was considered a symbol of the turbulent history of Germany and Europe.

Shortly after mid-day, Josh and Marissa left Rex and Catia to meet with Erhard Bachenheimer, the third contact on their list of interviewees.

From the background file provided by Rehka and Greg they knew that Erhard Bachenheimer was the son of Ernst

Bachenheimer, a German Jew and Holocaust survivor, a journalist who died two years ago at the age of 89. His wife died 6 months ago.

Erhard Bachenheimer, 65, had followed his father's footsteps in journalism. Like his late father, he worked for *The Berliner Kurier*, The Berlin Courier, a regional, daily tabloid founded on 15 June 1949. Bachenheimer was married. They had no children. His wife was a nurse.

After the experience with Sulzberger in Zurich, Josh was not willing to take any chances. When he and Marissa met Bachenheimer in his office, Josh gave him a handwritten note warning that his office and phone could be bugged and asked if there was a safer place to talk.

Bachenheimer read the note and didn't look shocked. He showed them a thumbs up and said, "What do you say we go for a coffee across the street?"

In chorus, Josh and Marissa said, "Excellent idea."

In the coffee shop, at their table, Josh took the same precautionary measures as with Sulzberger in Zurich; he surreptitiously scanned the table and surroundings and switched on the phone jammer app.

Marissa did the usual spinning of their cover story of doing research about the work of people who are still involved or were involved in the past in the recovery of Holocaust loot.

Bachenheimer's drawn out o-k-a-a-a-y after listening to Marissa's story, told them that he was skeptical. Maybe because they weren't Jews, or maybe because they weren't very convincing, or maybe it was just the second-nature skepticism of a journalist of forty odd years in the industry.

Nevertheless, to their surprise, he didn't pursue it. Instead he asked, "How can I help you?"

Josh asked him to talk about his and his father's work in recovering Holocaust loot.

Bachenheimer nodded and started. When he came to the end of his narrative, Marissa asked if he had any information about loot still not recovered.

"On that topic I can keep you busy for a very long time but let me give you the summarized version. At the end of the war, the Allies found loot hidden in vaults, warehouses, houses, basements, tunnels, salt mines, and secluded castles. They found it in more than a thousand repositories across Germany and Austria. They immediately set up collection points. One such collection point was Wiesbaden, which, at its height, housed about seven hundred thousand individual objects including paintings and sculptures.

"The identifiable works of art were returned to the countries from which they were taken. Each government had to track down the owners. But many of the owners couldn't be found and it landed in the hands of art dealers, galleries, and museums worldwide. Some of them deliberately or negligently didn't do any research about their collections' provenance.

"In 1998 the National Gallery of Art in Washington identified more than four hundred European paintings with gaps in their provenance covering the World War II era.

"The Nazis stole an estimated twenty percent of Europe's art. Not just Jewish art, all art. More than one hundred thousand pieces remain unaccounted for to this day.

"And last but not least, as you probably already know, death camp victims were stripped of all their personal belongings on arrival at the camps. Gold, coins, rings, spectacles, jewelry, and other precious items were sent to the Reichsbank for conversion to bullion and then credited to SS accounts. How do you even begin to restore that?"

Josh and Marissa were shaking their heads.

Bachenheimer said, "But that's not what you're after, is it? I have a gut feeling you're after something specific."

Josh, with a poker face, said, "We've recently come across an interesting piece of history, the libraries of the Jewish Ghetto in Rome. Apparently, they were stolen by the Nazis and moved to Germany. Have you ever come across that in your research?"

"Aha, I thought there was more to it. But you're not Jewish as far as I can tell. Why the interest in Jewish literature?"

Marissa said, "I have a friend in New York, an Italian-Jew. She has an interest in the history of the Italian Jews. It was fascinating to listen to her when she told us about the libraries."

Bachenheimer took a sip of coffee and stared at them over his wireframe glasses for a long, uneasy spell. "If the two of you and your friend in New York are on a quest to find those libraries, I'd like to commend you. It was one of the tasks I'd set for myself long ago, but I always got caught up in something else. I have collected information about it over the years. I'd be happy to share it with you but on condition I get the exclusive."

Josh and Marissa knew they had to give an answer, but they didn't know if Catia and Rex would be happy. Marissa thought quick and hard. She couldn't see any downside and said, "Agreed, provided my friend doesn't have a problem with it."

When they left the coffee shop, it was with the agreement that they would come by Bachenheimer's office early the next morning to pick up a flash drive with his research on it.

As they drove away to their hotel, they checked and doublechecked and were pleased to see they had no followers.

They were also relieved when Catia and Rex told them they did the right thing to agree to Bachenheimer's request for an exclusive on the story.

***

Berlin, Germany

Tuesday, August 30, 2016

THE NEXT DAY, after collecting the flash drive from Bachenheimer, the five of them spent most of the day visiting the East Side Gallery, a section of the Berlin Wall, covered in colorful murals, which was not destroyed at the end of the Cold War; the Pergamon Museum hosting the reconstructed Ishtar Gate of Babylon; and the Jewish museum, the largest of its kind in Europe.

In the late afternoon, they made another reconnaissance trip to the Bödekers' house and neighborhood, this time in Josh and Marissa's rented car.

Back at the hotel, Catia studied the information on Bachenheimer's flash drive. He had collected a lot of information, more than anyone of the other people they had interviewed so far. However, much of it was information he had collected from the work of scholars who had been speculating about the fate of the libraries over the past forty years or so. There was nothing she didn't already know.

CHAPTER 30 – IT WAS A NOVEL

BERLIN, GERMANY

WEDNESDAY, AUGUST 31, 2016

SUNSET WAS AT 7:56 P.M. An hour later, when the Bödekers' car pulled out of their garage, it was fully dark with a cloudless half-moon sky.

Rex, Catia, and Digger were in their car on the north side of the park bordering the Bödekers' house, close to that entry. Josh and Marissa were in their car on the south side of the park, also close to an entry.

They saw the lights in the Bödekers' house going out. Soon after, the garage door opened, and the car drove off.

"You're on, guys," Marissa said into her microphone.

Josh kissed her and got out of the car. He was clothed in black, and a ski mask covered his face.

Rex was similarly clad, and Digger had on his full harness, equipped with a video camera the size of a pencil eraser, which was located on the top of his head between his ears and practically invisible. Everything Digger would see would also be visible to Rex. Mini earphones were fitted in Digger's ears, completely invisible, and a mini microphone not much bigger than a pinhead was fitted on the harness between his front legs. All of it was wirelessly connected to an iPad mini, which Rex normally carried in a small backpack and had strapped to his forearm.

Marissa and Catia remained in their vehicles in the driver seats, ready to move quickly if required. On their phone screens they were tracking the Bödekers' mobile phones as well as Rex, Josh, and Digger approaching the house. The four of them were in contact with each other through CRC's standard tactical communications gear, consisting of throat mics and mini earpieces, provided by the CIA's technical labs.

Josh met Rex and Digger among the trees and shrubs directly behind the house. There was a five-foot wooden fence between them and the house. Not a big obstacle for any of them. Josh quickly inspected the other side of the fence, found no hindrances, and jumped over.

Rex said to Digger, "Go, boy, get over."

Digger took a few steps back, ran, and bounced over the fence with at least a foot to spare. Rex followed him a second or two later.

Inside the yard, Rex called Digger to him, scratched his ears, pushed his nose against Digger's wet nose, and said, "Clever boy. You think you can do a recce for us?"

Digger's answer came in the form of an uplifted, waving tail and a lick across Rex's face.

"Love you too, boy." He pointed to the left of the house. "Scout and hide."

Despite his size, Digger disappeared like a ghost. Rex removed the patch of cloth on his left forearm covering the six-inch screen to track Digger's movements.

Through the micro earphones located inside Digger's ears and the images streaming back from the night vision camera on his head, Rex directed him around the property. A few minutes later, Digger emerged out of the dark next to Rex and pushed his wet nose into Rex's face. The coast was clear.

"Clever boy. You're such a clever dog," Rex said as he ruffled Digger's ears and scratched his back. "Okay, now you have to guard the place while Josh and I go inside."

Digger looked at Rex in anticipation, and Rex said, "Guard and hide." Digger took off again, this time to the right side of the house. He would stealthily be circling the house while Rex and Josh were inside and would warn them if anyone approached.

Rex and Josh approached the back door. To their surprise they didn't need Rex's lockpicking skills—the door wasn't locked.

Inside the house they made sure all the curtains were drawn before they switched on their tactical penlights and started searching the rooms. They kept in touch with Catia and Marissa, reporting their progress, but it was slow going. The Bödekers' house was very neat and tidy, but there was no obvious place where the diary could've been. There was a small bookshelf in the family room, but it only contained a few novels and illustrated magazines. The Bödekers were obviously not avid readers.

Half an hour later, Rex and Josh met in the family room again. They both shrugged—nothing.

Catia said, "The attic, Rex. Have you looked there?"

"*Attic…*," Rex said slowly. "Of course. Thanks, Catia, I didn't even think about that. Hang on let me see if I can find the entry."

Rex and Josh went up the stairs again but found no entry.

"Look on the outside, Rex, there could be a staircase," Catia said.

Catia was right. The stairs to the roof space was on the outside, on the north side of the house.

Minutes later, Rex and Josh were staring at the dust-covered stacks of boxes and junk in the loft. With the dust of years covering everything, it was going to be all but impossible to hide the signs of their visit. But there was nothing they could do about it. They could only hope that the Bödekers would not set foot in their attic before the dust had covered their tracks again.

In the glow of their tactical penlights, they inspected the boxes in the shelves trying to figure out what was written on them.

A few minutes later, Josh said, "Hey, Rex, my German is a little rusty, but here on this box it says something about Onkel Karl, you think..."

Rex took two steps, cast the light on the box, blew the dust away, and read the German words; *Onkel Karl – Bücher und scheiße* and then translated it for everyone, "Uncle Karl - Books and shit."

"That's it!" Catia shouted in their earpieces.

They took the box off the shelf, placed it on the floor, and took the lid off. Inside they found everything, except for the cash and pocket watch, mentioned in the court record of Bauer's estate. The signed original manuscripts of the four books Bauer had published, the signed originals of his two Ph.D. theses, the bundle of all articles he had published, and the diary right at the bottom of the box. It was an A5 size leather bound book, tied with a piece of string that could once have been white. The leather was worn-out and dirty.

"Okay, we've got the diary," Rex said. "I think it's best if we don't remove it but rather take photos of every page."

"Agreed," Catia said, "but only if you boys can hurry up. You've been in there for over forty-five minutes. The Bödekers cellphone signals say they're still at the restaurant, but I think they might be heading home within the next half hour or so."

"On it, Missus Dalton," Rex quipped.

Catia laughed.

Rex took his mobile phone out, launched the camera app, and started taking photos while Josh turned the pages. After a few photos, Rex stopped and scrolled through the images on his phone to make sure he was capturing the pages properly. Bauer's handwriting was neat and tidy, and the quality of the images on the phone were perfect.

"Go for it," Josh said after he had a look at the images. "You're every bit as professional as a Cold War spy stealing blueprints."

They were making good progress, about four pages per minute, but it didn't feel like it. The stress of the moment made it feel like an eternity, especially for Catia and Marissa who had nothing else to do but watch the clock and the Bödekers' cellphone signals.

They were about two thirds through the diary when Marissa said, "Uh-oh, they're on the move. How much longer?"

"Maybe another ten minutes or so," Josh said.

"How long is the drive from the restaurant to the house?" Rex asked.

"It took them twelve minutes to get there," said Catia. "But let's be safe and make it ten minutes."

"Okay, we'll try to start packing up in eight," Rex said. "Please watch the time for us."

A minute later, Rex's phone beeped with a low-battery alert. He didn't panic. He had two spare batteries with him, but there was no time to swap them. "Your phone, Josh. Mine is out of power."

Josh had his phone out before Rex could finish his sentence.

Two minutes later, Catia was in their ears. "Boys, it seems as if the Bödekers are in a hurry to get home, they're about four minutes out."

"Okay, if it comes down to it, we'll take the diary with us."

But a few photos later, Josh turned another page and saw it was blank. He turned another one and found it blank as well. He quickly flipped through the rest of the pages—all blank.

"Great, let's repack the box and get out of here," Rex said. "If we've missed anything, we'll have to come back on Saturday night when they're out to the movies."

"Yeah, and in the meantime, we'll hope and pray they don't get a reason to come up here," Josh said.

Seconds after Rex, Josh, and Digger had landed on the other side of the fence in the park, the lights of the Bödekers' car illuminated the driveway.

They were back in the Daltons' hotel room half an hour later. Rex plugged his phone into the charger and started it up. When he was back online, he uploaded the images to the CRC server, and Josh did the same with the photos on his phone.

It took a little over twenty minutes before Rex started reading and translating. Within minutes they were so lost in Karl Bauer's diary, they forgot all about dinner.

Digger had given up on getting any special treats for dinner tonight. However, Rex gave him his kong stuffed with peanut butter. The kong was an oddly-shaped toy, part cylinder, part cone, with indentations that made it look like a hard-plastic snowman, with a hole running through it from top to bottom. The only toy ever known that a Dutch shepherd couldn't destroy in a few minutes. Rex always kept a few of them at hand. It was always a joy to see Digger's absolute ecstasy when he saw that kong. It was a special treat, reserved for times when Digger had done especially well, as he did tonight, and given sparingly. Digger worked for praise, not treats.

After emptying the kong, he ate some of his kibble, drank some water, and with a long sigh, plonked down on his bed in the corner of the lounge and went to sleep.

They were surprised to find that Karl Bauer's diary was not a chronicle of daily events, it was a novel, written in the third person, as if he were an ever-present but unseen observer, detached from the events he described.

PART III

THE NOVEL

CHAPTER 31 – THE BEGINNING OF THE END

STALINGRAD, RUSSIA

31 JANUARY 1943

OBERST WILHELM ADAM, aide to *Generaloberst* Friedrich Wilhelm Ernst Paulus, heaved a long sigh. *How did it come to this?* He shook his head slowly, opened his diary, and started writing:

31 January 1943 – 7:00 a.m. It was still dark, but day was dawning almost imperceptibly. Paulus was asleep. It was some time before I could break out of the maze of thoughts and strange dreams that depressed me so greatly. But I don't think I remained in this state for very long. I was going to get up quietly when someone knocked at the door. Paulus awoke and sat up. It was the HQ commander. He handed the colonel general a piece of paper and said, "Congratulations. The rank of field marshal has been conferred upon you. The dispatch came early this morning—it was the last one."

"One can't help feeling it's an invitation to suicide. However, I'm not going to do them such a favor," said Paulus after reading the dispatch.

Schmidt continued. "At the same time I have to inform you that the Russians are at the door." With these words he opened the door and a Soviet general and his interpreter entered the room. The general announced that we were his prisoners. I placed my revolver on the table.

"Prepare yourself for departure. We shall be back for you at 9:00. You will go in your personal car," said the Soviet general through his interpreter.

Then they left the room. I had the official seal with me. I prepared for my last official duty. I recorded Paulus's new rank in his military document, stamped it with the seal, then threw the seal into the glowing fire.

The main entrance to the cellar was closed and guarded by the Soviet soldiers. An officer, the head of the guards, allowed me and the driver to go out and get the car ready. Climbing out of the cellar, I stood dumbfounded. Soviet and German soldiers, who just a few hours earlier had been shooting at one another, now stood quietly together in the yard. They were all armed, some with weapons in their hands, some with them over their shoulders.

My God, what a contrast between the two sides! The German soldiers, ragged and in light coats, looked like ghosts with hollow, unshaven cheeks. The Red Army fighters looked fresh and wore warm winter uniforms. Involuntarily, I remembered the chain of unfortunate events that had prevented me from sleeping for so many nights. The appearance of the Red Army soldiers seemed symbolic. At 9:00 sharp the HQ commander of the 64th Army arrived to take the commander of the vanquished

German 6th Army and its staff toward the rear. The march toward the Volga had ended.

With the surrender, the Soviet forces captured 235,000 German troops.

One of Paulus's last actions, before surrendering, was to send his wedding ring back to his wife on the last plane. Paulus had not seen his wife in more than a year and would not see her again—she died in 1949 while he was still in captivity.

31 January 1943 was the beginning of the end for Nazi Germany.

By September 3, 1943, the first of the Allied forces landed in Southern Italy. By September 8, five days later, Italy's fascist regime had surrendered.

By October 16, 1943, when the ERR, under the watching eyes of Dr. Karl Bauer, removed the books from the Jewish Ghetto in Rome, the tide had well and truly turned against Germany.

By Christmas of 1943, German forces were in retreat on all fronts.

***

IN THE LATE summer of 1944, Heinrich Himmler, the Reichsführer of the SS, one of the most powerful men in Nazi Germany and one of the main architects of the Holocaust, in a last-ditch attempt to save the Reich, ordered the launch of *Unternehmen Werwolf,* Operation Werewolf—the creation of a covert special force trained to engage in clandestine operations behind Allied lines.

The Nazi *werwolf* was not the monstrosity of horror films that grew hair all over its face and body during the full moon. It was a figure out of Germanic mythology wherein the *werwolf* was a patriotic figure who stayed behind in the Fatherland when its people had to flee into exile to escape the invading forces, and who at night came out of the forests and terrorized the invaders, leaving only the spoor of the wolf in the snow.

Joseph Goebbels, Hitler's minister of propaganda, made a call on Germans to join the resistance. "The enemy will be taken in the rear by the fanatical population, which will ceaselessly worry him, tie down strong forces and allow him no rest or exploitation of any possible success."

But the German people were war weary. Their country was in ruins. They faced hard times and a harsh winter with little to no food or shelter and not much sympathy from their conquerors. In the end, Operation Werewolf's propaganda value far outweighed its accomplishments.

By early 1945, the SS realized there were not enough w*erwolves* to form an effective fighting force and decided to use the few they had, in the form of an underground railroad. Their job was to facilitate travel for SS fugitives along ratlines. At that they were successful as they helped thousands of SS officers and high-ranking Nazis to flee Germany as the Third Reich fell apart around them.

By April 1945, the Allied forces were steamrolling across Germany, rapidly taking control of the country as resistance from German forces crumbled.

CHAPTER 32 – PLEASE GIVE ME A BIT OF TIME

FRANKFURT, GERMANY

7 TO 13 MAY 1945

THE END OF all military operations had been set to commence at 11:01 P.M. Central European Time on 8 May 1945. The day that would become known as V-E, Victory in Europe, day.

Karl Bauer's wife, Gertrude, had been killed more than a year previously, on 22 March 1944, during the last days of a six-month Allied bombing campaign of Frankfurt when more than a thousand buildings of the biggest old Gothic town in Central Europe, most of them half-timbered houses, were laid to waste.

Bauer was at the Institute for Research on the Jewish Question in Frankfurt when the announcement of the armistice came on 7 May 1945. He was a troubled man— he had been for some time. Like many others, he had seen the writing on the wall more than a year ago.

An estimated 70 to 85 million people were killed during the war. The German army had been utterly destroyed, with 4.3 million dead and missing military personnel plus 350,000 to 500,000 dead German civilians. The country's infrastructure was devastated. And the Allied commanders had just announced the establishment of an International Military Tribunal under international law and the laws of war for the prosecution of prominent members of the political, military, judicial, and economic leadership of Nazi Germany; those who planned, carried out, or otherwise participated in the Holocaust and other war crimes.

Die Nürnberger Prozesse, the Nuremberg trials, would start in November.

I wish I could've done more to hide what I've done, was a thought that often crossed his mind.

Karl Bauer had little doubt, as the operations manager, the looter in chief of *Einsatzstab Reichsleiter Rosenberg*, ERR, a war crimes trial was in his future. In January he had approached Scharnhorst, one of the many covert organizations that had sprung up to assist senior Nazis escape from Germany and the consequences of the atrocities they had committed during the war.

The name Scharnhorst was derived from the name of the famous General Gerhard von Scharnhorst (12 November 1755 –28 June 1813), the first Chief of the Prussian General Staff, noted for his reforms of the Prussian army and his leadership during the Napoleonic Wars. The Nazis named one of their fearsome battleships after him. Bauer decided not to dwell on the fact that the Allied navy had sunk the Scharnhorst during the Battle of the North Cape on 26 December 1943.

Bauer didn't get an immediate answer—he was told that someone from the organization would be in touch as soon as possible. In the meantime, he was told he had to return to his work at the Institute and continue working, without drawing any attention to himself.

The uncertainty and the waiting were nerve-wracking. However, with no authority or means to get his application fast-tracked, he had to resign himself to waiting and agonizing.

His anxiety bourgeoned on 12 May 1945, when he received the news of the arrest of his erstwhile superior, Alfred Rosenberg. If the Allies were putting Rosenberg on trial, it was only a matter of time before the investigators would come knocking on his door. For a few moments he considered escalating his request to Scharnhorst but remembered he was told not to try to contact them. "Don't call us, we'll call you," the Scharnhorst man had said.

Hours later, he concluded the only thing he could do was to act like an innocent man. Make sure that all the loot under his control remained intact. Ensure none of it was carried away by anyone. He had to show that he cared about the books. Attempting to escape from Germany on his own was not an option. Not without a new identity, money, and passage to a new country— none of which he had. If he were caught, he'd be looking very guilty—something he had to avoid at all cost.

He tried to pacify his anxiety with the thought, *Maybe it'll all stop with Rosenberg.* But he knew that was wishful thinking.

***

FRANKFURT, GERMANY

MONDAY, 14 MAY 1945

IT WAS LATE afternoon on 14 May 1945 when Bauer looked at the small piece of paper folded to about an inch square, handed to him by one of his staff. "Where did this come from?"

The woman shrugged. "A man came in and said I should hand it to you. He didn't give a name."

Bauer unfolded the paper slowly. The message was in pencil, cryptic; *St. Leonhard 11:00 tonight.* There was no name.

At 10:45 P.M., Bauer, on foot, approached the St. Leonhard Catholic Church dating back to 1219. Of the nine churches in the Old Town of Frankfurt, this was the only one that survived the war almost undamaged. The streets were dark, so was the church—electricity was one of the first things knocked out by the Allied bombs early in the war.

On arrival, Bauer went up close to the building looking for the person or persons he was supposed to meet. The

240

previous time he had a meeting at the church was with the representative of Scharnhorst. At the last meeting, the man he met was covered in a monk's robe, Bauer never saw his face, nor was he provided a name. When he reached the back of the church, the spot where he had met the Scharnhorst man before, a voice called out softly, "Doctor Bauer, here, under the tree." It was the voice of a man, but not the same voice as previously.

He approached slowly, and in the dim light of the half-moon and starlight he made out a figure clothed in a monk's robe, head and face obscured by the hood.

"Come closer, we'll have to keep our voices down."

Bauer moved to within two yards of the man.

"I am Father Hermann Schürer, the envoy of Cardinal Siegfried Reinhart."

Bauer hesitated. Cardinal Reinhart was the head of the German episcopate—the leader of the German Catholic Church. He was also the man who in 1939 sent Hitler birthday greetings in the name of all German Catholic bishops. The cardinal was a man whom Bauer admired because of his understanding of the intricate role National Socialism would play in Europe and the threat posed by the Jews to the future of Europe. But those ideals lay in tatters now.

This is not the Scharnhorst agent.

"What does the cardinal want with me?" he whispered nervously. Although he had heard of Hermann Schürer and knew he was Cardinal Reinhart's aide, he had never met the man, never saw a photo of him either. It worried him that he couldn't see the man's face. But he had to trust *someone*.

Schürer, if it was this man's real name, said, "Your request for assistance is still under consideration. But you need to know there are many that need help, and our funds are drying up rapidly."

It was a lie. Bauer knew it was a lie because he knew of the vast sums of money, gold, and looted treasure stashed away in the banks and in the secret warehouses and hiding places of friendly countries. The value of it ran into the billions. He knew this because he had firsthand experience in sequestering and concealing some of it himself. However, it was not being lied to by a man of the cloth, if this man was indeed one, that had him on high alert; it was the involvement of the church, the leader of the German Catholic Church, no less.

Cardinal Reinhart involved in Scharnhorst? Helping Nazis escape from Germany?

He decided not to respond and waited for Father Schürer to continue.

"We are aware that your situation has become more urgent with the arrest of Alfred Rosenberg."

"What are the charges against him?" Bauer interjected.

"The charges have not been finalized as yet. We've heard he will be going on trial with other senior Nazi officials in November. From what we've heard, the charges will be vague. Such as conspiracy to commit crimes against peace; planning, initiating, and waging wars of aggression; war crimes; and crimes against humanity. There's no way he is going to be found not guilty."

Bauer shook his head in disbelief. "With those kinds of charges hardly any German citizen would escape conviction."

"We agree."

"Why is the cardinal now interested in me?"

"During your time at Rosenberg's ERR, a vast number of unique and valuable books, manuscripts, and documents went through your hands, and much of it is still under your control today. Those are items of tremendous value to the Fourth Reich."

"The Fourth Reich?" Bauer knew about the diehards' plans to resurrect Nazism. He thought them madness. But he didn't say so.

Schürer nodded and said, "You're regarded as Rosenberg's successor. You're one of the core group of people we'll need when the people of Europe come to their senses and realize the mistake they've made when they backed the Soviet Union instead of supporting Germany to destroy Communism. Let them experience the hell Communism is going to unleash on them and they'll come running back to us. They'll beg us to establish a new Nazi Reich."

Bauer nodded slowly. He couldn't afford to tell the man what he thought of the idea; it could cost him his place on the ship heading to South America and freedom. It was not as if he had had a change of heart about Semitism, if anything it was more intense than before, but for now the only important thing to him was to get out of Germany as quickly as possible.

"Yes, I worked for the ERR, it's not a secret. I executed orders, I never killed anyone. The books entrusted to me are still under my control and will be handed over to the new authorities if and when required." It was Bauer's turn to lie. First, the books at the Institute were not the only ones under his control. Second, on his orders, 12 Jews, one for each of the tribes of Israel, were sent to their deaths in concentration camps.

"Doctor Bauer, if you're sure you've done nothing wrong, why did you approach Scharnhorst to help you escape?"

Bauer clenched his jaw—he had said too much. But what he knew about the books that were not at the Institute couldn't help him. Or could it? Maybe it was worth exploring. "What is expected of me? That's if I survive and don't land in jail or worse, very soon."

"As I've said, we need to get all the books we can out of the way and hide them. We can't let them get back into the hands of those who used them to undermine us for so long."

"The problem is, I can't touch anything at the Institute. The Allies' investigators visited yesterday. They told me I'm responsible for keeping every book and every document and manuscript and every item in that building in its place until they come to remove it. They confiscated the catalogues. In other words, they know exactly what's there."

"We know all of that. But there are other books, not at the Institute, not catalogued. Are there not?"

Bauer realized they had finally gotten to the reason for the meeting. And in that moment Bauer knew his knowledge of the location of the missing books gave him the leverage he needed to get the ratline out of Germany that he was so desperate for, through Scharnhorst or one of the other secret aid organizations.

"None that I know of," he lied without blinking an eye. "Everything that I ever handled and shipped back to Germany are at the Institute. Minus, of course, the items destroyed by the bombs."

"Doctor Bauer, I know you are under a lot of stress lately, especially so since the arrest of Alfred Rosenberg. It is possible that the events of the past year or so, the loss of your wife, the fall of Germany, and other matters might have affected your memory. But it is critical that you calm yourself and think carefully. We *need* those missing books. You're the only one who can help us get them to safety."

And in exchange for that you might consider helping me escape or not?

"I'll do as you suggested, but I'm sure, despite the trauma of the past year or so, my memory is the one thing that's still functioning properly."

"Doctor Bauer, I'd like to caution you to not be flippant about this. Scharnhorst *can* help you in ways that you wouldn't believe possible."

"Such as?"

"Records can disappear, people can forget that they've ever met you or worked with you. When the investigators come for you, they'll find no evidence to use against you in a trial. You can get away scot-free."

Bauer felt emboldened by what he believed was his newly discovered position of strength to pressure them into finalizing his escape. But he wasn't thinking clearly. "I already told you what I know. I'm of the opinion I've got nothing to fear."

"I see. Should I let the Scharnhorst leadership know you're withdrawing your request for assistance?"

For the second time, Bauer regretted saying too much. He said nothing, only shook his head.

"Doctor Bauer, we know about everything you did and what you're facing if it were to be revealed. Just in case you doubt it, let me give you a very brief summary of a few things you should consider.

"You're the man associated with the concept of *Judenforschung ohne Juden*, Jewish Studies without Jews. When you search your memory later tonight and, in the days to come, remember to spend a few moments thinking about Salonika—I'm talking about the thousands of books and Judaica from the ancient Salonika *kehillah*. Also, don't forget the Jewish books of Vilna, Lithuania. By your own estimates, as reported to your boss Alfred Rosenberg, one hundred and sixty thousand of them, collected from Strashun, from YIVO, from synagogues and private collections, from the Lubavitch yeshiva and the Vilna Gaon's kloyz. Those are matters that would appear on the charge sheet in your trial. But there'll only be a trial if we don't help you.

"Last but not least, Doctor Bauer, Rome. The books removed from the Jewish Ghetto; the Rabbinical College Library, *Biblioteca del Collegio Rabbinico Italiano* and the Jewish Community Library, *Biblioteca della Comunità*

Israelitica. We know that you know where those libraries are."

A cold shiver ran down Bauer's spine. He was grateful for the darkness as he tried his best to remain calm. "You might be right about my memory. Please give me a bit of time to search my memory and review my notes."

"Thank you, Doctor Bauer. I knew you would understand. I'll be in touch."

Walking back to his apartment through the dark streets of Frankfurt, Bauer decided that it was time to start writing things down—the past and the present, including the events of that day, 14 May 1945.

CHAPTER 33 – SOME GOT CHARGED FOR WAR CRIMES

RHEINWIESENLAGER, SIERSHAHN POW CAMP, GERMANY

FRIDAY, AUGUST 17, 1945

KARL BAUER, COVERED in the only clothes he had—the same he had on when he was arrested two weeks before—pulled the dirty, stinking, ragged blanket, issued to him when he entered the prisoner of war camp, tight around his body in an attempt to fend off the predawn cold. He was cold, hungry, thirsty, dirty, and desolate. As far as his eyes could see there were men, former German soldiers, now prisoners of war, thousands of them. All of them cold, hungry, thirsty, dirty, and desolate.

Most of them had suffered much, much longer than he had.

Camp Siershahn was one of nineteen POW camps collectively known as the *Rheinwiesenlager,* Rhine meadow camps, constructed by the Americans along the Rhein River with big haste as the Allied forces rolled into Germany. Between April and September 1945 these camps would host almost two million captured German troops.

Bauer was one of the few who was not a former soldier.

In the two weeks he had been in the camp, he had experienced exposure to the elements and over-crowded conditions. He had suffered with everyone else as water and food were rationed strictly. They received no mail. It didn't bother him, as he expected none. Red Cross inspections of the camps were not allowed.

So, this is what it really means to have the shoe on the other foot. I guess I should count myself fortunate then— unlike the Jews, there's no hard labor for me, and there seem to be no gas chambers in my future. He grinned wryly at his own gallows humor.

Due to lack of contacts and financial means, his plan to escape from Germany never came even near to fruition. Since his arrest, he had come to regret his decision not to give in to the demands of Father Hermann Schürer, the envoy of Cardinal Siegfried Reinhart, that night of 14 May during their secret meeting behind the St. Leonhard Catholic Church. He had never heard from Father Schürer or any other representative of *Scharnhorst* since. And he had been unable to peddle his knowledge to any of the other secret Nazi aid organizations in exchange for his escape from Germany.

When the changing color of the eastern horizon announced the dawn of a new day, Bauer stood, wrapped the blanket around his shoulders, and collected his earthly possessions consisting of a metal spoon, tin plate, and tin cup. His notes, which he had started writing on the night after the meeting with Father Schürer, were concealed in the inner pocket of his ragged jacket. He started shuffling with his fellow prisoners in the direction of the main gate, where the trucks with their daily rations of food and water were expected to arrive by sunrise.

At the time of his arrest, he had loudly proclaimed his innocence. But they didn't charge him with anything. He was told to shut up and shoved into the back of a military truck at gunpoint. All the while he was protesting that he was a Christian, a biblical scholar, and priest. His captors ignored him. They must have thought his claims of being a Christian and a Nazi at the same time were mutually exclusive concepts—an oxymoron.

By the end of September 1945, when the *Rheinwiesenlager* POW camps were closed, the mortality rate in the camps would have reached 56,000. Karl Bauer was not among the dead—his name was called out that morning of Friday, 17 August 1945.

"Where am I going?" he asked the soldier in English, who was prodding him with his rifle in the direction of the truck.

"You're going into the back of that truck, kraut."

"Yes, but where are you taking me from here."

"To a gas chamber. Move it, swine! Oh, here's a tip for you. When you hear the sound of the gas coming through the nozzles, take deep breaths—it will be over quicker."

Bauer got onto the truck without another word. Names had been read out regularly in the past. The people who answered were bundled into the back of military trucks just like he had been. None of the prisoners knew where those people went. Rumors abounded. Some said it was payback time—those who were taken were executed and it would not end until there was one dead German for every person who was killed in the concentration camps. Bauer decided not to believe that.

Some rumors had it that the people whose names were called were all set free. Bauer decided not to believe that either.

He was about to find out some of them were indeed set free—after being questioned. Of those questioned and not set free, some were charged for war crimes and some were going to be witnesses in the trials of those who had been charged with war crimes.

Bauer would soon find out that he was going to be one of the latter—a witness in the upcoming trial of his former boss, Alfred Rosenberg.

After that it was probably going to be his turn to face justice.

CHAPTER 34 — A BLANKET

CAMP STALAG XIII-D, NUREMBERG, GERMANY

OCTOBER 2, 1946

KARL BAUER WAS a defeated man; he had been for a long time. The deterioration of his psychological condition had been a gradual but persistent process which started on the day of his arrest on 3 August 1945. After his arrest, during his first two weeks of internment at Camp Siershahn, he was convinced he would soon die from thirst or hunger or cold or some kind of disease or a combination of it all. But then he was transferred to the Stalag XIII-D Nürnberg Langwasser camp in Nuremberg where he got more food and water and better shelter.

Stalag XIII-D was a Nazi prisoner of war camp built on Hitler's party rally grounds in Nuremberg, northern Bavaria. Throughout the war, the Nazis imprisoned thousands of prisoners of war from Poland, Norway, France, and the Soviet Union at Stalag XIII-D. However, on 16 April 1945, the camp was liberated by the United States Army and turned into a POW camp for 15,000 captured members of the SS.

After a few weeks of better treatment, the fear of starving or freezing to death had subsided but returned with a vengeance a few months later.

It was shortly after breakfast when he became violently ill and so did more than 2,000 of his fellow inmates. All with the same symptoms which had set on within half an hour after breakfast—nausea, vomiting, and abdominal pain followed by severe diarrhea. They didn't have to speculate much; it was obvious they had been poisoned. But it didn't make much sense. If the idea was to kill them, why use poison and not bullets?

The rumor mill had gone into overdrive.

It would only be much later when Bauer would learn what had really happened. It was the work of a Jewish group who called themselves *Nakam*, the Jewish word for revenge. Their leader was Abba Kovner. *Nakam* aimed to kill six million Germans in retaliation for the six million Jews killed during the Holocaust—a nation for a nation. They had plans to poison the main water supplies of Germany, but that never came to fruition when Kovner was arrested by the British on his way back from Palestine with a boatload of poison which he had to dump overboard. Nonetheless, *Nakam* succeeded in infiltrating one of their members, a baker, into Camp Stalag XIII-D, where he managed to slip arsenic into 3,000 loaves of bread. However, in his eagerness to kill as many Germans as possible, he must have diluted the poison too much— more than 2,000 prisoners became ill, but none died.

Over the past thirteen months, Bauer had been interrogated several times, thankfully not violently, to collect evidence from him to use against his former superior, Alfred Rosenberg. Bauer was often tempted to let them know that he was willing to testify in person in exchange for his freedom. But he thought better of it. Trying to make such a deal would have been an admission of guilt, and *his* defense, if they charged him, was going to be, "I did nothing but execute orders and never killed anyone." Besides, the investigators never even hinted at charges to be brought against him. It was better to let sleeping dogs lie.

But uncertainty still nagged Bauer. The trials in progress now were only the first of many, they were told. Those on trial now were only the first tier of highest-ranking Nazi officials which included Hermann Göring, Rudolf Hess, Joachim von Ribbentrop, Wilhelm Keitel, Alfred Rosenberg, and 19 others. Once they were dealt with, the second round of prosecutions would start. The trials of the second tier of the Nazi hierarchy, which was where he fitted in. Deep down, Bauer feared it was just a matter of time before he would find himself in court facing a team of Allied prosecutors.

He was shaken out of his dispirited brown study when he heard his name called out. He got off the bench in the courtyard where he was sitting, approached the guard who called his name out, and identified himself.

The guard took him to one of the interrogation rooms where he was pushed into a chair beside a steel table, his hands were cuffed to the table, and his feet to shackles embedded in the concrete floor.

Bauer didn't know what to make of it when he laid eyes on the man who had entered after the guard had left. He had never seen the man before—no surprise there, he had received many visitors over the past thirteen months whom he didn't know from Adam. But this was the first visit from a Catholic priest; at least that was what Bauer assumed he was, based on his clothes—a long-sleeved black ankle-length cassock with the signature white clerical collar. The priest was a portly man of about five foot eight or so of very light complexion, bald head, round, almost puffy face, with silver wireframe glasses. Bauer guessed him to be around his mid-fifties and based on the man's plump physique concluded that the priest had not gone hungry lately.

The priest sat down in the chair on the opposite side of the table, leaned forward and said in a quiet voice, "I'm Father Hermann Schürer, the envoy of Cardinal Siegfried Reinhart."

Bauer instantly recognized the voice. For more than a year he had been hoping to hear that voice just one more time. "I've been waiting for you for a very long time, Father Schürer. Why have you never contacted me since our last meeting?"

"I'm sorry about that, Doctor Bauer, but we had a lot to deal with. I don't have to tell you, Germany has been utterly destroyed and left in absolute chaos. There are millions of people in desperate need of help. People are dying from lack of food, potable water, medical care, and shelter. The church has been inundated with the pleas of those in desperation. But we haven't forgotten about you."

"I've been ready to talk to you for a very long time, Father, long before I got arrested."

Schürer shrugged and said, "All I can say is I'm very sorry. There was nothing we could do to get to you earlier."

"How very convenient for you. Do you want me to believe you were so busy you couldn't even get a message to me? I don't believe it. Don't even try to explain it. As a man of the cloth myself I'd appreciate it if you don't lie to me. You've left me in the lurch for one reason and one reason only..."

"Now, Doctor Bauer, let's not descend to the level of accusations and blame. It serves no good purpose. I understand how you feel, but let's try and keep our conversation civilized."

"I'll try my best to be civilized, but don't you ever tell me again that you know how I feel. You don't."

"My apologies for offending you. That's not my intention. I'm here to help you."

"If your track record is any indication of what help I can expect from you it's probably better for me to rejoin my fellow prisoners out there in the courtyard."

Schürer shook his head and opened his mouth to reply, but Bauer interrupted him. "Last time I saw you, your parting words were, 'Scharnhorst can help you in ways that you wouldn't believe possible.' You were right, I don't believe it. You can't help me."

Schürer held his hand up to stop him, but Bauer ignored the priest again and continued. "It seems to me you're the one in need of help."

Schürer ignored him and changed the subject. "Have you received the news about the outcome of the trial yesterday?"

Bauer shook his head.

Schürer took a newspaper clipping out of the inner pocket of his cassock and read, "Twelve of the twenty-four were found guilty and sentenced to death by hanging; Göring, Ribbentrop, Keitel, Kaltenbrunner, Rosenberg, Frank, Frick, Streicher, Sauckel, Jodl, Seyss-Inquart, and Bormann in absentia. Hess, Funk, and Raeder were sentenced to life in prison. Doenitz, Schirach, Speer, and Neurath received prison terms ranging from ten to twenty years. Schacht, Von Papen, and Fritzsche were found not guilty." He paused and looked at Bauer over his lowered glasses for a while and said, "Those sentenced to death had all lodged an appeal to the Control Council."

"Waste of time if you ask me," Bauer mumbled.

"You may be right. I'm not holding out much hope that the council will reverse the tribunal's findings."

Bauer didn't reply. He stared at Schürer, waiting for him to get to the real reason for his visit. Bauer was sure he knew the reason, but he wanted the priest to say it.

After a long silence Schürer said, "We've been following the trial very closely and paid special attention to the charges and evidence against Alfred Rosenberg. His entire defense collapsed once the prosecutors presented those meticulous reports you've sent Rosenberg during the war."

Bauer understood the hidden meaning of Schürer's words all too well. He might as well have said, "If your own reports about your work were strong enough evidence to convict Rosenberg, they would surely be enough to convict *you* when you go on trial." The priest, however, said, "The speculation is that the next round of trials will start soon." He didn't have to add, "and we expect you would be one of the accused."

Another long silence followed as the men stared at each other. A battle of wills to see who would lay it on the table first.

"Despite what you might think, I want you to know we *can* help you, Doctor... if you want us to."

"What can you do and in exchange for what?"

"We want the information about those Jewish libraries."

"Of course you do."

"We can get you out of here. You will never stand trial. And we'll make sure no one will bother you ever again."

Bauer was tempted to throw a fit and tell Schürer it was something they could have done long ago. It would have avoided his arrest, maybe even Rosenberg's conviction. Be that as it may, he was the one in prison, and he was the one desperate to get out. "When?"

"It will take a bit of time."

Bauer decided to give the priest a piece of his mind. "Don't give me that. You had all the time in the world, or are you saying you still haven't done anything?"

Schürer grinned. "No, we've done our homework. We know exactly what must be done to get you out of here and keep you out for the rest of your life."

"I'm listening, Father."

"But we need your permission first."

"You have it. Get me out."

Schürer waved his finger. "It's a bit more complicated than that, Doctor Bauer. We need an undertaking that you'll cooperate with us."

"Ah, I see. By cooperation you mean the information about the libraries, right?"

Schürer nodded once, subtly.

"I'll cooperate, but I'll have some conditions of my own."

"Such as?"

"Let's start with exactly what it is you're going to do for me."

"I suggest we start with you telling me whether the two libraries still exist or not."

Bauer looked at Schürer for a few beats and whispered, "They exist."

"You've been interned for more than a year; how can you be sure?"

"Because I know where they are. No one would've been able to touch them. What I want to know is what you can do for me and how you're going to accomplish it."

"Doctor Bauer, over the past two years Scharnhorst was able to build a sprawling network of collaborators in important places. Some of them have access to official records, for instance the records of your work during your tenure at ERR. In your case it includes every file, every catalogue, every report, and every note you produced. Without those there is no case against you."

"I think you're over-optimistic if you think by destroying those records, I'll get away scot-free. What about the people who worked with me? What about the people who reported to me? What about the people who know me? Do you have access to their memories?"

Schürer smiled. "Doctor, you've obviously got no idea about Scharnhorst's reach."

"Obviously not. Even so, I'd like to see it in action, at least some of it, before I'll consider a deal. You'll have to excuse me, but I've got reason to be cynical."

Schürer stood and said, "I'll pass your message on and will get back to you as soon as possible. Is there anything we can do to make life here a bit easier for you in the meantime?"

Bauer was silent for a while before he said, "A blanket."

"I'll see to it," Schürer said.

Bauer was more than a little surprised when he crawled into his bunkbed that evening and found he had two blankets instead of one.

Maybe they can help me.

CAMP STALAG XIII-D, NUREMBERG, GERMANY

OCTOBER 17, 1946

FIFTEEN DAYS LATER, Father Hermann Schürer, Scharnhorst agent and aide to Cardinal Reinhart, was back at Stalag XIII-D to see Doctor Bauer again.

As before, Bauer was in a chair at a steel table, hands cuffed to the table and feet cuffed to shackles embedded in the concrete floor.

Bauer thanked Father Schürer for the blanket and then went quiet, waiting for the priest to explain the reason for his visit.

Schürer started. "Have you heard about Alfred Rosenberg?"

Bauer shook his head.

In a solemn voice, feigning piousness, the priest told him. "Seven days ago, on October 10, the Control Council rejected Rosenberg's appeal. He and nine others were executed yesterday. Bormann is still missing and Hermann Göring committed suicide hours before he was to be executed."

Bauer tried to remain calm and not show his panic, but Schürer's scare tactics were working. The symbolic significance of the date of the executions, October 16, also didn't escape him. It was, to the day, exactly three years after he had overseen the removal of the Jewish Libraries from the Ghetto of Rome.

"Our understanding is that the second round of charges and trials will soon start..."

Bauer interrupted. "Okay, okay, I get it. My neck is on the chopping block next. Are you going to get me out of here and safeguard me against prosecution or not?"

Schürer smiled. "Of course, we can do all of that, but we'll need your cooperation."

Bauer interrupted again. "Stop the vagaries. What exactly do you want?"

The priest nodded slowly and said, "We want the two Jewish Libraries you removed from Rome. In exchange we will get you out of here. No charges will be brought against you. Your records will be removed, and people who worked with you will not remember you."

"I'll walk out of here a free man and I will never face any charges?"

"Yes, and Scharnhorst will also set you up and pay for board and lodging in Cologne, the city of your birth. You will be a member of the West Cologne parish, where you'd be doing volunteer work for the Archdiocese of Cologne."

Bauer took a deep breath and opened his mouth to respond.

Schürer stopped him. "It's part of your cover, setting up a new life, reentering the priesthood."

Bauer started to talk again but the priest stopped him again. "Let me finish. You will receive a monthly stipend of one hundred Reichsmark for a period of three years."

Bauer was staring at the table, his mind working overtime. *Hundred Reichsmark, it's a pittance... Still better than prison or the gallows.* "I'd prefer to leave Germany," he said.

The priest cleared his throat, shook his head and said, "Doctor Bauer, this is a take it or leave it proposition. I am not authorized to offer you anything else."

Bauer went quiet for a very long time. He had no other options and no leverage. In fact, it was even possible that they would get him out of prison, take him to a secluded place, torture the information out of him, and kill him. He looked at Schürer, sighed, and in a low whisper said, "I'll take it."

"Thank you, Doctor. I knew you would cooperate."

"Don't patronize me, Father. You get me out of here, take me to Cologne, and after you've set me up as you have offered, I will give you the details about the libraries."

"That'll be acceptable," Schürer said. "But let me warn you, Scharnhorst will hold your records and not destroy them until they're in possession of the libraries."

"Understood," Bauer said.

CHAPTER 36 – WRITE IT DOWN

COLOGNE, GERMANY

MONDAY, OCTOBER 28, 1946

ON MONDAY 28 OCTOBER 1946, at exactly 11:05 A.M., Karl Bauer walked out of Camp Stalag XIII-D Nuremberg with only the clothes he had on his body and his diary in the inner pocket of his threadbare jacket.

Father Hermann Schürer was there to greet him and accompany him on the train to Cologne, two hundred and forty miles away. The priest was kind enough to bring a small bag of food with him, which Bauer appreciated. They didn't talk much during the five-hour trip. They both knew that this was not the beginning of a beautiful friendship—the only reason they were on that train was because Bauer had been blackmailed. And as soon as Scharnhorst had the libraries, there would be no contact ever again.

Bauer's accommodation in Cologne was, to put it mildly, spartan, like the room of a monk in a monastery where they have taken a vow of poverty.

He didn't complain. *At least it'll be me rather than a prison guard holding the key to the door.*

It was all but impossible to feel welcome after meeting the landlady, who was in her late sixties and rudely abrupt. The priest of the West Cologne parish where Bauer was going to do volunteer work was very friendly, excessively so, he thought.

Scharnhorst's watchman. Appointed to make sure I stay on the straight and narrow.

It was late that night when Father Schürer accompanied Bauer back to his room, gave him the first month's stipend of hundred Reichsmark, and said, "We've fulfilled our obligations in terms of the agreement. Now it's your turn. Tell me about the libraries."

Bauer was quiet for a few seconds before he started. "On October 16, 1943, we loaded the books of the *Biblioteca del Collegio Rabbinico Italiano*, the Italian Rabbinical College Library, and the *Biblioteca della Comunità Israelitica*, the Jewish Community Library, into two train wagons.

"There were between twelve and fifteen thousand books in total. We placed sheets of carton between each layer. Of the two libraries, the estimated seven thousand books of the Jewish Community Library were the most important to the ERR.

"The train was heading for Frankfurt. I was on that train. We made a stop in Zurich, where I had the Schenker Company on standby to unload and transport the books to the Freeport Geneva."

"Geneva?" Schürer sounded incredulous. "On whose orders?"

"Alfred Rosenberg."

"Doctor Bauer, I sincerely hope you're not going to tell me now that only Rosenberg knew the access codes to the storage facility in Freeport Geneva."

Bauer grinned slightly. "I accompanied the libraries to Geneva, Father. I'm the one who organized the storage and the access codes which I handed over to Rosenberg later."

"Do you have the access codes?"

"Yes."

"Where?" Schürer was becoming impatient.

Bauer tapped his index finger against the side of his head.

Schürer took a small notebook and fountain pen out of an inner pocket of his cassock. "Write it down."

Bauer took the notebook and pen and wrote: *Block·D warehouse 4007. Account number: AR102AH809HP715-X*

"How do I know Rosenberg hasn't moved it?"

Bauer grinned. "I would have known if he did. He didn't. But if you don't believe me, there's one sure way to find out."

When the door closed behind Father Schürer, Bauer sat down on his bed and sighed.

Maybe I should write a novel about my experiences. Who knows, it could become a bestseller.

PART IV

THE SWISS CONNECTION

Chapter 37 – Geneva, here we come

Berlin, Germany

Wednesday, August 31, 2016

WHEN REX STOPPED his narration, there was a protracted silence as they stared at each other with a mixture of astonishment and exuberance. And then, as if on cue, they all started talking at once, stopped, and started laughing.

Digger was on his feet, dashing toward Rex, ready for action. "No worries, boy," Rex said when Digger edged up to him. "We're all good here." He scratched Digger's back a few times, he relaxed and returned to his bed.

When the mirth subsided, Catia had her hand up as if in school trying to get the teacher's attention. They all looked at her and waited.

"There is so much going through my head right now," she said. "This is the first time we know that the libraries survived the war. They were together in Geneva. Not destroyed by bombs or carried away to Russia.

"We've made more progress than anyone else has in more than seventy years. It's a momentous discovery."

"Indeed," Rex said. "But I suspect you might not be able to use the information in Bauer's diary in your thesis unless you can show the original. Unless we can legitimately obtain that diary from Heinrich Bödeker, we'll have to find the libraries."

"You don't think if we show Bödeker a handful of greenbacks he will part with the diary?" Josh asked.

"He might," Catia said. "But keep in mind the information in the diary will only be part of my thesis. Right now, the cardinal question is: What happened to the libraries after Bauer handed them to Scharnhorst? If they still exist, where are they? If they don't, what happened to them?"

Rex said, "It's highly unlikely that the libraries are still in the Freeport. Well, at least not in Block D warehouse 4007. Nonetheless, I think we should start there. We need to confirm that Bauer didn't lie to the priest, although I doubt he would've. I got the impression from his novel that he would've met with a nasty accident if he did. So, if we can get confirmation that the libraries were there, we might also be able to get a lead as to what happened to them."

"Okay," Josh said. "But I get the feeling it's not going to be as easy as waltzing up to the reception desk at the Freeport, smiling nicely, and telling them, 'Hey, guys, we'd like to see your records about Block D warehouse 4007 going back to 1943. Oh, and while we're here, could you also check your records and tell us who removed the contents of that warehouse and where to?'"

Rex smiled. "No, I don't think it will go down exactly like that. But don't forget we have discovered new actors in this saga, Hermann Schürer, Cardinal Siegfried Reinhart, and Scharnhorst. They might have left us some answers."

"Yeah, well, putting it like that... maybe you're right," Josh said.

"What bugs me," Marissa said, "is that the Catholic Church was involved in this... well, at least two of its high-ranking clerics, Cardinal Reinhart and Father Schürer."

Catia nodded. "It's sad but true, Marissa. Some church officials *were* involved in underhanded activities with the Nazis, that much we know. There's little doubt that the pope of the time, Pius XII, knew when the libraries were removed from the Ghetto, and he knew when the Jews were rounded up and carted to the gas chambers a few days later. It all happened under the pope's windows and he did nothing about it."

"I can see why the church might want to keep that part of history buried," Marissa said. "I guess we should ask Greg and Rehka to do some research about Schürer and Reinhart."

"Agreed," Catia said.

"It looks like we're heading to Geneva," Rex said. "Wilhelm Jablonsky is the next guy on the list to be interviewed. He also happens to be a lawyer. I hope he'll be able to give us some ideas of how to go about getting information from the Freeport."

Josh nodded, took his phone out, and opened Rehka and Greg's research file with Jablonsky's background information. "According to this, Wilhelm Jablonsky's father was Gerhard Jablonsky, born in 1920 in Frankfurt, died in 2011 at age ninety-one in Geneva. He was married; his wife died in 2014.

"Gerhard was nineteen when the war broke out; he was arrested by the SS in 1943 and sent to Bergen-Belsen; he survived. After the war, he studied law and worked in the German Justice Department for a few years, until he realized that the new German government wanted to bury and forget the Nazis, the Holocaust, and the entire war. They turned a blind eye to war criminals. Gerhard was not happy with that and started his own practice, seeking justice for those who were wronged. That's when he moved to Switzerland and set up a private practice in Geneva.

"They had three children. Their oldest son, Wilhelm, followed in his father's footsteps and became a lawyer. He went into practice with his father. He's now sixty-six, divorced, two adult children."

Catia, who had opened and then closed her mouth several times during that recitation of facts, smiled demurely and added, "I also happen to know that Wilhelm Jablonsky is a *sayan*."

"Good. Looks like we're off to a good start in Geneva, then," Josh said.

"Geneva, here we come," Marissa chimed in. "At least I'll be able to communicate with the people for a change."

French was the *lingua franca* in the Geneva canton, and Marissa was fluent in French.

"Right," Rex said. "First thing tomorrow morning."

CHAPTER 38 – A CAUSE AS DESERVING AS THIS

GENEVA, SWITZERLAND

THURSDAY, SEPTEMBER 1, 2016

ALTHOUGH ABRAHAM HEILBRON gave them a letter of introduction and spoke to Jablonsky, Catia felt it would carry more weight if Yaron Aderet gave Jablonsky a call as well. When she called Aderet and told him about Bauer's diary, he was ecstatic and made the call to Jablonsky immediately. Aderet's confirmation text message reached Catia twenty minutes later.

At 3:00 P.M. that afternoon Wilhelm Jablonsky's secretary, Julia, looked at Rex, Catia, and Digger, when they walked into the office, smiled and said, in perfect English, "Mister and Missus Dalton?"

"Yes," Catia replied.

"Mister Jablonsky has been expecting you. You can go right through."

They introduced themselves to Jablonsky and shook hands, Digger got his obligatory paw-shake.

Jablonsky spoke fluent English.

Digger first made his habitual fragrance surveillance run of the room with all the new smells in it. Rex accompanied him, holding his leash in one hand and his mobile phone in the other, stealthily scanning the room for bugs. There were none. Still, Rex also activated the signal jamming app on his phone before he sat down.

Rex and Catia knew they could trust the man, a vetted *sayan* for the Mossad, and decided to play open cards with him about their research, but nevertheless divulged only as much as he needed to know to advise them.

Catia started by giving him a summary overview of her Ph.D. and their hunt for the libraries but made no mention of Bauer's diary.

Even so, what Catia told him had Jablonsky excited. "Amazing! I knew about the libraries, but always believed they were destroyed. What you're saying is that there's a chance they might still exist. That'll be a joyous day when you find them, Missus Dalton. I'll help you in any way I can. You just tell me what you need."

"Please call me Catia," she said.

"Only if you call me Wilhelm."

"Deal." Catia smiled.

"While we're discarding formalities, you can call me Rex. The dog told me he stands on protocol and wanted to be called Digger and nothing else," Rex deadpanned.

Jablonsky laughed. "Okay, but on the same condition as Catia, you call me Wilhelm."

"Wilhelm it is then," Rex said. "We actually have quite a few questions, but I'm afraid it will take much longer than the hour we've booked with you."

"No problem. Excuse me for one second." Jablonsky picked the phone up and dialed his secretary. "Julia, please reschedule my appointments for the rest of the day." He turned back to Rex and Catia and said, "I'm all ears."

Catia said, "If you don't mind, we'd like to start by getting an understanding of the work you and your father did for Holocaust victims."

"I don't mind at all," Jablonsky said. "Let me give you a bit of background first.

"The Swiss government made many promises after the war to cooperate with any inquiries, and even appointed their own teams of investigators. They promised to freeze German assets and investigate all accounts and activities.

"They did nothing of the sort. They dragged out every inquiry and made it prohibitively expensive for foreigners to reclaim stolen property. They introduced legislation which determined that after five years valid owners had no claim to ownership anymore.

"Another crazy piece of legislation they introduced gives protection to a buyer who acted in good faith. Which means, if a Swiss person takes possession of an object in good faith, and it later turns out to be stolen, it's rightfully that person's property after five years."

"Very convenient," Rex said.

"Unbelievable," Catia said.

"But true. To answer your original question, that's what my father did and I'm still doing—trying to help people who have legitimate claims to work through the Swiss legal labyrinth and infuriating bureaucracy."

"Sounds like a job with exasperation written into the job description," Rex said.

"You have no idea," Jablonsky said. "You must understand how Switzerland operates. They run the country like a business. They would take anyone's money into their banks and lend it out to anyone from whom they could make a profit. Drug money, terrorist money, secret money, dirty money, stolen money, they don't care. They'll take money from the devil. To the Swiss, that's what neutrality means.

"The bankers are the backbone of the Swiss economy.

"They are also the core of the Swiss deep state. They and their cronies have seats in the highest hallways of power in this country. And they don't take kindly to anyone investigating their affairs, especially their sins of the past. Their influence stretches far beyond the borders of Switzerland.

"I'd be remiss if I didn't caution you to watch your backs. What you're trying to unearth is going to ruffle the feathers of some very influential people across Europe."

"Thanks for that, Wilhelm. You're not the first to caution us. We'll certainly heed your advice," Rex said.

Catia told him that they had it on good authority, without telling him about the source, that the libraries were put into storage at the Freeport in October 1943 and that the Nazi secret organization Scharnhorst could have been involved.

Jablonsky raised his eyebrows when he heard the name Scharnhorst but didn't ask about the source of their information.

He lowered his glasses to the tip of his nose and was staring at the two of them in turn for a moment before replying. "Let me tell you a bit about the Freeport. Some of it you might already know, some you might not. Please bear with me.

"It's a warehouse complex with a total storage capacity of fifty-two thousand square meters. It's the oldest freeport in the world, dating back to 1888. It holds a guesstimated one hundred billion US dollars-worth of art collections, and that's not all you'll find in there. As the facility expanded in size and popularity, it adopted the obscure practices of Swiss banking, which made it the preferred storage facility for the international elite who value privacy and prison-like security.

"The facility is not owned by a single person or institution, but the Municipal Council of Geneva is the majority shareholder. To get the information you want by asking for it is a non-starter; they simply won't give it to you. You can go through the courts and try to get an injunction to open their records and that storage room. But it will take years to get to court, and the outcome would be dubious at best."

Rex got the feeling the lawyer knew of a way to get it done. "Is there another way?"

"Yes, there is. It's not legal. But it can be done."

"How?" Catia asked.

"I've got someone on the inside who did me a few favors in the past. Give me a day or so. I'll be in touch."

Rex and Catia thanked him. Rex gave him the number of his burner phone and offered payment for his time, which he declined with a very polite, "It's the least I can do for a cause as deserving as this."

***

A FEW MINUTES AFTER his clients were gone, Jablonsky called his contact at the Freeport, Eva Guggenheim, a Swiss Jew. After the greetings he said, "I'm phoning to find out if you've got any plans for tonight?"

Eva laughed. "Sounds like you're asking me on a date."

"It's because I am."

Hours later Jablonsky and Guggenheim were led to their table in the Il Lago, a Michelin-starred, Italian restaurant on Quai des Bergues, next to Lake Geneva, shortly after 8:00 P.M.

After the first course was served, Jablonsky leaned forward and said, "Eva, I need a favor. Some information about a certain storage facility in the Freeport."

She smiled. "It's true, then. There's no such thing as a free lunch, or in this case a dinner... I'm listening."

"Can you get access to records going back to 1943?"

"Yes, if the account is still operational, it's easy."

"If the account is not operational, can you get the information from the archives?"

"I'll need my boss's permission."

"Will he give it?"

"Not without detailed explanations and very good reasons and a written application from the requestor. Privacy and secrecy laws, I don't have to tell you anything about them, Wilhelm."

"No, you don't. The privacy and secrecy laws might as well have been written into the Swiss constitution. The country can't function without them."

"However," she added, "I may be able to get into the archives unnoticed. What am I looking for?"

"The shipment was handled by the Schenker Company. It came from Rome by train and was offloaded in Zurich on 17 October 1943. From Zurich, the Schenker Company transported it to the Freeport." He took his cellphone out, pushed a few buttons, and read from the screen. "It was placed in Block D, warehouse number D4007; and the anonymous account number is AR102AH809HP715-X. I'll write it down for you."

"It'll take me a day or two. I'll have to be very careful; I could get in a lot of trouble if they catch me."

"Thank you."

They spent the rest of the dinner talking about politics, family, and holidays.

When Jablonsky dropped her off at her apartment a few hours later, he thanked her again and again cautioned her to be careful.

CHAPTER 39 – THEY'RE STILL ALIVE AND WELL TODAY

GENEVA, SWITZERLAND

FRIDAY, SEPTEMBER 2, 2016

WHEN HER COWORKERS were out on their lunch breaks and it was quiet in the office, Eva took the chance of running the queries against the database of current accounts and the archived data. She made notes and called Jablonsky on her mobile phone.

"Got the information you asked for. I'm going on my lunch break in fifteen minutes. I can meet you at the coffee shop on the corner of your office block."

"Great. See you there in half an hour."

At 1:00 P.M. Jablonsky ordered and paid for the two coffees and a plate of toasted sandwiches and joined Eva at the table.

She got to the point immediately. "There was no record of that anonymous account number in the live accounts. And I couldn't find anything about it in the archives either.

"Then I ran searches on warehouse D4007, and what I found is weird, to say the least."

"What?"

"D4007 has been rented only since 12 November 1946. Some of the customers are anonymous, some aren't, and it shows as being still in use now. But according to the database, D4007 had never been used before November 1946—as if it didn't exist before then.

"The weird thing is storage spaces right next to and across from D4007 and throughout the entire D-block had been in use for more than two decades before 1946. Yes, some of them were empty from time to time but not for very long, two months at the most. But, as I've said, the computers are suggesting storage D4007 didn't exist before November 12, 1946."

"Bizarre," Jablonsky murmured.

Eva nodded. "Yes, it is. I checked the format of the account number you gave me, and it corresponds to the number format in use at the time. Obviously, there's something untoward going on here."

"Undoubtedly," Jablonsky said.

Then Eva had to leave to get back to the office in time.

Jablonsky called Rex and told him he had some information.

An hour later, Rex, Catia, and Digger were back in his office.

He told them what Eva told him.

When Jablonsky finished, Rex murmured, "November 12, 1946." *That's fifteen days after Bauer was released from Camp Stalag XIII-D. By then Scharnhorst had already moved the libraries and everything before that had been wiped.* "Wiped."

"Wiped?" Jablonsky looked puzzled.

"The records were wiped," Catia said. "I presume it is possible?"

"Ah, I see what you mean. Well, I guess it is possible. But I'd imagine it couldn't have been easy. It would've required authorization and cooperation at the highest level of the Freeport management and, I'm sure, external interference."

"Which is not entirely impossible, based on what you told us yesterday about the Swiss deep state," Catia said.

"And don't forget Scharnhorst," Rex added.

"But would they have had that kind of influence in Switzerland?" Catia asked.

"Oh, yes, Scharnhorst has wide reach," Jablonsky said. "I know they have a lot of sway in Switzerland."

"You make it sound as if they're still around," Rex said.

"It's because I believe they are. I've experienced it. Remember, it's here where they kept their money, and I believe they still do. In the secret bank accounts."

"Scharnhorst, really?" Catia sounded unconvinced.

Jablonsky grinned. "I don't think Scharnhorst ceased to exist sometime after the war; they've only changed some of their goals and membership over time. Over the years, some of my clients have dropped their name. I'm almost certain they're still in operation today. I've even heard a few names."

"Would you be able to share some of the details with us?" Rex asked. "Of course, without breaking any of the country's privacy and secrecy laws and attorney-client privileges."

"I'd be happy to. I'm sure my clients wouldn't mind as long as I keep their names out of it."

"That might be of great help," Catia said.

"Okay, I'll ask my secretary to find the files. I'll extract the information and you can come and pick it up by mid-day on Monday."

CHAPTER 40 – REASON TO BE CONCERNED

GENEVA, SWITZERLAND

FRIDAY, SEPTEMBER 2, 2016

EVA KNEW SHE had to be careful, and she was, but not careful enough.

What she didn't know was that the upgrade of the Freeport's computer systems a few months prior had included a security patch which logged and tracked all staff activities on the computer systems. Reports were generated and automatically sent to staff's supervisors when unusual activity was detected.

By the time Eva was in the coffee shop, imparting to Jablonsky the information she had retrieved from the system, her manager, Enzo Wanner, was looking at the exception report of her activities on the system earlier that day. From time to time staff had to access archived data, but they were not allowed to do so without completing the proper request and get *his* written permission and an access code that only *he* could provide.

Guggenheim had done none of it, yet she got access. How?

According to the report, she spent more than twenty minutes in the archives running queries about account number AR102AH809HP715-X and made quite a few queries about the D4007 storage block. What finally set off the klaxon in Enzo's head were the dates she used in her queries—1943 to 1946.

Something to do with the war... she's a Jew... something to do with the Nazis... why can't they simply leave the past alone?

Wanner picked up the phone and called Rolf Lauener, the deputy head of the FIS, the Intelligence Service of the Federation, in the Geneva office. FIS was the agency responsible for prevention of terrorism, violent extremism, espionage, proliferation of weapons of mass destruction, and cyberattacks against critical infrastructure. The FIS also helped the cantons to maintain internal security and supported the federal law enforcement authorities. They were not a law enforcement authority themselves; their core tasks were prevention and situation assessment on behalf of the political leaders.

As far as Wanner was concerned Eva Guggenheim could have been involved in espionage or terrorism or cyberattacks or extremism or a combination thereof.

***

WHEN EVA GOT back to her desk after lunch, a coworker at the desk next to hers told her she had to report to Herr Wanner immediately.

Among the highest-ranking officials of the FIS there was a tacit understanding that they had an unofficial duty to help with the protection of the business known as Switzerland. They had to make sure that Switzerland's past remained in the past; that embarrassing situations were best avoided, but if they had to be dealt with, then it had to be done swiftly and efficiently.

The Swiss preferred the world to think of their country in terms of green valleys, majestic Alps, ski holidays, Swiss chocolates, Swiss watches and, of course, the ever-popular children's book and TV series *Heidi* and the classic movie *Sound of Music*. And not to forget that Switzerland was also the country that had been protecting the Vatican and the pope with their Swiss guards for the past five hundred years. And that if one happened to have lots of money, Switzerland was the place where one could bank in secret.

The Swiss didn't want to be dragged through the mud of history. Discussing matters such as collaboration with the Nazis, SS gold in their bank vaults, stolen *objets d'art,* and such were taboo.

When Eva walked into Wanner's office she knew from the look on his face that she was in trouble, and she instantly knew why. She had no idea how her manager was able to find out about her prohibited access into the archives, but her heart started racing when she heard the title of the other man in the office, second in command of the FIS office in Geneva, Rolf Lauener.

"Sit down," Wanner said after the terse introduction. "I've asked Herr Lauener to be present at this meeting because of the gravity of the situation."

Eva said nothing. She simply stared at Wanner and Lauener, trying to hide her nervousness.

"Do you know why you're here?" Wanner asked.

Eva nodded.

"Then instead of Herr Lauener and me wasting time extracting it from you, why don't you tell us? Don't lie."

Eva knew she had been caught red-handed. "I used an unexpired passcode, which you generated in the past, to gain unauthorized access to the archives and collect information."

"What were you looking for?" Lauener asked.

"I wanted to find out if a certain account number and storage space had been in use in 1943."

"Why?"

"I honestly don't know. I did it for a friend, and he didn't tell me why he wanted the information."

"Who's your friend?"

Eva dropped her head and didn't make a reply.

"You're in serious trouble, *fräulein*," Lauener said severely. "You've broken several of Switzerland's security laws. My advice is to not withhold any information. Your friend's name."

"Wilhelm Jablonsky, he's a lawyer," she whispered.

"Why did he want this information?"

"I told you, I don't know."

"How much did he pay you?"

"Nothing. It was a favor."

"In exchange for?"

"Nothing."

"You've done this kind of favor for him before, right?"

Eva nodded.

Lauener looked at Wanner and said, "A quick word outside?"

Wanner nodded and followed Lauener out of the office.

In the hallway outside, Lauener said, "I don't think she knows much more than she's told us. You make sure she does not leave the premises or use the phone to warn Jablonsky, while I have a word with him."

Back in his office, Wanner said to Eva, "Hand over your mobile phone." Eva started shaking her head, but Wanner said, "You want me to call the police in?"

She shook her head again and very reluctantly took the phone out of her handbag and handed it over.

Lauener stood and said to Wanner, "I leave it to you to handle the internal disciplinary side of her misbehavior."

To Eva he said, "I'm going to have a word with Herr Jablonsky. You wait here until I get back."

When Lauener had left, Wanner explained to Eva that she would face formal disciplinary action in accordance with the Swiss labor laws. In the meantime, she would be allowed to continue working at the Freeport but not to do any work that required the use of a computer or phone. "In other words, you'll be doing filing, mail delivery, and cleaning. The alternative is that you go home and wait for the disciplinary hearing—without pay."

Eva decided to stay. She needed the money, but knew she had to get another job, urgently. *Maybe Wilhelm will be able to help me get another job?*

***

LAUENER TURNED UP at Jablonsky's office unannounced and all but forced his way past the secretary into the lawyer's office.

By the time Lauener had introduced himself and stated his title, before he could even begin to state the purpose of his visit, Jablonsky knew it was about Eva's data mining activities earlier in the day. In the past it hadn't caused any problems; something must have changed.

Jablonsky was worried, not so much about himself as for Eva. He knew the old tried and tested principle—when you find yourself in a hole, stop digging. In this case it meant, say as little as possible, preferably nothing.

Lauener tried the oldest trick in the book. "Fräulein Guggenheim told me everything."

Jablonsky grinned. "Which was?"

Lauener struggled to hide his frustration. "That you instructed her to extract data from the archives at the Freeport that is protected under the privacy and security legislation."

"Instructed?"

Lauener sighed in frustration. "Doesn't matter what word she used. Did you ask her to do it or not?"

"Yes."

Lauener looked as if he were about to explode. "Yes, you did ask her or no you didn't ask her?"

"Yes."

"Did you compensate her for it?"

"No."

"Why would she do it then?"

"I asked."

"In exchange for nothing?"

"We're friends."

"She's done this type of favor for you in the past?"

"Can't remember off the top of my head."

"She said she did."

"Her memory must be better than mine."

"Why do you want this information?"

"I have an interest in history."

"Herr Jablonsky, you might think you're very clever. Let me assure you, you're not. You and Fräulein Guggenheim are involved in a serious crime. It'd be in your best interest if you stop the conceit and answer my questions."

"Herr Lauener, I don't know what you've been doing the past few minutes since you've rudely forced your way into my office, but I've answered every one of your questions."

"You've been evading them, Herr Jablonsky. Now, who's your client?"

"You've obviously not been listening. I'm not acting on behalf of a client. And even if I did, I'm surprised that a man in your position doesn't understand the principle of attorney-client privileges."

Lauener shrugged and stood. "Have it your way, then. You'll hear from me again."

"I'm sure I will. Make an appointment next time."

When Lauener slammed the door shut behind him, Jablonsky took a long sip of his cold coffee. His mind was in overdrive. Lauener's exasperation was worrisome, not because of the possible legal consequences but because of the fact that the FIS was involved. Although Eva's queries had produced no direct evidence that the libraries were stored in unit D4007, they did reveal that the records had been tampered with. And that was more than likely the reason for the FIS's interest.

He suspected that Lauener, knowingly or unknowingly, was working for one of the secret cabals operating in the country.

These were groups of super rich and influential but nefarious individuals and organizations operating in the shadows for various purposes: money laundering, terrorist activities, dealing in unprovenanced art and relics. And Hitler worshippers. Yes, seventy odd years after the war, there were still some delusional Nazi hardliners hoping somehow to raise Adolf Hitler from the dead and establish the Fourth Reich.

Like his father, he had been on the radar of some of them for many years. He had received many threats to his life. He had narrowly escaped once when an assassination attempt on him failed. He had been harassed and assaulted.

He had reason to be concerned; he and Eva had violated Switzerland's sacrosanct secrecy laws.

CHAPTER 41 - CONTINUE THE INVESTIGATION

GENEVA, SWITZERLAND

FRIDAY, SEPTEMBER 2, 2016

WHEN ROLF LAUENER left Jablonsky's office, he angrily lit a cigarette. He needed the nicotine to calm him down. The two interviews had left him in a state of indignation. But notwithstanding his foul mood, after a couple of quick puffs he managed to take stock of what he had learned. Two Jews were interested in the history of storage unit D4007 in the Freeport, going back to 1943. Clearly Jablonsky was acting on behalf of an undisclosed client. But the required information was not in the computer system. Lauener was convinced it had something to do with the Nazis because of the date, 1943. And, of course, it struck him as odd that D4007 seemed to have not existed prior to 12 November 1946 although every other storage space in block D had been in use for twenty plus years by then.

Somebody was trying to hide something, to keep a secret from everyone.

Working for FIS and its predecessor for more than forty years, he knew full well there was a lot of unrecovered Nazi loot in Switzerland. But, as a true, self-aggrandizing bureaucrat, he took it upon himself—*because if I didn't do it, who would?* —to save his beloved Switzerland from the potential embarrassment that could be caused by the unveiling of the past.

His immediate problem was that unless he could find a way to coerce Jablonsky into revealing the name of his client, he wouldn't make much progress with the investigation. Guggenheim obviously had no idea who Jablonsky's client was or the reason the information was needed. On the other hand, Jablonsky obviously knew everything but was not going to impart that information— not willingly.

It was time to brief his manager about the case and get his guidance.

On the way to his office he phoned Enzo Wanner and asked him to put the phone on speaker so that Guggenheim could hear. When she was on the line, he told her that the investigation was ongoing and that she must keep herself available for further questioning when required.

When he arrived at his office, he immediately went to see his manager, Ruedi Meister, the head of the Geneva FIS office.

He gave Meister all the details and asked for advice about how to proceed.

Meister immediately said, "Continue the investigation, of course. We *have* to know who Jablonsky's client is."

When Lauener had left his office, Meister spared a moment in thought.

A pesky people, the Jews. They just don't know when to leave well-enough alone.

Then he picked up the phone and called a very rich and influential man, Joost Trauffer, and arranged to meet him at his house that night. It was part of his unofficial duties to his country to keep a look out, in the canton of Geneva, for anyone trying to dig up the past and report it to the Institute for the Preservation of Swiss Heritage. The precise details of the institute's goals, activities, and membership, he didn't know, except that Herr Trauffer was the chairman.

***

GENEVA, SWITZERLAND

FRIDAY, SEPTEMBER 2, 2016

JOOST TRAUFFER WAS 57. Ever since he completed his university studies at the age of 22, he had been working at Zehnhaus Consultants, an investment business established by his father and a friend in 1946. Over the years he had learned all the intricacies of the investment trade and got promoted up the ladder until he was appointed as assistant to the CEO, his father, in 2002 at the age of 43. In 2004, after his father had passed away, he became the sole proprietor and CEO of Zehnhaus Consultants.

Trauffer, like his father, was not a man for the limelight. He never gave interviews. He was the only person on the planet who knew what was really happening at Zehnhaus Consultants. In the public eye, even to those who made an effort to try and find out, Zehnhaus Consultants was a small, private investment company that didn't even use the word *bank* in its name. Zehnhaus's name was not on the official Swiss private bank list, a list of more than 300 authorized banks and securities dealers published by the Swiss Financial Market Supervisory Authority, FINMA.

But Trauffer was a rich man, one of the richest individuals in Switzerland. The Swiss banking laws allowed him to hide his riches from prying eyes. The total value of the cash, gold, precious stones, art works, and artifacts owned by Zehnhaus Consultants was somewhere north of $5 billion.

Despite his vast fortune, Trauffer lived in what the rich would certainly call a modest house, in Cologny, an affluent residential neighborhood on the shores of Lake Geneva. It was the most expensive living area in Switzerland, where prices reached 35,000 CHF (€32,000) per square meter compared to the Swiss average of 6,333 CHF (€5,800).

The property had set him back €17 million—petty cash for him. And certainly, it was a modest home for a man with so much money. It was a ten-room luxury villa of 565 square meters with half a hectare of beautiful gardens and magnificent panoramic views of the lake and the city.

That was more than enough room for him and his wife of twenty-five years, who had adopted a globetrotting lifestyle. The Trauffers seldom entertained. Trauffer didn't believe in friendship, being disinclined to spend time on nursing relationships unless he could profit from them. There had been a time when Trauffer had thought he and his wife were friends, but he was mistaken. She loved to do charity work in exotic countries. He loved only money and the acquisition thereof.

For his own entertainment he maintained a small circle of carefully selected lady friends, no more than four of them at any given time, replaced and rotated often, who entertained him, one and sometimes two at a time, a few times a week, when his wife was not at home, which was nine to ten months of the year.

He and his wife had discussed divorce but decided it would be too messy and too expensive. Instead they settled on an open marriage. They would use the utmost discretion in their extramarital affairs and Joost would fund his wife's overseas adventures of mercy. She knew her husband was a very rich man, but she had no idea of the full extent of his fortune. As long as he kept her in the luxury she had become used to, and didn't bring scandal on her, she didn't care what he did.

It was 8:30 P.M. He was in his study in an opulent reclining chair overlooking the crescent-shaped forty-five-mile *Lac Léman*, Lake Geneva, shared between France and Switzerland in the shadows of the Alps.

He took a slow sip of the special cognac from the snifter in his hand. The world over, cognac was associated with ostentatious elegance and wealth, justifiably so with this 1858 Cognac Croizet Cuvée Léonie which he bought in its original hand-blown bottle in 2011 for the bargain price of €112,700.

He had examined the bottle and its sealing with utmost care before making the purchase. One tiny security breach, such as a dried-out cork, would transform a magnificent achievement into an evaporating, stale, tasteless slurry. This one was perfect.

His mind went back to the last two years of his father's life. It was December 2002 when the old man was diagnosed with cancer. The doctors gave him eighteen months if he got treatment, less without. His father decided not to take any treatment and passed away in January 2004, fourteen months after the diagnosis.

Trauffer was ten when he was told who his father was. Although it was a bit of a surprise, he was happy and proud to have him as a father, a hardworking, respected, and very successful businessman. A role model for him.

But it was only in the last fourteen months of his father's life, after he had been diagnosed with terminal cancer, that Trauffer had learned the full story about his father.

PART V

A BUSINESS VENTURE

CHAPTER 42 - GERMANY WAS DOOMED

CHRISTOF GRESSMANN AND his lifelong friend, Arno Diederich, had been dreaming about setting up their own business since they were young. The Second World War delayed their plans by a few years. As boys of 12, in 1931, the two of them joined Scharnhorst, at the time a youth organization that later amalgamated with the Hitler Youth.

In May 1933 the two of them were enthusiastic participants in the public burnings of "un-German" books. Works of prominent Jewish, liberal, and leftist writers ended up in the bonfires that they were told would set Germany free from outlandish cultures.

By the time they finished university they were in love with the ideology of National Socialism, firmly believing it was the answer to the world's problems. Definitely beneficial to Germany, and, in due time, beneficial to Europe and the rest of the world.

On 1 September 1939, at the outbreak of the war, Gressmann and Diederich were 21, freshly minted from Berlin's Humboldt University, with Bachelor of Commerce degrees. They both joined the SS and in mid-1942, Gressmann was posted to Auschwitz where he was put to work as a bookkeeper responsible for keeping track of the possessions taken from the prisoners upon their arrival.

Diederich was assigned to the SS Main Economic and Administrative Office in Berlin, responsible for managing the finances, supply systems, and business projects for the SS. They were the receivers of the confiscated property of the prisoners in the concentration camps.

Although prior to his arrival Gressmann had never heard of Auschwitz, it didn't take long to find out what was really going on there. It was not a prisoner of war camp. It was an extermination camp. The possessions taken off the interned were never going to be returned to them. They were systematically worked to death on starvation rations, massacred in gas chambers, and their bodies cremated after removal of the gold fillings from their teeth.

His work as administrator and accountant didn't require him to interact with the condemned. He deliberately kept himself removed from the butchering, turned a blind eye, and tried his best to desensitize himself.

But that was not always possible, such as the day when he was told to be present when a new trainload of prisoners arrived. All of them Jews. Almost one third of them were dead on arrival. When those who survived the horrific journey stood in rows outside the train on the platform, he became aware of the incessant crying of a baby among their ranks. His eyes found the mother and baby just in time to see an SS soldier ripping the infant from its mother's arms, grabbing it by the feet, and smashing its head against one of the train cars. The crying stopped.

The traumatized mother fell to her knees, howling in terrible grief. A bullet to the back of her head stopped the shrieking.

Gressmann had known that the purification of Germany from its enemies was never going to be a bloodless endeavor. He had nothing against the annihilation of the enemy; that was, as far as he was concerned, the purpose of war. But he wanted it done in a humane, structured, and disciplined manner. Smashing babies' heads against train cars and shooting prisoners in the back of the head in full sight of everyone was not disciplined—it was barbarity, behavior unbecoming to even the lowest members of the Aryan race.

It troubled Gressmann to no end that the SS officers in charge had tacitly approved the cold-bloodedness by failing to lift a finger to stop it. If nothing else, the incident shocked him out of his self-imposed ignorance and left him wholly disillusioned. In the days that followed, Gressmann couldn't help but quietly question the Nazi leadership's "Final Solution of the Jewish Question," in particular their methods, which were sheer savagery. He finally reached the point where he became convinced that Germany was going to lose the war—because you reap what you sow. The citizens of Germany were going to pay the price at the end of the war, and the war was not going to end until Germany was utterly destroyed. And then the

Allies would come for everyone who worked at these death camps.

During his leave, at the end of 1942, he went to Berlin where he met with his friend Arno Diederich. It was the first time they had seen each other since their postings. He told Diederich what was going on at Auschwitz. And he was not surprised when Diederich told him there were many of these extermination camps throughout Nazi-occupied Europe. The numbers of the dead were mindboggling—in the millions, some estimates were as high as ten million and counting, according to Diederich.

They didn't know whether to believe the numbers or not, but that prisoners were being killed *en masse* was certain. The two of them agreed that it was not the extermination that horrified them, but rather how it was done. Diederich told him about gruesome medical experiments on prisoners in addition to starving and working them to death. And if that was not enough to leave them nauseated, there was the story about one of the officers in one of the camps who had prisoners tattooed and then killed to use their skins for book covers.

Gressmann and Diederich agreed that Germany was doomed and so was anyone who had anything to do with the death camps, irrespective of what roles they played.

That's what steered them to devise a plan of escape and survival.

The first step was to get Gressmann transferred from Auschwitz to the SS Main Economic and Administrative Office in Berlin so that the two of them could work together on the execution of their plan. Diederich, in good standing with his commanding officer, managed to get his friend transferred to Berlin within two months.

CHAPTER 43 - ZEHNHAUS CONSULTANTS

WHEN FIELD MARSHALL Paulus surrendered to the Russians in January 1943, Gressmann and Diederich knew they had been right. The writing was on the wall.

A year later, by Christmas of 1943, German forces were in retreat on all fronts. However, by now Gressmann and Diederich's scheme was in full swing. In their positions as custodians and accountants of the property looted from the prisoners at the extermination camps, they also had to see to the deposit and safekeeping thereof in secret SS accounts in Switzerland. That was the ideal opportunity for them to siphon some of it off into their own secret Swiss accounts.

By January 1945, when the walls of German resistance started to crack and the enemies breached the German borders, Gressmann and Diederich decided it was time to execute the final stage of their plan. They put in a request for transfer to a fighting unit. "To help defend the Fatherland against the invading hordes, Germany needs every able-bodied man and woman who can shoot. Put wounded or crippled people in our places; let us go and fight," was how they motivated their request.

"Two real patriots! Germany could do with more of your kind!" Their commanding officer praised them and signed the transfer papers.

Pulling a few more strings, the two managed to get transferred to the same unit on the Western front "to fight the advancing British and American forces." They handed their SS uniforms in at the quartermaster store and got kitted out as regular infantry soldiers. On their way to their new unit, they made sure to lose their transfer papers, rank insignia, and ID papers. They reported as privates to their new commander, who had neither the time nor the inclination to care about their paperwork or their training. His orders to them were to "get a rifle in your hands, point it at anyone not in German uniform, and start shooting."

It was April 1945.

Two days after their arrival, while out on a night patrol, their platoon was surrounded by an American company. In the ensuing skirmish, half of their platoon were either dead or wounded by the time Gressmann was able to convince the platoon leader, a young lieutenant, that it would be wise to surrender.

So far, their plan was working out exactly as they had intended.

Within twenty-four hours they found themselves in the Koblenz prisoner of war camp, one of the *Rheinwiesenlager* camps constructed by the Americans along the Rhein river. Life in the camps for the next ten months was hell and often a grim reminder of what the prisoners in the death camps had gone through. There were many days when they believed they were not going to survive. But they did and were set free in February 1946. Their release papers stated that they were privates Tim Taussig and Erhart Treich.

By the time of their release, the Allies were vigorously hunting war criminals, especially those involved in the Holocaust. That included anyone who worked at or had anything to do with the death camps in any manner.

The two friends, knowing they had to get out of the way before anyone recognized them, approached Scharnhorst. Although it had the same name as the youth organization they once belonged to, it was now a secret organization helping erstwhile Nazis escape from Germany and the Allied prosecutors.

All they wanted from Scharnhorst were new ID documents and Swiss passports. With their new names, Petri Zehnder, the former Christoff Gressmann, and Daniel Neuhaus, the former Arno Diederich, made their way over the border to Switzerland in mid-1946.

By the end of that year, Zehnder and Neuhaus fulfilled their childhood dream when they started their own business, *Zehnhaus Berater*, Zehnhaus Consultants.

In Switzerland there were two kinds of banks. There were big banks with nice offices in multi-story glass-façade buildings with bright signs, among them the most powerful and influential financial institutions in the world. The second kind of bank, of which Zehnhaus Consultants was one, were the type that stayed out of the limelight, had offices in side streets, and were prohibited by Swiss law from soliciting deposits. Even so, they were allowed to call themselves banks if they wanted to. They were private banks. And many of them wanted to remain private.

Zehnhaus Consultants had an abundance of startup capital—many millions in Swiss francs, SS gold, and looted *objets d'art*. After arriving in Switzerland, they had quickly moved their stolen treasures to new secret accounts and then reached out to Scharnhorst to send them clients. Zehnhaus's deal with Scharnhorst was that they would be happy to sponsor the escape of vetted Nazis who were in hiding and on the run. Many of them had money that they wanted in offshore accounts. Zehnhaus would be happy to give them the best possible investment advice and administer and secure their investments—for a fee. Some of the refugees were penniless but had valuable information about secret accounts and the location of stashes of paintings and other works of art held by elite Nazis. Those were the kinds of refugees that Zehnhaus welcomed with open arms. They had no shortage of clients.

The two of them married Swiss citizens within a few years. Neuhaus and his wife had no children and didn't want any. Zehnder and his wife had one child, but he died within a week after birth and they were unable to have another.

Zehnder then got himself a mistress, one of the secretaries working at Zehnhaus, and with her he had a son. His name was Joost and he carried his mother's surname, Trauffer. Zehnder, having learned his lesson about marriage, didn't marry the secretary, although he loved her and his son and made sure that they lived in luxury.

Not unexpectedly, the moment Frau Zehnder discovered her two-timing husband's betrayal, she divorced him. She got enough in the settlement to live in equal luxury and never bother him again.

Daniel Neuhaus and his wife died in a tragic car accident in 1999. Under the terms of the partnership agreement, Petri Zehnder inherited everything, which included Neuhaus's stake in Zehnhaus, his house in Geneva, and his holiday cabin in the small ski town of La Clusaz, France.

Petri Zehnder passed away in 2004 at age 86.

CHAPTER 44 - INNATELY SUPERIOR TO OTHERS

GENEVA, SWITZERLAND

FRIDAY, SEPTEMBER 2, 2016

WHEN JOOST TRAUFFER, at the age of ten, was introduced to his father, the latter had immediately taken up his paternal responsibilities and assured that his son understood his lineage and was proud of it.

Joost Trauffer didn't partake in politics; he had better things to do than spend time on endless discourses and promises no one intended to keep. Begging people to vote for him was below him. He never talked politics with anyone, neither his clients nor his associates. But that didn't preclude him from having political views. Under his father's influence he had become a purity of his Germanic origin, part of the Nordic Aryan race—the *Herrenvolk*, the Master Race, innately superior to others. He didn't care for other races, illegal immigrants, Jews, Muslims, or anyone other than his own kind.

Though he didn't mind accepting money from any of them.

Trauffer had been surprised but not shocked to learn that his dad and his business partner, Daniel Neuhaus, were former SS officers and that they had been living under false names since 1946. That they had played a role in the death camps didn't bother him, neither did he spare any thought for the fact that the Zehnhaus fortune was built on possessions ripped from the hands and bodies of the condemned.

Under the tutelage of his father, he had come to believe that those killed in the camps, particularly the Jews, were not innocent. They had been pilfering the wealth from the people of Europe who were kind enough to let them live among them for centuries. No, the Jews had it coming for a very long time. The so-called Holocaust was payback time, the comeuppance for the Jews. Besides, what punishment better befitted the greatest crime in human history? —the killing of Christ.

And what was more, the Holocaust served a useful purpose. It was the single reason the Jews got their own country—Israel. The rest of the world, even the non-Germanic types, was fed-up with the Jews.

But Trauffer never spared a moment to assess his own hypocrisy. He was an atheist. If he ever worshipped a god, its name would have been Mammon, not Jesus.

Finally, what the world had to understand was that Switzerland was the one country in the world that managed to produce good from evil. The money from the international drug trade, from terrorism, from dictators, from the Nazis and any other ill-gotten sources, was deposited in the country's banks and lent out to businesses across the globe. Businesses that produced goods and services and employed millions of people. Therefore, Switzerland had to protect the unsavory aspects of the past. Everyone in their right mind knew there were things of the past that were better left alone, because the end justified the means.

The convoluted nature of his reasoning passed his notice.

His father and his business partner, Daniel Neuhaus, took over Scharnhorst in 1957 when Cardinal Siegfried Reinhart passed away. By then the organization had served its purpose of aiding and abetting Nazi war criminals. It was time to reinvent Scharnhorst. To that end they had reestablished the secret headquarters, this time in Geneva, and formulated its new goal—the protection and expansion of the wealth of its members. Of course, that required them, among others, to conceal the past, such as the whereabouts of Nazi loot.

The five members on the board of Scharnhorst, with Joost Trauffer as the chairman, were in control of vast fortunes, all of it built on the ill-gotten gains of the Shoah. They held sway over powerful people in the highest hallways of power in the country, including the Federal Police, Canton Police, Department of Defense, the FIS, Justice Department, Border Guards, politicians, and many others.

PART VI

ONE FLEW OVER THE HORNET'S NEST

GENEVA, SWITZERLAND

FRIDAY, SEPTEMBER 2, 2016

TWO MINUTES BEFORE 9:00 P.M. Trauffer saw the lights of Ruedi Meister's car coming up the driveway to the house. He was alone at home; his wife was away on some do-good mission in an African country of which he couldn't be bothered to remember the name. He took another sip of the cognac, got up from his chair, and walked to the front door.

He shook hands with Meister, invited him in, and steered him to the study where he offered him a cognac from a fancy-looking bottle, but not the bottle of 1858 Cognac Croizet Cuvée Léonie, which he had put back in the liquor cabinet before he went to meet Meister at the front door.

Settled in their chairs with drinks in hand, Trauffer started. "What brought you to my house, Herr Meister?"

"People snooping around in the past, Herr Trauffer. Earlier today an office worker at the Freeport, a Jewish girl, Eva Guggenheim, tried to extract information from the archives about a storage space in use during 1943."

Trauffer felt a little icy chill running down his spine. *The Jewish libraries.* He kept his composure. "What made you think that it would be of interest to me?"

"The date, sir. 1943. It could be something to do with World War Two."

"I see. What did she find?"

"Nothing, sir. The report shows that unit D4007, the one she seemed to be interested in, didn't exist prior to November 12, 1946."

"What's the problem?"

"She told my deputy she did it on behalf of Wilhelm Jablonsky, a Jewish lawyer specializing in the recovery of Nazi loot."

"Interesting."

Trauffer had never met Jablonsky but knew much about him. Over the years the irksome Jewish lawyer and his equally annoying father had been a thorn in Scharnhorst's flesh. On a few occasions the Jablonskys came very close to unearthing some utterly damaging information. The kind of information that would have not only caused colossal embarrassment to Switzerland but would also have landed some Scharnhorst members and a few very influential officials in prison. Fortunately, thus far, Trauffer had been able to outsmart them.

Trauffer maintained an impassive demeanor. "What did Jablonsky have to say?"

"According to my deputy he was very uncooperative. He said he has an interest in history and was acting for himself. Obviously protecting his client."

"Naturally," Trauffer said. "But it seems to me they were on a wild goose chase."

"Indeed, sir. The only thing that bothers me a bit is the fact that the computer records show that unit D4007 didn't exist before November 1946. However, all other units in the D-block existed, and were in use, for many years before that date."

Damn those idiots who wiped the records instead of altering them. If Meister can figure it out, so can Jablonsky and his client.

"Way back then information was kept in handwritten records. When things were computerized the information had to be entered by hand. I'm sure there are many more discrepancies such as this one, caused by human error."

Meister got the message. Trauffer was not interested in this matter. He had done his duty. A few minutes later, he finished his drink. Trauffer accompanied him to his car and thanked him for his diligence.

Shortly after 9:20 P.M., a few minutes after Meister had left, Trauffer punched the number of a secret message service into his mobile phone. He keyed in responses to the various voice prompts until he was asked to key in his message and typed: MEET AT 10.

He sighed, poured himself another serving of the world's most expensive cognac, took a sip, and leaned back in his recliner.

Jablonsky must have been acting on behalf of a client.

Who is the client?

What information does his client have about those libraries?

How did the client know to look for them at the Freeport, unit D4007 specifically?

This is too close for comfort.

Five minutes later he got a text message with a thumbs-up emoticon from the message service on his mobile phone.

***

TRAUFFER HAD A few possessions that he couldn't bring himself to sell. They were worth obscene amounts of money, but sentiment was an almost equal part of the issue.

One of those assets was a painting by Vincent Van Gogh; *The Painter on His Way to Work*. Property of Kulturhistorisches Museum in Magdeburg, Germany, formerly the Kaiser-Friedrich Museum, removed on 12 April 1945. Financial value: inestimable. Consequences of being found in possession: financial ruin, disgrace, and prison.

Another was the contents of a secret vault the size of a ten-foot shipping container below his office in the city. It was stuffed to the brim with an assortment of ancient Etruscan terracotta pots, decorated vases, busts, and bas-reliefs removed by the Nazis from the ancient Etruscan city of Tarquinia and other archaeological sites in the Italian areas known as Umbria and Lazio. Financial value: between fifty and a hundred million euros. Consequences of being found in possession: financial ruin, disgrace, and prison.

In March 2014, the Italians got a sniff in the nose about some Etruscan artifacts stored at the Geneva Freeport. With the help of Swiss prosecutors, they got access to the Freeport storage facilities, and by the time they put their crowbars down they had uncovered a trove of looted Etruscan antiquities. Those were linked to Robin Symes, a disgraced British art dealer who was sent to prison.

Trauffer's third and by far most precious possession was two Jewish libraries removed by the Nazis from the Jewish Ghetto in Rome in 1943. The libraries known as the *Biblioteca della Comunità Israelitica* and the *Collegio Rabbinico Italiano*. In total, more than 15,000 books, ancient, unique, and irreplaceable. Financial value: inestimable. Consequences of being found in possession: financial ruin, disgrace, and prison.

Trauffer only learned about the existence of the libraries in the last few days of his father's life. Why the old man had waited so long to tell him, Trauffer could not explain. But by the time his father told him, the morphine was dripping into his body to alleviate the pain and his mind was not functioning properly anymore. His speech was slurred, and most of the time he was incoherent.

Nonetheless, over a period of days, Trauffer had managed to piece it together.

When Scharnhorst was revived as a secret organization helping Nazis escape, their leader was Cardinal Siegfried Reinhart, and his right-hand man was Father Hermann Schürer.

Scharnhorst learned about the libraries through an SS officer who worked for ERR. With the information they got from the SS officer, they were able to track down Karl Bauer and make him a deal. In exchange for the libraries, they had sanitized his personal and war records, put him up in a job in Cologne, and assured that he was never prosecuted for war crimes.

In those days, the libraries were of immense value to those who earnestly believed in the imminent resurrection of the Fourth Reich, such as Scharnhorst. But by 1957, when the founder, Cardinal Siegfried Reinhart, passed away, the Fourth Reich was no more than a fanciful dream. It was clear that the Fourth Reich was not going to happen, not in their lifetimes, probably never.

That's when the leaders of Scharnhorst agreed that their organization had served its purpose. They had helped hundreds of war criminals escape, and it was time to disband the organization and destroy any evidence of their existence. Some of them wanted the Jewish libraries to be included in the destruction.

However, at the time, Petri Zehnder and Daniel Neuhaus were members of the board of Scharnhorst. They agreed with the idea that Cardinal Reinhart's Scharnhorst had reached the end of its usefulness in terms of helping Nazis escape from Germany, but argued that there was a need for a new Scharnhorst with a new mission and that the libraries should be kept for posterity. They convinced the board to let them take possession of the libraries.

Ever since learning about the libraries, as much as Trauffer cherished them, he was also troubled about the possibility of discovery and the catastrophic outcome it would have for him, the Zehnhaus empire, and the members of the modern-day Scharnhorst. They had no idea about the existence of the libraries and would be caught up in the storm that was sure to ensue.

According to his father, the libraries were placed in storage unit D4007 by Karl Bauer in the Geneva Freeport in October 1943. They remained there until November 1946 when Scharnhorst took possession and moved them to Frankfurt, where they were kept under the protection of Cardinal Reinhart. In 1957 Zehnhaus took possession of the libraries and moved them to their new location where they had remained to this day. He cherished those libraries for no other reason than his intense dislike of the Jews. It gave him a psychological superiority over the Jews to be in possession of something so precious to them.

Trauffer poured more cognac into the snifter, a somewhat unrestrained shot this time, and took a rather large gulp of it. For close on seventy years no one caused any trouble. No one came even close to the secret. People were searching for the libraries, but over the years their enthusiasm had withered as scholars concluded that the books were destroyed during the war. But now, out of the blue, people with unnervingly accurate information turned up, and if they were not stopped could turn the whole applecart over.

Who was it and where did they get that information?

As the 158-year-old cognac muddled his brain and his logic, Trauffer spent a few moments to curse the idiots who had wiped instead of altering the records of the storage unit. It was a massive error of judgment, a potential disaster, seventy years in the making. It was too late to fix it retrospectively. The cat was out of the bag, and out there were at least two Jews, Wilhelm Jablonsky and Eva Guggenheim, who knew about the discrepancy and, of course, Jablonsky's client as well. At least three too many. There could be more. An intolerable situation.

By now, close to €30,000 worth of cognac had gone down his throat. Instead of calming him down, it rather helped to stoke his growing trepidation.

"This could cause a shit storm," he mumbled. "An embarrassment to Switzerland with Joost Trauffer the epicenter of it all.

"Zehnhaus's books will be opened, Scharnhorst will be exposed. I'll be prosecuted and find my ass in prison... for a very long time. My Scharnhorst colleagues would join me in prison, that's if they don't cover their own asses and sell me out or kill me before. There's only so much influence we have in high places. The moment the shit hits the fan we'll be disowned and abandoned by those who have lived in our pockets for so long."

His body was ravaged by waves of cold shivers as his already deeply troubling thoughts turned to the Jews— the rightful owners of those libraries. He had no doubt, the state of Israel would get involved and would have a field day pointing fingers at Switzerland about its collaboration with Nazi Germany. Not to mention what awaited him when the Mossad, the most efficient and fearsome intelligence agency on the planet, got wind of this.

CHAPTER 46 - THE TROUBLESHOOTER

GENEVA, SWITZERLAND

FRIDAY, SEPTEMBER 2, 2016

BY THE TIME Trauffer joined the secured teleconference at 10:00 P.M., in his befuddled mind there was only one solution for his problem. Those who were nosing around in his affairs had to be interrogated to find out what they knew and then eliminated.

The secured communications system was hosted on the Darknet. The voices of the two participants on the call were scrambled and encoded from end-to-end and decoded by a special app installed on the phones on each side. The voices were computerized in an attempt to outsmart voice identification systems. The signals traveled through a mesh of proxy servers across the globe to hide the locations of the callers. All that technical stuff caused the conversation to be delayed by a few seconds, requiring them to talk like they would on a two-way radio. A bit of an annoyance, but worth enduring for the security it offered.

Trauffer liked to think of the man he was talking to as a problem solver. A man who could get information that was difficult or impossible to get through normal channels. A man who could make people change their minds or make them disappear. And sometimes this man literally had to shoot the trouble.

Trauffer called him the Troubleshooter. The Troubleshooter's security protocols dictated that no names would be asked for or given. The Troubleshooter, as far as Trauffer knew, also didn't know what *his* name was. They'd never met in person, also part of the tight security measures.

But Trauffer was mistaken. The Troubleshooter knew exactly who he was. Part of his security protocol, unbeknownst to his clients, was to vet them thoroughly before contracting with them. Another fact his clients didn't know was that he kept extensive electronic surveillance tabs on his clients' emails, internet usage, phones, and cars.

Trauffer didn't know that the Troubleshooter's real name was Horst Klenst, 50 years old, a highly-skilled former special forces operator of the German KSK, Kommando Spezialkräfte, an elite special forces military unit composed of special operations soldiers selected from the ranks of Germany's Bundeswehr and organized under the Rapid Forces Division. Klenst specialized in covert surveillance, information gathering, assassinations, abductions, interrogations, and finding people who wished not to be found.

All Trauffer knew was that the Troubleshooter had never failed to deliver a successful outcome for him or his predecessors at Zehnhaus Consultants or any of Scharnhorst's members, and that was all Trauffer cared about.

Trauffer knew the Troubleshooter was not a man for small talk. He liked it and was in no mood for it either. He got right to the point.

"You have two targets. I want information from them. First target, Wilhelm Jablonsky, a lawyer practicing in Geneva. Second target, Eva Guggenheim, an office worker at the Freeport. I don't know their addresses."

"I'll find them," Klenst said.

"I want to know who is Jablonsky's client that instructed him to extract information from the data archives at the Freeport and why the information was needed.

"Oh, and while you're at it, find out how the client knew to look for the information at the Freeport. Make sure you gather every scrap of information, name, address, description, photos, etcetera."

"And when I'm done?"

"Terminate them. Make it public. I want to send Jablonsky's intrusive client an unambiguous message."

The conversation was over in less than three minutes.

Trauffer didn't give Klenst any background information such as the history of the libraries. He was going to find out about it during his interrogation of the two Jews.

331

***

GENEVA, SWITZERLAND

A LITTLE OVER seven hours later, at 5:15 A.M. Trauffer got a text message to join a secured teleconference.

Klenst started without introduction. "The woman didn't know much of anything. She did what the lawyer asked her to do without questioning. She hasn't met the clients, had no idea who they were, and didn't know why the information was required."

"Clients, more than one?"

"Yes, Rex and Catia Dalton. Recently married. No photos but I got descriptions."

"Continue."

"They're not Swiss. The conversations were in English. Rex Dalton had an American accent. His wife, Catia, is Italian, a Jew from Rome. She's apparently doing research for a Ph.D. at Sapienza about some lost Jewish Libraries.

"According to Jablonsky his clients wanted the information from the Freeport because they believe those libraries had been stored there between 1943 and 1946 and could perchance still be there. He had no idea where his clients got that information from and never asked.

332

"Jablonsky had no current address or whereabouts or any other information about his clients. That's all I got out of them."

"No loose ends?"

"Taken care of."

"Good."

"Anything else I can do for you?"

"Yes, find the Daltons and take them into your custody. Let me know when you have them. I have a few questions for them."

"Consider it done."

The call ended. If Klenst had any idea who Rex and Catia Dalton were, he might not have made a promise like that. But most likely, he was under the impression that he was going to deal with two students. How much of a threat could they be for a man with his skills?

Neither Klenst nor Trauffer had any way of knowing that Jablonsky had left out a vital piece of information about Rex and Catia: their companion, a big black dog who went by the name of Digger.

When the call ended, Klenst started planning how he was going to track down the Daltons. There were several options. He could try and find out from Sapienza if they had students registered under the names Rex and/or Catia Dalton. Catia could be registered under her maiden name. Nonetheless, he could make enquiries about the Ph.D. topics of students—how many of them would be working on lost Jewish Libraries?

He would put his Russian hacker team to work to find out from border control databases when and where the Daltons had entered or exited the country. There could be pictures of them from the security camera footage. They also had to check out the computer systems of hotels and guesthouses in Geneva and surroundings to find out where the Daltons were staying.

About an hour later he started giving orders.

CHAPTER 47 – I CAN ALREADY SEE THE HEADLINES

GENEVA, SWITZERLAND

SATURDAY, SEPTEMBER 3, 2016

DETECTIVE MARK WINKLER of the homicide division of the Swiss police in Geneva was dispatched by his supervisor at 8:00 A.M. to the scene of a double homicide discovered by locals in Parc La Grange in the Quai Gustave Ador neighborhood. It was Geneva's largest park. Situated along the lake, it contained the largest rose garden in the city, and a horticultural center.

On this Saturday morning Detective Winkler didn't notice any of the serene beauty of the park. His attention was focused on the gruesome scene in front of him. The naked and entangled bodies of a man and woman in a seated position on one of the park benches. In his 30 years on the force, he had seen some grisly scenes. This one ranked right up there with the most macabre. It was as if the killer wanted to express his or her hate in the manner the victims were mutilated. With all the blood and wounds covering the bodies it was difficult to estimate their age, but the male was definitely much older than the female. The causes of death for both victims were clear, a bullet between the eyes—it would have been a coup de grace for both of them.

The fact that they were both naked and the woman in a straddled sexual pose on top of the man could possibly have been a message from a shocked and outraged spouse or partner or lover—a killing of passion. But Winkler's experience dictated that it was not good practice to take anything at face value until all the facts were known.

About twenty minutes after his arrival on the scene, Winkler was somewhat surprised at the arrival of Rolf Lauener, the second in command of the FIS office in Geneva. The FIS was only interested in criminal cases where there was a potential espionage or terrorism connection.

"Morning, Herr Lauener. What brings you to such a messy scene so early on a Saturday morning?"

Lauener returned the greeting and grinned. "My boss thought there was no better way for his deputy to start such a lovely Saturday morning."

"I take it," Winkler pointed to the bodies, "that the FIS has information that makes you suspect there might be more here than meets the eye?"

Lauener shook his head. "We're reliant on your expertise. We have an interest, at least an initial one, in all serious criminal cases."

Of course, how stupid of me.

"You wouldn't want to venture a guess about the identities of the victims, would you?" Winkler said.

"No idea," Lauener said over his shoulder, as he turned and approached the bodies.

Winkler could see Lauener was lying but decided it would serve no purpose to confront him about it.

The two of them circled the bodies in silence for a few more minutes. Lauener took a few photos on his cellphone, waved goodbye, and left.

"He knows who they are," Winkler mumbled to himself. "But he's a spook. Obfuscation is what makes them tick."

The forensic team turned up and started their work while Winkler stood around and tried to figure out how it all happened. He had already worked out that the park was not the scene of the crime; the victims were tortured and killed at a different location and their bodies dumped in the park after.

Lauener had phoned his manager, Ruedi Meister, and arranged to meet him at the office.

As soon as they were both seated in Meister's office, Lauener started. "The deceased are Eva Guggenheim and Wilhelm Jablonsky. The two people I interviewed yesterday. They were viciously tortured."

He took his cellphone out and showed Meister the photos.

Meister must have had an inkling of who was behind the killings but would never discuss it with his underling. "Damn, as if a double murder is not enough, it had to be Jews. I can already see the headlines: Anti-Semitism raising its ugly head in Switzerland."

"On the way here, I couldn't help but wonder if there could be a connection to their snooping around in the Freeport," Lauener said.

"And your conclusion?"

"It's possible. But that means..."

Meister interrupted. "It means you're speculating. The photos you showed me tell the story. It's obvious. Jablonsky, the old goat, was shagging this girl half his age. They got caught by a spouse, partner, lover, whatever, and got killed for it."

"Yes, but..." Lauener started.

Meister interrupted again, a bit irritated this time. "Lauener, we're not a law enforcement agency. We have no authority. We work *with* the police...," he paused for effect before he continued, "and we *don't* get in their way. Let them do their work and give us their findings."

"Yes, sir."

"Well, that's it, then. We wait for the police to complete their investigation and apprehend the killer. We will then know if we have any interest in the case. I doubt we will.

From what you told me yesterday, there's no reason to believe that the unfortunate souls were a threat to national security."

Lauener nodded and stood without expressing his thought that Jablonsky's client could very well be a threat to national security. There was no point. It was clear that Meister had no appetite for the matter. It suited Lauener, he could go home and enjoy the rest of the weekend with his family.

Meister was wondering if he should update Joost Trauffer. He decided not to, it was all over the news, Trauffer would know soon enough, if not already. Besides, he had a niggling suspicion that Trauffer already knew.

CHAPTER 48 - THEY NEVER FORGET WHAT THEY'VE SMELLED

GENEVA, SWITZERLAND

SATURDAY, SEPTEMBER 3, 2016

SWITZERLAND HAD ONE of the lowest homicide rates in the world; 2.9 per 100,000 (244 homicides) per year. Every murder still got a lot of press. A double murder was a media blockbuster.

The Daltons and their friends, Josh and Marissa, had planned to spend the day sailing on Lake Geneva. They had a late breakfast at their hotel that morning and were back in their rooms getting ready for their outing. It was 10:00 A.M. Rex already had Digger on the leash and was waiting for Catia to finish when a Breaking News alert flashed on the TV screen.

Within minutes they knew there was not going to be any sailing on Lake Geneva. In shocked silence they took in the news of the horrific deaths of Wilhelm Jablonsky, a well-known Jewish lawyer of Geneva, and Eva Guggenheim, an office worker at the Geneva Freeport. The broadcast was in French, the main language of the Geneva area. However, the English subtitles and the translations provided by Rex and Marissa, both fluent in French, were enough for Josh and Catia to get the full story.

Although Jablonsky never gave them the name of his contact at the Freeport, they now knew her name was Eva Guggenheim.

Rex became aware of Digger's soft whining, turned his head, and saw him with his feet on Catia's lap, trying to comfort her. She had tears in her eyes. Rex put his arm around her shoulders and pulled her close to him. The host announced a short commercial break after which an expert would join them in the studio to give his opinion.

"They're dead because of us," Catia whispered.

Rex nodded slowly. "Tortured and killed to get our names and whereabouts."

Catia wiped the tears from her eyes and said, "Rex, we're going to find the animals who did this and..."

"Put them down," Rex interjected.

"And it can't be soon enough," Marissa added, her voice loaded with emotion.

"Their death warrants have been signed," Josh said.

The commercials were over, and they turned their attention back to the TV.

The expert was a retired homicide detective with more than 40 years' experience. His opinion was that the public all too often was given to conspiracies and mysteries. The result of watching too many movies. In his experience, ninety plus percent of murders were committed on the spur of the moment in a fit of rage. The evidence he had seen so far told him this homicide fell into that category. There was no reason, as far as he could see, to complicate the matter. It was a crime of passion. The top suspect on the police's list should be whoever would have been insulted by the betrayal, such as a spouse, partner, lover etcetera.

"Hogwash," Josh said, holding a middle finger up to the TV screen.

"Exactly," Rex said.

In the weeks to come, the Geneva homicide detectives were going to find themselves wholly frustrated, left clueless, as they would learn that the 66-year old Jablonsky and his wife had divorced more than a year ago. There was no love lost between them. None of them had another love interest in their lives. If anything, Mrs. Jablonsky might've been a bit relieved that her share of the divorce settlement, the payment of which her ex-husband had been delaying to her utter annoyance, would now probably be paid much quicker. The detectives would also learn that the 32-year old Eva Guggenheim was a lesbian, had not been in any relationship at the time of her death, and had not been in the past eighteen months.

Rex turned the sound down.

Josh said, "Obviously we've poked a stick into the hornets' nest."

"Yep," Rex said. "Our foray into the Freeport's historical records drove them to murder…"

"But you didn't find anything," Marissa said.

"Yes, we didn't find what we were looking for, but don't forget we learned that the records could've been tampered with. I'd say now we can be sure it's the case," Catia said.

"This could be a big jump, but I'm of the opinion this also proves that the libraries are still in existence," Rex said.

"Good point," Josh said.

"And we have to assume," Marissa said, "the killers got the information they wanted. Your names and whatever details about yourself you had given Jablonsky."

"He knew our real names and that we're married, that we're from Rome, about Catia's Ph.D., and he met Digger. There was nothing else he could've given them apart from descriptions of us. We haven't met Eva Guggenheim. She would only have known what Jablonsky told her," Rex said.

"We have to assume they're out there right now looking for you," Josh said. "Fortunately, we've been operating with fake IDs."

"Yes, but don't forget we only did so since we visited Abraham. They'd be able to get our photos from that visit, and with facial recognition software they'll track us down quickly. We never used disguises on any of our trips," Rex said.

"Maybe you should consider quietly slipping out of the country," Josh said. "We need to figure out who they are before you come back and take care of them. You could use a boat to travel across Lake Geneva to France without having to go through a border control post."

Rex was quiet for a while, thinking about Josh's idea before he said, "I agree, we should leave. And although they're probably only looking for Catia and me, you should also get out. But I'd suggest we leave the same way we came in. Through customs. If they manage to track down the records of our entry, we want to let them find the records of our exit. That way they won't know that we know they're looking for us."

"What about our escorts, Bulldog and his friends, in Zurich? I'm sure they took photos of us. I can't help but wonder if they are connected to these killers," Marissa said.

"They might be," Catia said. "But they'd only have photos of you and Josh. They probably have no idea that Rex and I are involved. Even though we know they're amateurs and probably part of some crazy new-Nazi group bent on intimidating and harassing Jews, doesn't mean we should ignore them."

"Our immediate problem is a lack of information. Leads," Josh said.

Digger must have sensed the change in the emotional state of his pack. He was sitting on the floor between Rex and Catia, staring at them in turn in anticipation. Rex was deep in thought as he gently scratched Digger's back and ears.

Catia noticed the look on Rex's face as he was staring at Digger and said, "You've got that I've-got-an-idea-look, Rex. What's up?"

Rex shook his head slightly and said, "I'm not sure. It might be a long shot. But…"

"Maybe worth a try," Josh completed for him.

"Yep."

Catia smiled. "You're keeping us in suspense, Rex."

"Okay, you have all heard of my late friend, Trevor Madigan, Digger's owner and handler."

Josh nodded and in a solemn voice said, "The former Aussie SAS operator, the guy who served with you in Afghanistan and was killed in that ambush that only you and Digger survived?"

"Yes, that's the one," Rex said and paused for a few beats as the horror of that night of the ambush flashed through his mind. "He once told me how he and Digger were called out to a crime scene on a military base.

345

Apparently one of the soldiers was stabbed in the neck with a broken bottle. The soldier survived, but it happened in some dark corner and he had no idea who his assailant was.

"As a last-ditch attempt to find the culprit, Trevor and Digger were called out two days after the incident when the MPs couldn't make any progress with the case.

"He told me that when he arrived there, he told the investigating officer that he wanted to be taken to the spot where the crime took place, but that he didn't want any other information. He explained to me that it was important to let Digger 'tell' him what happened. Kind of a fresh perspective, untainted by human speculation and deductions.

"He said when they got to the scene of the stabbing, he told Digger to 'have a look around' and 'report his findings.' Well, maybe not exactly like that, but you know what I mean. What he told me happened then I'll never forget. Digger sniffed around a bit, stopped at a certain spot, sat down and looked at Trevor clearly distressed about something. It turned out that was the exact spot where the soldier was stabbed, where his blood was spilled on the ground, except there was no blood visible to the human eye anymore. The spot had been cleaned.

"Trevor said he told Digger to find the culprit. Digger put his nose to the ground, made a few circles around the spot, and then headed in the direction of the nearest fence. On the way, Digger stopped at a culvert in the road. That was where he 'showed' Trevor a broken beer bottle in the grass.

"From there, Digger took Trevor to the spot where the attacker went over the fence and off to the main road from where he had apparently hitched a ride."

"Wow!" Catia exclaimed.

"Hang on, there's more. Digger then took Trevor back to the spot where the stabbing took place. Trevor told me it was as if Digger was saying to him, 'Okay, I've shown you what happened after the stabbing, now let me show you what happened before.' Digger then tracked the assailant's scent from the scene of the stabbing, backtracking him to one of the singles' quarters, and sat down in front of the door, telling Trevor that the attacker came out of that room and went along the route that he had just showed him to the place where he had stabbed a fellow soldier."

Marissa was staring at Rex incredulously.

Catia was staring at Digger, who was smiling as if he had been following the entire discussion about him.

"It sounds like a fairytale," Marissa said. "I accept Digger is a genius, but there must have been scents of many other people; how would Digger have known which one belonged to the culprit? Not to mention two days after the incident."

Rex shrugged. "I've got no idea. All I know is Trevor told me that these dogs can smell emotions: fear, hate, deceit, lies, sadness, joy, all of that and more. I've experienced some of it over the years. Digger has pointed out nefarious people to me on more than one occasion."

Josh grinned. "I know it sounds incredible, Marissa, but I've seen Digger in action, he's brilliant. I'm prepared to believe that story."

"Well, according to Trevor, the MPs confronted the guy in that room, took him on the route Digger had shown them, and he confessed even before forensics matched his fingerprints with those on the broken beer bottle."

They were all staring at Digger in amazement, and he, of course, enjoyed all the attention, as if happy to confirm that Rex gave a true and accurate account of what happened.

"Let me guess," Josh said. "You want to take Sherlock Digger to the park and let him have a bit of a look and a sniff?"

"Right. As soon as the police finish their work in that park."

"Okay, but what will you achieve?" Marissa was still skeptical. "The killer is long gone. He must have gotten there in a car and left in a car. Surely Digger won't be able to track the people once they got into a car and drove off, would he?"

"No, he won't, but he will get the scent of that person, and when he gets that scent again anytime in the future, he'll let us know."

"C'mon, Rex. How long could he possibly remember the scent?"

"For the rest of his life is what Trevor told me."

"Are you serious?"

"I am. Trevor explained to me that humans have five million olfactory receptors, dogs have two hundred and twenty million. We remember what we see, dogs remember what they see and smell, and they never forget what they've smelled. We can be deceived by what we see, dogs won't be deceived by what they smell. They've got no problem telling identical twins apart and are never fooled by disguises."

"In other words, at least one member of our team would be able to identify the scumbags if they happen to come close to us," Josh said.

"Exactly. Remind me, when we have time, to tell you the story of how Digger proved the Croatian police wrong when they accused an innocent man of murder on the Island of Olib a few years ago."

"Well, then we have to do it," Josh said.

"Okay. Let's bring John Brandt up to date," Rex said and took his satphone out.

Half an hour later they had their plans in place. Josh and Marissa would check out of the hotel and fly back to Berlin where they would change their looks and passports and fly over to Dubrovnik, Croatia, where the TOMATS was at anchor.

Rex and Catia would also check out and find a place where they could wait for the police to finish their work at the crime scene in the park. After Digger had been taken for a visit to the park, they would take the same route to Dubrovnik as Josh and Marissa.

CHAPTER 49 – FIND THEM

GENEVA, SWITZERLAND

SUNDAY, SEPTEMBER 4, 2016

IT WAS 10:00 A.M. on Sunday when an old couple with a big black dog entered Parc La Grange. The man was slightly bent over, walking with the aid of a cane. The woman had her right arm hooked into the left arm of her companion and the leash of their big black dog in her left hand.

There were quite a few people in the park, but it was not overcrowded. It didn't look as if any of them were aware of the gruesome crime discovered there in the early hours of the day before. The police had cleared out an hour earlier.

The old couple strolled slowly along the pathway toward the bench where the bodies were found. There was no blood anywhere – the police must have cleaned it all up. The old man bent down to the dog and said, "Digger, tell us what happened here. Search."

He unclipped the leash.

Digger wagged his tail, looked at the old man, and licked him in the face once.

"Thanks, Digger. Love you too. Search."

Digger turned around and started sniffing the ground and the bench. He circled the bench twice before he sat down in front of the bench at the spot where the bodies were found. He looked at the couple and whined softly. His ears were laid back and his tail was down on the ground. The hair on his back and neck made an uneven black ruff.

Rex bent down and rubbed Digger's back. "I know, Digger. It's terrible. I'm so sorry to put you through it." He clipped the leash back on and said, "Find them."

Digger whined once more, turned, and headed back the way they came, towards the gate, with his nose close to the ground. He took them out of the park into the parking lot and ended up in an empty space designated for the handicapped where he sat down and let out a soft yelp.

"If I'm not mistaken, this would be where the killers parked their car," Rex said.

"Rex, it's unbelievable. How could Digger know what was on that bench? Can he smell death?"

"It certainly looks like it."

"And how did he know which scent to pick out from all those in this park? It's as if he can smell evil."

"I don't know, Catia. I asked Trevor some of those same questions, but he didn't have the answers either. He always told me that I must realize that dogs were created to serve and protect humans. They would never lead us into danger—not consciously."

"If I understand what just happened here correctly," Catia said, "Digger is telling us, 'there's danger here, and I know what the perpetrator smells like'?"

"Yep. That's what I make of it," Rex said.

"Okay, let me get on the phone and see when is the soonest we can get a flight to Berlin," Catia said.

***

UNDISCLOSED LOCATION

SUNDAY, SEPTEMBER 4, 2016
HORST KLENST FELT like a general on the battlefield, moving his troops around with succinct commands over secured communication lines. Klenst's troops had never met him, didn't know what he looked like, and only ever communicated with him through the anonymous and impersonal secured messaging service on the Darknet. They addressed him as Nordwand, the German word for the north face of the Eiger mountain, the biggest north face in the Alps.

Klenst though, unbeknown to his troops, knew everything about them. He had photos of them, knew their real names, where they lived, everything about their families, their telephone numbers, and every little detail about them.

His Russian hacker team provided the first report by 2:00 P.M. Sunday, a little more than 24 hours after receiving their orders.

"We can confirm that their real names probably are Rex and Catia Dalton, as you've told us," said Oleg, the nom de guerre for the team lead of the hackers.

"They've been in Switzerland three times over the last four weeks. The first visit was to Geneva on 9 August, when they arrived on an Alitalia flight from Rome and left again for Rome the same day. That was the first and only time they traveled on their Rex and Catia Dalton passports.

"Using facial recognition, we discovered they made a second visit to Switzerland under the names Ronald and Cate Winthrop, arriving in Zurich from Cologne on a Swiss Air flight on 26 August and left for Berlin two days later.

"On their last visit, they used the names Roland and Catherine Bream, arriving in Geneva on a Swiss Air flight from Berlin on Thursday last week, 1 September. They left on an Alitalia flight for Berlin two hours ago."

Damn! Too late to get them followed from the Berlin airport. Klenst let out a string of German swear words under his breath, almost inaudible.

"Sorry, what was that?" the Russian asked.

"Nothing. Continue."

"We got good quality video footage of all their visits on their way in and out as they went through customs. I'll upload the footage as soon as we finish the call."

"Where did they stay while on those visits?"

"We're working on that now. I'll get back to you within the next twenty-four hours."

For now, Klenst was happy to get the video footage of his targets and didn't think to ask Oleg to collect more security camera footage in the baggage collection areas or car rental companies. Had he done that, he would have discovered that the Daltons had a big black dog with them on all three occasions they had been to Switzerland.

When the call ended, Klenst sat back in his chair and considered the information he got from the Russian. The Daltons had been busy the last few weeks. Rome to Geneva and back to Rome. Rome to Cologne to Zurich. Zurich to Berlin. Berlin to Geneva to Berlin. Switzerland was the common denominator on all their trips.

Why are those libraries so important to them and Joost Trauffer?

He woke his laptop computer from sleep mode, opened the browser, and in the Google search box he typed, "Jewish libraries of Rome."

PART VII

INTO THE HORNET'S NEST

CHAPTER 50 - WHAT'S THAT BOY UP TO?

DUBROVNIK, CROATIA

MONDAY, SEPTEMBER 5, 2016

ABOARD THE TOMATS, John, Christelle, Declan, and Simona were listening without interrupting as Rex and the team gave them a detailed account of the events of the past three weeks since Rex and Catia had visited them in Venice.

Rex concluded the narrative with his summation. "The killing of Jablonsky and Guggenheim, as far as I am concerned, is proof positive that those libraries are still in existence."

"I tend to agree," Brandt said. "And if that's correct, when you find them, you're going to have a major international scandal on your hands. Switzerland, Germany, the Catholic Church, and who knows who else might come out of the woodworks."

"Whoever holds those libraries seems to be well-aware of the dire consequences that will follow if caught in possession. That's why they'd kill to prevent the discovery," Spencer said.

"I'm worried they might destroy them... wipe out all evidence of their existence," Catia said.

"What's to prevent them from selling them or giving them away?" Simona asked.

"I don't know about selling or giving away," Christelle said. "Anyone who knows even just a little about the history of those libraries knows that owning them means running the risk of the vexation of the world's Jewry."

"Those books are worth billions," Catia said. "Some people *might* be willing to take the risk of dealing with the wrath of the Jews if they could make that kind of money. Besides, Jablonsky explained to us that under Swiss law if a Swiss citizen takes possession of an object in good faith, even if it later turns out that object was stolen, it's rightfully theirs after five years."

"I'm aware of that stipulation in the Swiss law," Christelle said. "It's been a royal pain in the backside for us for many years. But in this case, because they're so aggressive about protecting them, it's clear there's little chance that they'd be able to show they got the libraries in good faith."

"Good point," Catia said.

"If we could find them," Rex said. "I think, with the help of the governments of Italy, America, and Israel, and maybe a few other European countries, enough political pressure can be brought to bear on the Swiss or any government in whose jurisdiction they are, to cooperate..." He paused for a beat. "And who knows, maybe even the pope could be persuaded that this would be a good opportunity for the church to make amends for their scandalous lack of action during the war when those libraries were removed from right under the windows of Pope Pius XII."

"Brilliant strategy, Rex. That could very well be the way to handle it once you find the libraries," Christelle said.

"That's if they are to be found on European soil," Rex said.

Brandt frowned. "Do you have reason to believe they might not be?"

"No, I don't, but it gives me the cold shivers whenever the thought crosses my mind that the libraries already are or might come into the hands of some fanatical Muslim group. Getting their hands on the heritage of the Jews, such as those libraries, would be like an erotic dream come true for Muslim extremists of any ilk."

"Oh, my God!" Christelle shrieked.

"Wait," Brandt said. "Let's not borrow trouble. Let's work with what we have. Thus far, we know we stepped on someone's toes when that Guggenheim girl conducted the queries in the Freeport's archives. I'd say for now, the Freeport holds the lead we're looking for."

"There *is* another possible lead," Rex said.

"Yeah?"

"Jablonsky told us that he was convinced that a modern-day version of Scharnhorst exists. He told us some of his clients had mentioned the names of people who could be involved in it. He was going to ask his secretary to go through the old files and extract the names for us. We were supposed to go and pick them up at his office today."

"I'm sure Jablonsky's office will be under surveillance now. Maybe even broken into and ransacked to find out more about you and Catia. We'll have to work out a plan to get that information without them knowing," Brandt said.

"I'll talk to Yaron," Catia said. "He might be able to get us a *sayan* in Geneva who could get the information from Jablonsky's office."

"Good. In the meantime, let's talk about the Freeport," Brandt said.

"The challenge is to get in there," Josh said. "My understanding is it won't be as easy as rocking up there with crowbars and opening storage units to have a peek at the contents."

"Jablonsky told us the whole place is compartmentalized," Catia added. "The government owns the land and the buildings and rents out space to anyone who pays. They're not required to give names or addresses or what they're storing. Total anonymity. Every visit to the facilities is recorded and videotaped."

"Yep, it might be easier to get into Fort Knox," Marissa added. "But we could try to get into the Freeport's and their customers' computer systems. Greg and his team, with the help of the computing power of security agencies such as the CIA and NSA, should be able to overcome that problem."

"That *can* work," said Brandt. "But all of it will be illegal. We won't have the backing of the CIA or any US government agency without the say so of their directors who in turn would need a nod from the President. And I'm not sure we'll get it. They'll argue that this is a Jewish problem, not an American one."

"Yes, but in the past," Rex said, "when we were working for the CIA and other US security agencies, CRC almost always operated under the if-something-goes-wrong-we-don't-know-you principle. Their lack of official backing never stopped us then."

"That's true, but we don't have the same situation now. We've never initiated an operation without them asking us to do so. You see, part of the terms and conditions of CRC's contract is that we're not under any circumstances to initiate our own operations. We can only act when authorized by them, even though they might renounce us if we get caught.

"So, if we act on our own, even if we find the libraries and return them to the Jews of Italy, instead of getting a hero's welcome, we'll have our asses dragged before the courts."

"C'mon, John, they won't do that. Would they?" Christelle said.

"Christelle, I don't have to tell you what the politicians are like these days. If I am on a sinking ship ten miles from the coast, and I jump off and walk back on the water to dry land, I'll get prosecuted for not being able to swim."

Everyone exploded in laughter.

When the laughter receded, Christelle smiled and said, "John, I get the feeling our holiday might get truncated."

"Only by a day or two," Brandt said. "I'll make a few calls and see if I can line up all the necessary meetings in DC and get it over within a couple of days."

Rex said, "John, don't make any calls or book any flights yet. I might have a better idea."

"Spit it out," Brandt interrupted.

"Need-to-know, John. You don't need to know yet."

Everyone, including Catia, was staring at Rex.

Then Catia started laughing as well.

"What do you two find so damn funny?" Brandt growled.

"Patience, John, patience. It's a virtue," Rex said as he stood, took Catia's hand, and helped her up. "Give us twelve hours. In the meantime, relax and enjoy yourselves. There might not be much time for that once we get this mission going."

Everyone was quiet as they looked at each other, found no answers, and watched Rex, Catia, and Digger leave the lounge.

"What's that boy up to?" Brandt asked of no one in particular, his brow furrowed in a frown.

He only got blank stares and shrugs.

It was 8:00 P.M.

***

ROME, ITALY

MONDAY, SEPTEMBER 5, 2016

ON THE SATURDAY morning after they had completed an errand for Klenst, he dispatched two men to Rome who he had often used in the past when wetwork was required. Wetwork was the euphemism for the use of heavy-handed tactics such as the battering and killing of subjects.

The errand they were required to run in the early hours of Saturday morning before getting on the train to Rome, was to collect the bodies of a man and a woman from a warehouse and place them on a bench in Parc La Grange.

The duo now had orders to visit Sapienza in Rome and use whatever means necessary to find information about the Daltons. Klenst was more than a little irritated at the same message he got every time he called Rex Dalton's number which was found on Jablonsky's cellphone: *We're sorry, you have reached a number that has been disconnected or is no longer in service. If you feel you have reached this recording in error, please check the number and try your call again.* He gave up after the tenth, it could have been the fifteenth, attempt and returned to his research about the Jewish libraries.

A plan was slowly taking shape in his head.

Klenst didn't expect any news from his Rome team over the weekend. But by 8:30 P.M. on Monday, he was getting prickly. He had expected a progress report two hours ago. Just when his mood was shifting from cranky to incensed, the text message came through.

"Nordwand, I'm sorry to have kept you waiting," Lenny, the pseudonym for the team lead in Rome, started when the call was connected. "It took a little longer than anticipated, but we've got some information."

"Don't make me wait any longer," Klenst snarled.

"The woman is registered as a Ph.D. student under her maiden name Catia Romano. She's a Jew. Rex Dalton is not a student at the university. We don't know if he's Jewish.

"According to one of her fellow students, they got married in May of this year.

"We have confirmation that her Ph.D. thesis is about the Jewish Libraries removed by the Nazis from the Roman Ghetto in 1943.

"Her study supervisor is Professor Zechariah Nachum. He has an office at the *Centro Bibliografico*, owned by the Union of Italian Jewish Communities. Incidentally that's also the only address on record for Catia Romano."

"What the hell does that mean?"

"We got a copy of her student application form. It's a masterpiece in vagueness; no home address, no email, no phone number, no next of kin, only contact details for Zechariah Nachum."

"Nachum will know how to get hold of her. Here's what I want you to do."

CHAPTER 51 - WELL PLAYED DALTON

DUBROVNIK, CROATIA

TUESDAY, SEPTEMBER 6, 2016

REX WAS OFF by four hours; it didn't take twelve, it took eight.

It was 4:00 A.M. when Chris McArdle, the second in command of CRC, roused Brandt and patched him into a secured video conference with Martin Richardson, deputy director in charge of CIA operations.

"John, I know what time it is over there, but we've received an urgent request for help from Israel. Their Prime Minister phoned the President, on the red phone, no less."

Richardson was referring to the Moscow–Washington hotline established in 1963 that allowed direct communication between the leaders of the United States and Russia. Over the years it became known as the red phone, although the hotline was never a telephone line. At first, the communications link used Teletype equipment, later it was a fax machine, and now it was a secured computer link over which messages were exchanged via secured email. Nonetheless, the moniker red phone stuck and came to mean the ability for world leaders to make a call to the President of the United Sates directly in times of a crisis.

"What's the crisis, Martin?"

"I see you've got a mug there in front of you. I hope it's filled with strong coffee, you're going to need it. It's a long story."

"Now that you've disrupted my sleep, I've got nothing better to do than drink coffee and listen to you. Go for it."

Richardson launched into a long exposition about two Jewish libraries stolen by the Nazis during World War II and how an Italian Jew, a lady by the name of Catia Romano, while doing research for a Ph.D. at the University of Rome, inadvertently stumbled across information that indicated that those libraries had survived the war and, in all likelihood, still existed.

John Brandt couldn't recall that he ever had to exert so much effort not to explode in raucous laughter. It was only sheer willpower that let him keep a straight face while trying to ask intelligent sounding questions at the right moments.

"Now CRC has become a research arm of the University of Rome?" Brandt managed to get out while still keeping an impassive face.

"John, the President wants this taken care of. Two people have already been killed for it. The Israelis are worried that the libraries might fall into the hands of their enemies. Can you imagine what a shit storm that's going to unleash if Hezbollah or one of those fanatical Muslim groups get their hands on them? And let's pray that, God forbid, they don't already have them."

"Mhh, not a very comforting thought. But why don't the Israelis take care of it themselves?"

"Well, as their prime minister rightly pointed out, this is an issue that originated before the state of Israel came into existence. Their PM is of the opinion that it's an issue to be taken care of by the international community. However, taking it to the UN is a nonstarter. The President agreed. The PM also asserted that America would have a lot more economic and political clout with the European governments when the chips are down. And, as usual, they've made it known that, being the skunk of the world, they'd prefer to take a backseat while their big brother fronts this one on their behalf. Nonetheless, they promised to give us all the backing we need, but we're in the driver's seat."

"I could only hope the President extracted some quid pro quo."

"No, no, no, John. Haven't you heard? Presidents don't do quid pro quo. They only do things that'd earn them the eternal gratitude of their counterparts."

"Of course, how stupid of me. What's our brief?"

"Simple. Get those libraries. Yesterday."

"Okay, where do I get hold of this Catia Romano? And who's the Israelis' contact person?"

"Your old friend Yaron Aderet at the Mossad. He'll brief you fully. He knows how to get hold of the woman."

"Will do."

"Oh, and John..."

Brandt held his hand up. "Don't worry, Martin, I know the drill; If we get caught, you don't know us. Right?"

"You're always so perceptive, John. Keep me posted."

"Have a good one, Martin."

Two minutes later, Rex, Catia, and Digger were rudely awakened by thunderous knocking on the door of their stateroom. It was Brandt shouting, "Wakey-wakey, Dalton, wake the missus and the pooch and get your asses down to the comms room."

A minute later, Brandt repeated the same routine outside Josh and Marissa's room.

"Well played, Dalton. Especially the part about the Muslim fanatics," were Brandt's first words as soon as they were all seated in the communications room, each with a big mug of coffee in hand.

It was clear that Josh and Marissa had no idea what Brandt was talking about. They were staring at him with what-are-you-on-about expressions on their sleepy faces.

"Oh, you're not accomplices?"

"To what?" Marissa snarled.

"Let me enlighten you then. You see, Mark Antony and Cleopatra here, somehow, I suspect through Yaron Aderet, managed to get the Israeli Prime Minister so riled up he phoned the President of the United States. On the red phone, mind you, and asked for help to get those libraries back before fanatical Muslims could get their hands on them."

Marissa and Josh were shaking with laughter.

Rex and Catia were pokerfaced. Digger let out two short barks and smiled, probably because he wanted to make sure his pack knew he was excited to be part of the fun, or maybe he was just letting them know he was pleased that his pack was happy.

"John, you *have* to give them some credit for creativity," Josh said when he managed to stop laughing. "They saved you a trip to DC. Not to mention saving you from your favorite activity, hobnobbing with the mandarins of the Beltway."

"And I'm sure Madame Proll is very happy about it too," Marissa chimed in.

"She doesn't know yet," Brandt growled. "Nevertheless, I'm eternally grateful. It's only that I would've liked to have some warning before I got the call from Martin Richardson. Do you have any idea how much effort it required not to start laughing during that call?"

"Tsk, tsk, Rex, I'm disappointed," Josh deadpanned. "Knowing the Old Man's fragile state of health, how dare you put our fearless leader through such an ordeal? He could've blown the mission out of the water."

Brandt smiled and shook his head. "Okay, you've now all had your fun at my expense. I'm going to wake the others and get Yaron on the line. We've got a mission to plan, bad guys to find, asses to kick, and Jewish libraries to salvage."

***

SIBERIA, RUSSIA

TUESDAY, SEPTEMBER 6, 2016

OLEG WAS OFF by more than twelve hours; it took him and his team closer to forty hours instead of the twenty-four he had promised Klenst.

"Nordwand, this was a much bigger challenge than I thought it would be," Oleg started. "It's as if the Daltons, after their first trip to Geneva, all of a sudden become security conscious."

"Get to the point, Oleg. I don't have all day."

"On that first trip to Geneva they rented a vehicle from Europcar in the name of Rex Dalton. The GPS records of the rental car they used show that they visited a house in the suburb of Lancy. The property is registered in the

371

name of Abraham Heilbron. They were there for more than four hours."

"What's your problem?"

"Well, the problem is, on each of the subsequent visits they used different passports and their tracks, so to speak, dead-end at the airports every time after they cleared customs. There are no records of car rentals or accommodation. They must've been getting help from friends, family, acquaintances and such to get vehicles and accommodation."

"I see."

"I think we've reached the end of the road of what my team and I can do remotely. The only way to get that information would be to send someone around showing their photos at the office of each car rental company and the reception of every place offering accommodation. But by the looks of it that might be a waste of time. They've obviously taken care to cover their tracks."

"Okay, send me the address of that property in Lancy and everything you have about Abraham Heilbron."

Five minutes later, Klenst had Abraham's details and address. The man was 94 years old, probably senile. He saw the Daltons almost a month ago. He might not even remember them. Was it worth shaking that tree?

He opened the application on his laptop with which he kept electronic surveillance on his customers and selected

Joost Trauffer's name. The GPS coordinates for Trauffer's phone and car showed him to be in La Clusaz. He had been there since Sunday morning.

Taking a bit of break. Probably in the company of one or more of your floozies.

He remotely activated the microphone on Trauffer's cellphone and clicked the record button. Every sound made within five yards of that phone would be picked up by the microphone and transmitted to Klenst's computer. It was like standing next to Trauffer.

He decided to wait until he got more information from his team in Rome before reporting to Trauffer.

CHAPTER 52 – INITIATING THE MISSION

EN ROUTE TO VENICE, ITALY

TUESDAY, SEPTEMBER 6, 2016

SOON AFTER THEY had started the planning session, Rex and the others agreed that the answers to their questions were likely to be found in Switzerland. Hence, they decided to immediately lift anchor in Dubrovnik and set sail for Venice, where they would be within an hour's flying of both Geneva and Zurich.

The seas were calm, and the weather forecast for the next twenty-four hours excellent. At its cruising speed of 15 knots the TOMATS would cover the 364 nautical miles to Venice in about 24 hours.

Brandt would direct the operation, and Chris McArdle would provide the administration and support services. As in Brandt's rescue operation and the Badr operation, they immediately activated their virtual war room, which consisted of a continuous secured video and audio link between CRC headquarters, the Ops Room on the TOMATS, and for this operation also Yaron Aderet's office at Mossad headquarters in Tel Aviv, Israel.

Christelle Proll, vacationing on the TOMATS, was there in a personal capacity but would monitor the situation to see if French involvement was required at any stage.

Rehka was on her way from Mumbai to Venice where she, Marissa, and Catia would work with Greg Wade's ELINT, electronic intelligence team, backed by CIA analysts with the world's most powerful computers and most extensive databases available to them.

When Brandt and his longtime friend Aderet were finally able to talk to each other, it started off with a good chuckle about the Daltons' audacious scheme to get official approval for the mission.

"John, on a serious note," Aderet started when the hilarity abated, "the Muslim fanatics angle presented by Catia and Rex might sound like a ruse on their part. But we, the Prime Minister and I, don't want to ignore that possibility. I'm sure you'll agree it would be a disaster if that ever happened. Retrieving those libraries intact and returning them to the Jewish people would go down in the annals as one of the great moments in the history of our people."

"You're preaching to the choir, Yaron. We're all very much aware of the gravity of the situation and what an ignominious failure it will be if we can't keep those libraries out of the hands of your enemies."

Aderet made two of his top computer experts based in Tel Aviv available, and they were immediately linked into the virtual war room and introduced to the ELINT team. He also tasked a three-man *kidon* team under Yakov Jessel, the man who was involved in the Badr operation the year before, to fly over to Geneva and set themselves up in the embassy where they were to be on standby to join Rex and his team on short notice if necessary.

Jessel and his men were from the top-secret Kidon department. *Kidon* was the Hebrew word for *bayonet* or *tip of the spear*. They were an elite group of specialist operators, some said the very best in the world, responsible for serving the Mossad's needs in operations against the enemies of the state of Israel.

The ELINT team went to work right away. Their brief was to get into the Freeport's computer systems. They had no illusions; there was a massive amount of information they'd have to work through, if they got access to it to start with. A long shot, they all agreed, and one that would take a lot of computing power and some nifty programming to scan through all those records.

"But definitely worth trying," Rex said, "seeing that we have nowhere else to turn to for more information at the moment."

The only other potential source for a lead was Jablonsky's secretary, who had access to the records in his office. To that end, Aderet made a call to the Mossad's COS, chief of station, in Geneva to get in touch with one of their *sayanim*, in this case a female lawyer, who was to get in touch with Jablonsky's secretary to see if she had managed to extract the information about the

Scharnhorst members. If not, would she be able to give them access to Jablonsky's files?

The COS phoned back within a few hours and reported that the lawyer told him she had known Wilhelm Jablonsky personally for many years and what a terrible shock his death was to her and the legal community in Geneva. She was more than happy to help bring the perpetrators to justice. She also knew Jablonsky's secretary, Julia. She promised to get back as soon as possible but told him to expect the circumstances to be very sad and chaotic and that it might take a few days to get the information.

CHAPTER 53 – WHERE IS CATIA ROMANO?

ROME, ITALY

WEDNESDAY, SEPTEMBER 7, 2016

LENNY AND NIKLAUS, Klenst's henchmen in Rome, had rented an SUV from Hertz, checked into a ramshackle Airbnb, left their luggage there, and went to stake out Professor Zechariah Nachum's office during the day on Tuesday. Late that afternoon they followed the bus that he took to his apartment. There they set up their surveillance again.

It was shortly after 2:00 A.M. Wednesday when they made their move. All lights in the small apartment block were out, and they were sure everyone in there was fast asleep.

There were no electronic security systems of any kind. The door to the foyer was locked and each apartment owner had a key to unlock it. Zechariah's apartment was on the ground floor. There was an emergency exit door on the side of the building. That was the door through which Lenny and Niklaus entered. Neither the lock of the emergency exit nor the one on Zechariah's apartment door posed a challenge to the two experienced criminals.

The old man was asleep in his bed when they entered. He only became aware of them when a big gloved hand clamped over his mouth and smothered any sounds.

There were two ski-masked men. The one who had his hand over the old man's mouth was enormous. His companion was a short, squat man, stocky body, with buckled legs and exceptionally long, hairy arms.

At 86, Zechariah had less strength than a ten-year-old. His resistance was feeble at best.

In heavy accented English the big man said, "Nachum, if you want to get out of this alive, you'll make no noise and answer all our questions truthfully.

"Let me demonstrate what's going to happen if you don't do it."

The short one sat on Zechariah's legs, took his cigarette lighter out, flicked it on, and held the flame to the sole of the old man's left foot.

Zechariah shrieked in pain but only a soft muffled sound could be heard.

The short one, still seated on Zechariah's legs, retrieved a pack of cigarettes from his shirt pocket, took one out, and lit it.

"Where is Catia Romano?" The big one asked.

Zechariah shook his head.

The short one burned Zechariah's leg with the cigarette.

Within half an hour of being subjected to the sadistic fantasies of his tormenters, Zechariah started giving them information, in drips and drabs. At times, he passed out from the pain as they broke some of his fingers, punched him in the face, ribs, and stomach, and scorched him with the lighter and cigarettes. But they revived him with cold water and smelling salts.

He confessed that he knew the people in the photos they showed him, Catia and Rex. He told them that the woman was one of his students, Catia Dalton, née Romano, and Rex her husband. He wasn't shown a photo of Digger or asked any questions about him, so he didn't tell them anything about the dog. He was also not asked whether the Daltons had any associates; thus, he didn't mention anything about Josh and Marissa. He was, however, forced to elaborate on the topic of Catia's Ph.D. thesis.

When they asked him about the Daltons' address, he was not lying or withholding information when he told them he didn't know. But they didn't believe him. Another round of intense pain followed until the big one must have realized that inflicting more pain wouldn't make the old man remember what he had no knowledge of.

"Okay, what's her telephone number?" he asked.

"In... office," Zechariah mumbled almost inaudibly.

"Where's your cellphone?"

He shook his head. "Ahh... no... no... cellphone."

The truth was that he had a cellphone, but he hated cellphones and computers. He was of the opinion those were the cause of the corrosion of social interaction that would eventually lead to the downfall of civilization. He almost never used his cellphone. It was only on the persistence of his daughter, Hannah, that he had a cellphone, so that he could use it in case of an emergency. It did him no good in the emergency he found himself in now.

His tormentors didn't know whether to believe him or not. There was no cellphone in sight. The only way to confirm he was not trying to mislead them was to administer more pain. But this time they overdid it. The punch to the crop of his stomach was the final straw. Zechariah's body went limp, he was unconscious again, but no amount of cold water or smelling salts got him back. His breathing was shallow and rapid. His heart was racing.

They had no knowledge of medical matters. The old man could have suffered a stroke, heart attack, brain damage, or whatever, and they wouldn't know. To them it looked as if Zechariah was about to die.

Their instructions were to rough up the professor, get information out of him, but not kill him. Nordwand thought that the news of the attack on the old man would reach the Daltons and draw them out of hiding.

Nordwand was not a man who tolerated failure. They had to find something to make up for the fact that they had ruined Nordwand's plan. They ransacked the apartment but found nothing to tell them where to get hold of the Daltons. In their fervor to get information that could resolve their dilemma they never looked under Zechariah's pillow. If they had, they would have found his cellphone where he always put it before going to sleep.

Half an hour later, at 4:30 A.M., they had found nothing, Zechariah was still unconscious, and by the looks of it his condition was worsening. They were seriously worried but agreed there was nothing more they could do. They had to leave.

They walked a few blocks away to where they parked their SUV and drove to the Airbnb, about half an hour from the apartment. They were starved and bone tired. But first they had to report to Nordwand, not something they were looking forward to at all.

ROME, ITALY

WEDNESDAY, SEPTEMBER 7, 2016

ZECHARIAH WAS AN early riser, 5:00 A.M. every morning. So was his neighbor, Luisa Cipolla, a widow in her late seventies with whom he had become good friends. It was a platonic friendship, formed over the years they had been living in the same apartment block. They would often watch a movie on TV together; sometimes they would go out for a walk or a meal at one of the nearby restaurants.

Over the years, they had developed an early morning ritual – they took turns to have their first espresso of the day while watching the news at each other's apartments at around 5:30 A.M. every morning, before Zechariah would catch the bus to his office at 6:30 A.M.

By 5:20 AM., while Luisa was busy getting the espresso machine ready and placing a few pieces of the biscotti, Italian almond biscuits, which Zechariah liked so much, on a small plate, it didn't strike her that she hadn't yet heard the usual early morning rumbling noises made by the building's antiquated water pipes when Zechariah took his shower.

It was about 5:35 A.M. when she looked at the clock on the wall that she realized she hadn't heard the usual noises from his apartment and mumbled, "Zechariah is late. I better go and find out if he's okay." She went knocking on his door. There was no answer. She went back to her apartment and got the key that Zechariah's daughter, Hannah, had given her a few years ago.

"Just in case," Hannah had said at the time.

Luisa unlocked the door, took one step inside, and instantly saw that something terrible had happened. She rushed to his bedroom and found him unconscious, bloodied, and battered on his bed. She didn't panic; she was a former nurse. Instead, she hurried back to her apartment, got her cellphone and dialed 112, the Italian emergency number, while scurrying back to Zechariah's.

The police and ambulance sirens could be heard within minutes from Luisa's call. She was visibly shaken when she spoke to the police officer, while the paramedics examined Zechariah and started preparing to lift him onto a gurney.

Notwithstanding her state of distress and tears streaming down her face, Luisa made it clear to the police and the paramedics that she was going with her friend in the back of the ambulance to the hospital. When the police officer tried to stop her from getting into the ambulance, she issued a stern warning to him. "Officer, you'll have to drag me out of here by force. I'm going with him to the hospital. If you want a statement from me, you know where to find me. Now get out of my way."

The officer, obviously knowing what was good for him, relented and stepped aside.

On the way to the hospital, Luisa phoned Hannah and told her what happened and that her father was being transported to the Salvator Mundi Hospital in Viale delle Mura Gianicolensi, not far from the apartment.

On arrival at the hospital, Zechariah was still in a coma. A team of doctors and nurses attended to him immediately. All Luisa could do was to sit in the reception area and wait for the doctors to let her know what their diagnosis was.

An hour and a half later, after Hannah had arrived, the doctor came out and told them that apart from the visible bruises and burn wounds, the MRI scans and X-rays had revealed three broken ribs, two broken fingers, and a slight concussion but, thank God, no serious brain damage.

The combination of pain, shock, and his hypoglycemia, a condition also known as low blood sugar, were what put him in a coma. He explained that although hypoglycemia was usually treated with diet, when a patient went into a coma because of low blood sugar levels, it was necessary to administer glucagon injections to raise the blood sugar levels, which was what they were doing. They were also administering pain medication and light sedatives in an intravenous drip.

He was confident that, barring any unforeseen complications, Zechariah's injuries, although extremely painful, were not life-threatening. Due to his age it was to be expected that it would take some time, but he should be able to make a full recovery.

***

ROME, ITALY

WEDNESDAY SEPTEMBER 7, 2016

IN THEIR ROOM at the Airbnb, Lenny and Niklaus had finally mustered the courage to call Nordwand.

Lenny, their spokesman, explained what had happened.

Nordwand quickly surmised that they got no new information and had screwed up his plans. He launched into a profanity-laced rebuke, the likes of which they hadn't had since undergoing their six months of compulsory service in the Austrian military more than twenty years ago.

Nordwand left no doubt that if the old man died, the two of them would never work for him again.

Lenny and Niklaus had no illusions about what that meant. They were not religious at all, but in foxholes there are no atheists. They looked at the spire of St Peter's Basilica in the distance, crossed themselves, and said a silent prayer for themselves and for the old professor.

By 6:45 A.M. Lenny and Niklaus were back outside Zechariah's apartment. The police were on the scene. Surreptitiously, Lenny questioned some of the shocked bystanders and was told that an old man was assaulted in that apartment in the early hours of the morning, that he had been taken to the hospital, and that he was still alive at the time when he was loaded into the ambulance.

They let out their first half-sigh of relief, but knew they were not out of the woods yet. They went back to their car and headed to the hospital. All the way they prayed quietly that their victim was still alive and would remain so until the Daltons showed up.

At the hospital, Lenny managed to convince the receptionist that he was one of Zechariah's friends, living in the apartment block next to his, and was very upset when he heard what happened to his dear friend.

The receptionist told him in great confidence that the doctor had pronounced Zechariah's condition to be stable and satisfactory. She leaned over and in a confidential tone whispered to Lenny, "That means he is out of danger and should regain consciousness soon. But he will not be allowed any visitors other than his daughter and his caretakers for at least the next twenty-four hours."

Lenny and Niklaus, when they got back into their car, let out another sigh of relief. Now they were very eager to get Nordwand on the line and tell him that his brilliant plan was back on track.

Nordwand was still in a bad mood, extremely rude when they spoke to him again, but at least he didn't swear at them or threaten them.

All they had to do now was hope that Zechariah would stay alive and the Daltons would turn up. They went to a nearby street café, got themselves bags of food, coffee, and soft drinks, and returned to their car where they settled in for the wait, which they knew could be a long one.

Nordwand decided it was time to update Trauffer again.

CHAPTER 55 – WARN CATIA

ROME, ITALY

WEDNESDAY, SEPTEMBER 7, 2016

SHORTLY BEFORE 10:00 A.M. Zechariah stirred. Hannah and Luisa were next to him. It took a minute or so before he was fully aware of his surroundings. An almost imperceptible smile reached his lips as he recognized his daughter and his friend Luisa. He tried to say something, but Hannah told him to rest and that the doctors said he would be okay.

But it soon became evident Zechariah was not going to relax until he had his say, despite the fact that he was struggling to get the words out.

Hannah thought he wanted to tell them who did it. "Do you know who did this to you, Papà?"

He shook his head slightly.

"How many were there?"

Zechariah slowly raised two fingers.

"Two?"

He nodded.

"Don't worry, Papà, you're safe here. They won't get near you. The police have posted a guard outside your room."

He nodded, closed his eyes for a few seconds, and then tried to say something again.

Hannah leaned in close to hear him.

"Ca... tia... dang... danger... warn..."

"Catia is in danger?"

Zechariah nodded.

"You want me to warn her?"

He nodded again.

Hannah had met Catia a few times and knew how dearly her father held her. "What's her number?"

He shook his head slightly and whispered, "Ce... Cell..."

"Her number is on your cellphone?"

He nodded.

Luisa also knew Catia, but she was wondering if her friend was hallucinating. She had never seen him with a cellphone. Besides, she had seen the apartment. The thugs had pulled it apart; they would certainly have taken the phone. "Hannah, does he even have a cellphone?"

"Yes, he does, I gave to him, but he almost never uses it. He hates the thing. I've set up a few speed-dial numbers for him. He always puts it under his pillow at night so he can hear it ring and vibrate and it's close by if he needs to dial the emergency number—his version of a panic button. My number and Catia's and his office and a few others are on it."

Luisa left the room to ask the policeman on guard outside to help her get in touch with the lead detective at Zechariah's apartment. Within minutes she was talking to him and asked him to try to find the cellphone. "Have a look under his pillow first." She was holding her breath while the detective complied with her request.

"Got it," he said less than a minute later. "Strange place to keep a phone."

"Wait till you reach the professor's age, then it might not be so strange anymore. Now, can you please do me a favor and read to me the telephone number of Catia Romano from that phone? She's one of his students, I need to get a message to her."

A few moments of silence followed before the detective said, "Got it."

Luisa wrote the number down, thanked the detective, and called Catia.

CHAPTER 56 - FLAMING WITH A
FRIGHTENING RAGE

VENICE, ITALY

WEDNESDAY, SEPTEMBER 7, 2016

A FEW HOURS before Luisa was on the phone with Catia, the TOMATS had moored in Marina Santelena, Venice. The team was looking at the first bits of information produced by Greg's ELINT team.

It was 10:20 A.M. when Catia saw the Unknown Caller message on the screen of her phone. For a moment she considered ignoring it but decided against it. She apologized to everyone, got up, and took a few steps to the back of the room.

Although Rex didn't know who called or heard what was said to Catia, he saw the terrible toll the caller's words were taking. Her face was contorted in anguish, and tears were streaming down her face.

Rex went to her, tenderly placed his arm around her, and pulled her tightly against his chest. He took the phone from her and explained to the caller who he was.

He knew about Luisa and her friendship with Zechariah but had never met her.

Brandt was watching the blood slowly drain from Rex's face and his right hand tightening into a fist, the knuckles white. When Rex turned, Brandt saw his eyes; they were flaming with a frightening rage. And he was sure of one thing; someone was going to get hurt or killed.

When the call ended, Rex led Catia back to her chair. He sat down, and in a soft, measured tone told everyone what had happened in Rome.

When he ended, Declan asked, "How could they've known to go to Rome? And how did they know about Zechariah?"

"The scumbags could have gotten it out of Jablonsky," Rex said. "We told him that Catia is a student at Sapienza. I imagine it wouldn't have been too difficult for them to find out from the university that Zechariah is her study mentor."

Catia said, "Zechariah couldn't have told them much more than that he's my study mentor, that he knows us, my university email, and my phone number. He doesn't know where we live or any other way to get in touch with us."

"According to Luisa, they haven't taken his phone. The police have it," Rex said.

"Start packing for Rome," Brandt said, looking at Rex and Josh.

They nodded.

Catia and Marissa spoke in chorus. "We're going with them." It was not a request; it was a statement of fact.

No one argued with them.

Aderet immediately offered to instruct one of his underlings to organize a private jet to fly Rex and company to Rome.

But Rex said, "Before Yaron arranges our ride, let's consider the possibility that we could be walking into a trap. I'm of the opinion it's quite possible that this could be part of a scheme to get us out in the open, knowing that we'd visit him as soon as we learned about the attack on him."

"Yep," Brandt said. "And that's exactly what I hope they'd be doing. In which case they'd have watchers at the hospital, maybe also at Zechariah's apartment. If we can get eyes on both places before you get there, we might be able to identify the watchers and you can surprise them."

"I'll get our Chief of Station in Rome to immediately dispatch surveillance teams," Aderet said.

"That'd be good," Rex said. "I'd like to have a look inside Zechariah's apartment, unnoticed." He didn't tell them that the main reason for wanting to visit the apartment was to let Digger have a look and a sniff around. As far as he was concerned, Digger's ability to sniff out miscreants was beyond doubt. But what he had in mind now was still only a theory, yet to be proven. Digger would have to get the scent at the crime scene, remember it, and at a later stage, which could be days, even weeks apart, point out the criminals if he happened to cross paths with them.

Aderet called the Chief of Station, COS, in Rome and told her to organize a private jet from Venice to Rome and to dispatch agents to set up surveillance at the hospital and Zechariah's apartment. They had to try to identify any observers. She also had to arrange for accommodation, weapons, and a few other tools of the trade that the Rome team might require.

Aderet was still on the phone to the COS when Rex thought about Abraham Heilbron. Although he knew Zechariah could have given up Heilbron's name under duress, he also remembered that he and Catia, when they traveled to Geneva to meet with him, did so on their real passports and rented a car with GPS tracking in his real name. It would have been child's play for the bad guys to track Heilbron down—he could be in mortal danger.

When Aderet finished his call, Rex told them of his concerns about Abraham.

Twenty minutes later, Aderet had arranged with the COS in Geneva, where Israel had a permanent diplomatic mission to the United Nations and other International Organizations, to send a security detail to Lancy to keep a watch over Abraham Heilbron.

* * *

EN ROUTE TO ROME

BY 11:30 A.M. Rex, Catia, Josh, Marissa, and Digger were on a private jet on their way to Rome.

An hour and ten minutes later, at 12:40 P.M., their plane touched down at Rome Urbe Airport, a small civilian landing strip on the north side of Rome.

Shortly before landing, Aderet reported that Abraham's home in Geneva was under the watchful eyes of his field agents and so were the hospital and Zechariah's apartment.

When they stepped off the plane, they were met by a *sayan* who gave them the keys to an SUV with heavily tinted windows and a large canvas bag. The bag contained four fourth-generation 9-mm Glock 17s with silencers and three fully loaded 17-round magazines for each gun plus four boxes of spare ammunition. Between the four of them there was enough firepower to start a small war. Inside the bag were also disguising paraphernalia and other handy tools such as four black KA-BAR military knifes, two 50,000-volt Taser guns, two bottles of sedatives with syringes and needles, a big bundle of zip ties, and ten rolls of duct tape.

Half an hour later, they were in adjoining rooms in a neat and tidy but nondescript backstreet hotel owned by one of Aderet's *sayanim*. No ID was required; in fact, no check in was required. They drove straight into the underground parking and took the elevator up to their rooms on the third floor, the keys to which were handed to them by the *sayan* who met them when they got off the plane.

CHAPTER 57 – PROST

LA CLUSAZ, FRANCE

WEDNESDAY, SEPTEMBER 7, 2016

JOOST TRAUFFER TOOK a deep breath as he stared out the window at the Aravis mountains from the comfort of his luxurious reclining chair in his living room. He had taken a few days off from the office to spend time alone at his house in La Clusaz. He had been a troubled man ever since receiving that first report from Ruedi Meister of the FIS, five days before. As the Troubleshooter unearthed more information, instead of pacifying him, his angst grew in leaps and bounds with every new report.

He took his cellphone out of his pocket to see if there was any message from the Troubleshooter—there wasn't. He sighed and put the phone back in his pocket.

The Troubleshooter's latest report dashed all of his hopes that the Daltons had come to Geneva looking for information about the Jewish libraries, didn't get what they wanted, and left, and that would be the end of it.

The identities of the Daltons were confirmed, and he now knew what they looked like. He had the name of Mrs. Dalton's study supervisor and the name of Abraham Heilbron, a nonagenarian living in Lancy, who would probably not even remember much more than the names and faces of the Daltons.

Although, it can't do any harm to put surveillance on the old fossil, just in case the Daltons pay him another visit.

But the bottom line was, the Daltons remained at large, present whereabouts unknown.

It was the Daltons' frequenting of Switzerland and Germany over the past four weeks that ruined his hopes of having heard the last of them. Their visit to Cologne, specifically, got Trauffer's hackles up. That was Karl Bauer's place of birth and the place he returned to after Scharnhorst got him out of the POW camp. He had to assume the Daltons must have somehow figured out Bauer's involvement with the libraries.

When he got out of his chair and approached the liquor cabinet, he remembered his previous solo deliberation session, the terrible headache, and the exorbitant cost in acquiring it—all of it self-inflicted. Now, while he was contemplating what to drink, he recalled the words of Steve Jobs on his deathbed in 2011: "Whether we drink a bottle of $300 or $10 wine – the hangover is the same."

He chose the five-hundred-dollar cognac and resolved to not overindulge again.

As an accomplished businessman he knew that problem-solving was essentially an exercise in defining options, weighing the pros and cons of each, and selecting the best one for execution.

His first option was to do nothing; the trail ended with the lack of information in the Freeport databases. Yes, the discrepancy of the data about unit D4007 certainly must have looked suspicious to the Daltons, but what was there that they or anyone else could do about it? Even if they managed to get unfettered access to the Freeport's computer systems, they would find nothing more than they already knew. Even if they managed to get physical access to each and every storage unit in the Freeport, which they wouldn't get, not legally, even in a hundred years, there was nothing to be found. A lot of other companies and individuals could be in trouble, but not he or Zehnhaus or his fellow Scharnhorst members. None of them stored any of their treasures at the Freeport.

He had just started on his third cognac. He was not a man that ever approached his problems with a *laissez-faire* attitude—he just could not bring himself to stand by and let things take their own course, hoping for the best. The do-nothing option was crossed out.

The second option was to move the libraries to a new location. But the question was why would he do that? In the 59 years the libraries had been stored at the house in La Clusaz, no one, not Neuhaus's wife, not his own mother, or his wife, or any of his lady friends that he took to the house regularly, had even the slightest idea that their favorite weekend retreat held what some scholars called the most important Jewish library in Europe, maybe the world.

Ten feet below the garage floor was a spacious climate-controlled vault. The entrance to the secret subterranean storage was so well concealed that it was all but impossible to find unless one knew where and what to look for. And even then, to get access to the vault, one had to know how the intricate lock mechanism operated. First, one had to know about the invisible door hidden at the back of the built-in wardrobe in the basement. Then one had to know that the door could only be opened by flipping off the switch marked HWC, hot water cylinder, on the house's electric circuit board in the linen cupboard in the laundry. Once the lock on the hidden door was open, one had to know that the button marked Auxiliary Mains on the switchboard, usually in the off position, had to be switched to the on position. That would disengage the electronic lock on the vault door. Finally, one would be able to enter the vault, after entering the five-digit sequence on the combination lock.

On the other hand, it was the first time in almost six decades that someone got enough information, and he still had no idea how, to send them on a search for the libraries at the Freeport.

What information do the Daltons have, and where did they get it?

Up until a few days ago he had always believed that he was the only person on the planet who knew that the libraries had survived the war. But now, it was highly likely that the Daltons had figured out as much.

Thinking through it, he came to the realization that since Bauer had handed the libraries over to Father Schürer of Scharnhorst in 1946, there had always been more than one person who knew of the whereabouts of the libraries. He had no way of knowing whether his father or his business partner had taken someone into their confidence.

Could that be how the Daltons came to know about the libraries?

He was busy with the fifth cognac and up to five options; do nothing, move the libraries, destroy them, sell them, or kill everyone who had been asking questions about them.

The do-nothing option he had discarded more than an hour and two cognacs ago. The idea of destroying the libraries left him nauseated.

The thought of selling them, at this level of inebriation, was more appealing; it would put many millions, maybe a billion, in his pocket. But he was still sober enough to understand that the risk of discovery would be very high. And the consequences ruinous. Enough reason to park this option for now.

With his pledge not to overdo it completely forgotten, Trauffer poured the sixth cognac and turned his mind back to the move-the-libraries option.

He would have to do it himself, without any help. Fifteen thousand books, give or take, he'd have to pack and carry up two flights of stairs and unpack at the destination. But that was not the biggest issue.

La Clusaz was a very small town, about 1,800 inhabitants during the off season, growing to many thousands during the ski season. That would have been the best time to make the move, when there were many people around. In normal years, the ski season started in September. This year, however, it was forecast to be the driest season in 150 years, and with the ski season in all likelihood not starting until January. Global warming, some said. Part of the normal long-term weather cycles, others said. Whatever the cause, it was very inconvenient. La Clusaz was still a virtual ghost town inhabited only by nosy locals with the small-town mentality of making it their business to know everything about everyone else's business.

By now he was so intoxicated and caught up in his dilemma he didn't even realize he was having a boisterous, audible, conversation with his other self.

"Shit. That means, irrespective of which option I choose, I still have to get the Daltons, find out what they know, how they know it, who they told, and then kill them all."

"You'll have to, otherwise, you'll forever be looking over your shoulder for someone hunting for the libraries."

"Yeah, better to kill them all now and stop it once and for all."

By the time half of the bottle was gone, and he didn't realize his arguments were going in circles, another thought entered his mind.

"I've never cared for those Muslim crazies. But I don't mind taking their money."

"And your point is?"

"Well, my point is, if it comes to it, I'd rather sell the libraries to the crazies... I'll even consider gifting them to them... just as long as the damn Jews don't get them back."

"I like that! Brilliant idea. The ultimate insult to the God-killers."

He got up from his chair, and with the glass of cognac in his hand he staggered down the stairs to the basement. "I haven't been to visit you in months."

"Shame on you."

"Yeah, yeah, don't rub it in."

A minute or so later, he said, "Ah shit, the switches on the circuit board." He turned around and lumbered back up the stairs to the laundry. "Why the hell did they *have* to put it in the damn laundry and not somewhere downstairs?"

There was no answer.

Unsteady of hand and feet, he swore a few times as he struggled to open the cover of the switchboard. "Now what was it again? Hot water off, auxiliary on? Or was it... mhh... hope that worked."

With muffled moans and groans he descended the stairs to the basement again.

"Ah, great, it worked." He stepped through the hidden door and held onto the rails with one hand, cognac in the other, as he went down the stairs. He stopped in front of the eight-inch steel reinforced vault door and started turning the dial while calling out the numbers. "Seven left. Four right. Nine left. Six right. Two left. Open sesame!"

For a long while he was quiet as he stared at the shelves filled with thousands of books. The literary, religious, and cultural legacy of the oldest Jewish congregation in Europe. The written history of more than two thousand years of Jewish presence in Rome, dating from before the birth of Christ, from the time of the Caesars, the emperors, and the early popes.

"If I can't have them, neither can you," he said as he raised the half empty glass of cognac. "Prost!" he shouted, gulped the remaining cognac down in one swig, and hurled the glass against the nearest wall. Then he turned around and left, closing the doors behind him as he went.

Trauffer might have been surprised, even shocked out of his drunken stupor if he could have heard the words spoken by the man he called the Troubleshooter.

Two hundred and seventy miles away, Horst Klenst had raised his *U-Boot* and said, "Prost, Herr Trauffer. I agree. The Daltons can't have them."

U-Boot was a popular German cocktail made with beer and a shot glass filled with vodka that was sunk into the beer mug. The shot glass with vodka dropped into the beer resembled a submarine, hence the name, *U-Boot*, the German abbreviation for *Unterseeboot*, literally undersea boat.

CHAPTER 58 – JOSH'S PRIMATES

ROME, ITALY

WEDNESDAY, SEPTEMBER 7, 2016

SOON AFTER ARRIVAL at their hotel, Aderet arranged for the lead agents of the surveillance teams at Zechariah's apartment and the hospital to be put in direct communication with Rex and his team.

The lead agent at the apartment told Rex that the police had wrapped up their work and left about an hour ago and that they hadn't spotted anyone watching the apartment. It was good news, as they would have little trouble getting in and out of the apartment. But it was a little disappointing that there was no one they could capture and question.

The lead agent at the hospital, however, had the news they were hoping for. There were two men in a red SUV, a Hertz rental car, parked under a huge umbrella pine tree. They were obviously waiting for someone. They had been there when the surveillance team had arrived more than two hours before, and from the bags of food they bought, it was reasonable to assume the two were not planning to leave soon.

A few minutes later Rex et al were studying the surveillance photos and video clips received from the agent. One of the men was a dark-haired bearded hulk of about 6′ 5″, almost two meters. He had an upper body like a professional heavyweight wrestler, a cone-shaped head which seemed to be mounted directly onto his shoulders, and a rotund midriff attesting to his love of food and beer, and lack of exercise.

Josh had one look and dubbed him Gor.

"Gor?" Marissa frowned.

"Short for gorilla."

"And this one?" Rex laughed as he pointed to the photos of Gor's companion, a stocky man of 5′ 8″ or so with almost red hair, buckled legs, and extraordinary long arms.

"Tan," Josh announced without hesitation. "As in orangutan."

When they stopped laughing, Josh said, "On a serious note, Rex, if those are indeed our guys and we were to get into a scrap with them, you have my word, I'll come to you and Digger's rescue as soon as I've dealt with Tan."

Rex grinned. "Geez, thanks, Josh. It means a lot to have the assurance of a comrade in arms who wouldn't hesitate to let his buddy have the honor of being ripped apart by a gorilla."

Even though Catia and Marissa knew it was their way of dealing with mission tension, they couldn't help but laugh at the sudden bout of wit that had besieged their men.

Over the next half hour, they planned their next steps. Rex, Catia, and Digger would take the SUV to visit Zechariah's apartment first and then make their way to the hospital. Josh and Marissa would take a taxi to the hospital and get eyes on the suspects while they waited for Rex and Catia to arrive. They would remain in contact with the Mossad agents onsite but would not meet with them. The agents would be their counter surveillance teams, watching their backs.

Rex and Catia used the same disguise they had used in Geneva a few days before—an old couple. Rex slightly bent over, walking with the aid of a cane. Catia had her right arm hooked into Rex's left arm and Digger's leash in her left hand.

The agent told them the coast was still clear as they approached the apartment. The front door to the lobby was not locked, but the door to Zechariah's apartment was covered with red and white crime scene tape with the words POLIZIA ZONA SBARRATA, Police Zone Barred, printed in big letters.

Rex and Catia ignored the message and entered after Rex picked the archaic lock in a few seconds.

Inside the apartment, in less than thirty seconds, it was clear Digger must have figured out what had happened there. His soft yelps, whining, and snarling as he worked his way around Zechariah's bed and the rest of the apartment made it evident that he was more distraught than in the Geneva park a few days ago. What they had no way of knowing then, but realized later, was that Digger had recognized the scent of the villains he got in Geneva and was trying to tell them about it.

As it was, Catia thought Digger's behavior was because he could smell Zechariah, and the old man's blood on the sheets and floor must have been as tormenting to him as it was to her and Rex.

When Rex, after a few minutes, told Digger to "Find them," he was already raring to go. He immediately headed for the front door and led them through the emergency exit onto the street. Two blocks away, he sat down at a parking space off the sidewalk. The hair on his back and neck were raised. He looked at Rex and Catia, looked back at the parking space, and let out a low growl and bared his teeth as he started down the street.

"This must be where the thugs got into their car," Catia said.

Rex nodded. "And they went that way." Rex pointed down the street in the direction Digger was looking. "Okay, let's go over to the hospital and let Digger have a sniff at Josh's primates."

ROME, ITALY

WEDNESDAY, SEPTEMBER 7, 2016

THE TAXI DROPPED Josh and Marissa off at the hospital shortly after 3:00 P.M. A few minutes later Rex told them that he and Catia had gained access to Zechariah's apartment.

Josh and Marissa knew they were probably not on the radar of the bad guys, but they didn't want to take any chances; therefore, they disguised themselves as American tourists from Texas, complete with leather boots, jeans, large shiny belt buckles, and Stetson hats. Marissa's dark hair was now blonde and shoulder-length, and she sported large sunglasses. Josh's blond hair was now black, and he was wearing wraparound sunglasses.

The lead agent onsite told them that they would find Gor and Tan sitting in a red SUV in the shade of a big tree facing the main entrance of the hospital. He also told them about a little street café from where they would be able to get a good view of the suspects. According to the agent, Gor and Tan were quite relaxed—clearly not expecting any trouble at all, and wholly unaware that they were under surveillance. "They've been sitting in that car, eating, drinking, smoking, and sleeping for hours already," the agent said. "There are no other watchers around."

411

Josh and Marissa didn't hesitate to take the agent's word for it. Mossad's agents had a reputation for being the best in the business. And, of course, it helped that Aderet had spoken very highly of the men his COS in Rome had assigned to the task.

On their way to the street café, Josh and Marissa got eyes on Gor and Tan in the red SUV when they passed within less than two yards from them. Josh noticed that Tan had an Italian newspaper over the steering wheel but surmised that Tan could either not read or didn't understand Italian. Most likely it was the former—the newspaper was upside down.

But the mystery of Tan's literacy was resolved a few minutes later when Marissa asked Josh if he also got the whiff when they had passed the car. But Josh, afflicted by a mild case of sinusitis the last day or two, had not smelled anything.

Tan, according to Marissa, apparently liked to blend his tobacco with a globally popular hallucinogenic herb known by many different names, depending on the country and the age of the users thereof, but most often referred to as pot or weed, also known as marijuana or cannabis.

They found a table outside the café and ordered espressos and cannoli as they settled in to keep a clandestine watch on their targets while waiting for the Daltons to arrive.

The plan was for Rex and Catia to get close enough to the red SUV so that Digger could have a sniff at the occupants and tell them if the men were indeed the hoodlums who attacked Zechariah.

To Marissa's question of how exactly Digger was going to tell them, Josh only shrugged and said, "Rex and Digger have developed their own language over the years. Trust me. I've seen them talk to each other."

"Yeah, right. Did I ever tell you about the long chats I've had with the Easter Bunny and Santa?"

Truth be told, none of them knew if the plan would work. They only had Rex's recollection of a story told to him by his late friend Trevor. Rex had told them that Digger was more than competent to follow a scent once he was given a scent to follow, such as a piece of clothing worn by the person he had to find. According to Rex, that was exactly what happened in Vanuatu a few years before when Rex saved Margot Lemaire, currently a deputy minister in the French parliament. Digger apparently also showed his prowess in Croatia when he sniffed out the true killer of a young woman and saved an innocent man from landing in prison for life.

Shortly after 4:00 P.M. Rex parked their SUV in a space off Viale delle Mura Gianicolensi, opposite the hospital. On the way to the hospital, Josh and Marissa brought them up to speed with what the targets had been up to since they had been placed under the watch of the

Mossad agents up till now, which was that they had been eating and drinking and sleeping, and Tan was a chain smoker. At that moment Tan was in the driver's seat. Gor was on the passenger side. He had reclined his seat; apparently it was his turn to take a nap.

Rex and Catia, still in their disguises, with Digger on his leash, struck out from their car across the parking lot on a route that would take them past the primates' SUV.

Josh and Marissa were watching from their position at the café across the street. This was the moment of truth— would Digger live up to their expectations or would it turn out to be wishful thinking?

When the three of them were a few yards away from the car, Digger started growling softly, the hair on his neck and back standing on end. He moved out in front of Catia and Rex, positioned himself between them and the car, and stopped. He stood there with his gaze fixed on the car, tail in a vertical position, moving stiffly from side to side, slowly. His ears were erect and pitched slightly forward, toward the car. When Rex took a step forward, Digger took a step to his right and blocked him. He kept staring at the car, snarling softly, throwing quick glances back at Rex and Catia as if to make sure they were not doing anything stupid, such as getting any closer to that car.

Across the road, Josh and Marissa glanced at each other. They didn't have to say it; there was no other explanation. Digger was blocking Rex and Catia from getting any closer to that car. He was protecting them from danger. And for that there was only one explanation; Digger had sniffed out the bastards.

"I'll be damned," Marissa murmured.

Josh grinned. "I won't tell you I told you so."

"You better not."

Rex whispered to Catia, "Digger has identified Zechariah's assailants."

"Without doubt," Catia whispered back. "It's amazing."

It was only later when they would come to the realization that for Digger it had been the third time in four days that he had gotten the scent of those evil men.

When Rex and Catia started walking again, Digger kept shielding them from the car and forced them to take a wide berth around it. As Digger herded them away, he continued looking back as if to make sure no one from that car would attack the members of his pack.

Both Rex and Catia took note of the fact that Gor and Tan were oblivious to their presence. Both front windows of the car were rolled down. Gor's seat was still down, presumably he was asleep. Tan's head was resting against the doorpost, he could have been asleep as well.

***

415

Rome, Italy

ABOUT HALF AN hour later, any observer who might have been interested in what was happening in the parking area, of whom the Mossad's lead agent had assured them there were none, would have noticed an American couple, doubtlessly from Texas, entering the parking lot. The couple stopped about twenty yards away from the red SUV. They took their cellphones out, ostensibly to look at online maps. It was apparent from their body language that they were not only lost, but at odds as to which direction to go.

A minute or so later, an old couple with a big black dog also entered the parking area, and when they passed the American couple, the latter stopped them, undoubtedly, to ask for directions. But it would soon have been clear that the old couple was unable to help the Americans. The old man shook his head and pointed in the direction of the red SUV under the tree. The Americans nodded, seemed to thank the old people, turned, and walked toward the SUV.

The old couple followed a few paces behind, probably to make sure the Americans got the information they were asking for from the occupants of the red SUV.

The shade of the large umbrella pine tree and the shadows of the hospital building reaching the parking lot against the setting sun had rendered the area where the

416

red SUV was parked in semi-darkness. Therefore, what happened next would likely have been a bit of a blur to an observer.

What happened was, Josh approached the passenger side, Marissa the driver side.

Gor had only managed to get a strange, muffled, growling sound out as his body convulsed a few times before it went limp. It was the result of 50,000 volts from Josh's Taser gun hitting his body. It was highly unlikely that he felt the needle plunging into his thigh shortly after.

At the same time, on the driver's side, Tan didn't require the rough treatment his buddy got. On approach it became clear to Marissa that Tan was so stoned it was quite possible he could have gone through surgery without the need for anesthesia. He certainly didn't feel the needle going into his arm dangling out the window.

With their charges out cold, Rex and Josh moved quickly to zip tie wrists and ankles and gag them with duct tape. Gor was pulled over the backrest of his reclined seat onto the backseat and Tan was shoved over into the passenger seat. Josh got in the back with Gor, and Rex got into the driver seat. Fortunately, Digger, although clearly not happy to do so, obeyed Rex's commands and got into the baggage area of the SUV without making a noise. It was clear that if Digger had his way, he would rip the men apart there and then.

While Rex and Josh took care of the seating arrangements, Catia disabled the GPS tracking on the vehicle.

Less than two minutes after the American couple approached the SUV, it could be seen pulling out from under the tree and leaving the parking lot.

The old lady had her arm hooked into the arm of the young American woman as the two of them walked to the hospital's main entrance.

Chapter 60 – It's Them

ROME, ITALY

WEDNESDAY, SEPTEMBER 7, 2016

WITH THE ASSURANCE that there were no more threats and that they were still under the watchful eyes of the Mossad team, Catia and Marissa entered the hospital to visit Zechariah.

He was asleep when they entered the room. Catia's hand flew to her mouth to stifle a cry of shock when she saw the appalling condition of her beloved mentor.

Marissa stood a few paces away, from where she stared at the battered face and body. The expression on her face was unmistakable; she was furious.

Hannah and Luisa, in whispered tones, told them what the doctor had to say about Zechariah's condition and the prognosis that the old man was not in mortal danger and was expected to make a full recovery.

Their talking, although they tried to keep their voices down, must have been loud enough to wake Zechariah. His eyes darted around the room, and the moment he recognized Catia despite her disguise, a delighted smile broke across his bruised face.

Catia was struggling to keep her emotions in check as she took Zechariah's hand and said, "I'm so sorry..." But that was as far as she got before tearing up again and becoming unable to speak.

With a labored voice, Zechariah started to speak, but Catia said, "Shh... don't talk. You need to rest. Don't worry, you are safe and so are Rex and I. They won't harm you again."

But Zechariah still had a will of his own, and he made it clear he wanted to talk to Catia, alone.

Luisa, Hannah, and Marissa left the room.

Catia took the seat next to Zechariah's bed where she was close enough to hear him, took his hand in hers, and gave it a tender squeeze.

Over the course of the next twenty minutes or so, during which Zechariah had to stop often to regain his breath, he told Catia that the men who tortured him did it to get information about her and Rex and their search for the libraries. He had a wry, pain-filled smile when he said, "But... I... I think I... dis... disappointed them... couldn't tell them much." He sighed and closed his eyes.

When he opened his eyes again, Catia took her phone out and showed him the photos and video clips of Gor and Tan provided by the Mossad agents.

"Couldn't... see faces... bal... clavas..." But he continued to tell her the clothes and the physiques of the men in those photos were those of the men who had tortured him. "It's them," he reiterated before he lapsed into sleep again.

Catia texted Rex. IT'S THEM. Z RECOGNIZED THEM. THEY TORTURED HIM TERRIBLY.

Catia took photos and a video of Zechariah's injuries and transmitted them to Rex. "You better pray that God will have mercy on you. I won't."

***

TIVOLI, ITALY

WEDNESDAY, SEPTEMBER 7, 2016

THE INTERROGATION ROOM was a sizable rumpus room in the basement of a large house on a twenty-acre estate outside Tivoli, a historic town about 19 miles north-east of Rome. The estate belonged to an affluent Italian Jewish businessman, a *sayan,* who leased the property to the Mossad for the token amount of one euro per year.

Upon their arrival, Rex and Josh were met by one of Aderet's agents, who helped them get their captives into separate cells in the basement. He then parked the red SUV in one of the lock-up garages, locked the door, and rejoined them. He took them on a tour of the property, explained all the security measures, and told them that he had instructions to remain on the property but to stay out of their way.

421

Gor and Tan were still unconscious when Catia's text message and the photos of Zechariah's injuries reached Rex. The images immediately put both of them in a murderous mood and made them more than just a little impatient to wait for the vermin to wake up.

Digger seemed to be equally irritated, as he all but refused to leave the guard position he had taken up in front of the doors leading to the cells.

The agent helped them set up the interrogation room with two video cameras and microphones, all of it linked via secured satellite connection to the TOMATS ops room, Aderet's office in Tel Aviv, and CRC's headquarters in Arizona.

Although Brandt and the others in the TOMATS ops room, Aderet and his people, as well as Chris McArdle and his team, were kept informed with summary progress reports as events unfolded in Rome during the day, they now expected Rex and Josh to provide them with a more detailed account. And that included an elaborate exposition by Josh, no less, because not even Rex could tell it as well as he could, about Digger's heroics in sniffing the scumbags out so effortlessly.

Throughout Josh's telling, Rex feigned unsurprise, as if he never expected anything else.

"I've always admired and believed in Digger's abilities," Josh said. "But I have to confess I thought what we expected of him today was going to be a bridge too far for him."

"Don't worry, I'll talk to Digger and ask him to forgive you for doubting him," a straight-faced Rex said to the amusement of all.

Josh smiled. "While you're at it, could you put in a good word for my lady as well? Marissa has never been a believer, doubtful at best, but I know for a fact Digger converted her today."

"I'll hear what he thinks about that. I suspect he'd insist on a proper apology."

Just then they saw Catia and Marissa's car approaching the house.

Rex and Josh didn't have to be told when they saw the expressions on the ladies' faces. It could not be mistaken; they were on the warpath.

"Are those scumbags awake?" were Catia's first words.

Before Rex or Josh could answer, Marissa said, "We," she pointed to herself and Catia, "would like to have a word with them right away."

Rex, although also in a foul mood, knew Catia and Marissa were not in the right frame of mind to conduct an interrogation. There would be no interrogation at all; in their current state they were more than likely to put a bullet between the eyes of each of them. Which, Rex thought, was not a bad idea at all, but not before he and Josh had extracted the information they wanted.

It took a combined effort from Rex and Josh to persuade the ladies to let them first question the prisoners before they had their retribution. In the end they reached a shaky truce when Catia relented and said, "Okay. You can question them first. But if you haven't got them talking within the hour, Marissa and I are taking over."

Catia and Marissa agreed to watch the proceedings on a big TV screen from the living room upstairs.

Chapter 61 – He'll Have Us Killed

Tivoli, Italy

Wednesday, September 7, 2016

THE TIME WAS approaching 6:30 P.M. when Gor, because of his size and with no THC coursing through his system, was the first one to stir as he started to regain consciousness.

Tan, by the looks of it, was going to be asleep for a while longer.

When Gor opened his eyes, after the bag was removed from his head, he looked unnerved as he found himself with hands and feet tied to a sturdy metal chair bolted to the cement floor and his mouth obstructed by duct tape. He shook his head a few times, mumbled, then blinked a few times when he looked at Rex. His eyes bulged when he recognized him. Gor must have been deeply troubled by the fact that *he* was the one tied up in the chair, and not Rex Dalton.

Josh ripped the duct tape off Gor's face brusquely, tearing out part of his beard and hair with it.

Gor screamed in pain and immediately launched into a profanity-laced tirade. In German.

Digger stood in front of Gor, snarling and growling, body language unambiguous; waiting only for a finger snap from Rex so that he could rip Gor apart, which he had been begging Rex to let him do since the carpark.

Seeing that Rex was keeping Digger at bay and his swearing having no effect, Gor switched tactics and issued a challenge. "Untie me and let's have a fair fight, I'll take on both of you. C'mon, Dalton, let's do it. Or are you scared of me? Be a man. If you beat me, I tell you everything I know; you lose, I walk out of here. What do you say?"

Rex and Josh ignored him. They had seen Gor's kind before, many times. Either of them could take Gor apart in a fight. Instead of answering, Rex calmly translated Gor's ranting into English for Josh's benefit while he put on an elaborate act of picking up a baseball bat from the table and wiping it with a cloth, as if he was sterilizing it. He took a few practice swings.

All the while, the verbal diarrhea kept flooding out of Gor's mouth, and Rex calmly translated.

Rex put the bat down, took out his Glock, slowly fitted the silencer, ejected and checked the magazine, inserted it back, pulled and released the slide.

By the time Rex placed the loaded gun on the table in front of him, Gor had gotten around to insulting the dignity of his and Josh's mothers, sisters, and the rest of their lineage.

And Rex had enough.

He stood, took the baseball bat and gun, handed them to Josh and said, "Hold on to this for me, will you? I'll only be a minute. I'm going to grant this piece of shit his wish.

"I want you to stand there in the corner and be an impartial referee. If he tries to escape, shoot him in the knee. If he beats me, shoot me between the eyes and set him free. Understood?"

"Yep, got it," Josh said with a broad grin. What Gor didn't know, but Josh did, was that Rex had a fearsome reputation in hand-to-hand combat. Gor was about to get the beating of his life, but he had no inkling about it.

Rex took his KA-BAR knife out, cut the zip ties, returned the knife to its sheath, took two steps back, and said to Gor, "Ready when you are."

Digger moved to the corner with Josh. He had on his face what could only be interpreted as a big smile, as if he already knew precisely how this scene was going to play out.

Gor shook his head as if he couldn't believe his luck and maybe he even thought Rex was bluffing. Very confidently, he jumped to his feet with a smug grin on his face and started moving toward Rex, bobbing and weaving like a boxer.

In the ops room on the TOMATS, in Aderet's office in Tel Aviv, at CRC's headquarters in Arizona, and in the living room upstairs, everyone but John Brandt and Chis

McArdle, who had big smiles on their faces, were holding their breath. Catia had her hand over her mouth, her eyes wide with fear.

None of the spectators had thought of keeping the time. Therefore, in the aftermath, there was disagreement about the duration of the fight. It was Greg who settled the matter when they replayed the video for the umpteenth time in slow motion, and he pointed to the electronic clock on the video. "Exactly seven and a half seconds, from the first punch to when Gor hit the floor."

In that 7.5 seconds, Gor got his nose broken with the first punch. His eyes tilted in their sockets, but he had stayed on his feet. Watching it in slow motion, they could see the momentary look of surprise on Gor's face. It was obvious he had no idea where that blow came from. Next, three of his ribs broke from the roundhouse kick that followed the nose job. His eyes were probably too teared up to see the kick coming. He had let out a long noisy grunt when Rex's next punch struck him in the solar plexus and took his wind out. Rex's final kick struck him in the groin, sending him to the floor making a loud gurgling sound.

Gor never even got around to attempting to block a punch or kick, let alone throw a single punch of his own. He stayed down on the floor, in a fetal position, and cried like a baby.

Rex grabbed Gor by the hair, dragged him back to the chair, and shoved him back into it as he yelled out in pain.

Josh stepped over, handed the baseball bat and gun back to Rex, retrieved a bottle of smelling salts from the pocket of his cargo pants, and held it under Gor's nose. "You're doing great, man. I'm impressed," he said, while massaging Gor's shoulders as boxing coaches do between rounds. "When the bell rings for the next round, I want you to rush him and let him have everything you've got. He won't last ten seconds. I can tell, he's pretty much out on his feet."

Gor shook his head vigorously. Through the sobs, with blood and snot dripping from his face, he mumbled, "I'm done. What do you want to know?"

The beating not only persuaded Gor to cooperate but must also have improved his language skills dramatically. He was now fluent in English, albeit with a pronounced Austrian accent. He sounded a bit like a world-renowned professional bodybuilder who became a very famous Hollywood actor and went on to become the governor of California. However, the similarities ended with the accent—the former governor and action-movie hero would've been very disappointed with his sound-alike.

Josh tied him up to the chair again and stepped aside so Rex could start the questioning.

Gor said that he would tell them everything, but Rex had to promise not to hurt him or kill him. His secret was out; he was a bully and a coward. He could hand it out but couldn't take it. His gigantic physique had always given him the advantage, but no one had ever put his fighting skills to the test like Rex did.

"Okay," Rex said, "no more pain, but only if you don't lie. You'll start with your real name, address, family and such. Then who you work for and how long you've been working for your employer. You'll tell us about all the operations you've done for your employer up till today."

Digger was back in his position in front of Gor's chair snarling and growling. He knew the drill. His job was to scare the daylights out of the man in the chair but not attack him unless Rex told him to do so.

Gor nodded enthusiastically. "I'm ready to tell you everything, but please calm down the damn dog first."

Rex shook his head. "No can do. That dog has got a mind of his own. I can't control him when he's pissed off at someone. And you've definitely managed to piss him off big time. What I do know, which might help you, is that he hates lies. He'll rip your throat out the moment he detects a lie, and I won't be able to stop him. Oh, and one more tip. He's very sensitive; he detests being called a damn dog."

Across the globe the onlookers were laughing. Catia and Marissa looked at each other and smiled. "Maybe it's best that they went in first," Marissa said. "I don't think you and I could've inflicted so much pain and damage in such a short time. Not to mention Digger's antics."

Catia said, "Although I'm not entirely satisfied yet, I do feel a lot better already."

"Can you give me something for the pain?" Gor asked Josh.

"Did you give the old man you attacked in his bed this morning anything for *his* pain?"

Gor shook his head. He didn't even attempt to deny knowledge of it.

Josh took his Glock out, chambered a round, and pointed it at Gor's knee. "Then you better start talking before I put a bullet in your knee so you can experience real pain."

Gor immediately launched into a narrative, starting with his name, which he said was Uwe Althaus; he was originally from Salzburg, Austria, now living in Annecy, France, 26 miles out of Geneva. He was 42, divorced, and had two children who were living with their mother.

However, he had no idea who he was working for. Honestly. The man was known to him only as Nordwand, but he had never met the man. He and Tan, whose real name was Dieter Kraus, also from Austria, Vienna originally, now living in Geneva, met while they were doing their military service in Austria.

They were recruited by Nordwand six years ago.

Rex glanced at Digger and he started growling.

Althaus had gone pale. "What? I've been telling you the truth. What's with the da... ah the dog?"

Rex said nothing, he frowned and looked at Digger and back at Althaus.

Digger got the message; he snarled and with raised hair started moving slowly toward Althaus.

"The Darknet!" Althaus shouted. "The Darknet. We found Nordwand via a website on the Darknet. Call the dog off!"

Digger glanced at Rex. Rex nodded slightly, and Digger stopped growling, took a step back, and sat down again.

"Be careful, Uwe. He can read your mind, and he doesn't like it when you leave things out. To him that's the same as lying."

Althaus looked as if he didn't believe what Rex was saying about Digger's mindreading abilities. Nonetheless, he continued to tell them about the work they'd been doing for Nordwand over the years. But Rex looked at his watch, stopped him and said, "We'll get back to that later. For now, tell us only what you've been up to the last week up till today."

"Early on Saturday morning last week, Nordwand sent us to a warehouse on the outskirts of Geneva to pick up two bodies, a man and a woman." He quickly added, "Please note, we didn't kill them, they were already dead when we got there. Our instructions were to move the bodies to Parc La Grange in the Quai Gustave Ador neighborhood and put them on a bench. After that we caught a train to Rome to find you and your wife."

Despite Rex's admonitions and Digger's growling threats, Althaus steadfastly maintained that he and Kraus didn't kill those people.

He told them that he and Kraus got Catia's student records at the university by bribing one of the staff in the student administration office. They were hoping to learn where to get hold of Catia and Rex but couldn't find any of that information in the records. They did, however, learn about Zechariah Nachum and his whereabouts. The next day, Tuesday, they had kept a watch on Zechariah the whole day and followed him to his apartment that night.

He stopped talking, looked at Rex and said, "You know the rest."

Rex said nothing. He only raised his eyebrows, looked at Digger and then at Althaus.

Digger was on his feet, snarling and growling as he took a step toward Althaus.

"Stop him!" Althaus yelled.

Rex said nothing. He only looked at Digger and nodded.

Althaus shouted, "We went into his apartment early this morning!"

Rex nodded at Digger and he backed off.

"We questioned him to find out where we could get hold of you and your wife. But he didn't know, so we left."

Rex shook his head slowly. "Uwe, I've warned you not to leave things out." He looked at Digger, pointed at Althaus, and said, "All yours, buddy."

The next moment, before Althaus could get a word out, Digger was on him. He stood on his hind legs growling and snarling, with his front paws pushing against Althaus's chest and his bared teeth mere inches from the man's hysterical face.

Althaus was screaming at the top of his lungs. Moments later, his urine started collecting in a puddle on the floor below his chair.

"Stop! Please! I beg you, please stop him!"

"Digger, stand down," Rex ordered. But this time Digger wasn't happy to back off. Rex had to repeat the command before Digger retreated.

Althaus was sobbing.

"You've got something else to say, Uwe?"

"Yes, we had to use force to get the old man to talk."

"What kind of force, Uwe?"

Althaus dropped his head and mumbled something inaudible.

Rex nodded for Josh to switch on the wall-mounted TV screen and said, "Show him."

Althaus kept his head down and refused to look at the screen.

Josh grabbed him by the hair and jerked his head back, "Look at the screen, chicken shit. There's a movie we want you to watch and comment on."

Josh clicked through the photos and video that Catia took of Zechariah's injuries.

"Uwe, I'm going to give you one more chance, one only. Who of you did this to that harmless, innocent, 86-year-old man? I want to hear specifics, Uwe. The next time I'm not going to call the dog off."

It took Althaus about ten minutes to provide all the details. Ten minutes during which Rex struggled not to untie the man and beat him to death.

"Nordwand wanted us to hurt the old man. He thought if we harmed him enough, you and your wife were bound to come and visit him. That's why we were outside the hospital. We were waiting for you to turn up so that we could capture both of you and hand you over to him."

"And now that you've ruined Nordwand's plans?"

"He'll have us killed."

435

"Just like that?"

"Yes, he's a man without compassion."

"As opposed to you and Kraus, kindness incarnate, the male versions of Mother Teresa," Josh said.

Rex looked at Josh. "Well, seeing that they've already been sentenced to death and they're no use to us anymore, I see no reason we shouldn't execute the sentence. What do you say?"

"Now that's an idea that makes me very excited," Josh said as he retrieved his Glock slowly.

But before he could bring it to bear on Althaus, Althaus yelled, "Stop! Don't shoot me! I beg you, don't do it."

A fresh stream of urine splashed on the floor.

"You and Kraus are dead men walking," Josh said. "I'm saving you from the agony of waiting for your execution. Besides, there's the score to settle for what you did to that poor defenseless old man this morning."

Rex held up his hand. "Wait. I've got an idea..."

"Anything. Just tell me what you want me to do," Althaus interjected.

Rex looked at Josh. "You want to hear it?"

Josh shrugged nonchalantly. "I'm really bent on shooting this asshole, so your idea better be good."

"So, Uwe, there you have it. Your life is now in my hands. If my friend likes my plan, you live. If he doesn't, you die. Want to hear my plan?"

Althaus nodded fervently.

Josh replaced his gun in its holster and Rex explained what he had in mind.

Ten minutes later, Althaus was still alive and back in his cell, gagged and tied to the bed.

***

Tivoli, Italy

Wednesday, September 7, 2016
TAN, DIETER KRAUS, was fully awake by now, and his muffled protests could be heard as Josh dragged him by his hair into the interrogation room, shoved him into the chair, duct-taped his arms and legs to it, and removed the bag from over his head.

Kraus swore loudly in German when Josh tore the duct tape from his face. He squinted against the bright light and shouted, "Mein Gott!" when he recognized Rex's face. However, he was not nearly as loquacious as his buddy, Uwe, and definitely not in a fighting mood at all.

Digger didn't scare Kraus as much as he did Althaus, maybe slightly unsettled but not terrified. Althaus's blood on the white walls, chair, and floor, as well as his urine on the floor and the smell thereof must have induced some anxiety. Nevertheless, he started by refusing to speak English.

But, unfortunately for him, Althaus had used up all of Rex and Josh's patience. In short order, Josh kneecapped him with the baseball bat which instantly equipped Kraus with fluent English abilities and an intense desire to talk to them. As expected, he also spoke English with a prominent Austrian accent, but sounded nothing like any famous person, at least not one that Rex or Josh knew of.

Unlike Althaus, instead of asking for pain killers, through the moans and groans of the excruciating pain in his knee, he begged them to let him have one of his cigarettes.

Josh placed Kraus's pack of special cigarettes on the table and said, "You can have as many as you want as soon as you've shared your memoirs with us."

Over the course of the next half hour, Kraus confirmed to them that Althaus told them the truth. He was dragged back to his cell, and despite his demands to have his cigarette as promised, Josh told him to shut up or he would have the other kneecap done. He went quiet at once.

It was 8:10 P.M. in Italy.

CHAPTER 62 – I WANT THEM ALIVE

TIVOLI, ITALY

WEDNESDAY, SEPTEMBER 7, 2016

IT WAS ALMOST 9:00 P.M. in Italy when Rex dialed the secret conference number from Althaus's mobile phone.

They were back in the interrogation room, Althaus was back in the chair, arms and legs tied to it. Digger was on his left. Rex, on his right, with the business end of his Glock buried in Althaus's ear. Josh was on the other side of the table, across from Althaus, his Glock trained on a spot between his eyes.

From their remote locations, the rest of the mission team watched with bated breath. If Rex's plan worked, they were about to locate Nordwand, the killer of Jablonsky and Guggenheim and mastermind behind Zechariah's torture. Locating Nordwand and getting their hands on him could bring them a step closer to the libraries. Failure meant they would be back at square one.

The biggest risk, the single point of failure, was the plan's reliance on the lowlife, Althaus, to convince his phantom employer that he and Kraus had succeeded in tracking down the Daltons and that they would soon be in custody.

Greg and his specialists had the tabs on that secret conference number. The location of the server that hosted the secret teleconference facility had no name that appeared on any official maps but was visible on satellite images from which it looked like a cluster of four farmhouses in the middle of nowhere in the Siberian wilderness in Russia.

They were ready the moment both parties were online to quickly weed out the mesh of proxies and fake exchanges and get a bearing on the location of Nordwand.

Althaus had a script in front of him that Rex et al had prepared. The script was designed to take as much time as possible so as to give the eavesdroppers time to find Nordwand's location without raising his suspicions.

Although sweating and shaking nervously, Althaus had no illusions about what awaited him if he failed to convince Nordwand of the authenticity of the scripted report he was about to give him. For the fact that his voice would be computerized and that there was going to be a slight delay in the communications, he was grateful.

Althaus swallowed once when Nordwand's curt, synthesized voice, "Report," came over the speaker.

"Good news, Nordwand. We've been staking out the hospital since this morning."

"Get to the point, Lenny. I've been waiting all day."

Althaus must have wished he could have wiped the sweat dripping from his face. "The Daltons turned up at the hospital to visit the professor at about seven thirty tonight. We waited outside, and when they left an hour later we followed them."

"Where are they now?"

"They're at Taverna del Ghetto on Via del Portico d'Ottavia. It's in the Jewish Ghetto. The Jewish Ghetto is..."

"I know where it is. Continue."

"We're outside watching them. Ready to follow them again when they leave."

"And they have no idea they are being followed?"

"They've got no idea. Niklaus and I'll take them as soon as an opportunity presents itself."

"Do you have guns?"

"Yes, and Tasers. We won't have any trouble taking them down."

"I want them alive. Understood?"

"Yes."

"Don't make a mess of it, Lenny."

"We won't."

Rex and Josh looked at each other. So far so good. Despite his angst, Althaus had been doing an exceptional job. They were well aware that he could have slipped a prearranged, coded, distress signal into the conversation without them knowing about it. But they bargained on Althaus's comprehension of the fact that when the call ended, he would still be in their custody, and his genuine belief that he would be executed on the spot if he put a foot wrong.

"Okay, follow them when they leave that restaurant. See where they live and grab them as soon as you can do it without being seen. If at any stage you think you might need help, let me know. Don't muff this up, Lenny, you have one chance and one only."

"You can count on us, Nordwand."

"Your earlier performance doesn't exactly instill a lot of confidence in me."

"We won't let you down. Where do you want us to take them?"

"First, make sure you get them, then I'll tell you where to take them."

"Understood. We'll keep you posted."

"Do that. And one more time, Lenny, don't disappoint me."

The line went dead while Althaus was still saying, "I promise we won't."

Horst Klenst smiled when the call ended. "Lenny, you and Niklaus might earn me a big bonus, and you wouldn't even know about it. I certainly hope you're not going to disappoint me."

He opened the tracking program on his laptop and clicked on Joost Trauffer's name. The next screen showed him that Trauffer was still in La Clusaz, France.

CHAPTER 63 – MODERN-DAY
SCHARNHORST MEMBERS

SECURED VIDEO CONFERENCE

WEDNESDAY, SEPTEMBER 7, 2016

LESS THAN THREE minutes after the call with Nordwand ended, Greg joined them in the video conference and told them his team had a location for Nordwand. It was a surprise. Everyone thought from his pseudonym being the German word for the north face of the Eiger mountain above Grindelwald in the Swiss Alps, that would be his location. They were wrong.

According to Greg, Nordwand was in Vaduz, the capital of the Principality of Liechtenstein; a German-speaking microstate of 62 square miles, with a population of about 38,500, bordered by Switzerland to the west and south and Austria to the east and north. Europe's fourth-smallest country, with limited natural resources but a strong financial sector, one of the few countries in the world with more registered companies than citizens. It was also one of the most prosperous nations in the world.

Vaduz was one of the very few capital cities of the world without an airport; their nearest was Zurich Airport, about 60 miles away by road.

Greg's team had no trouble in finding out that the property in Vaduz was registered to a Liechtenstein incorporated company, HK Group. It didn't surprise them that HK Group was owned by a company incorporated in Luxembourg, and they expected if they delved further, they would find an elaborate scheme to obscure the true ownership of the property.

"Let's not get sidetracked," Brandt said. "The ownership of the house is not important; the occupants are. What we need is a surveillance team in Vaduz as close to right now as possible."

"I agree," Rex said. "But I want to caution that we should approach Nordwand with great care. If he is what I think he is, a professional contract killer, he'll be very security conscious and lethal."

Everyone agreed.

"Okay, I've got Yakov Jessel and his team on standby in Geneva," Aderet said. "They could be in Zurich within the hour and in place in Vaduz under two."

"Make it so," Brandt said.

Within minutes, Aderet had issued instructions to Jessel and they were on their way to the airport, where the Israelis kept two private jets to transport officials and agents around Europe and other parts of the world on short notice.

The team turned their attention to the second part of Rex's plan. Assuming that Nordwand was oblivious about the true state of affairs, they agreed that they had about two to three hours before they would have to make another call to Nordwand. This time it would be to inform him that the Daltons had been captured.

Rex said, "Greg, I trust you guys are continuing to monitor that conference number and Nordwand's?"

Greg looked affronted. "Of course we are."

"Sorry, no offense intended," Rex said. "It's just that Nordwand is probably not the kingpin, as I've said earlier, but rather a hired gun to do someone else's dirty work. Which means he'll be reporting progress to that someone else. And there is a good chance that he'll be using that same conference facility to do so."

"Don't worry, we're ready for him," Greg said.

Aderet cleared his throat and said, "I've just received information that might help us figure out who that someone else could be. Want to hear it?"

"The suspense is killing us, Yaron," Brandt said with a grin on his face.

"My COS in Geneva got those names from Jablonsky's secretary. I'll put it up on the screen."

Jablonsky's client files produced seven names of potential modern-day Scharnhorst members. Three of them had been dead for a few years already. The remaining four were:

Manuel Lanz, a main player in biotech investments, lived in Geneva. Reported worth, around $8 billion.

Werner Stuber lived in Zurich, a retired politician and former vice-chancellor of the Federal Council of Switzerland. Reported worth, around $3 billion.

Joost Trauffer, lived in Geneva, CEO and sole owner of Zehnhaus Consulting, a small financial consulting company located in Geneva. No information about his wealth.

Maja Bolliger, CEO of a well-known international pharmaceutical company in Basel on the border of Switzerland, France and Germany. Reported worth, over $6 billion.

It was Catia who noticed it first. "All but Joost Trauffer are listed among the top ten richest people in Switzerland."

"Birds of a feather flock together," Declan Spencer murmured. "What's Trauffer's business with this flock if he's a pauper?"

"Precisely," Catia said.

"Good point, Catia, Declan," Brandt said. "Greg, put some of your people on to collect every bit of information about those four. Start with Trauffer."

"On it, John."

Brandt turned and faced Aderet. "Surveillance teams to cover them?"

"Yep, I'll get teams onto it first thing in the morning," Aderet said. "At the current rate, I might soon have to send in reinforcements."

"Just make sure we don't run out of surveillance teams, Yaron," Brandt said with a smile.

CHAPTER 64 – WHERE SHOULD WE TAKE THEM?

THURSDAY, SEPTEMBER 8, 2016

SHORTLY AFTER MIDNIGHT, they were back in the interrogation room, and Rex dialed the secret conference number from Althaus's mobile phone again.

Half an hour before, Aderet had reported that Yakov Jessel and his team of *kidons* were in position outside the house in Vaduz, Liechtenstein. Jessel had reported that the house was dark; however, their infrared human sensor equipment had detected the body heat of one person inside, apparently asleep. There were no guards on the outside. It was an extravagantly large house, surrounded by a lavish garden without a fence of any kind.

Althaus was back in his chair, tied up as before. Digger was in position on the left of Althaus. Rex and Josh back in their old positions, weapons trained on Althaus.

Althaus seemed to be slightly less anxious than before.

The rest of the mission team were back in front of their TV screens, watching, quietly hoping and praying this part of the plan would also work. Ten minutes before Rex

449

dialed the conference number, he sent a text message to Nordwand. MEET IN 10.

Seconds after the text message, Jessel reported that the body in the house had moved to a room on the south side.

"Report," Nordwand said when he got online.

"Good news, Nordwand. We've got them."

"Excellent. Any problems?"

"None. We took them down with the Tasers and had them hogtied, gagged, and in the back of our car in under thirty seconds. No one saw us."

"Photos?"

"Stand by, I'm uploading them now."

A silence of more than two minutes followed while Rex uploaded the photos to the secured server in Russia and gave Althaus the thumbs up.

"They're there; you should be able to see them now," Althaus said.

"Let me have a look."

The line went quiet as Nordwand presumably studied the photos. There were four. Two showed Rex and Catia with hands and feet tied, on their backs in the back of a red SUV, seemingly unconscious. The remaining two photos were selfies; one showing Rex held up in a sitting position by a smiling Althaus, the other showing Catia in the same posture with Kraus.

Catia recoiled with revulsion at the memory of being touched by Kraus during the photo shoot earlier.

Rex had more photos and even a short video clip ready in case Nordwand needed more convincing. He didn't.

"Excellent," Nordwand said. "You're working your way back into my good graces. Keep it up and you might earn a bonus."

"Where should we deliver them?"

"Geneva."

"Okay, no problem."

"Don't get careless, Lenny. You've got more than eight hundred kilometers to drive. It'll take you eight to ten hours, and you have the border to cross. Make sure you keep them sedated and out of sight. There's a lot that can go wrong from now until you deliver them."

"We'll be careful."

"You better be. Call me an hour before you arrive in Geneva. I'll give you the final address then."

The call ended while Althaus was still busy saying he and Kraus would be hitting the road soon.

Klenst opened the tracking application on his laptop and clicked on Trauffer's name. When the next screen appeared, he smiled and mumbled, "I'm so glad you're back home on the shores of Lake Geneva. One less thing for me to worry about. But how you got that drunken ass of yours back home without killing yourself on the road, beats me. Who would've taken care of my payment if you'd killed yourself?"

CHAPTER 65 - THE SIX-HOUR MYSTERY

SECURED VIDEO CONFERENCE

THURSDAY, SEPTEMBER 8, 2016

THE TEAM WAS back in video conference a few minutes after the call. They were cautiously optimistic that the plan was on track.

They were still busy discussing it when Greg said, "Nordwand has just sent a text message, through the Russian server, to a mobile phone currently located in Geneva. The message is on the screen."

MEET IN 5

"Greg...," Rex started.

But Greg held his index finger up in a give-me-a-moment gesture and continued typing on his keyboard.

Rex waited.

Greg finished and said, "We should have more details about the location of that new mobile phone shortly. Apologies, Rex. You wanted to say?"

Rex grinned, slightly embarrassed. "Please get us more details about the location of that new mobile phone."

Everyone started laughing.

By the time the laughing had died down, Greg said, "Okay, got the details. The new phone has been tracked down to a house in Cologny, Geneva. Now hold onto your skirts... the house belongs to Joost Trauffer, one of our four Scharnhorst members."

"Bingo!" shouted Josh.

Rex looked at Catia. "I think Greg and his team have just found the custodian of your libraries, Missus Dalton."

Everyone started talking at once.

Greg shouted, "Quiet! The conference number has just gone active." He hit a few keys on the keyboard, and the next moment they heard Nordwand's computerized voice.

"I have the Daltons in custody."

"Excellent! The best news I've had in many days. Where are they?" Trauffer's voice sounded gruff.

"On the way from Rome to Geneva. They should arrive by around 4:00 P.M."

Rex frowned. *A ten-hour drive from Rome to Geneva will take until 11:00 A.M. not 4:00 P.M.*

That frown didn't escape Catia's notice.

"You want to do the interrogation, or do you want me to take care of it?"

"God, no! I don't have the stomach for it."

"What do you want to know?"

454

"A full and detailed account of how they came to know about the Jewish Libraries. Every detail of how they've been able to find out they had been stored at the Freeport between 1943 and 1946. Do they have any ideas about where the libraries are kept at present? And the names and details of everyone they've told. Get me that information first, then call me. I might have more questions."

"What do you want me to do with them after?"

"Unlike that lawyer and his slut, the Daltons have to disappear. Completely. An acid bath should do it. Understood?"

"Yep. Got it."

The line went dead.

"What was that frown about?" Catia wanted to know from Rex immediately after the call ended.

"The six-hour mystery..."

"What?" Brandt interjected on behalf of all.

"Well, according to Althaus," Rex said, "Catia and I would've left Rome about half an hour ago, around one. By Nordwand's calculations it's an eight- to ten-hour drive. We should be arriving in Geneva by nine, eleven at the latest, not four in the afternoon."

"Mysterious indeed," Aderet said.

"I think he's only giving himself enough time to get from Vaduz to Geneva once he knows the Daltons have arrived at their final destination," Brandt said. "But let's not get hung up on that for now. We've got planning to do and arrangements to make. Rex and his team have to get to Geneva. A welcoming committee has to be organized for Nordwand at the delivery point. And Joost Trauffer is screaming for attention."

It was 1:30 A.M. in Italy and Switzerland.

In Vaduz, Horst Klenst took his second secured cellphone out and sent a text message to the leader of his team who had interrogated and killed Wilhelm Jablonsky and Eva Guggenheim.

MEET IN 10.

Ten minutes later, he logged onto a different secured conference facility. He had four different mobile phones and four different secured conference facilities hosted in four different countries which he alternated between missions. This facility was hosted on a server farm in Ahmedabad, India. To convey his instructions required almost half an hour.

CHAPTER 66 – TRAUFFER WAS ASLEEP

ROME, ITALY AND GENEVA, SWITZERLAND

THURSDAY, SEPTEMBER 8, 2016

IN SHORT ORDER, Aderet had commandeered the Mossad private jet in Rome and instructed two of his agents to accompany Rex and his team to Geneva. Althaus and Kraus were sedated, tied up, gagged, and loaded into the cargo hold.

The lack of sleep in combination with the almost non-stop traveling and the oversupply of adrenaline caused by the day's activities were taking their toll. They all settled in and tried to take a nap as soon as they boarded the plane at 2:15 A.M. The flying time to Geneva was 90 minutes.

Aderet immediately dispatched a three-man surveillance team to Trauffer's house.

The plane landed at Geneva International at 3:45 A.M. and taxied into a hangar, hired by the Mossad through a front company. Althaus and Kraus stayed on the plane under guard of the Mossad agents.

Rex and the team cleared customs through Terminal 3, the designated terminal for private jets at Geneva International Airport. They were all in disguise, using matching fake passports. They were relieved to find border control at Terminal 3 staffed by a single customs officer for whom it was too early and too boring to be vigilant. Rex thought they could've dragged Althaus and Kraus through customs without raising any suspicion. She would probably not have noticed them. She didn't even look at Digger.

Outside the terminal building, they were met by the Mossad's COS in Geneva, Ariel Dayan. To Rex's question, he replied that he was indeed distantly related to the former Israeli Defense Minister, Moshe Dayan, the hero of the Six-Day War of 1967. Dayan provided them with a black Mercedes SUV and a big canvas bag loaded with the same type of items they got from the *sayan* in Rome the day before.

Dayan told them that the Trauffer surveillance team was in place and reported that Trauffer was fast asleep. The team had taken control of the house's security system: there were no dogs, no guards, and no fences. The nearest neighbor's house was almost a hundred yards away. One of the neighbors was not at home, and those who were at home seemed to be asleep.

Dayan then patched Rex through to the surveillance team lead and introduced them to each other.

CHAPTER 67 – THE POWER OF SUGGESTION

COLOGNY, GENEVA, SWITZERLAND

THURSDAY, SEPTEMBER 8, 2016

TRAUFFER'S BLADDER IGNORED all messages from his brain to not let go of its contents when he opened his eyes and looked into the snarling face of a vicious big black dog inches from his own face. Then behind the dog he saw the outline of a man whose face was covered by a black balaclava and pointing a gun at him.

He uttered not a single word as he was bound with zip ties and gagged with duct tape. He was hauled out, still in his urine-soaked pajamas, by another man whose face was also hidden behind a black balaclava. He made no attempt to resist when a needle plunged into his neck. By the time he was loaded into the back of a Mercedes SUV with tinted windows, he was unconscious.

***

MOSSAD SAFEHOUSE, GENEVA, SWITZERLAND

THURSDAY, SEPTEMBER 8, 2016

IT WAS A few minutes past 8:00 A.M. when he regained consciousness and found himself in a room with plain white walls and ceiling. The floor was polished concrete with no covering. He was in a swivel office chair with wheels. His arms and legs were strapped to the armrest and legs of the chair with duct tape, and his mouth taped shut with the same.

In front of his chair, about two steps away, were two cheap, white plastic chairs. The lights in the room were exceptionally bright. There was only one door and no windows. In the far corner of the room, up on the ceiling, was a video camera. A flickering red light indicated it was busy recording. In the same corner, on the floor was an old-fashioned four-legged enamel bathtub. In front of the bathtub sat a pallet with ten one-liter black plastic bottles. The labels were easy to read, the lettering was in white. SULFURIC ACID DRAIN CLEANER

His pajama pants were wet and smelled of urine.

The door opened, but instead of a human entering, a big black dog strolled in, casually. Trauffer felt as if his bladder was going to give up on him again when he recognized the big black dog from what he thought was a nightmare. He now realized it was not a nightmare.

The dog went and sat down between the empty chairs and stared at him without making a single sound.

What felt like an hour later but was in reality only seconds, a man and woman, both clad in black, faces covered in black balaclavas, walked in, closed the door, and sat down in the chairs across from him. The man had a gun with a silencer in his right hand. In a choreographed motion, as if they had practiced it, the couple removed their balaclavas.

Trauffer drew a sharp breath and his eyes threatened to pop out of their sockets as he recognized them.

Rex skipped all the niceties that usually preceded these kinds of situations such as introductions and the reason Trauffer was there. He didn't even remove the duct tape from Trauffer's mouth. He held up the index finger of his left hand for Trauffer to see and said in English, "Only one question, Trauffer. Nod your answer. Are you going to tell me where to find the libraries?"

Trauffer didn't move his head.

Rex sighed. "Before I throw you in that bath and pour the drain cleaner over you, let me make sure there are no misunderstandings.

"You understand English?"

Trauffer nodded.

"Good. Now let's make sure you know which libraries I'm talking about. I'm after the Jewish Libraries. The ones stolen by the Nazis from the Jewish Ghetto in Rome in 1943. They are the same ones about which you hired a contract killer to interrogate, torture, and kill Wilhelm Jablonsky and Eva Guggenheim. The same ones for which you had the 86-year old Professor Zechariah Nachum of Rome mercilessly tortured. The same ones for which you ordered your killer to track my wife and me down, capture us, interrogate us, kill us, and dump our bodies in an acid bath. Those libraries, Trauffer. Now, are you going to tell me where to find them, or does your body become part of the Geneva sewage system?"

Trauffer didn't move his head.

Rex grabbed the back of Trauffer's chair, wheeled him to the bathtub and tipped him, chair and all, into the empty tub.

Trauffer wiggled and screamed but the duct tape ensured that only muffled sounds could be heard.

Catia had an impassive look on her face. Digger had a smile on his.

Rex ignored Trauffer's obvious attempts to say something, bent down, picked up one of the bottles, unscrewed the top, and started pouring the contents on him.

If Rex and Catia didn't know what was landing on Trauffer was nothing but tap water, they would have sworn under oath that it was indeed sulfuric acid.

Trauffer's abject terror was testimony to how real it was in his mind. Psychologists called it the power of suggestion. For ages, physicians had known about it and used it to cure patients of their ailments by administering nothing but sugar-coated pills—the placebo effect. It had also been used by doctors who hypnotized patients; helping women to give painless birth, helping dental patients with painless tooth extraction, and allowing surgeons to perform operations without any anesthetics. Tibetan monks placed in a room with a temperature of 39 Fahrenheit, naked, were able to increase their body temperature to a little over 100 degrees, using only their minds. A man who got so drunk on pure Coca Cola, which he believed had generous shots of brandy in it, his friends had to carry him home. He woke up with an enormous hangover the next morning.

Catia and Rex would not have been surprised if Trauffer got out of that bath with actual acid burns on his skin.

Rex got a little worried that Trauffer might suffer a heart attack before he got any information out of him. He stopped when the bottle was half empty. He held the bottle up, read the label, smelled it and said, "Catia, did you put water in this one?"

She shook her head.

"Just hang in there, Trauffer, the real drain cleaner is here, I know." He put the half-empty bottle down and picked up a new one.

By now the room was starting to fill with a new and nauseatingly pungent odor. Medical experts would have explained that normal functioning of the human stomach and intestines were inhibited during situations of extreme fear. In layman's terms, Trauffer had soiled himself.

Tears were streaming down Trauffer's face. He was nodding his head vigorously, his whole body was shaking, and he was making unearthly, high-pitched sounds.

In a room upstairs from the interrogation room, Josh and Marissa were watching on a big TV screen, and so were the rest of the team in the remote ops centers in Tel Aviv, CRC headquarters, and on the TOMATS.

Aderet was shaking his head slowly. "John, will you please remind me to never upset that boy of yours."

Brandt grinned. "Yaron, don't ever upset that boy of mine."

Rex had been ignoring Trauffer while he slowly unscrewed the top of the new bottle. He took a quick sniff. "Ah, there you go. Now we're in business."

Trauffer's kicking, wriggling, trembling, and screaming increased exponentially as Rex started tilting the bottle.

Rex looked down at him. "You wanted to say something?"

Trauffer nodded with great vigor.

"Well, say it then."

Trauffer nodded enthusiastically and made more incomprehensible sounds.

"Oh, you want to tell me about the libraries?"

Trauffer nodded and blinked his eyes.

Rex screwed the top back on the bottle, replaced it on the pallet, and ripped the duct tape off Trauffer's face.

Trauffer screamed when the duct tape came off with some of his skin, and immediately said, "I want to make a deal."

"I don't deal with murderers. Where are the libraries? The next words out of your mouth better be the location of the libraries or you'll be going down the drain."

"La Clusaz!" Trauffer yelled in a high-pitched soprano-sounding voice.

"Details, Trauffer."

"They're stored in a vault below the double garage of my holiday home in La Clusaz. That's across the border in France. Both libraries are there. All the books are there... in the same condition they were in 1943. I took good care of them. I saw them only yesterday."

Trauffer was still on his back in the bathtub.

Rex was about to say something when Digger's soft whining made him glance at Catia and pause. He had never seen her face like that. A mixture of rapidly changing emotions: sadness, anger, jubilation, and then a single tear streaked down her cheek. He took two steps, pulled her up from the chair, wrapped his arms around her, and whispered, "It's over, Catia. The libraries are as good as on their way back home, to Rome. Just imagine

Zechariah's face when you tell him. Imagine the joy of the people in the Ghetto."

She only nodded and held on to him as if she had no intention to let him go, ever.

Digger had wormed his way in between them and was making soft noises as if he too wanted to tell Catia it was over.

The team members from across the world were watching in silence.

Trauffer had gone quiet.

Rex looked over his shoulder and said, "Keep talking, Trauffer. Don't stop unless I tell you to."

Trauffer immediately continued and told them about the hidden door, the electronic switches, and the numbers for the combination lock of the vault.

Over the course of the next hour, requiring only the occasional encouragement from Rex, Trauffer went into a detailed chronicle of the journey of the libraries from the day they were removed from the Jewish Ghetto in Rome, to the Freeport Geneva, to Frankfurt, Germany, and finally, 59 years ago, to La Clusaz, France.

Fortunately, every single word was recorded; Catia would have no need to interview the murderer again. Besides, she would most probably not be allowed to quote Trauffer as a source in her thesis – definitely not, if her professors knew the circumstances under which she got the information.

With a little prodding, in the form of Rex holding the bottle of drain cleaner up for Trauffer to see, Trauffer also told them everything about Zehnhaus Consulting, his father and his father's partner, the two thieves who stole the Nazis blind and built their own empire with the spoils.

He didn't leave anything out in his account of the history of Scharnhorst and its members—past and present.

However, no amount of prodding could make him give up the personal details of the man he called the Troubleshooter—simply because he had no idea who the man was or where he was, not even a guess. He had never heard the name Nordwand.

When Trauffer came to the end of his telling, John Brandt had the proud grin of a father watching his son win an Olympic gold medal.

Aderet had his handkerchief out, wiping the tears from his face, and said in a soft voice, "My God. It's real. They still exist, and they're coming back to our people..." His voice cracked up and he stopped talking.

All the while, Christelle Proll had been vigorously taking notes on facial expressionism to accompany the recording on her tablet. Undoubtedly, she would have a lot of questions to answer when she informed her director about the saga of the Jewish Libraries of Rome and that they were on French soil. She expected that the explanations wouldn't end with the director but would have to be repeated to the President and Prime Minister of France.

Rex pulled Trauffer out of the bathtub and wheeled him out of the interrogation room to the shower in the bathroom next door. He cut the duct tape off and tipped the chair over. Trauffer fell into the cubicle, landing under the faucet. Rex opened the cold water tap and said, "Get out of your pajamas and clean yourself; you smell like shit."

Trauffer got out of his pajamas, grabbed the bar of soap, and did as he was told. When he was done, he stepped out of the shower. He stood there in his birthday suit, water dripping from his body, looking around for a towel.

Rex ignored the man's obvious dilemma and shoved him out of the bathroom, down the hallway into a small room with a small, old-fashioned metal frame bed bolted to the floor. Rex pushed him onto the bed and used zip ties to secure his hands and feet to the bed's railings. Rex injected him with a sedative, and when Trauffer's body went limp, he left the room.

It was 9:30 A.M.

CHAPTER 68 – WHAT LIBRARIES JOHN?

THURSDAY, SEPTEMBER 8, 2016

REX, CATIA, AND Digger joined Josh and Marissa in the family room upstairs where they were linked into the secure video conference with the rest of the team.

"We've got about ninety minutes to make the next call to Nordwand," Brandt started, but Rex interrupted.

"John, I've been wondering about that," Rex said. "We don't have to play games with Nordwand anymore. I'm thinking we should ask Yakov to go and pick the bastard up at his house right now. In the meantime, we go to La Clusaz and get the libraries out of Trauffer's house and on their way to Rome."

"I'm inclined to agree with Rex," Aderet said. "We know where Nordwand is right now. We've got a very capable team on site. Let's take him now."

"Anyone seeing any issues with that?" Brandt's gaze moved from person to person. There were no issues. "Okay, Yaron, give Jessel his orders. Ask him to take Nordwand to Zurich.

"Dalton, you and your team get over to La Clusaz, make an assessment of what we need to move those books without damaging them, and let us know.

469

"Christelle, seeing that the libraries are on French soil, is there a need to inform the French authorities?"

Christelle thought about it for a while. A smile spread across her beautiful face and she said, "What libraries, John?"

John grinned. "Did I say libraries? Apologies. I must have misspoken."

Just then Greg shouted, "Got the sonofabitch!"

"Which one, Greg?"

"Nordwand. His name's Horst Klenst. Ex KSK, Kommando Spezialkräfte, a German elite special forces military unit." Greg loaded three pictures of Klenst on the screen. "That's the snake who's the real owner of that house in Vaduz."

"Great work, Greg," Brandt said. "Forward all the information and pictures to Jessel right away."

"Done," said Greg a few seconds later.

***

EN ROUTE TO LA CLUSAZ, FRANCE

THURSDAY, SEPTEMBER 8, 2016

UNDERSTANDABLY, JOSH AND Marissa thought Catia would be the most excited of them all. But the expression on her face did not correspond with what they thought it would be. She was quiet, withdrawn, a touch of melancholy. Not the bright-eyed and bushy-tailed Catia they had come to know.

Josh decided to break the ice. "Catia, you're about to graduate with a Ph.D., undoubtedly summa cum laude, from one of the world's foremost universities. Apart from that, you're about to make history as the first Jew in three quarters of a century to lay eyes and hands on one of the most significant artifacts of Jewish heritage. Why does your face look as if Digger has stolen your gelato?"

Catia laughed. "Oh, no. Not the stolen gelato look. It's horrendous. I'll try to change it right now." But the serious look resettled on her face shortly after. "Apologies, everyone. It's just... I... I don't even know how to say it. I'm totally overwhelmed. I'm struggling to even believe it's real... I... it's just... well, too much too quickly for me to process. It's as if I can't believe it until I see it. I'm trying to visualize it, but all that comes up is a dark empty space."

Marissa laughed. "Poor thing. Sounds much worse than your surprise wedding."

Within minutes, their witticisms had Catia out of her somberness.

In the back, Digger was smiling. He had reason to; his pack was happy.

Marissa saw Digger's smile and asked Rex, "Is it perhaps possible that Digger could be wondering what his reward is going to be? After all, he's the one who led us to the bad guys, which is what triggered the chain of events now leading us to the libraries."

Rex tried not to laugh. It was unquestionable; Marissa had been converted to a devoted believer in Digger's exceptional intellectual powers. With feigned seriousness he said, "I don't know. Digger never talks to me when I'm driving. Why don't *you* ask him?"

Marissa looked at Rex, then turned and looked at Digger, incredulously. She started, "Digger, tell me..." then hesitated and everyone else in the car exploded in laughter.

Digger let out a short yap as if to say, "Hey, do you mind? I'm trying to have a conversation with Marissa over here." But it had no effect. A little while later he apparently gave up, turned his head, and stared out the window.

CHAPTER 69 – A SPEEDY APPREHENSION

LA CLUSAZ, FRANCE

THURSDAY, SEPTEMBER 8, 2016

THEY ARRIVED IN La Clusaz shortly after 11:00 A.M. and drove past Trauffer's house—it looked quiet.

Rex made a U-turn farther down the road, came back to the house, parked in front, and they all got out. Conversing in English, Rex said loudly enough for anyone in the vicinity to hear, "This is my friend Joost's house. Now let's hope he remembered to leave the key where he said he would."

They went to the front door. Rex bent down, lifted and dropped the doormat in quick succession, and said, "Yep, his memory is apparently still serving him well."

The lock to the front door surrendered to Rex's lock picking tool in a few seconds. They stepped inside. Josh, bringing up the rear, had a quick look up and down the street before he also stepped in and closed the door behind them. There were a few people on the street wandering in different directions, but no one was paying them any attention.

Rex moved quickly and disabled the alarm system with the code Trauffer had supplied.

They had their guns out while they swept the house and basement. There were no surprises.

Finally, they stood in front of the built-in wardrobe in the rumpus room, staring at the door for a long moment in pious silence, until Catia whispered, "It's behind that wardrobe... would you allow me the honor of opening it?"

"We wouldn't have it any other way," Marissa replied on behalf of everyone.

The next moment, Catia tore away and sprinted up the stairs with Digger on her heels. A few seconds later the three of them heard the electronic locks clicking.

Seconds later, Catia was back. She stepped forward, opened the wardrobe door, stepped in, and pushed against the wall at the back. The invisible door swung away and revealed the flight of stairs going down – exactly as Trauffer described. She took a step forward, reached out, switched the lights on, and started down the stairs, slowly.

The others looked over Catia's shoulder as they followed. At the bottom, the vault door came into view.

Catia stopped in front of the door and extended her right hand to the combination lock – her hand was shaking. In chorus, the three of them called it out loudly, slowly, and rhythmically, so that she could keep up. "Seven left. Four right. Nine left. Six right. Two left."

The lock clicked and Catia pushed against the door, it opened to the inside. She stepped in and switched the lights on.

There was an eerie silence before they heard it, "Oh, God, no. No! No!"

Rex and Digger were practically flying through the door into the vault at the same time. Catia was sitting on the floor staring at the empty shelves. Not a single book in sight. Not even a scrap of paper.

The area of the vault, by Rex's quick estimates, was about the size of four garages – twice the size of the double garage above.

Josh and Marissa entered. Rex heard them drawing their breaths, sharply, and letting them out with a loud hissing sound.

"Trauffer, you sonofabitch," Marissa murmured.

"Herr Trauffer is in desperate need of a *real* acid bath," Josh said.

Catia was silent, as if they were not there.

Digger was on the floor with Catia, his head was on her lap, trying to comfort her. She was stroking his head, slowly.

Josh and Marissa were looking at Rex, waiting for his reaction.

But he didn't react. He was turning around very, very slowly. When he had made a full circle and faced Josh and Marissa again, he said, "Here's what happened. Nordwand, Horst Klenst, moved the libraries out of here in the time between when Trauffer left here yesterday afternoon and our arrival."

"C'mon Rex. How is that even possible?" Josh said. "He's at his home in Liechtenstein. He's been there the whole time. And what makes you so sure Trauffer didn't lie?"

"Your second question first," Rex started. "One, Trauffer genuinely believed he was going to die this morning in that bathtub. No human can piss and shit himself on demand just for the show – in his mind he was about to die. Two, the details he gave us, those that we had prior knowledge of, such as that in Karl Bauer's diary, we know were one hundred percent correct; so were all of the details about how to get in here. Three, the code for the alarm system; the system is connected to a security company. All he had to do to get us arrested shortly after arrival, was give us the wrong code. Four, Trauffer is still in our custody. He knows what would happen to him if he lied to us. That's why I'm sure he told us the truth.

"Now your first question. The fact that Klenst has been at his house all this time doesn't mean he couldn't have someone steal the libraries for him. Think about it; he has been doing everything via subcontractors like Althaus and Kraus. He subcontracted the killing of Jablonsky and

Guggenheim. He subcontracted the placement of their bodies in that park. He subcontracted Zechariah's torture. He subcontracted the killing of Catia and me. That's his modus operandi, and that's why I'm convinced he also subcontracted the removal of the libraries from this vault. He's the puppet master who makes the puppets dance."

Josh was nodding slowly. "Dammit, you have no idea how I hate to admit it when you're right and I'm wrong.

"And, of course, now the mystery of the six-hour time gap has been solved," Josh continued. "Klenst wanted the extra time to get the libraries out of here, kill you and Catia, and get rid of your bodies. Then he could go on and live happily ever after."

"Exactly. He has no intention of calling Trauffer ever again. Trauffer has no idea who he is and where to even begin looking for him. Happy ever after indeed."

"I only need three things to get you the libraries," Josh said and held up three fingers. "A flight to Zurich, the address of the safehouse where Yakov is taking Klenst, and a few gallons of real drain cleaner."

Catia got to her feet and said to Rex, "And how do you suppose Klenst managed to find out where the libraries were and how to get through all these doors?"

Rex put his arm around her shoulder and said, "That, I don't know. It's possible that Trauffer was careless, maybe he wrote it down somewhere, maybe he has it on his computer or phone and Klenst himself or his hackers got to it. Moreover, Trauffer was smelling like a brewery when we picked him up this morning. Maybe he divulged the information to someone while he was in a drunken stupor."

Catia was calm and collected, no signs of stress or anxiety. "Okay. What are we waiting for? Why are we not on our way to have a chat with Horst Klenst already?"

Her question got them out of their state of inertia and back into action immediately. They were back in their vehicle and on the road to Geneva within minutes.

Catia dialed into the TOMATS's conference facility and put the call on the car's speaker.

As expected, while hearing the news and Rex's theory about who was responsible, the rest of the team reacted the same as the four of them had earlier. And they were in agreement about the fate that they would like to befall the man known as Horst Klenst.

Aderet was on the line to Jessel shortly after. He told Jessel what had happened and how critical a speedy apprehension of Klenst had become.

CHAPTER 70 – THERE WAS NOTHING TO SAY

MOSSAD SAFEHOUSE, ZURICH, SWITZERLAND

THURSDAY, SEPTEMBER 8, 2016

TWO HOURS LATER, at the same time Rex and his team descended the stairs of the private jet that transported them to Zurich, Yakov Jessel reported that Horst Klenst was in custody. A little worse for wear; apparently Klenst was stupid enough to attack Jessel instead of surrendering when the latter walked into his study. Klenst had a broken elbow, and he couldn't see properly through his swollen left eye. Other than that, he was in good condition and in the interrogation room of a safehouse, awaiting Rex and his team's arrival.

Catia and Marissa didn't protest when Rex and Josh asked them not to be present when the two of them interviewed Klenst. They understood it was going to get ugly.

Rex and Josh were tired, hungry, and irritated in the extreme when they walked into the interrogation room with Digger in tow. Rex and Josh each had a silenced Glock 17 in their hands.

Neither of them said a word. There was nothing to say; they were there to listen to Klenst, and as far as they were concerned, Klenst knew precisely which topics to address. No introductions were required either; Klenst knew who Rex was and vice versa. For the purposes of this meeting, it didn't matter that Klenst didn't know Josh or Digger.

Even if Klenst didn't steal the libraries, he still had to talk about the work he did for Trauffer.

Rex simply walked up to Klenst where he sat on the chair and shot him in the left knee. He waited for Klenst's screaming and shouting to subside before shooting him in the right knee. All the while, maintaining his silence.

After the second shot, when Klenst was able to speak again, still moaning and groaning in pain, stuttering from fear and cursing in frustration, he started by telling them where the libraries were; in the Freeport, and he didn't need another bullet hole in his body to give them the unit number, block number, lock number, anonymous account number, and passwords.

Aderet immediately wanted to send agents in Geneva to check.

But Rex said, "Hang on. My wife is going to be the first Jew in 73 years to see those libraries. You can send your agents, but they are not to open that place. Understood?"

Aderet smiled and nodded.

Now Rex had something to say to Klenst. "I'm going to Geneva to the Freeport with my wife. If the libraries are not there, I'm coming back, and I'm going to find out what is the maximum number of bullets your body can take before you die. So, do I go to Geneva or don't I?"

"They're there. I'm not lying. Please give me something for the pain."

"I'll consider it after I've seen the libraries. In the meantime, my friend here will listen to the rest of your story."

Rex, Catia, and Digger were back on the plane to Geneva. It was a 50-minute flight.

Josh and Marissa continued the interview. There was a lot they wanted to hear. Klenst was extremely keen to talk and do it as quickly as possible so that he could get something for the excruciating pain. Anything.

***

THIS TIME, ON the second final journey to get the libraries, Catia had no portents of empty spaces. In her mind's eye was a picture of a warehouse packed to the brim with boxes filled with ancient Jewish books and manuscripts. This time her mood was as if she had an injection of high spirits. Her excitement was approaching the levels of that late afternoon of Saturday 7 May earlier in the year, when she was led down the short aisle by Yaron Aderet to get married to the most amazing man she had ever known.

Aderet ordered two of his agents to go to the Freeport, find the storage unit, and wait for a couple with a big black dog to arrive. In the meantime, no one was to enter that unit.

Rex and Catia found that the account number and access codes and every other detail were exactly as Klenst had said.

Catia's vision about the boxes and the books was spot on.

Rex opened one box. Catia stood there with tears streaming down her face when she saw the contents. "Zechariah, how I wish you could be here. I want you to get better quickly. You and I are going to put them back in the shelves from which they were removed."

***

BY NOW, IN Zurich, Klenst had told Josh and Marissa everything about the murders and the assault on Zechariah. He gave them the names and addresses of every one of his henchmen. He told them how he kept close electronic surveillance on Trauffer and learned how to get access to the vault in La Clusaz.

He told them about his plans to sell the libraries on the black market. His research showed he could get 10 to 15 percent of their market value. At least $50 million. His idea was to run an anonymous auction through one of his secured conference facilities, where only he would know the real identities of the bidders. And he thought buyers from the Middle East would be very keen to get in on the opportunity. And he thought, they would be prepared to pay a whole lot more than buyers from elsewhere.

After that he started talking about his clients all over Europe and the missions he did for them, including members of Scharnhorst—dead and alive.

It was clear that it was going to take weeks, if not months, to get him properly debriefed. And the information he had, if law enforcement acted upon it, was going to make life extremely uncomfortable, in some cases downright dangerous, for a number of rich and famous people.

Josh and Marissa kept listening to Klenst until they got word from Rex. Then they put him under sedation and handed him over to the Mossad agents to arrange for medical attention and safekeeping until a decision could be made about his future. It was probably not going to be a bright one. But then again, when politicians get involved, the outcome can be all but predictable.

Chapter 71 – The Aftereffects

ADERET INFORMED THE Israeli PM at the same time as Brandt informed Martin Richardson, who would in turn inform the President of the United States.

Aderet's report took less than an hour. Brandt's took almost three.

Brandt started with a summary. "We got the libraries. Thus far, they seem to be intact. Aderet is making arrangements for their transportation to Rome as we speak. He believes the quickest and best way is via cargo plane. Aderet is in charge of that. Mission complete. Over to you to handle the rest."

"Excellent work, John. But why is it that your words, 'Over to you to handle the rest' have such a dampening effect on my joy? As if you're trying to tell me the problem's been solved but the real trouble is about to start?"

"Martin, you seem to forget that missions have three stages: planning, execution, and close out. In the close out stage, the stage we're in now, any fallout from the execution stage is addressed. Sometimes political interference is required, sometimes only administrative intervention, and sometimes none at all."

Richardson sighed. "Okay, let me have the details. I have a feeling I'm not going to like it." Richardson remained quiet, like a landmine, while Brandt gave his very detailed report.

When Brandt finished, Richardson, still the epitome of impassiveness said, "Let me summarize. The libraries are safe and will be on their way back to their rightful owners soon. That takes care of stages one and two. Right?"

"Yep."

"The scenario in the aftermath is as follows:

"In a hangar in Geneva, held in captivity, are two Austrian citizens. They were abducted from a hospital's parking lot in Rome, on the say so of a big black dog. One of the prisoners has a broken nose, broken ribs, and a pair of crushed nuts. The other blocked a baseball bat with his knee, resulting in a smashed kneecap. Right?"

"Yep."

"In a Mossad safehouse in Geneva, one of the richest people, if not *the* richest person in Switzerland is being held captive. Physical harm; only a few minor bruises, but his psyche is so damaged he could be a candidate for the funny farm. Right?"

"Yep."

"In Zurich, in a Mossad safehouse, a citizen of Liechtenstein abducted from his house in Liechtenstein, one nine-millimeter bullet hole in each knee, is also being held in captivity. Right?"

"Yep."

"There are also four more men, Swiss citizens, not in custody yet, but who you suggest should be, who are apparently responsible for the killing of two people in Geneva a few days ago and the theft of the libraries. Right?'

"Yep."

"Finally, there's the trivial matter of three, hitherto still free and in good health, thank God, revered members of the Swiss society, who apparently are members of a secret organization with Nazi roots. And it's your suggestion they are to be arrested forthwith. Right?"

"Yep."

"John, please excuse me for only a few minutes. I just want to go and issue the orders for a firing squad to execute you at dawn," Richardson announced in an emotionless monotone. "I have however, one last question before you get shot. Do you have any suggestions I could give the President of how he should go about not getting skinned alive and his scalp draped behind the door of the Swiss president's toilet to keep the flies away?"

"That bad?"

"You have no idea, John. I can't imagine that it's possible to have made a bigger mess of things than you have done. And the irony is, you will live until dawn. I, on the other hand, will be dead immediately after giving the President the sensational news."

"Missions are sometimes like medicine, Martin. They have side effects. You know that as well as I do."

"I do indeed. And sometimes the side effects are worse than the disease itself. Which of course calls into question the wisdom of trying to cure the disease in the first place."

Brandt shook his head. "That's called the wisdom of hindsight, Martin. Let's be serious. I am well aware that we might have an international political situation on our hands. That's the reason I told you every single detail and gave you the tapes.

"What we've unearthed here is not only the Jewish libraries; there're some seriously dark stories with far-reaching consequences on those tapes, Martin. Listen to them before you go to the President. Although they'll never be allowed as evidence in a court, it can't be ignored—what's on them is the truth. To me it was more than just a little disturbing to find out what's been going on under the noses of the governments of Europe. I suggest the President should also be concerned."

Richardson nodded slowly, in silence.

Brandt continued. "The options, as far as I'm concerned, are: One, you can throw CRC under the bus. All you have to do is say; we didn't know, we had nothing to do with it, we certainly would never have sanctioned it. We don't know the people involved.

"Two, the President, while denying any involvement, very discreetly says, 'irrespective of how the information was obtained, we certainly hope that the story of the libraries is not really true. Because we would be very shocked and very upset if it proves to be true.'

"Three, the President mans up and owns it. He calls a secret summit of the heads of state of Switzerland, Germany, Austria, Israel, France, Italy, and the Vatican. He tells them the truth, all of it. My prediction is Italy, France, and Austria would be out of it quickly. Switzerland, Germany, and the Vatican are the ones running the risk of major international embarrassment and backlash if the full story comes out. Therefore, they'll have a vested interest in an outcome that will cause as little as possible damage to their standing in the international community.

"The fourth and final option; we capitulate, open the cages, let the thugs out, and hope for the best. We hope they're so scared they won't want to talk about it to anyone, ever.

"One or more of those options should take care of the issues of the libraries. As for the real bad stuff we've discovered, there're only two options I can think of: Ignore it or do something about it."

Richardson was quiet for a long while after Brandt finished. "You're right, John. Those are the options. And it's as you've said, missions always have an aftereffect, some worse than others. You and I know it from experience. Unfortunately, the politicians don't have our experience and don't always see things in a logical way. I just wish the aftereffects could've been a bit less severe."

CHAPTER 72 – THE SUMMIT

THE PRESIDENT WENT with Brandt's third option—a secret summit and the full story. The summit was called within hours from Richardson's report.

The first order of business, after hearing the full story from the President of the United States, was what to do with the captives. They were all in Switzerland, and the Swiss, for obvious reasons, were very keen to let their Federal Police take them into custody. The accusations against the alleged killers of Jablonsky and Guggenheim, as well as the rich and famous Swiss citizens belonging to Scharnhorst, would be investigated and acted upon. Any alleged crimes committed in other countries would be investigated by the respective law enforcement agencies of the relevant countries, and they promised to cooperate with each other in the process.

Everyone was happy with those arrangements, especially the President of the United States.

The next item on the agenda was the libraries.

The French were the first to declare disinterest, saying something along the lines of: thanks for the invitation to the summit, but we don't think this is our problem. We're very happy the Italian Jews will get their libraries back. There's no charge for the 59 years they were stored on our soil. *Au revoir.*

The Italians said that they were elated about the discovery of the libraries and offered to send planes to collect them. *Addio*.

The Austrians explained that their involvement was limited to the fact that a citizen of their country, a guy who was a corporal during the First World War, by the name of Adolph Hitler, caused World War II and all its horrors, including the looting of the libraries. Those iniquities had been dealt with long ago, and the corporal had committed suicide. They were also very happy for the Jews of Rome. *Auf Wedersehen*.

The Israelis said, "It goes without saying, we're over the moon with joy that the Jews of Rome will have their libraries. But please keep in mind, being a Jew doesn't mean you're automatically a citizen of Israel. The Italian Jews are Italian citizens. Furthermore, the state of Israel didn't even exist when this crime was committed. We are, however, extremely pleased that those responsible for the crime are all present at this summit. You now have a golden opportunity to confess your sins, do restitution, and get absolution. Oh, and don't forget the promise to never let it happen again. *Shalom*."

By now, the President, a skilled negotiator and political gladiator of more than thirty years, was in a much better mood than a few hours before. He had achieved his major goals: he got the captives off his neck, redirected the attention away from America and Israel, and convinced the Swiss, the Germans, and the Vatican that it was in their own best interest to reach an agreement, speedily.

Off the hook, the President told them that he didn't want to be the middleman in an issue that was clearly none of the USA's business. He was however, as a gesture of goodwill, more than happy to facilitate the negotiations. An offer that was accepted immediately and unanimously.

Within the next four hours, under the guidance of the President of the United States, an amicable agreement was forged. The precise details of the agreement would never be made public. Actually, the fact that the summit took place would never be published. Even so, it was part of the agreement that some information, albeit sketchy, had to be released.

The next day, the Italian government issued a press release stating that it was with indescribable joy that they could announce that the long-lost libraries of the Jewish community of Rome had been found at the Geneva Freeport and had arrived in Rome only hours before.

The Swiss government's statement followed the Italian announcement a few hours later. It confirmed that the Italian story was indeed true. The Swiss government, although somewhat embarrassed, was very happy for the Jews of Rome, and promised they would immediately launch an official investigation to get to the bottom of it and determine what should be done to prevent something like this from happening again. To a question from a reporter whether that meant the banking secrecy laws of Switzerland would come under review, the spokesperson stared over his glasses at the journalist for a long while before he said, "No comment." No one asked and no mention was made whether the investigation would look into the possibility that the Freeport could be holding more Nazi era loot.

The German Chancellor went on TV shortly after the Swiss announcement and expressed her profound gratitude for the recovery of the libraries. She apologized profusely for the role of Nazi Germany in the affair. And she concluded with a solemn pledge of openness and cooperation from her government in any investigations.

Although the evidence suggested two Catholic clergymen clearly operated way outside the boundaries of their calling, there was no evidence to suggest the Vatican was involved in any official capacity. Therefore, the Holy See took a vow of silence. A few years later though, in 2019, Pope Francis would announce that the secret archives of Pope Pius XII would be opened in March 2020.

CHAPTER 73 – DISCLOSURE OF A SECRET

THE LIBRARIES ARRIVED in Rome on board an Italian military cargo plane. Catia and Rex, Josh and Marissa, and Digger had special permission, thanks to a request from the President of the United States, to be present at the arrival of the libraries and to accompany the convoy taking them to a staging area where they would be sorted, catalogued, and scanned. Many of the books and manuscripts were in desperate need of restoration. Experts estimated that it would take eight months to a year before the books would be ready to be placed back into the shelves from where the Nazis removed them.

The fact that the Jewish community of Rome couldn't see the libraries immediately didn't suppress their spontaneous mood of jubilation. In the Jewish Quarters, an old man watching the reports on TV the morning the plane landed in Rome, summed it up best when he said, "Like the phoenix, they have risen from the ashes of the Shoah."

The arrival of the libraries did wonders for Zechariah's recovery. A week later, when he was discharged, Rex, Catia, Digger, and Julia took him to the staging area where an army of volunteers were working on the books. Zechariah had special permission to see the libraries; he was the only person alive who had seen the libraries on the day in 1943 when they were removed. And now, 73 years later, seeing them again, he couldn't help but weep with joy.

With the libraries back in Rome, and Catia feverishly at work on her thesis, Rex had time to fulfill a promise he had made to himself, in secret, the last time he was in Berlin. It was actually Josh who planted the idea in his brain then.

He told Catia he had a matter to attend to, but it meant, unfortunately, he would have to be away for one night.

Of course, she immediately wanted to know what was so important that it required him to forsake her, even if it was only for one night.

Rex said he couldn't tell her, not yet. However, he gave her his solemn promise that she would be given every iota and tittle when he got back the next day.

She agreed and said, "Okay, you can go, but remember, no secrets."

"No secrets, Catia, only delayed disclosure. You see, some secrets can only be disclosed in the fullness of time."

"Well, Rex Dalton, you have..." she looked at her watch, "thirty hours before I'm applying the thumbscrews. Fullness of time or not."

***

THE NEXT MORNING, Rex and Digger were picked up by a taxi outside the apartment and dropped off at the departure terminal of Leonardo da Vinci International Airport well in time for their flight to Berlin.

Heinrich Bödeker was of medium height and build. He had greenish eyes. His hair must have been dark when he was younger. Now it was silver gray. He was a friendly man, as could be expected from a salesperson.

Over lunch, in a nice restaurant close to Bödeker's work, in Munich accented German which he acquired from his mother, Rex told him about his interest in history. How he stumbled across the work of Dr. Karl Bauer. How he had tracked down Bauer's last will and testament and learned about his uncle's research. He didn't mention the diary; Bödeker was probably not even aware of his uncle's part-written novel.

Bödeker had to dig deep into the recesses of his memory before he could confirm that he still had the inheritance from his uncle, "In a box somewhere."

Rex almost said to him, "I know you've still got it. I had it in my hands just a week or so ago."

Rex's sales pitch was simple but effective. He started with feigned unease. "I was wondering... mhh... how can I put it... I don't want to offend you... for some people, inheritance... has sentimental value... beyond money..."

The mention of money did it. Rex could almost see Bödeker's ears pitching and his nose wiggling as he smelled money. "Would you consider selling it to me?"

Bödeker was struggling not to smile—Rex could see it.

"Well, I am not much of a history buff, but as you've said, there's the matter of sentiment."

It was written all over Bödeker's face: he had made up his mind; it was now only a matter of the price. "I understand. So how much is your sentiment worth?"

Bödeker shrugged. "Probably a lot less than it should be. But with all the trouble you've gone to, to track me and the books down, clearly, you'll attach much more sentiment to it than I do. Between you and me, I was never fond of my uncle Karl. He thought he was better than us. In other words, he was a bit of an asshole. How about five thousand?"

Rex had to use restraint not to let a very big smile take over his face. He had fifteen thousand in cash in his backpack. "It's a bit more than I had in mind," Rex started, but saw Bödeker was not going to budge, not easily. "But let's not bicker over the price. I really want it. I'll have one condition though."

"What?"

"You'll have to give me a letter, in your own handwriting, to state that you've sold it to me for five-thousand out of your own free will, that you have received fair compensation for it, and that I'm now the rightful and unencumbered owner."

"No problem. You dictate the letter. I'll write and sign it. And as long as you pay in cash, I'm happy."

They shook hands on the deal. Bödeker gave Rex his home address and invited him to have a drink with him and his wife that night at their home at 7:00 when they could finalize the transaction.

The expression on Bödeker's face told Rex he was going to kick himself the moment he was alone, because he realized he could have gotten more. Rex could only hope he wouldn't change his mind between lunch and 7:00 P.M. He could also only hope that when Bödeker visited the attic, he wouldn't see the telltale signs of an intrusion.

But Rex was relieved when he turned up at the Bödeker house and saw the box marked, *Onkel Karl – Bücher und scheiße* on the dining room table, and no mention was made of anything untoward discovered during Bödeker's trip to the attic.

***

REX AND DIGGER walked back into the apartment in Rome the next morning at 10:00. Catia was there, and she barely gave Rex enough time to put the box on the kitchen table before throwing her arms around his neck and kissing him as if he had been away for a month.

And he couldn't get enough of it.

After a few minutes, Catia and Rex still entangled in an embrace, Digger started wiggling himself in between them while making funny noises – they concluded it was his way of telling them Rex had gotten enough attention, it was his turn.

Catia laughed and gave Digger his hug and back rub and his kong stuffed with peanut butter. When Digger was happy, she turned back to Rex, put her arms around his neck again, and with a knee-buckling smile said, "Start talking, Mister Dalton. Start with her name and address."

Rex laughed. "Well, there're actually two."

"I see..."

"Both married."

"Rex Dalton..."

"To each other."

"What!"

"I think it would be better explained if you opened that box. I can see it in your eyes, you've been dying to know what's in it since I walked in with it. It's yours; you might as well open it."

A minute later Catia held Dr. Karl Bauer's original diary in her hands in a state of disbelief. "You didn't..."

"No, I most certainly didn't." He handed her the handwritten letter from Bödeker and took a step back so that he could see the color of her eyes change to aqua

marine—the color when she was happy—another
attribute of her that he couldn't get enough of.

CHAPTER 74 – TYING UP LOOSE ENDS

SIX WEEKS LATER, Catia handed in the first draft of her Ph.D. thesis. A week after that, she was sitting in a state of anxiety in front of a panel consisting of the three professors overseeing her studies: the primary supervisor, an advisor, and her promotor, Professor Zechariah Nachum. The fact that they wanted her to appear before them so soon after submitting the first draft was the cause of her stress.

It took more than one double take from her to understand what they were saying when they told her that the approval of her thesis was a foregone conclusion; she only had to make a few minor changes which would take her less than an hour to do, and resubmit.

"One of the most exciting, and without doubt, the most far reaching thesis I've had the honor of reading in all my life," the primary supervisor told her.

The advisor concurred.

"Ah... thanks... sorry, I mean... thank you so much, Professor."

"Catia, I don't know if you have any idea what a momentous piece of work this is," Zechariah started. "You've brought back sources of information covering more than two-thousand years of history of the Jewish people of Italy. We were convinced it was lost for eternity. Scholars of history are grateful to you. The academic world is grateful to you. We," he pointed at his colleagues, "are grateful to you. The three of us are *ad idem*; if ever there were a student who had earned the right to be proud of an achievement, it's you. We regard it as an honor to recommend to the rector the acceptance of your thesis."

Catia was speechless as she wiped the tears from her eyes.

Rex and Digger were waiting for her when she walked, or rather, glided, out of the building. She didn't have to tell them what happened in the meeting, it was on her face. She told them nevertheless.

"Time to celebrate, Doctor Romano," Rex said. "But why don't we go back home first and finish it?"

"Finish what?"

"Your thesis. Let's get it out of the way, then we have the rest of the day and night and as long as you want to celebrate."

Driving time included, it took exactly one hour for Catia to make the changes, mark the document as final, and submit it.

They started the celebrations with dinner at their favorite restaurant in the Jewish Quarters and paused it when they fell asleep in each other's arms after midnight.

***

REX AND CATIA decided to hold off on letting John Brandt know of the outcome of Catia's meeting with her professors. They were not ready to talk about the CEO job at CRC yet. The agreement with Brandt was to talk about it the day Catia graduated, and that would only happen in May the next year.

Josh and Marissa's wedding was less than a month away. Catia had never been in America and was excited to go. But before they could go, they had one final item on their to-do list. It was the fulfillment of the promise made to Erhard Bachenheimer, the journalist at *The Berliner Kurier*, in Berlin.

The Daltons turned up at his office in Berlin unannounced early in the morning and invited him for a coffee at a nearby restaurant. He was a little apprehensive at first. He had no idea who they were but agreed to give them a few minutes of his time. Within twenty minutes after they had sat down at the table, Erhard called in sick. He had been in journalism all his life; he knew the makings of a Henri Nannen Prize, the most prestigious journalism prize in Germany, the equivalent of the Pulitzer Prize in the United States.

Hours later, when Rex and Catia walked away from the restaurant hand in hand with Digger on Catia's side, Rex heaved a deep sigh.

"What's wrong, Rex?"

"We've been successful in our mission; the libraries are back in Rome, but I can't shake the feeling that we haven't seen the end of the saga."

"Why is that?"

"We've unveiled some of the deepest and darkest secrets of some of the most powerful and influential people in Europe. Corruption in the hallways of power will assure that many of them will never be called to account, but that doesn't mean they won't have their daggers out for us. We've embarrassed them; they'll be bent on revenge."

Catia nodded. "You're right. But we're not going to run and hide from them. Are we?"

"Never. I'll fight them as long as I have breath left in me. It's just that I was hoping we'd finally be able to live like normal people."

Catia smiled and looked at him. "*Carpe diem*, Rex. Seize the day. One day at a time."

Rex stopped and took her in his arms, kissed her and said, "Have I ever told you that I love you?"

"Never." She laughed.

FACT OR FICTION

FACT: The *Biblioteca della Comunità Israelitica,* the library of the Jewish community of Rome, and the *Biblioteca del Collegio Rabbinico Italiano*, the Italian Rabbinical College Library, existed as described in this book.

FACT: The libraries were seized by the Nazis as described. The character, Doctor Karl Bauer, is vaguely based on a real person who played a major role in the book looting ventures of the Nazis, Doctor Johannes Pohl, chief of the Hebraica collection at the Frankfurt Institute's library, head of the Rosenberg Taskforce, *Einsatzstab Reichsleiter Rosenberg,* ERR.

FICTION: The rest is lost in the mists of time and myth. The libraries were never recovered.

REX DALTON'S NEXT ADVENTURE

THE SHANGHAI STRAIN

REX, CATIA, AND DIGGER didn't need any persuasion to accompany Declan Spencer aboard the TOMATS on a trip to a part of the world none of them had ever seen, the 'Pearl of the Orient' better known as Hong Kong.

Their friends Josh and Marissa joined them. The nature scenes were breathtaking, the people enlivening, and the shopping exhilarating.

That was until the day when Catia, Marissa, and Digger went shopping at Stanley Market where two ladies were attacked by members of a triad group known as Sun Yee On. Seeing it happen right before their eyes, without hesitation, Catia, Marissa, and Digger jumped into action and rescued them.

But no good deed goes unpunished.

Their idyllic holiday came to a violent end. They and the women they rescued were now the targets of the Chinese government who wanted them dead to prevent them from uncovering the diabolic scheme devised by the President of China to get control of the world.

MORE REX DALTON AND DIGGER

Here's what readers are saying about the series:

Here's what readers are saying about the series:

"A great read, started and couldn't stop until the end!!!"

"Just gets better and better. Can't wait to read the next in the series."

"Rex and Digger return. The continuing story of Rex Dalton and Digger is a suspenseful and intriguing work."

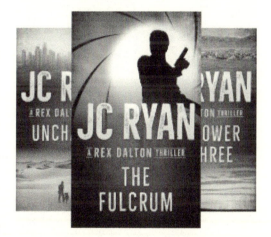

"What's A Dog To Do? 5 stars. I love reading about Rex Dalton's exploits, but my favorite character has to be Digger, his military trained super intelligent dog."

"JC Ryan scores again. I was not a fan of the first Rex Dalton book but plunged ahead with the second hoping JC Ryan would not disappoint. I loved it. Now here I am after reading the third book in this series. I had a hard time putting it down and found myself wondering about it when I was not reading. Rex has added several new ports of call to this adventure. He sure gets into more trouble than any person I know who just wants to become a sightseer. With the help of Digger (his new comrade in arms), we are once again trying to correct the wrongs inflicted on the weak."

See all the Rex Dalton books here
http://viewbook.at/RexDaltonSeries

ALSO BY JC RYAN

THE ROSSLER FOUNDATION MYSTERIES

http://myBook.to/RosslerFoundation

Here's what readers are saying about the series:

"All in all, a brilliant series by a master of the techno thrillers turning old much debated mysteries into overwhelming modern engrossing sagas of adventure, heroism and a sense of awe for the many mysteries still unexplained in our universe. Enjoy!"

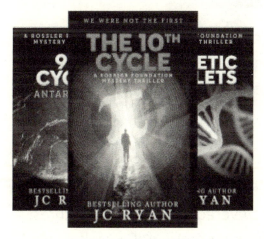

"I LOVED this series! It's readily apparent that the author drew from a large body of knowledge in writing this series. It's just believable enough to think it could happen someday, and in fact, aligns quite well with some of the current relationships that exist between present day countries and the USA."

THE CARTER DEVEREUX MYSTERY THRILLERS

myBook.to/CarterDevereux

Here's what readers are saying about the series:

"Omg this series is awesome. Full off adventure, action, romance, and suspense. If you start reading you are hooked. Carter and all characters are awesome, you will fall in love with all of them they become like family. I love the way J C weaves the human and animals together in the story. Try it you will love it."

"The best! What a joy to read these four books about Carter and Mackenzie Devereux bad their adventures. A very good read. I will look for more of JC Ryan's books."

"Suspenseful! Fabulous just fabulous! I enjoyed reading these books immensely. I highly recommend these books. Bravo to the author! You won't regret it."

"What a wonderful and intriguing book. Kept me glued to what was going to happen next. Not a normal read for me. But a very enjoyable series that I would recommend to everyone who likes adventure and thrills."

THE EXONERATED

http://myBook.to/ExoneratedTrilogy

Here's what readers are saying about the series:

"J.C. Ryan is an author that writes tomes. The great thing about that is that you get great character development and the plots are all intricate, plausible, suspenseful stories that seems to draw you in from the first scenario right up to the end.

The Exonerated series is no exception. Regan St. Clair is a judge. Together with Jake she has her own way in pursuing justice in ensuring that the legal system is applied ...well, justly."

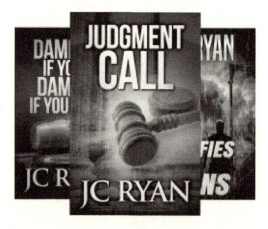

"What if you had the power to make a difference? Would you? Could you? What if in order to do so you had to join a super-secret organization that might not always play by the rules? What if you stumbled across this mysterious organization only to find out it had been polluted? What if you were a judge that has been worn out and disillusioned by the very justice system you thought you loved?"

"What a great series of books. It seemed like one book instead of three books. The story flowed seamlessly through the three books."

No Doubt

Rex Dalton and his dog, Digger, visited the island of Olib in Croatia.

A girl was murdered.

The police said it was her boyfriend who stabbed her to death, but Rex and Digger had no doubt they were making a big mistake.

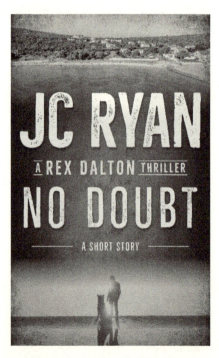

Rex decided to conduct his own investigation and bring the real killer to justice.

A thriller with quirks and twists that will keep you guessing until the end.

Get your free eBook

http://dl.bookfunnel.com/9frvkrovn5.

ABOUT JC RYAN

An interview with the author by the editor of Books 'N Pieces Magazine, http://www.altpublish.com/jc-ryan/

JC Ryan

Editor's note: "JC Ryan and I enjoyed an extensive two-hour Skype session where we spoke of all manner of things, especially his ranking as an author. The visibility of an author is often at the hands of readers. If you look at JC's ratings, each book enjoys several hundred or more four and five-star reviews, enough to make him notable, and on par with mainstream novelists. I encourage you to read one of his books, or listen to his audiobooks, now in production. You'll be hooked."

COPYRIGHT

Made in the USA
Monee, IL
27 December 2021